THE CERTAIN HOPE

Also by E. C. Jackson

A Gateway to Hope
A Living Hope
Pajama Party: The Story

THE CERTAIN HOPE

a novel

E. C. Jackson

ISBN: 978-1-7329592-0-0

Editing: amberbarryeditor.com and angela.trent@sbcglobal.net
Cover design: FormattingExperts.com
Typesetting: FormattingExperts.com
Book blurb: angela.trent@sbcglobal.net

The Write Way – A Real Slice of Life: ecjacksonauthor.wordpress.com
Author Page: facebook.com/ecjacksonauthor
Designed by Standoutbooks

Acknowledgments

My fourth book, book three of the hope-themed series, is behind me. Another labor of love is completed. I enjoy writing inspirational books that inspire me and encourage the people who read them.

I thank my family and friends for their prayers and support, as well as my editors, book formatter and book cover designer. Without the team God has blessedly provided, I would be an unknown author.

For at one time, we too were foolish and disobedient, deceived and enslaved by a variety of passions and pleasures. We spent our lives in evil and envy; people hated us, and we hated each other.

But when the kindness and love for mankind of God our Deliverer was revealed, he delivered us. It was not on the ground of any righteous deeds we had done, but on the ground of his own mercy. He did it by means of the *mikveh* of rebirth and the renewal brought about by the *Ruach HaKodesh*, whom he poured out on us generously through Yeshua the Messiah, our Deliverer.

He did it so that by his grace we might come to be considered righteous by God and become heirs, with the certain hope of eternal life.

You can trust what I have just said, and I want you to speak with confidence about these things, so that those who have put their trust in God may apply themselves to doing good deeds. These are both good in themselves and valuable to the community.

Titus 3:3-8
Complete Jewish Bible (CJB)

Chapter One

Tara Simpkins nibbled her balled fist, hoping to turn a rout into a win. Andy had spent three days installing her roof. He'd come into her life last Friday and was the perfect man. But unless she developed a way to keep him close, his exit would be speedier than his entrance had been.

The handsome roofer had captured her attention his first day on the job. He had even appeared mesmerized by Tara. That had never happened before. Men ran from her, not to her. She couldn't tell what prompted his interest in her, yet he continued to hang around. She loved the chase but was unsure how to get herself caught. And that dilemma wouldn't get resolved soon.

Andy seemed like her dream man. He was adept at keeping a conversation going, even though she wasn't. Plus, he'd seemed curious about his customer in a non-threatening way. He resembled an old friend. The charisma he oozed added to his appeal.

Andy engaged her in conversation, despite her ignoring his charm. Thoroughly smitten, she downplayed his attention. Because of that, he seemed to slow the hunt. But he still knocked on her door each evening after the work ended.

Tara had come to expect those knocks. How would she survive once they stopped?

Now, the dreaded last day had arrived. Could she keep from becoming an afterthought?

The crew labored on the roof as Tara fretted on the sofa.

She didn't know how to reclaim the ground she'd lost. Ground she'd thrown away, she reminded herself. Her ruse of indifference had created a gap she didn't know how to close. Of course she was interested in Andy. No sane woman rejected a personable man who wanted her. Especially if the interest was mutual.

She longed to cement a relationship, but she hadn't spent time with a man on a personal basis. Because of that, Tara felt awkward making small talk while Andy made advances. Her insides quivered whenever he drew near. Her thoughts went haywire, and her stomach somersaulted against her ribs. This was an unfamiliar situation for her thirty-two-year-old self. The man had eons more experience than she had. She had none.

Thirty-something women shouldn't feel awkward talking to magnetic men.

Tara had taken three personal days off from work to snag him while he worked on her house. Instead of spending the time endearing herself to Andy, she'd daydreamed throughout the house. She couldn't think of a coherent plan. Days had been wasted with moping. Her gaze was riveted to the window. Knowing Andy was there consoled her. She sneaked peeks as he scurried up and down the ladder. At least the crew's jovialness lifted her spirits. They sang and joked as they worked.

The doorbell chimed what she termed his signature ring: one long peal, followed by two shorter ones. Saying goodbye might ruin her. Hair patted into place, she opened the door with an unsteady hand.

Andy leaned on the rail, watching the door fling open. The six men who worked with him stood at his side. Silence reigned. They stood there, grinning at her.

Tara couldn't resist returning the smiles. Their noisy camaraderie while they worked would be missed.

"We're finished." Andy watched her closely, as if hoping she'd take the fiftieth chance to make it personal.

A lump formed inside Tara's throat. "Ahem. Ahem." No reply croaked out.

The workers' gazes switched from her to Andy.

Their eyes showed laughter. Their lips were silent.

Tara wanted to sink through the porch.

Andy winked at her. An impish grin spread across his face. "The men wanted to say goodbye."

Oh my goodness. The workers cared enough to wait and say goodbye.

So did Andy. Maybe there was still hope for a relationship with him. Uncontrollable joy pushed her into speech.

"Thanks, guys. You all did an incredible job. Now I can't see the sky from the third floor."

She laughed. And the men laughed with her.

Their liveliness brought memories of good times in my life. My mind came awake with each song. Their playful words made me want to live again. It reminded me that everything good hasn't been lost.

"Goodbye," the men chorused in unison.

"See you in fifteen years," the tallest man added.

With a hand wave, they headed toward their vehicles, anxious to get away. The crew was tired after three days of physical labor.

Andy studied her as the group broke up. "Remember, flat roofs need a yearly wipe down for longevity." Eyes gleaming, he paused and leaned closer. "But why wait? I'll make a house call sooner if you ring me."

Tara felt like a tongue-tied five-year-old.

Andy, make it simple. Ask for a date, if you want one. I'm uncertain, not disinterested.

He sighed and offered the papers he held. "I look forward to the next visit. Don't make me wait. A year is three hundred sixty-five days away."

With a salute, he left the porch and didn't look back.

Tara agonized over her next step. She held up the papers he'd given her and shouted after him, "I'll grab my checkbook. Jackie in your office requested payment upon completion. Hold on."

Andy turned toward her. "Don't bother." His gaze followed the vehicles driving off. He faced her in slow motion. "The ever-efficient Jackie will send a bill. I promise. See you later."

With a lopsided grin and another salute, Andy made his last exit.

Tara closed the door, but held on to the doorknob. No plausible excuse to stop Andy from leaving hit her mind. Slumped against the door, she considered the options. The truck pulled away while she reasoned with herself.

She walked onto the sunporch and sat in her favorite chair. In the back yard, a cardinal perched on the birdbath and dipped a wing into the water. Watching it brought back memories. Observing birds frolic had been her mother's favorite pastime. In the early morning, her mother would discard birdseeds in the feeder for a fresh batch. Then, she would refill the stone basin with fresh water, adding ice cubes in warm weather and an immersion heater in winter. Tara supplied both water and food, but not daily—and no ice cubes or immersion heater. Her goal was solely to save the birds from hunger or thirst.

She sighed into her hands. Her shoulders slumped.

Andy. I missed the chance to see where a relationship might take us.

He hadn't made it clear what he wanted. She could tell Andy wasn't a shy person due to the way he'd engaged her. But an interested man wouldn't have given up. Had hitting on her just acted as entertainment while he worked? No. His conversation had remained consistent even after the job was completed.

* * *

That night, Tara rolled onto her back. A smile was pasted on her lips.

Andy's love-filled eyes bored into hers. Love rose within her heart. Their chemistry couldn't be denied. If love dust existed, it had bound her and Andy. Forever.

"I love you, Tara. You're the woman I've waited for."

His intense expression unchecked her emotions. Battles raged within. Butterflies rippled her stomach. There wasn't a way to quench the joy inside her heart.

"I'm falling in love with you." Tears sparkled in her eyes. "No. I've fallen. I love you, Andy."

Her whispery voice sounded breathless.

"Andy ..."

It happened in a snap. The man's titillating smile vanished.

Tara struggled to sit up in bed. Wide awake, she sighed into the silence. Confusion settled around her. Her hands slid up and down her arms. She stared around the darkened room.

"It was a dream all along. Life, please, imitate my dreams."

A streetlight filtered brightness into the room. Her eyes closed. Maybe complete darkness would revive the vision. She replayed the scene in her mind. Romance thrived. She and Andy shared an intimate table inside a dimly lit café. His expression revealed what his words conveyed. Love seized him, for the first time ever. Neither he nor Tara could speak or break away.

Let it go. It was a dream. Nothing more.

Eyes open, she brushed hair off her face. Lying to herself wouldn't work. Dreams sufficed while asleep, but once awake ... reality must prevail.

Her mind dissected the real-life man. Andy's interest had appeared genuine from the moment their gazes met. Even a seasoned actor couldn't fake his obvious reaction. It marked the first time a man had looked at Tara with open admiration. His appreciation intensified her awareness of him.

The bonhomie she'd just experienced had been a dream. Throes of love and admiration seeped away. Tara still lived alone inside a three-story house, no longer teeming with familial love.

A lone star outshone the other stars in the smoke-colored sky. Beautiful twinkling lights mocked the despondency that invaded her soul.

She flopped to her other side, squirming on the full-size bed.

Numerous times Tara had ignored her shyness to mingle with men. When reinventing herself failed, she kept to her current friends. This latest failure had wasted three personal days from work; it was time off she might need at a later date.

I should've hogtied Andy to the porch.

Tara buried her face underneath the covers. Familiar teardrops seeped through closed eyelids. Her mind resisted further Andy notions.

* * *

On Friday, Tara and a co-worker exited their office building, grumbling about the weather. Rain had Tara wishing for an umbrella. Their complaint fest continued until Shelli stopped beside her husband's car.

"Hello," she said to the man who opened the car door for his wife.

"We're in for a storm." He went back to the driver's side of the car.

As Shelli waved, hair raised on Tara's neck. She eyed a stranger in the back seat of Shelli's car, but the tinted windows obscured her view. Her body trembled the way it had around Andy. Was it wishful thinking? She wasn't sure, but she stood with her eyes focused on the shadow.

Raindrops increased in volume and intensity. Tara stood without an umbrella in a downpour. Water streamed over her body and pooled at her feet. Her toes squeaked inside her sandals. Soaked clothing itched her skin. Drenched, she watched the vehicle round the corner. Only a thunderclap pushed her into action.

While other people waited at the corner for the walk signal, she sprinted across the street in a dash to her car.

Tara didn't stop until she reached her vehicle. Her keys fell into a puddle at the door, and after retrieving them, she slipped inside. Water dripped onto the cloth seat and muddied the floor mat.

"Ugh!"

Her palm whacked the steering wheel.

What gives with me? I got soaked watching a bogus Andy.

* * *

Luke Cassidy stared at Tara's soaked body as Rick's car pulled away. What was on her mind? That dramatic reaction validated his pursuit. Did she suspect he was inside the car? He was fascinated by her expression. Luke considered the implications of whatever she'd been thinking.

His friend's wife, Shelli, had come to mind on his second day at Tara's house. Tara had said she worked at the same multistate payment center for utility companies. Customer service, he thought. Could Shelli become a facilitator and permanent link to Tara? He hoped they were friendly or at least knew one another. A channel to Tara was essential now that her roofing job was completed.

Shelli's unrepairable car benefitted him. Rick worked the afternoon shift and escorted her home on his lunch break each evening. Luke asked to tag along on this trip in hopes of convincing Shelli to set him up on a date with Tara. In case he saw Tara while they waited, he hunkered in the back seat to escape recognition.

Plans had fallen into place with one master stroke. Only God could have the women walk out of the building together the day he was in Rick's car. Discipline restrained Luke from speaking to Tara as she had peered into the back seat. Her perplexed expression had intrigued him. She'd worn that same look whenever he approached her.

Tara appeared bereft. Luke watched her until the car turned the corner.

Two days ago, he'd completed a life-changing roof job. When he'd driven to the residence to bid the work, he'd developed a crush on the house. It struck his fancy. He coveted the vintage three-story building. Every feature appealed to him. Wrought iron framed the porch, and gargoyles were etched into the bricks.

The house needed only a minor overhaul. He was the man for the task if he was able to buy the place. Luke enjoyed restoring old houses. Especially one he hoped to make his own. As he'd climbed the steps, he was assessing the fair market value.

Then Tara had opened the door.

Luke had fallen in love on sight.

Entrapped by her guileless smile, he'd eyed her ringless finger.

Something about her says she's single.

Luke was hooked. There was no turning back.

His attention now shifted to Shelli, who was talking nonstop to her husband.

Goodness, woman, take a break. I have important questions.

He bided his time until the conversation stalled.

Luke spoke up quickly. "Who was that lady you were walking with?"

"Tara. We work in the same office. I was asking how she's getting along. She's gone through hard times lately."

Hmm ... Shelli enjoyed gossiping. What else does she know?

Luke tried to extract helpful information. He managed to learn that Tara's mother had died last month and her father had passed away the previous month. Personal details were scant, but Tara's tremendous loss affected him. He understood her reluctance to encourage a new relationship. No wonder indecision warred with obvious warmth.

She's reeling from the loss.

Shelli peered around the car seat. "Are you listening?"

"Thinking about your co-worker," he answered. "I understand the tremendous loss of losing both parents. Does she have family support?"

"I heard that only her parents' friends were at their funeral. She's an only child whose parents were only children. Both sets of grandparents had passed away."

Ten years ago, Luke's parents' death had altered his life. Their departure left him with a family to raise and support. Despite the newfound responsibilities, that same family had made life worth living.

Where were her friends? Tara can't be all alone. Personable people had relationships. Did Tara? What is her mindset? Is she happy?

Luke thought so. She was reserved and a bit withdrawn, but her behavior didn't signal depression.

He eyed Shelli. "Do you like her?"

"I don't dislike her. Sometimes we eat lunch together. She's blunt, but nice about it. Just don't ask her opinion unless you want to hear the truth."

"Pretty candid, huh?"

"She's standoffish, but only at work. I once saw her eating dinner at a restaurant with a family. While she's reserved on the job, Tara laughed and teased with the kids nonstop. Tara was the life of the party. It seems she has several close friends."

"And ... what else?"

She turned around, facing the windshield. "She's nice to people even if she doesn't really like them. She's like that with my sister, Olivia."

Few people liked Olivia. Shelli could be annoying, but she wasn't as vexing as her sister. Loose-lipped herself, Shelli normally told the truth. Olivia seldom did.

"Tara's lack of family interests me. No grief compares to losing loved ones. Perhaps I can help her through the grief. Will you set up a date between us soon?"

Luke scowled when her head shook.

"No, for two reasons. We don't talk about our life outside of work; Tara likes it that way. And, she's not your type." Shelli swiveled in her seat to face him. "Hey, come to the baseball game with us Sunday. My brother's team is playing the Bobcats. We'll have a tailgate party in the parking lot before the game."

Maybe going will give me another crack at Shelli.

While acquiring further information or lining up a potential date was a long shot, Luke accepted the invitation.

"I'll call Pete and Molli," Luke said. "Her father was recently released from the hospital. She spends much of her time at her parents' house. An evening watching a ballgame might take her mind off his sickness."

* * *

On the afternoon spent at a local baseball field, Luke's best friend, Pete, and Pete's wife, Molli, provided a buffer against Olivia's constant play for Luke. The bothersome woman plopped onto Luke's lap as soon as he sat down. His reflexes automatically kicked in. Luke lifted her off his lap to a spot on the bench, as far away as his arms could reach.

Stop acting brain-dead. A romance between us won't happen. "Stay there. No game playing today."

The gruff voice that came out of him was ominous enough to frighten even himself.

Everyone laughed except Olivia and Shelli. The foolish woman grinned and scooted closer.

Maybe I wasn't harsh enough. How about this? "Down, girl. We've been a no-go since we met."

Molli left her seat on the far side of Pete. She crossed directly in front of Luke and sat beside him. Her action boxed Luke in between herself and her husband.

Olivia rolled her eyes. "Protecting Luke, or making a play yourself?"

Molli grinned. "You can't be bold *and* stupid. Choose one or the other."

That remark successfully blocked Olivia's antics. Still, she simpered at Luke throughout the evening.

At the end of the seventh inning, Luke's ears perked when Olivia told Molli about Tara's parents' deaths. It was a clumsy attempt to reassure Molli about her father's sickness. Luke's antennae rose. It should be simple to ask Tara out himself, but she clammed up whenever Luke made the conversation personal. Shelli had declined to hook him up with Tara. Olivia might, too, if she realized he and Tara had previously met. Olivia wanted him for herself.

Luke strategized the path forward during the game. Even though her sister had refused to set him up on a date with Tara, Olivia would do it if only to have a pipeline to Luke. She would see it as a favor she could cash in. She was his last option to reach Tara indirectly. Once the game ended, Luke offered her a ride home so they could talk.

"The woman you and Shelli mentioned. Tara Simpkins. It must be hard to live without family. Tomorrow, will you set me up on a date with her?"

Olivia glanced at Luke but didn't speak. She slid inside the car and shut the door.

Luke maneuvered the vehicle across the parking lot while he waited on her response.

"Why suggest a date with a woman you haven't met?" She twisted in her seat and stared at him.

"She needs a friend. I've lived through a similar loss. I caught a glimpse of her Friday when Rick picked up Shelli while it was raining."

Olivia jerked her head toward Luke. "Tara isn't your type. Besides, she doesn't date."

"Is that an assumption or fact?" he asked.

"I don't think she's ever dated." Her sneer imitated a grin. "And I'm not your water girl. Get someone else." Her lips clamped together.

Luke observed her inner debate.

Contempt suddenly marked her curled lip. "Okay, I'll do it. I can't wait until you see her in person. A glimpse of her through a window during a downpour doesn't count. We'll critique the big date over dinner."

Luke chuckled. "No. We won't. You can refuse to ask, if you like."

"I said I'll do it. So I will."

The spiteful grin exposed Olivia's self-absorption. Her words welcomed a comparison between herself and Tara. That would be balloon-deflating time.

Luke pulled in front of Olivia's apartment building. Mindful of good manners, he walked her to the door.

"Here's a tip," he said. "Enjoy the chase. The mystique ends once you give in to the moment."

Now let her figure that one out.

After dropping off Olivia, Tara consumed his thoughts on the drive home. All roads led to her. She was the most gracious woman Luke had ever met.

Good thing he was free to do as he pleased these days. Familial responsibilities were behind him. His sister, Steffi, had tied the knot three months ago. She'd been the last sibling to leave the homestead. Luke's family trials were over.

His parents' vision of seeing their children happily settled into adult life wasn't snuffed out with their lives. Luke had placed his life on hold, relinquishing dreams of becoming a doctor. Four days after they celebrated his medical school acceptance, the Cassidy family had planned a double funeral. That morning, a propane truck had exploded on the highway. The accident claimed their parents' lives.

The driver of the propane truck, newly married, had traveled with his wife. A rider in the cab might've caused a distraction, lessening the driver's ability to react in emergencies. Due to that factor and others, their attorney had argued "contract breach," and the settlement was substantial. Monetary compensation failed to eradicate the pain of losing their parents. Nothing can replace loved ones.

Luke had borne the news stoically that day. He then explored his options and took over the family's roofing business. He'd worked in all phases of the job since his youth. He and his three brothers knew the roofing process inside and out. The family drifted into a workable solution.

Their grandparents' and aunt's input provided a stabilizing force. Now his brothers had spouses and children of their own. Only Steffi remained childless.

Enormous responsibilities had hammered him for ten years. His siblings' needs no longer topped his own. Luke would follow his destiny wherever it led.

His number two thought gained traction. It was time to lease his suburban home; urban living beckoned. He welcomed new opportunities. And his future wife occupied his dream house.

Chapter Two

At the side entrance, Tara swiped her badge then hesitated. But the line queued behind her swept her into the building. She almost tiptoed through the customer service department.

Monday morning rolls around like clockwork. Can't it ever miss a week?

Her wish didn't matter. People with jobs worked.

She trudged an indirect route toward her cubicle. Was life worth the effort it took to live it? Her weekend had been a total bust. Even the matinee movie she'd sat through hadn't been worth the trip—or the eight dollars she'd paid to watch it. If she'd wanted to hear kids scream and holler, she would've visited her neighbor. That show was free. Thumb twiddling and house wandering had occupied her evenings.

She took a deep breath and sat at her desk. "Here we go. Back to the weekly grind. Countdown time begins now."

"Tara, don't take the first call!"

She took a brave peek over her shoulder.

Olivia, the co-worker she least wanted to see, resembled a predator on the hunt. Her constant "please help little ole me" expression irritated Tara. And the woman's tongue was toxic.

Olivia, why today? I can't take your shenanigans.

Tara hurriedly averted her gaze, then her eyes widened at the call queue. Over one hundred vexed customers waited on hold to jump her. Who would give the worse attack: a trouble-making co-worker or an unknown customer?

Olivia stopped at Tara's desk. "Don't take the call; we need to talk."

Tara cringed. Her finger hovered over the "ready" button. Oops.

"Hello, my name is Tara. How may I help you?"

An assault arose with the first call. A man yelled, "I smell gas throughout the house."

Her eyes opened wide. "Sir, you've called the wrong number. You've reached the payment center."

A loud clang when the caller hung up caused a pain inside her ear. Tara rubbed the area above her jaw. She glanced at the computer. No pop-up showing the caller's phone number appeared on the screen.

Irritation rose within her. It was way too early for drama of any type. Running for home sounded good at this point. Even being stuck alone inside an oversized house was better than a minefield of disgruntled callers.

Hmm ...

"Tara! Are you listening to me?"

Oh. She's still here.

She spun her chair around. "Did you need me for some reason?"

Please say no. Go away. What an exhausting morning.

Olivia took a step backward, eyed Tara, then appeared resigned to whatever she planned to say.

"*Even you* won't believe what happened yesterday."

She's insulted me with the first sentence.

Olivia pushed Tara's banana and apple aside and sat on the desk. "Wanna know what happened?"

"I have a headache." Tara rubbed her temples. "I need to concentrate on the next call. Tell me later."

Olivia shook her head. "Here's what happened. Ricky's friend, Luke—he's a close friend of mine, too—well, Luke asked me to set him up on a date with you. Don't look stunned. He was serious."

Tara leaned back in the chair, fully engaged in the discussion. This was unheard of news. "Shelli's husband, Rick? What piqued his friend's interest?"

"Maybe he felt sorry for you or something." Olivia shrugged. "Shelli and I told him your parents passed away within one month of each other." She frowned at Tara. "Anyway, he appeared concerned that you are all alone. That's what he implied."

Olivia leaned closer, but her voice rose an octave higher. "You'll never believe what else Luke said. Guess. Stop glaring at me. That you weren't alone. You have him." She peeled Tara's banana and took a bite. "Can you believe a man you've never met thought that? Why should he care?"

Tara moved her apple to the other side of the desk. Olivia was a pathological liar. She doubted the man said anything close to that.

"I don't believe you. Why did you and this guy discuss my parents' deaths? How did my name come up? Neither of you know me."

Olivia rolled her eyes. "I knew enough to whet his interest. Here's what else he said."

Tara's curiosity died with each word Olivia spoke. If only a person who told the truth had brought the offer. She barely listened as the woman prattled on.

* * *

Later, Tara signed off the telephone. Some days seemed longer than others. Today felt extra long. Too many problem calls in one morning. She thumped her watch. Was it running fast? A quick glance at her cell phone proved the work day was almost over.

Whew. Too bad it isn't four o'clock. Well, it's time for a late lunch. The cafeteria should be empty. Whoopee for me.

She grabbed her lunch sack out of the refrigerator and placed it in the microwave. The cafeteria was on the other side of the building and Tara turned in that direction. The place should be practically empty.

Time for a nice quiet meal.

"Over here, Tara. Sit with me."

Shelli. Some people refused to be ignored.

Lunch with her might place me into Luke overload. I'd rather remember Andy.

Tara had finally met a man she liked, but then she blew it. Maybe Shelli just wanted to talk about work. One could always hope.

Her trip across the room reminded Tara of a movie where a woman had struggled in a trek across the desert in a sandstorm. She felt invisible debris pummeling her face and body. The death march came to mind.

With a silent sigh, she snagged a seat across the table from Shelli. "You're eating lunch late."

"It's my day off. I actually came in to talk with you. Your normal lunchtime started forty minutes ago. Were you on a long call?"

"Yeah. But this customer had a real problem I could fix." Tara unpacked her lunch and glanced at Shelli's bakery box, frowning at the gooey concoction in Shelli's hand. She looked back at her broccoli stir-fry. "Saved from starvation."

"Me too. By chocolate-covered doughnuts." She tilted the box toward Tara. "Want one?"

"No thanks. I ate too much ice cream over the weekend."

"So did I, plus too much cake. I won't eat any dessert this weekend. This morning, I dropped off Rick at work and kept the car ... and got doughnuts." She took a bite. "Mmm. Delicious." Shelli gulped the sugary drink she held. "I hoped you were eating lunch late and hadn't gone home." Wily eyes observed Tara. "It's my turn to convince you to date Rick's friend." She paused for effect. "Luke is a good guy. Olivia told me you didn't believe her. Why not?"

Tara coughed and patted her chest. She spat her half-chewed roll into a napkin. She stared at Shelli with water-filled eyes. "Is that a serious question? Olivia lies."

Shelli set her drink on the table, stirring ice inside the glass with her straw. "I am her sister. Pretend you like Olivia, even if you don't."

Tara reprimanded herself for her abrupt comment. *Behave. Don't rub her sister's shortcomings in Shelli's face.*

Tara donned what she hoped was an apologetic smile. "Who said anything about disliking her? But I won't play pretend games with you: Olivia tells lies. I don't believe anything she says."

Shelli's jaw slacked. "I can't believe you actually said that. What if I tell her?"

"I'll explain why I made the comment if she asks." Tara laughed then gave her best contrite look.

"Let's go back to what we were talking about first." Shelli pushed the doughnut box aside. "Luke is a close friend of Rick's. We were at my brother's baseball game Sunday. He asked about you while taking Olivia home."

"He doesn't know me. How did my name come up?"

"Molli, Luke's best friend's wife, has an extremely sick father. She and her husband were at the game. Olivia mentioned you recently lost both parents from the same virus, although it is different from the one Molli's father had."

Olivia spoke the truth for once. Still, why did she tell death stories to a person with a sick relative?

"Don't you think that story was a bit morbid for a person whose father is ill?"

"It was her way of telling Molli how lucky she is that her father is still alive." Shelli swept her hand aside, and then picked up another doughnut. "Let Olivia be. What about you and Luke?"

Me and Luke? A stranger? I'd rather date Andy. He liked me. Too bad I messed things up.

"Come on, Tara. How can one date hurt anything? Accommodate Rick's friend. Luke's sincere request surprised me."

Could this new development convince Tara to go out with Luke? Her fingernails clicked on the table. Perhaps a date with him would banish Andy from her brain. So far, nothing else had. Should she give in? There wasn't anything left to lose.

Then her thoughts filled with her abominable nineteenth birthday spectacle. *Don't go there. All blind dates don't end in disaster.*

"Come on. Go out with Luke."

Pressed for a response, Tara's resolve to say no lost steam. She stalled for time. Dating a stranger was a difficult proposition for someone her age who had only gone on one date that ended badly. A younger woman without the negative baggage might've agreed without hesitation. So would Tara. The knowledge that Luke was Rick's friend satisfied her objections.

Ignoring my difficulties is an inane way to solve a problem. Plus, a break in the monotony might help.

"I'll go." Tara spoke before her mind changed.

Shelli swished her balled napkin into the receptacle. "I suggest we eat an early dinner at my house on Saturday. It's easier to talk that way." She rose, studying Tara. "Will that setup work for you? Or would you rather have a one-on-one date with Luke?"

Tara worked out the fine points in her mind. One decision always led to others.

A group setting will feel less intimidating for a date with a stranger.

Two dates in thirty-two years. The first one occurred thirteen years ago.

Any date is overdue—blind or otherwise.

"It's odd that he wants a date with a stranger. But set up a date at your house." Curiosity overtook her. "What's he like? How old is he?"

Shelli snickered. "You're working from behind. Those are questions you ask in advance." Her grin was conspiratorial. "You'll like Luke. Most people do."

Shelli filled Tara in on his exploits as they left the cafeteria.

* * *

The next evening, Tara's four married friends sat around the kitchen table, pumping Tara for information. The group hung out at her house every Tuesday at six o'clock. The weekly routine had developed right after Tara's mother's death.

Deep-rooted relationships ruled with these women. Long ago, they proclaimed themselves friends for life. Best friends Abby and Tara had lived across the street from each other since before they started kindergarten. Identical twins Mindy and Marcie came to their school in seventh grade. Suze joined the gang their freshman year in high school.

Tonight, the women gorged on chicken broccoli casserole and chocolate cake. Marcie pointed to the half-empty cake plate. "Dessert overload. Someone will have to roll me home. Now, Tara, bring us up to date. Give us the lowdown on the new guy, Luke. What did Shelli tell you?"

Tara stacked her cup onto the saucer. "Not much. He and her husband have been friends since high school. At thirty-two he's never had a serious girlfriend. Maybe he's a serial dater."

Suze glanced at Abby. "You aren't reacting. Guess you heard a preview." She turned to Tara when Abby nodded. "Is that it? You didn't find out particulars? Where does he work?"

"I didn't ask. Where he works won't matter unless we hit it off."

"Which means it counts in case you do. Always find out beforehand," said Marcie. "Advance knowledge tempers a better response."

Not for me. "Only job snobs do that. Not everyone goes to college or has a white-collar job like Stan."

"So you prefer dating a man who works at McDonald's?" Marcie asked.

Mindy laughed until she coughed.

Giggles erupted around the table.

"Tara would if his name was Andy," Mindy finally said.

Tara batted dream-filled eyes. "I love a man I'll never see again." She paused, eyeing Mindy. "Honest enough for you?"

"Too real for me." Abby pushed aside her saucer. "The man you described earlier isn't a quitter. Somehow, he'll wind his way back to you. Premature love declarations spell disaster."

"Abby's right. You let Andy walk away last week," said Marcie. "If he reappears, you'll keep him close regardless."

"Meeting Andy again is concerning because you're desperate to keep him." Suze frowned, tapping her lips. "Dating Luke will provide interaction with another man and level the playing field somewhat. Especially if he's likable."

"I agree with Suze," said Mindy.

Wow. Opposition regarding a man I won't see again. "Perhaps Luke and I will have an enjoyable date on Saturday. But Andy's the man I prayed for."

* * *

The blind date day approached much too quickly for Tara's taste. Two separate incidents tempted her to cancel it. First off, Shelli didn't ask for her phone number to give to Luke, which wasn't necessary, but would've been nice. Maybe Shelli hadn't passed on Luke's request. However, the worst offense was Olivia inviting herself and a date to the dinner.

Thursday, before meeting Luke, Tara ate lunch with Shelli and Olivia. Neither one had taken a breath since they'd joined her. She concentrated on the spicy chicken sandwich she'd prepared last night. Savoring each bite while the sisters gabbed, Tara tuned into the conservation when Olivia named co-workers she said were undatable. Shelli switched subjects to an upcoming holiday.

"Memorial Day's coming. Olivia, did you—"

"Hush. I was talking." While Olivia chewed a tater tot, smug eyes focused on Tara. "Luke probably broke up with the woman he's dated for five years. But she wasn't his girlfriend, or so he claimed. You aren't his usual type. I can't wait until he sees you in person."

Tara shuddered. Vegetables fell onto her lap. She laid her fork on the table, then pushed aside her half-eaten sandwich.

I may look ordinary, but I treat people right. You never have.

Shelli rolled her eyes at Olivia before smiling at Tara. "Luke has always dated the wrong women. Rick explained he did the same thing in high school. We both agree he needs someone grounded in his life; like you."

The backhanded compliment annoyed Tara. Yesterday she'd suppressed the urge to cancel the date. But today's lunch with these two placed her back into retreat mode. Her friends' opinions and her anxiety had been troublesome enough. Olivia's rudeness forced Tara to reconsider going. Again.

Still, she refused to bail at the last minute. Besides, it would feel good to get out of the house, regardless of why it happened. The old home she loved was filled with nostalgic and sorrowful memories. Both of her parents had died agonizing deaths at home.

* * *

On Saturday, Tara lingered in bed until mid-morning. Nothing she tried tapered her anxiety. She pounced on the ringing house phone and found Abby on the other end.

"Get out of bed. Eat something delicious. Then read a good book."

"How did you know I was still in bed?" Tara propped herself against the headboard. "I'm a nervous wreck."

"Dibbling in bed becomes your safety net when you're feeling confused.

I was halfway out the door and on my way over until Craig insisted I let you figure it out on your own. Hold on." Muffled voices conferred in the background. "Here's Craig."

Craig? Tara waited with her hand splayed across her chest.

Abby and Craig had steady dated since their junior year in high school. Fourteen years ago, the couple married two months after their high school graduation.

"Enjoy the evening. Think positive thoughts." The deep voice struck the right tone. Craig's steadiness calmed her nerves. "Be the lovable person you always are," he continued. "Consider Luke as a potential friend so you won't become flustered."

His suggestion surprised Tara. "You still think I tense up when men show interest?"

"Now I finally understand why. They weren't for you. You'll figure it out once you meet the right man."

Tara hugged herself. "Ah! Thanks, Craig. One day I'll marry a caring man like my friend did."

"Keep those thoughts. I'm rooting for you. Here's Abby."

Tara smiled. "I knew I liked that woman," she heard him say.

Back on the phone, Abby blurted out a pep talk before hanging up.

When her stomach gurgled louder than usual, Tara slid beneath the cover, massaging her abdomen.

"Feasts calm tension. Get up."

Her mother had insisted that the family dine on gourmet meals whenever their daughter became antsy.

* * *

An old idiom proved true. Watched pots never boiled. The hands on the watch dial had barely moved each time Tara looked. Edginess plunged her into tidy-up mode. A thorough house cleaning consumed her afternoon. Sometime later, she put her cleaning supplies away and headed toward the staircase, checking her watch on the way upstairs.

"One hour until time to get dressed. Almost there."

* * *

Five minutes later, Tara sauntered from the bedroom, but her cell phone rang before she reached her destination. She answered inside the bathroom.

"Hey, Suze. What's up?"

"Has Luke called?"

Tara studied her reflection in the vanity mirror. With a silent sigh she opened the top drawer.

"No. Shelli doesn't have my cell phone number."

"Don't make excuses for him—or yourself. He could've requested it. And you could have offered yours."

"Stop provoking me." She blew bangs off her face. "You don't like him. Do you?"

"Haven't met him. Josh suggested that talking down about Luke might minimize your anxiety."

Tara frowned at the phone then replaced it to her ear.

"Although a bit more positive sounding, Craig spoke similar words earlier."

"Uncanny. Well, anyway, take free advice. Don't be nervous—think of me. That'll make you laugh."

A bona fide smile curved Tara's lips. A quick glance in the mirror showed twinkling eyes gazing back at her. "Oh, Suze. I love you. Wish we were double dating. Hmm ... That's an idea I should've thought of on Friday."

"That would've been fun. Call me the moment you get home."

* * *

Ready earlier than she'd expected, Tara lounged on the settee in her bedroom, casting aside her e-reader within minutes. Maybe a cozy mystery would've better suited her mood than the chosen romance novel. Her hope-filled morning vanished. She'd gotten over her stress a bit, but now it was back. She and Luke should've met at a neutral location. But then she reminded herself that hindsight never worked for anyone.

A lack of a phone number kept her from canceling dinner. Besides, Suze was right. Pretending that dating a stranger was normal had been a mistake. Even though Tara downplayed the date, she was antsy. Dinner being at Shelli's house made it worse.

Tara moved onto the sofa in the living room and sat with her hands folded on her lap. Her gaze darted around the room without anything registering. She tried to calm herself but was too tense to wait it out. Children playing outside the house drew her to the window. Neighborhood girls jumped double-dutch rope across the street. She laid her forehead on the window pane, watching while they played. Her mind drifted over her life when she was young. Those were the good ole days. In elementary school, her biggest problem had been not being able to play outdoors longer.

A four-door sedan slid into the parking place in front of her house. One hand clenched the curtain when a man of medium-height exited the car. Tara gasped into her other hand. Her heart was racing by the time he crossed the sidewalk to her house.

It's Andy. Shelli and Olivia said my date's name is Luke.

Wait. Is Andy paying a surprise visit? How odd he arrived at the exact time Luke was scheduled to come. Her brain froze up. *Forget coincidences. Andy must be Luke.*

Is his name Andrew Lucas or Lucas Andrew? Did he tell me his name when we met? The shirts he wore had Andy embroidered on the pockets.

If I was mistaken, it was a reasonable error any person could make. Good thing I never called him Andy.

She flinched at her silliness.

What foolish thoughts. Relax. It'll be okay. No, it won't.

Tara stared down the empty street in both directions. Her lips mashed together when he reached the front door. She released the curtain once the chime sounded one long peal followed by two shorter ones.

Andy's signature ring reverberated throughout the house.

Rational thought eluded Tara. Her gaze darted around the room as if she sought a place to hide. Inhaling deeply, she stumbled across the floor, steepling her fingers over her mouth and nose.

"Okay. You can do this. You can handle any crisis with ease."

Somewhat calmed by the pep talk, she opened the door and tried to smile.

Laughter twinkled in Andy/Luke's eyes. He held out his hand. Did he expect a handshake?

"Stop looking irate. I come in peace." His hand rose higher then fell at his side.

Perhaps something in her expression made him pause. What? She was still standing. She hadn't cut and run or burst into tears.

"I figured you would be surprised to see me, but you're shocked."

Tara ignored the direct gaze. "I—I thought your name was Andy. Andy was embroidered on your shirts."

"Oh yeah. My younger brother." The grin returned full force. His gaze slid over her face until he chuckled. "I grab the first shirt hanging in the laundry room if I'm running late. That happened three days in a row last week." His voice lowered. "I had late nights and couldn't sleep. Too much Tara Simpkins on my mind. On Friday you forgot my name after the introduction. But, you remembered me. When I arrived Monday to replace the roof, anticipation had snared us both."

Luke likes me enough to involve my co-workers. Tara tuned out his last remark. *Stick to basics. He set up the date through Olivia. Don't let him weasel out of his deceit.*

"Why set up the date through a third party?"

"You ignored my attempts to make it personal." With eyes that sparkled in natural lighting, he gestured toward the foyer. "May I come inside? Or are you sufficiently angry to send me packing?"

Although distrust sent Tara's emotions into overdrive, the unrepentant man was allowed entrance.

Chapter Three

Four hours later, Tara stood alone on Shelli's balcony, squinting at the horizon. Different location, same scenario. She was lonely although not alone. However, avoiding the social scene years ago had eliminated rejection. Before wising up, pre-teen Tara had put herself forward, praying for male attention. At outings in her teens, she remained aloof, retreating to wherever adults gathered, even though her friends mingled. As an adult, after a few fervent tries to socialize, Tara chose quiet alcoves hidden in secluded corners.

Years of this made one thing clear: Males chatted with her, but none had asked her out. Marriage dreams disappeared after her twenty-fifth birthday.

In her muddled thinking, Andy had been her last hope.

No. Luke was. Had her last chance come and gone?

Vivid colors transformed the sky into a delicately understated vision. Each night's display offered a new, quiet beauty of its own. Tara ogled the pale pink and purple sunset streaking across the skyline. Her mind cleared as she studied the picturesque view.

In the evenings, she often sat in her bedroom until the last plum streak faded. Tara was awestruck by the peace she felt while watching sunsets. Her gaze poured over the sky. Hearing laughter inside the apartment reminded her she wasn't at home. She glanced over her shoulder at the group seated in the living room, resisting the pull to join the lively discussion. Her gaze reverted to the scene that always boosted her spirits.

She let the amazing sky show curb her loneliness. Her joy then floundered once the colors began blending with the slate-blue sky. This last transformation was indicative of her day. The morning's promise had drifted into evening's impossibility. In love with Andy, she'd hoped for friendship with Luke, but they were the same person. Tara was still in love with him.

His actions toward her hadn't missed a beat but had intensified since their last meeting. Each word he spoke displayed genuine affection.

What would my parents think of Luke? I miss them so much.

After her mother had become bedridden, Tara sat beside the woman wasting away before her eyes. Each evening, they observed nightfall together. Her mother leaned on the headboard while Tara cuddled her mother to her chest. The fragile lady's tired eyes fixed onto the sky until the last stroke of color disappeared.

"Don't close the curtains, dear," she always reminded Tara, when Tara stirred. "The star show is sure to launch soon. And I won't fall asleep before it does."

Inevitably, her mother fell asleep minutes later. Her energy was depleted by simply sitting up in bed.

Watching sunsets helped Tara stem pain. But the two people she loved most in the world were gone, and she knew she must adopt a different lifestyle soon.

Whenever she considered her parents' deaths, a recurrent thought from her younger years surged. *Someday I'll be blessed with a family of my own. People I love will love me back.*

She peered through the patio door, seeking the man who was impossible to figure out.

Her gaze latched onto Luke, who stared at her. She wanted to look away but couldn't.

Luke ogled Tara as if they were alone.

Her legs quivered like a bowl of gelatin. She clasped her hands behind her back to regain balance.

Have you fallen as hard as I have? Tell me. So I can stay or say goodbye.

A whiny voice repeatedly called her name.

Tara cringed.

Olivia, please go home. Stop bothering me. You've done enough to ruin my evening.

Should she call a cab and go home? Why leave if the Andy/Luke confusion propelled her there? She'd accepted that her reticence might've sparked his desperate action. It at least showed Luke cared enough to conjure up a plan.

"Hey, Tara. Come back inside," Shelli said while sitting next to Rick. Her voice carried through the open door. "My husband claims you've only spoken five words. It's your turn to carry the conversation load."

Sighing, Tara poked her head inside the door.

"Cooperate, or Luke might think you don't like him." Shelli stood, pointing to the amused man. "See? He's lost without you by his side."

Tara glanced at Luke. Lost? He wasn't. The self-satisfied man appeared smug.

Shelli reclaimed her seat once Tara sat next to Luke. "Luke didn't tell us he'd met you already. He kept that secret to himself."

Luke touched Tara's hand, winking when she looked up.

Shelli pointed a crooked finger. "Stop grinning. Admit you tricked me."

"I tricked Olivia. But thank you for the reinforcement. I appreciate both of your efforts."

Olivia used the acknowledgement as an excuse to hoard the conversation.

Tara glanced at Luke when his elbow nudged her side. His lips touched her ear while he whispered.

"She'll fizzle out in thirty minutes."

Tara refused to agree with him, even though she did. He'd tricked her into a date but not blind allegiance.

She was happy to wait until Olivia petered out.

* * *

Tara's hopeful nonchalance intrigued Luke more than it ever had. He'd finally found his sassy, laidback lady that would love him. She was a snappy work of art he couldn't resist. Her projected innocence snagged him the first time they met.

Things are moving in the right direction. How do I bring my lovely lady along for the journey?

Before long, Olivia took a much-needed breath. The lull in the conversation reminded him about the other people in the room. He leaned his mouth close to Tara's ear while speaking in a stage voice.

"Since you've hardly spoken, Rick wants you to critique the sunset for us. I prefer a soliloquy while we watch together."

Tara's audible breath intake surprised him. His sister, Steffi, did that same thing when insecure. The lady was indeed a hard sell. By now she should view him as a keeper like he did her. Luke had invested way too much of himself in their relationship to let her go. Was he getting ahead of himself by expecting too much, too soon? Still, what brought on her reaction? His words or the intent behind each one he spoke?

It's time to spend the rest of our evening alone.

Luke smoothed Tara's hair with his hand, smiling when her teeth nipped her bottom lip. His finger lingered in a tangle that curled around her ear. Tara's facial expression depicted determination—but to what end?

She cleared her throat. "Have you ever attended an interactive sky show at the planetarium? If so, did you like it?"

Her lips quivered. Did she want to laugh? No. Her eyes are solemn. She's sad.

"Not since my elementary school days. We could go next week."

Tara studied her hand instead of him. "Tell us about your previous blind dates." Her gaze sought his when her lips trembled. "Am ... I the first? ... Do you normally ... date strangers?"

Her awkward retort to a simple response about a potential date location bothered Luke. Tara should be more at ease by now.

Luke stretched out his hand, palm up. Perhaps his body language would elicit trust where his words hadn't.

Without looking at him, Tara lay her palm on his.

Luke enclosed her hands in his grasp and tugged her arm.

Her gaze centered on him as she rose. The ambivalence in her eyes compelled Luke into action.

He gazed at the room at large. "I thoroughly approve of Tara changing the subject. However, my response may cause her embarrassment."

Bewildered eyes focused on Luke. Tara tugged away from his hold.

When he held her hand tighter, the question in her gaze flipped. Her body trembled as the pulse in her thumb throbbed.

Maybe she understands the depths of my feelings after all.

"After answering Tara's question, we'll be leaving." Luke clasped her other hand in his. The luminous glow in her eyes robbed his speech. He was enthralled for the first time in his life. As the yearning in her gaze pulled him in, he shook his head to clear his thoughts.

"Tara, you're the only blind date I've ever had or will have."

Mist entered her eyes. *She wants to believe I meant it.* Overcome by Tara's expression, Luke placed an arm around her waist, pulling her closer. His lips brushed her brow. "No need to get up, Shelli. I'll let us out."

Olivia's mouth hung open, and so did her date's. Shelli sat in stunned silence.

Only Rick appeared unfazed. He turned to his wife. "What did I tell you. Luke's in for the long haul." He grinned at Tara. "Brace yourself. Prepare to get swept off your feet. Invite us to the wedding."

Shelli jabbed her husband. "Rick, stop. Who knows if they'll see each other again."

"I do." He laughed, nodding to his friend. "I'll mark the calendar in advance. Next month? Or sooner?"

Luke joined in his friend's laughter and held up two fingers. "Sooner. Two weeks. Pray God answers."

* * *

Tara felt the pinkish tint that rose on her cheeks. Her gaze settled on the sunless sky through the balcony glass door. She struggled to detach herself from the conversation around her. Her legs wiggled. The toe of her shoe dug into the carpet.

Let me out of this nightmare. Luke can have a great laugh and tease me on the ride home.

With her hand enclosed in his, Luke headed toward the door.

Tara matched his steps the entire way. She barely had time to say thank you and goodbye before he closed the door behind them. Neither one spoke, yet the companionable silence knitted the couple together. Luke held her hand while he led her to the car. Whipping open the door, he guided her gently inside.

Her mind went numb. Unwilling to launch a conversation, she waited for Luke to speak.

Luke glanced her way a few times but drove in silence. Even though no one spoke, the mood inside the vehicle remained peaceful.

In her mind, Tara rehashed the scene at Shelli's apartment. Chaotic thoughts relived Luke's performance. A confounding episode had transpired, but the unabashed man seemed sincere. Each action toward Tara conveyed care and respect, and his eyes displayed love.

Luke turned right at a corner instead of making the left turn to her house. She'd assumed he was taking her home. Three blocks down the road, he pulled into an ice cream shop's parking lot.

He released his seat belt. "Since we didn't have dessert at Shelli's house, I thought we could get ice cream and cookies to eat at your house." He brushed a thumb across her cheek. "I love your house. I can't wait to live there."

Move in? We haven't finished the first date.

She just couldn't figure him out. Did he operate from a scripted plan?

Luke left the car and hurried to the passenger side. Opening the door with a flourish, he did everything except bow.

Tara couldn't help laughing, and he laughed along with her. Grabbing her hands, he made small talk until they stepped inside the shop.

Back inside the car, Luke explained the roofing business while Tara listened. She was on nonconsequential-information overload. Plus, she was still reeling from the marriage bombs he continually dropped into their conversations.

Tara thought back to Tuesday's conversation with her friends. Each one had had reservations about her meeting up with Andy again.

He wants marriage. I love him more than ever. Mom would've liked Luke. Would Dad?

Mental shoulders shrugged. Maybe.

She peered into the grey night. *I miss you guys so much. Your sound judgment is much needed. Especially now.*

Luke commented on neighborhood houses while he parked. Holding her hand, he escorted Tara up the steps to her house.

The sunporch was her favorite hangout spot. A desire to share the space with Luke hit her full force. She unlocked the front door and walked into the house, stopping her stroll inside the kitchen.

Extracting the bag from Luke's clinging fingers, she nodded toward the connecting room. "In there, Luke. Sit wherever you like. I'll be right there."

Tara left him standing in the middle of the sunroom and lifted a tray and sherbet bowls from cabinets, humming while she worked. Ice cream was her favorite dessert, but she preferred it paired with birthday cake instead of cookies. Had she been alone, Tara would've picked up a small cake at the grocery store.

Luke had chosen chocolate ice cream while Tara had gone with vanilla. She layered cookies on a dish and transferred each item onto the tray. After spoons and napkins were added, she exited the kitchen, thinking up conversation topics.

Luke stood exactly where she'd left him, but he was now studying the water-damaged ceiling.

"I love your space, although we should enlarge it and add a deck outside."

Her mouth gaped. *What?*

Luke ignored the reaction. "Were all the floors in the back of the house water damaged?"

His keeping up the banter inside her house made it more personal. Tara nodded while overlooking his previous remark. Had she misheard him? Time would tell.

"The damage must be worse upstairs. The quicker we make those repairs, the better."

Tara's mind froze in thought. *We?* Marriage bombs freely flowed. Rooted to the spot, she stared until her inaction increased his action. Luke bypassed two chairs and set the tray on a glass table in front of a wicker loveseat. Once he chose a spot, obviously hoping she would join him, Tara squeezed beside him into the tiny space left.

He grinned and handed her the bowl heaped with vanilla ice cream.

He'd realized she was reluctant to sit near him. Was he a mind reader too? There wasn't a way to stop thinking. Her brain teemed with impractical reflections.

Still grinning, Luke's weight shifted on the cushion. He took off his shoes, picked up the dessert bowl, and crossed his ankles on the table. Then he crumbled four chocolate chip cookies on top of his chocolate ice cream. Once he had finished, he faced Tara. A light shone in his eyes when Tara licked her lips.

"Hope you're comfy. I'll tell you my life story before I propose."

Plonk!

Luke's eyes narrowed as Tara's spoon hit the floor.

The room became claustrophobic fast. Limp arms hung at her side. "Excuse me," squeaked past the lump inside her throat. "I'll grab a clean spoon. Be right back."

As Tara circumvented the far side of the loveseat, she tripped over the threshold that led into the kitchen. Disregarding the twinge in her right ankle, she kept moving until the spoon was flung into the sink.

This can't be happening. While pinching herself, her mind filtered through the dream she had had the night Luke finished the roof job. *I'm trapped inside a dream masquerading as my life.* An absurd thought, Tara. Stop it.

She laid her head on the counter but sprung up quickly. *Luke might see me. He'll think I'm overwhelmed.* She was. Her gaze darted toward the door. She couldn't hide inside the kitchen until he left.

Deep breaths. She collected her thoughts and moved to the utensil drawer, selecting a green-handled spoon from the drawer. *Back to the lion's den. My beloved space won't be the same.*

Sitting beside Luke, Tara picked up her bowl, frowning at the melted mess. She set it down and cleared her throat while Luke watched.

"Too many surprises," she said, sighing.

With a tender smile, Luke placed a finger on her lips.

Kind eyes. One look was like a peek into his soul. Every expression, word, and movement conveyed one simple message. Once Luke removed his finger, the sensation it brought lasted. His warmth bound Tara with an invisible cord.

"I feel like a school boy." Luke placed the empty bowl on the table. "We're soul mates. I accepted that our relationship would be atypical the moment we met."

Tara watched him without speaking. She felt the same way. The fulfillment of her dreams was presented on a gilt-edged platter.

Luke massaged the bridge of his nose. His self-confidence depleted before her eyes.

"Your facial expressions send mixed messages. What are you truly think-ing?" he asked, smiling as Tara looked down. "Do you want to get more ice cream?" He continued after she shook her head. "I'll toe the line and do what I hate most: talk about myself." He snoozled a comfortable position on the cushion. "Here goes the life story. I'm thirty-two and live alone. Due to past disappointments, I hold two non-negotiable expectations: marrying the right woman and raising godly children. I am the eldest sibling of three brothers and one sister. As always, their well-being remains important. Our parents died in an auto accident ten years ago. Not long after celebrating my accep-tance into medical school at Washington University, a propane truck smashed into a median strip on I-70. The explosion caught everyone unawares. My parents didn't have a chance."

"Oh no! I remember the accident." *Luke lost his parents at a young age. His brothers and sister were even younger. I had thirty-two happy years with my parents.* Tara touched his hand.

"Compassionate, just as suspected." He leaned closer. "I've learned to live with the loss."

Tara inched forward then went back to the vacated space. "Mom and Dad, plus my old pastor and his wife, knew your family. They all attended the funeral. Now, I wish I had gone." She rested her forehead on her palm.

The couple who lived in our area belonged to Luke.

Tara touched his hand again. "I understand the horror of losing both parents. But my parents' sickness provided me with time to adjust. You got blindsided."

Luke brushed a lock of hair off her face. "How did your parents become ill? I've heard they died within one month of each other. Facts were fuzzy. Tell me what happened."

One of his hands massaged her shoulder.

"It's a long and involved story. Well, it feels that way to me."

"Tell me everything. Getting another person's insight can work wonders and will bring us closer."

He's right. I'm already connected. Tara fidgeted under his smile. "Luke Cassidy is a sweet talker."

"It's all good if my words ring true. I'll finish my story after hearing yours."

Balance. Where to begin and how much to tell? Her right hand pulled the fingers on her left hand. "Here's the short version. Mom and Dad retired last year. They'd never left Missouri, and traveling the world was their goal. Mom kept a hope log of places she and Dad planned to visit. My parents lived by the motto, 'never spend a dime you can save,' so they had some good savings for the travel."

"Planning for the future is practically unheard of these days. I can tell by your demeanor that you were raised in a stable environment, with lots of love thrown in."

Luke grinned.

Tara offered a teary smile.

"My parents lavished love on me. Guess who dropped in on my mother's thirty-fifth birthday after they'd given up hope of having children? Dad professed I was heaven's gift."

When teardrops overflowed from her lids, Tara wiped her cheeks with her index fingers, and Luke blotted the rest with his thumbs.

"Heaven's gift. Well, gifts give pleasure, and so do you. Continue."

"Well, Mom happily planned their vacation: a Caribbean cruise." She wiped her eyes with a napkin and sighed. "They begged me to go along, but it seemed like they should take the trip they'd wanted for a lifetime alone." *They'd doted on me long enough.* "Their first vacation became their last one."

"What else happened?"

Saddened eyes bored into his.

"Mom became ill on the return trip to Florida. She didn't see a doctor until she got back to St. Louis. Multiple negative test results brought the standard diagnosis: She'd caught a virus on the trip. It happened all the time, they said. However, Mom got steadily worse. A week later my father became ill as well. Dad grew sicker than Mom in a short time span. My parents became roommates in isolation. I had to wear a mask and gloves inside their room. And still the doctors couldn't detect what was wrong."

She shrugged. "Out of ideas, I contacted the cruise line. Thank God I did. Four other passengers on the same cruise had taken ill. Two vacationers had died within days of returning home."

"An epidemic?" Luke shook his head, frowning. "They released culpable information over the phone?"

"Evidently the employee on the other line had a heart. Six passengers had been affected on that cruise. I told the doctors, and the hospital contacted the Centers for Disease Control and Prevention in Atlanta. The center requested blood and tissue samples as they had with the other patients, which the hospital sent."

Luke appeared perplexed then produced a blank expression. "Their sickness was caused by a rare virus instead of a known bacterium?"

"My parents might've recovered if bacteria had been the culprit. Most bacterial infections can be cured with antibiotics. The CDC believed more people were infected than fell sick. The passengers who died had immune systems that weren't strong enough to survive the infection." Tara studied Luke. His concerned expression emphasized his sincerity. He didn't listen out of a sense of duty. Luke cared. The tenderness he generated towards Tara made her explanation flow easier.

"What else?" he asked when she hesitated.

"After the CDC verified the virus wasn't airborne or transmitted by touch, the hospital discharged my parents and recommended hospice."

Luke became suddenly still. "They kicked them out even though they were still sick? That seems odd. Hospitals don't usually do that—especially if the patient is severely ill."

"The administrator said there wasn't anything else doctors could do for my parents. That hospice would keep them comfortable at home. Dad died two months later, and Mom passed away last month." Tara wiped away tears. "Enough about me. Your turn."

"In a moment. Were you your parents' only care provider?"

"Mostly. A home health aide visited three hours per day during the week. My practical dad either figured they would die, or he had a strong suspicion that they might. Before Dad entered the hospital, he tied up loose ends on the home front and placed a portfolio in their safe deposit box with these instructions: 'Hire an attorney and an accountant.' Do you know anyone?

The couple my parents used retired."

"You're covered. My brother Colton will handle the legal part, and Andy is a CPA. We'll talk with them Monday."

Andy. I want to meet the brother who owns that name. Tara closed tear-filled eyes when Luke signaled he wanted her to continue.

"Dad left insurance policies on the dresser in their bedroom. He knew they were dying." She sniffed into one napkin and dotted her eyes with a different one. "Even now, it's hard to believe my father's strength failed him. Sometimes I stood out of sight in the hallway and watched him cry. It would've crushed Dad to know I saw him. Towards the end, Dad sat in front of the oven, dressed in pajamas and robe, enshrouded in blankets. The thermostat stayed set on 90 degrees, but he was cold and shivered as sweat poured off his body. I placed two quilts and one blanket over him while he slept at night. Their last days were very different from each other's." A sigh seeped through trembling lips. "My parents took their dream cruise in January. Dad died in March and Mom in April."

And now it's May. I'm raw. I can't bear any more pain.

Grief gripped her body until Luke kissed her hand and cradled her fingers. He gently lifted her face toward his. "Sorrow can't outlast cherished memories built with loved ones."

"I know." A huge teardrop rolled down her neck. "My parents lavished love on me even with their death sentence. Dad insisted we strip the place to the bare minimum. Unused articles were donated or thrown away. The third floor is empty. Only the washer and dryer are in the basement. Mom took over where Dad left off and had the house cleared of their clothes and personal items. She freed me from sorting through memories after her burial."

Only the items I wanted remain. She blinked at the memory. "Your turn. For real this time."

Chapter Four

Tears flowed when the back of Luke's hand caressed her cheek. Her heart skipped a beat as his fingers tangled loosely in her hair. Unbelievable emotions she'd never imagined were aroused.

His gentle strokes produced relaxing effects. Heat radiated throughout every inch of her body. *His touch and my love act as a balm against endless pain.* Breathe. Rushing into tomorrow while living in today won't work. Life isn't over.

Luke pulled back his hand. "Your thoughts? Many expressions flickered across your face."

"That the first day we met changed my life. I can't get over your being here." Pausing, Tara smiled. "Tell me about the real you."

"At the beginning—" Luke laughed. "Look. My life is an open book I want you to read. Ask questions, if you like, at any time." He paused. "When our parents died, Andy was twenty-one, Colton seventeen, Benton fifteen and Steffi twelve. We come from a generation of roofers. Granddad founded Cassidy Roofing in his twenties and passed the company to Dad after Granddad's retirement. I inherited the business, surrounding property, and the house outright. All assets were left to me with the directive to equally divide anything unrelated to my inheritance. Every asset, which included the insurance settlement, was split five ways. Several rental properties are the only possessions left undivided. I've been advised against dawdling."

Tara felt complete ease for the first time since Luke arrived. "You'll split the rental property as evenly as you did the other assets."

Luke's lopsided grin made Tara rethink her bold declaration. Only quality time spent with a person revealed their true character. Assuming a person's intent without knowledge was illogical.

Somehow, I know I'm right about Luke.

"I think you try to do the right thing if you know what that right thing is," she continued.

"Which means I mess up." A bemused smile highlighted his features. "Sometimes I'm ill-informed. I love that vote of confidence, though." His hand reached out to Tara. "I want to live an upright life. Nevertheless, I'm eons away from being a selfless person, although I hear a few exist."

"My parents were selfless," Tara said. "You've never met anyone who did the right thing just to do it?"

"In one word, no. People do good things based on multiple motives."

Thinking over his reply, Tara chose to change subjects. "Tell me more about your business."

"Five years ago, I revamped Cassidy Roofing and developed the surrounding land. A three-story office complex replaced the old warehouse and storefront. Three utility buildings were erected in the rear parking lot. They contain the roofing business, a plumbing company, plus a shared warehouse and shop."

"Does the office complex and surrounding property belong exclusively to you?"

"Yes. Granddad purchased the property very cheap fifty-six years ago. I simply implemented plans Dad had drawn. My brother Benton owns the plumbing company. Granddad's friend ran his plumbing company in Grandad's warehouse alongside the roofing business. He sold to my brother three years ago. Cassidy Roofing is debt-free. The office complex is fully occupied and paid for. Andy's CPA firm and Colton's law practice also are housed inside the complex. Steffi manages their offices."

Tara couldn't stop grinning. She was right. Luke was trustworthy. "So you put everyone through college with shared assets."

"Absolutely not." His head shake emphasized the point. "I'd put myself through college with roofing. I lived at home, studied relentlessly, *and* worked hard. I graduated college debt-free. My parents paid whatever my salary and scholarships didn't cover. My siblings adopted the same plan. Proceeds from Cassidy Roofing and our rental properties paid expenses that scholarships and salary failed to cover."

"The rental properties are shared assets, but you also used funds from Cassidy Roofing. You're a nice guy."

"I wanted my parents' vision to live on even though they didn't. Andy had followed the same pathway. Other than hard work, scholarships were key." He paused when she sighed. "I see sadness. Why?"

Gripping Luke's hand, Tara squeezed his fingers. "You were accepted into medical school after years of hard work and dedication."

The hand he raised brushed off her comment while his thumb stroked her wrist. "My second choice proved better than the first one. In the end, I kept the family business afloat. Next Cassidy generations will benefit from what Granddad initiated and Dad continued. Staying the course provided everyone an easier life."

Luke uses practicality to cover disappointments.

She quietly listened when he continued speaking.

"Granddad passed the business to his only child who passed it on to me. I'm looking forward to our oldest son following the same path."

"Stop making me blush." Giggles escaped pursed lips.

Quit showing your gauche side.

Luke's eyebrow rose.

Had Tara spoken out loud? Quick. A diversion.

Tara picked up Luke's empty bowl. "Seconds on ice cream?"

Luke removed it from her hand. "Perhaps later. I intend staying put until I'm banished."

Shifting position, Tara drew her legs beneath her. "When will you divvy up the rental property?"

"You switch topics better than I do. The plan is to pay everyone the nominal value when funds become available."

"Then you'll keep the property for your personal portfolio."

Tara's houses came to mind. *Rental property. Lord, where are You leading us?* Her lips pressed together. Tara had rarely consulted God since her mother's death. Even after her father passed, she'd prayed for her mother's healing. After that failed to happen, her hope for a happy family life crashed. Tara had buried many expectations along with her mother.

"An appropriate ringtone," Luke said when Tara's cell phone rang.

Celine Dion's "Because You Loved Me" filled the air.

She barely glanced at where it laid on the table. Abby. Likely with questions about the date. After it pealed three successive times, she placed the phone on vibrate. Time spent with Luke surpassed giving her friends up-to-the-minute updates.

During their conversation, Luke drew out details on her nonexistent social life. Tara even supplied details on the horrific nineteenth birthday blind date.

"Let me see if I understand what happened. You agreed to date the brother of a woman you met at the library?"

"I'm wiser these days. But, she wasn't a total stranger. We'd talked there on several occasions. My foolishness became apparent once we ended up in the parking lot of an X-rated movie theater. I didn't know how to react until his two friends met us at the ticket window. One look at those sleazeballs and I ran across the street into a restaurant. He and his friends followed behind me, forcibly trying to make me leave with them. They ran off after several male customers intervened. The manager called the police, who were there in five minutes. My father arrived fifteen minutes later. Carl, my pastor and surrogate brother, pulled up behind him. That was my first and last date. It was scary."

"I can imagine your fright, but you can't give fear a stronghold. What happened to the men?"

"Nothing. They were gone when the police arrived. I handed over his and his sister's phone numbers. I never saw any of them again, including the man's sister. Maybe she switched libraries."

"So, you had one date. Then the other men you've met lacked perspective."

Practically drowning in Luke's compassion-lit eyes, Tara pondered where their conversation was headed. "What do you mean?" *Why did I ask?* She braced herself for the answer.

"Those guys should've known a keeper when they saw one. I understood the moment you opened your door. Don't let nitwits define you."

"Maybe they couldn't see beyond the ordinary."

Tara peeled nail polish off her thumbnail. What else could she add to avoid sounding like an absolute reject?

"Does that remark refer to yourself? The men in question had lousy judgment."

Uncontainable joy bubbled within Tara. "Has anyone complimented your marvelous way with words?"

"You're the first one to suggest it. And I hope we'll have many more firsts."

"Aw. Stop it. My cheeks are hot. Do you enjoy flustering me?"

Luke's thumb touched the pulse throbbing in her neck. "Your chest has a pleasing pink streak."

Tara snapped the top button on her blouse. Thrilled by Luke's appreciative gaze, she almost undid the button.

"OK, so I told you about my nonexistent dating life. What type of women caught your attention?"

"Women who understood that marriage wasn't on the table."

That's curious. Luke hyped family life, especially in his talk about his siblings.

"Why date if you didn't want marriage?"

"Just because you date doesn't mean you'll get married. But I'll think about your question and let you know."

"Uh-uh. Now. Facts please."

"We don't play by the same rules." The corner of Luke's eyes crinkled when he chuckled. "Blame my folks. Solid relationships like theirs only happen between the right two people."

Please mention the woman Olivia said you dated five years. How do I bring that up? "Ever been engaged?"

One eyebrow slowly rose. "It seems you're doubting a truthful man's word. I haven't had any serious relationships. Women came and went with me. I did date a woman off and on; mostly off. She flits between St. Louis and her home in California, visiting family for three months during the summer."

Tara's heart seized within her chest. Did Luke just admit to having a special lady in his life? No one dated a woman for five years just to fill time.

"Stop overthinking. Until meeting you, I'd never considered marriage."

Then explain the woman you dated for five years. "It's late. Do you live nearby?"

He took the topic change in stride. "Thirty minutes away. A straight shot out Highway 40. Eat breakfast with me in the morning."

A date set for less than twelve hours from now. Luke wants to accelerate our relationship. *I hope it works. Here goes another sleepless night.*

Tara's life's mission was to fall into deep love with an adoring husband. This night counteracted all her lonely yesteryears.

"Hello? You didn't answer. Do you attend church on Sundays? Tara?"

Luke's questions penetrated her discussion with herself. *Pay attention. Don't run him off.*

"You caught me daydreaming." *That comment makes it sound like I'm bored. Do better.* "I haven't in a long time. Since my parents couldn't attend, we all stayed home."

"Do you blame God for their deaths?" His expression softened.

What a strange question. Carl had once implied the same thing. Hmm.

Tara stood, then sat back down. "I don't blame God. Yet, I—I don't understand *why* they died. He knew my parents were all I had in the world. And Jesus is the healer." Confusion filled her mind. "I prayed for their healing day and night. But Mom and Dad died. They expected to live. Miraculous healings take place daily. Why were they an exception?"

"Only God knows the why, and only He knows the future. Did you turn away from God because He didn't answer your prayers as you expected? That's the question Granddad would ask if he were here. Regardless of our desires, God does what's best for the people we pray for."

Lowering her eyes, Tara glanced away.

"Just think about what I said."

She double blinked then sighed. "Sure will," she said, not meeting his gaze. *I lost everything precious to me; others didn't.*

"Back to our plans. I haven't attended a church service in ages. What time does your service start?"

"Ten o'clock." *Thank goodness you changed the subject before I wept all over you.* "Breakfast first?"

"Sounds good. The entire day belongs to us. Agreed?"

Tara laughed. "You're incorrigible. Tell me about the rest of the agenda."

"Lunch and a house tour."

"Perfect! I get to see your stomping grounds. And ...?"

Luke's thumbs stuck up. "An introduction to my family."

"Already?" Tara's heart fluttered against her chest.

"It's time."

Luke leaned in closer, securing her hand in his. His passionate gaze undid Tara's self-control.

"Visions of us together soothed me until we met. I already love you, Tara. Will you marry me—and quickly?"

Luke's intense expression penetrated Tara's numbness. Her hands throbbed within his grasp. Her brain froze. Her teeth nipped the inside of her lip.

"While working on your roof, beliefs that you were like-minded spurred me on. Watching you stand in the rain clinched it for me. Somehow you suspected that I was inside the car. We're destined for each other. Love me back. Say yes."

Love me back. Hearing the exact words she'd prayed so many times coming *to* her from someone else almost changed her mind. She wanted to love a man who would love her back. *Why now and not when I was younger?* Tara jerked her hands from his grip. Rampant emotions stripped her speech.

She hoped to avoid making a crucial error. "Please. Slow down. Let me catch up. Until today, I thought your name was Andy. I doubted we would connect again."

"I tried to make my intentions clear from the beginning. All I needed was to re-enter your life." A lone finger stroked her lips. "Did you miss me after the work was done? That was the outcome I prayed for."

I love Luke, and he loves me. Two rational adults can't both be wrong, even if it does feel fast.

Until this moment, Tara had equated quickie marriages with fool's gold. Funny how personal involvement skewed perspective.

"Truthfully, you're an answer to many years of prayer. I constantly think about you." Unshed tears filled her eyes. Tara's finger dotted her lids. "Sorry. I'm feeling overwhelmed at the moment."

"I delight in you. We're building memories that will last."

Precious words from a man claiming love. Luke is kind.

"Tomorrow, I'll go along with each suggestion except the family introductions. It's too soon to meet the people closest to you with marriage talk."

Luke brushed his lips across Tara's mouth, kissing her once she relaxed against him.

Fireworks exploded. The air sizzled. Her body was aflame. Did her hair stand on edge?

She felt secure within his arms. Now Tara understood why people succumbed to sexually charged moments even while recognizing right from wrong.

She slid from his embrace. "Are you trying to coerce me, Luke? My mind should say yes instead of my body."

"Why not both?" he asked, laughing.

"My brain's fuzzy. There's an overpowering ... something. Love? Hopefully, yes. I played hooky from work for three days while you replaced the roof. I didn't want to leave knowing you were here."

Luke sat straight up. "Now you tell me. I could've spent three days inside the house instead of sweating on the rooftop."

"I'd hoped you would guess why I was home and knock on the door more often."

"Marry me soon. I've waited a lifetime for you." Luke caressed her neck.

Would a smile suffice when she was speechless? Imagine being loved for no other reason than the man thought her lovable.

"I want to build our lives together. I could leave for the night without hesitation if you were mine."

Tara laughed. "It's the twenty-first century. People can't own each other."

"In spirit they can. Say yes. Don't leave me in doubt."

"*But,* dating allows us to see where the road leads."

Luke touched her cheek. "Hopefully to a quick stroll down the aisle."

Their foreheads brushed together just before his lips found hers.

Tara lost herself in Luke's kiss. He spoke volumes with minimal words. Her head flopped onto his chest once he released her. Her mind felt defenseless, so she sought a diversion.

"Do you attend church? If so, which one?"

Grinning, Luke quirked an eyebrow.

"Oh yeah. You've answered that question."

"I haven't gone lately, for good reasons. My mind strays from the sermon, planning activities I should avoid."

That remark revealed his mindset. What did his expression reveal?

Tara shuffled in his arms for a closer look.

Luke's placid features hadn't altered.

"You're supposed to be absorbed in the pastor's message instead of planning itineraries." She paused. "What thoughts cross your mind? Naughty or nice?"

"My choirboy days passed years ago. But I'm a good person, if not honorable."

"Try again. No person can live an admirable but immoral lifestyle."

Mirth filled his eyes. "That's the main reason I keep my personal beliefs private. I don't want anyone going to hell from observing me. Although, even people without a relationship with God can attend church and speak the lingo like people who truly know Him." He leaned closer. "Here's a secret. I've already slotted you. Sincerity is important to you."

"That's right. I admire honesty. Care to explain your rating system?"

"It classifies people as anywhere from authentic Christians to hypocrites and then to the nonbelievers. As for me, I don't want to mislead anyone or dishonor God with sinful habits. Hypocritical Christians can and do push nonbelievers away from the true God."

"Forget the rating-system question. Tell me about your sinful habits. Actually, um, may I guess which ones you have?"

"There are a handful. I know you're well-behaved in general. Don't act smug over your exemplary behavior," he retorted. "But let's get back to us.

What other objections are there? I want to get married sooner rather than later."

He was expressionless. How did Luke's facial expressions not mirror his thoughts?

"It's simple enough," Tara said. "My main objection is you and me. This is our first date. We're not ready for marriage. You feel like someone I've known a long time, and yet we're strangers."

Tara leaned her head on the cushion.

Luke gently squeezed her fingers, grinning.

That smile did it every time.

"Be reasonable," she continued. "Let's date for a while. Our relationship is too new to contemplate anything further. I can't promise forever already."

"There's always tomorrow. I want to see you every day. Spending time together will make you feel more comfortable."

"Exactly. We'll get to know each other. Knowing the basics beforehand decreases buyer's remorse."

"Granddad's parents died in a boating accident when he was nineteen. His parents and my grandmother's parents were great friends, yet he and Grandma met at the funeral and married three weeks later. The Grands were inseparable, with genuine love lasting sixty-three years. We're in love now. They didn't waste time, and I don't think we should either. I'd like to get married in two weeks."

"I can't adapt my life to someone else's story. Two weeks is too soon. We must get better acquainted."

The relief that Tara was at least willing to get married showed on Luke's face.

A private battle raged within her. She felt like a wishy-washy numbskull. Nonetheless, for the first time in her life, Tara was appreciated by a man other women wanted.

She feigned serenity, but her pulse raced. Did her facial expression shout a resounding yes? She tried to keep a blank look.

"Goodnight, Luke." She hesitated. "Tonight was wonderful. Our having a relationship will make me happy."

Luke rose, and Tara stood beside him. With linked arms they headed toward the front door. Once there, Luke bestowed a lingering kiss.

"Sure you don't want me to stay?" His grin was enticing.

"Nice try. That's one of the few things I am certain of."

When Tara stepped onto the porch, Luke followed behind her.

"Lock the door, then watch me from the picture window in the living room." His voice lowered. "See you in the morning, love."

Luke waited on the sidewalk as Tara followed his directive. Then he waved and stepped into the car.

Hands framing her cheeks, Tara sagged against the wall, contemplating their conversation after Luke drove off. He was persistent, thoughtful, easy-going and fun. She'd fallen swiftly under his spell but had declined his marriage proposal several times. Had her demeanor screamed "yes"?

Still, the owner of Cassidy Roofing had fallen in love with her on sight. That development defied life as Tara lived it. How long could she deny her own desires?

Was declining his offer the correct choice? Perhaps. But she could be wrong and had been wrong before.

My hopes repeatedly die untimely deaths. But I'm too tired to think about it more tonight.

Tara cleaned up the kitchen, turned off lights downstairs, and switched on the foyer nightlight. On the bottom step, she noticed her cell phone had logged fourteen messages. Four friends waited to hear the report. No one expected Tara's news. Andy was her blind date. The roofer she'd talked about was Luke. They were the same person.

Her hands waved in the air on the upstairs landing. An urge to cheer ensnared her. "Whoopee! The man I love proposed fifteen days after we met. Yay!" She laughed in the bedroom doorway.

Tara sat on the bed, kicked off her shoes, and yawned.

"Oh boy. I'm tired. But it's texting time." Giggles abounded as she wrote the news.

Anyone standing, take a seat. Quickly. Guys, Luke is Andy. He wore his brother's shirts last week. Must've overlooked his name during introductions. He proposed!!! And wants us to marry in two weeks. I declined. We're spending tomorrow together. Breakfast, church, etc. My body is popping inside. The man I love loves me!!! Goodnight. We'll talk later.

Chapter Five

The cell phone instantly pealed.

"Ab, you're still awake. Or did I interrupt your sleep?"

"You expected me to sleep without talking to you? Now tell me details."

"Luke told me his name on Friday, but evidently I missed it." Her hands clenched the quilt. "Andy was the name on the shirts he wore."

"Okay. Meeting him overwhelmed you. You were off-balance and missed his name. I even understand the shirt mistake. But why did he set up a date through a third party? There doesn't seem to be a good reason for that."

"I shied away each time he came close." Tara slid beneath the covers. "That happened three days straight."

"Stop making excuses. Let him stand on his own feet. Somehow, he guessed your feelings and took advantage of your attraction, laying on the charm."

"Abby—"

"Do. Not. Marry. Luke. Say no. Mean it. Stick to that position."

Suze's phone number popped on Tara's screen. Mindy's number followed.

Whoa, guys. Lay off. Whatever happened to turning in early?

"Suze and Mindy are calling."

"And ..."

Tara sat up, sighing. "I've chosen to date Luke. Please withhold judgment until meeting him. Promise?"

"Only if you agree to tread lightly. We're on the same side here. How about we have lunch tomorrow?"

"I told Luke we would spend the day together."

"Bring him over tomorrow so Craig and I can meet him."

"Thanks, Ab. The invitation means you'll keep an open mind. We'll schedule a visit another day."

"Oh, Tara. You are schoolgirl giddy in love. I don't like the way Luke played his hand. Please, come over tomorrow, if possible."

Tara ran over Luke's stated itinerary in her mind. "Will do. I'd better go."

"Nighty-night before your phone rings again."

The phone immediately rang. Suze's call was next.

I'm Ms. Popularity tonight. Here goes everything.

"It's late. You still awake?"

"Skip the chitchat. Tuesday, you claimed you were in love with Luke. So fall out of love with him."

So much for politeness. One down and three to go. "Claimed? I poured out my heart Tuesday. It was hard saying I love a man I barely know."

"His using different tactics complicates things. The sleight of hand stacked the deck against you, Tara. You have to wonder why he didn't just ask you out."

"You had to be here. His approach wasn't what I wanted, but he's sincere."

"The man's a stranger; don't pretend otherwise."

"Luke and I deserve an opportunity to make this relationship work," Tara replied.

"Tara ... Okay. I can't take any more. Goodnight. Call me tomorrow."

The next call immediately buzzed in. "Hey, Mindy. Somehow I expected a chat with you tonight."

"Indeed. Haven't you learned how to answer incoming calls?"

"Abby hates being interrupted by another call. She was in a talkative mood."

"We all are. Marcie's calling you after their company leaves. Fill me in."

Tara launched into a synopsis of the evening, ending with, "Luke loves me. And you know how I feel about him."

"Here's my perspective, even though you may not want it: You're lonely; so get out of the house and meet people. Don't fall for smooth talk from someone you just met. How fast can you set up a visit with me and Woody?"

"I'll run it by Luke tomorrow. Marcie's calling now."

"Ask my sister to call me."

Tara took the incoming call. "Mindy said call her. Late night?"

"Just had a few people over before Mindy and family descend on us next week," she said. "I can't believe the blind date was a ploy."

"Not in a negative sense. Luke tried multiple ways to reach me."

"For what? A quickie wedding? Why the big rush?"

"You seem to forget that you married Stan after dating for two months."

"Mindy married his brother three years before. I knew the man."

"Gotcha. Luke and I are committed to making our relationship permanent."

"Then decide about marriage *after* euphoria wears off. There are horror stories associated with men like Luke taking advantage of unsuspecting women."

"Marcie ..."

"Don't become another statistic because you're stubborn."

"I dislike being called stubborn."

"OK, just keep me posted."

Sprawled on her back, Tara shimmied under the light quilt. Her arm dangled over the bed's edge. Telling about her evening had unleashed a tsunami of negative advice complete with warnings. No one offered congratulations. Don't marry Luke had been their consistent theme.

Grudgingly, Tara admitted her friends offered sound advice. She'd declined Luke's proposal, then punted the ball into tomorrow.

How can I learn the difference between hits and misses without previous experiences?

An exhausted Tara fell asleep at one-thirty.

* * *

Luke's thoughts were filled with Tara throughout the drive home. He refused to accept the barrier erected against him. Despite her constraints, the perfect couple had fallen in love. Tara's actions demonstrated the significant nature of her attraction. Missing work for three days revealed hope. Thus far their courtship was progressing better than expected.

Before this date, he'd only wanted to secure more, even though a quick marriage had been his preference. Now he sought marriage within two weeks. It safeguarded Tara's allegiance before second thoughts invaded. One date had set his life on the proper course. Genuine love was awe-inspiring.

He was in love for the first time, and marrying Tara was the only thing he wanted to do.

Luke parked in his circular driveway instead of in the garage. Glancing next door, he entered the ranch-style house. His keys clattered into the empty candy dish. Endless Tara images consumed his mind.

Moseying toward his bedroom, he stopped short of the door and turned in the opposite direction.

There was no point in trying to sleep. He knew he was too worked up. He headed to the kitchen and stared into the refrigerator, pushing the six-pack of beer aside. He only drank maybe one can if watching sports with friends. He pulled out ingredients for a sandwich and put it together. Carrying it into the bedroom, Luke propped his back up on the cushioned headboard.

A barrage of text messages told him he couldn't put off sharing how the date went until tomorrow.

As he took his last bite of sandwich, Luke alerted his brothers, sister, and best friend, Pete.

Heads up. Tara said no to the proposal. But we'll be a solidified item in two weeks. Mark the calendar. Spending Sunday together. Stay tuned!

Response messages exploding Luke's cell phone left him speechless. Seconds later, everyone except Steffi had replied.

It's almost two. Why are they still awake?

Luke himself was usually asleep by now. He seldom stayed up late. But there he was, sleepless, and so were they. Since his one text message led to more questions, Luke spent the next thirty minutes responding.

* * *

Kerplunk. The cell phone vibrated off the nightstand bright and early. Luke dragged himself awake. His fingers inched across the floor. Raised on an elbow, he peered at the caller ID through one eye.

"Steffi. Might've known."

He flopped onto his back, cell phone in hand. Better end the conversation before his sister provoked him.

"You woke me at an ungodly hour. Whatever the reason, it had better be beneficial *and* necessary."

"And what if it isn't?" Steffi spat back. "Humor me. Okay?"

Massaging his temples, Luke turned on the speaker. "It's too early to yak. Call back at a decent hour if that's what you want to do. My future wife and I had a long night." The poorly stated comment had him tossing off the sheet and sitting up straight. "That came out wrong. I didn't sleep with Tara."

"Good. You met the woman two weeks ago. Wake up. This *yak* may take a while, so deal with it until we're finished."

A half smile quirked his lips. Perhaps Steffi would hang up after she slammed him. "Yeah. Let's hear it." He frowned at her breath intake.

"You warned me off marrying a man I've known since childhood. Scott has been Benton's best friend since elementary school. But you objected to *my* marriage and then proposed to a stranger. Explain yourself."

Luke rested his back on the headboard. "Either I can speak, or you can continue ranting. Which will it be?"

"You can defend these juvenile actions, but they won't persuade me and Grandma. And you're only kidding yourself into thinking this makes sense."

"Stop projecting your views onto Grandma. I gave sound advice concerning Scott. You fell in love with Benton's best friend, but he was wild in his younger years, and it wasn't clear he was done being so." Luke may as well voice all his thoughts. "You inherited a good sum of money. Don't let Scott blow it."

Clanging erupted in the background of the call. Luke checked the time. What was she doing? It was too early to cook breakfast.

Steffi sniffed into the silence. "You're implying Scott married my money."

"Scott loves you. But plan for the future even if he doesn't."

Luke thumped the headboard as his comment penetrated.

"Whew. Hey, don't swap topics. You met Tara on a Friday and then saw her for a few minutes over three days while replacing her roof. There was no other contact until yesterday."

"Stef—"

"Who are you? Where did you hide my brother?"

"I don't make willy-nilly decisions." Leah popped into his mind. Luke rubbed the bridge of his nose. "Scratch that remark. Trust my intuition."

"Why did you propose? *I* should've allowed Scott to settle down and you do this? What if Tara's going through her own transformation period?"

"She is. Her father died in March, and her mother passed away in April."

"Oh, Luke. She's depressed. Tara needs support, not a husband."

"She deserves both, and that's where I come in. And you, along with the rest of our family." He switched off the speaker, placing the cell phone to his ear.

"I get it. Her circumstances are heart-wrenching. But marriage? How could you hoodwink yourself and a woman you profess to love?"

Luke stretched his shoulder muscles. He was ready for this meaningless conversation to end.

"We'll choose the best option for us. I'm out of the dating scene, and Tara has never been in it."

"She turned you down."

"I love Tara and won't back down. Get ready." A grin spread across his face as he waited for her response.

"You've never followed your feelings before. Your decisions are always well planned. Something's wrong. Talk to me. Do I need to come over?"

Luke grimaced into the cell phone. "No. Surprise your husband with breakfast in bed. That'll give you something to do."

"All right, smarty. Level with me. We're all married while you're still single. Do you feel left out?"

"It's love, Stef, not depression." Luke laughed. "View me as a satisfied man."

Steffi rushed into speech so fast that her words ran together. "No, you aren't. I won't be fooled. Leah's at fault. Grandma's my next call. Goodbye."

Luke snorted when the phone connection severed.

"Shower time. She'll come around."

* * *

The house phone rang as Luke stepped out of the shower. Grabbing a robe, he hurried into his bedroom. Only his grandmother let the phone ring at length. The caller ID blinked her number.

"Hello, Grandma. Just out of the shower and about to call you."

Never one for preliminaries, his grandmother plunged right in. "You omitted your grandfather and me from the marriage loop."

An audible sigh escaped his lips. Luke maneuvered inside the closet, grabbing the first things he saw off the hangers. Barely acknowledging his selections, he turned the speaker on. "Steffi threatened to call you right away. I'd thought she might decide to be discreet."

"Why? No time is too early if she's worried."

"Well, I'd hoped marriage had added wisdom."

"Blame the marriage proposal instead of your sister. The nervous wreck dropped an egg carton before hanging up. What are your plans today?"

Here we go. May as well get on with the inquisition.

Luke continued dressing. "Spending the day with Tara. Breakfast, church, lunch, and then a house tour. The plan is to win her over by evening." Luke practically heard his grandmother's brain spinning.

"Bad behavior on steroids. Why rush to wed a woman who's trapped inside a difficult season?"

"Because I can and will help her overcome grief."

"A third major snappy judgment won't cut it. Forgoing medical school to run the business and renovating the warehouse are numbers one and two."

Luke restrained himself from preening. Two slam dunks. "Excellent decisions. This present gem surpasses them all."

"You're mighty sure of yourself. Marriage is a team sport that requires each participant's full cooperation. Those other ideas relied on you alone. Future outcomes rest on Tara's efforts and your own resolve. Bring her by today. Bruce and I want to meet her."

"Working on it. Tara declined an earlier offer." A hand raked through his hair. Maybe it would happen today. One could hope. "She's shy around strangers. Perhaps we'll drop by after the house tour. Don't be concerned if we don't show. But do you have a moment to hear some things I've learned?"

Luke provided details concerning Tara's lifestyle.

* * *

Tara switched outfits several times that morning. None of the clothes in her closet were right for special time spent with Luke. Her business casual wardrobe typically worked fine for all events.

She slid hangers from one end of the rod to the other. "Ugh! I've already discarded two dresses and a skirt and blouse." Her bottom lip jutted. "Nothing works. I need more clothes."

Tara stepped out of the closet then went back inside. Forget fantasies of wearing Sunday best. She never dressed up for church, and Luke had proposed to a woman who wasn't a fashion plate.

She grabbed a camisole from a drawer and slipped into a newer pair of jeans and a crimped shirt. Next, she retrieved a pair of low-heeled strapped sandals off the shoe rack. Fully dressed, she turned her body side to side in the vanity mirror. Her reflection passed the "I look okay" test, although she wanted to wow Luke, not be just okay.

"At least it's an upgrade from the day I met Luke. That was a T-shirt, paint-splattered jeans and ponytail day."

With a long sigh Tara rubbed her thighs then walked into the bathroom.

Presentable enough to be seen in public, but at church, everyone's gaze will follow us down the aisle. Glad I sit in the last row and come in from the back.

"It is what it is. Top priority: hair and face." She tapped her nose while glancing around the room. "Got it!"

Tara rushed to her bedroom and retrieved her laptop off the desk.

Ten minutes later, she was back in front of the bathroom mirror. Her eyes squinted as she made a valiant attempt to mimic the hairdo on a Facebook video.

Abby, her self-proclaimed fashion advisor, had sent the link last month.

After several clumsy attempts, her locks were loosely braided and fashioned into an intricate topknot. Loose hair tendrils framed her face like clouds.

Tara rubbed her aching arms. "Whew! Those maneuvers wore me out. Now it's makeup time!"

Light strokes brushed flawless skin until an attractive glow enhanced her looks. Tara winked at her smiling face.

"Wow! I always forget how makeup can emphasize my best features. Hmm. Some ... thing ... is missing." She snapped her fingers. "Earrings. I know just the pair."

Tara zipped into her parents' bedroom. Only the bed, dresser, and chest of drawers remained. Pictures lined the chest of drawers, and a jewelry box was left inside the dresser. Her father had gifted his wife with ruby earrings on their fortieth wedding anniversary. She reverently hooked the studs into her earlobes.

Would Mom have celebrated Luke's marriage proposal?

Once Tara's father had passed on, her mother had spoken differently regarding Tara's social life, wanting her to be more social.

She sank onto the stripped mattress with her mind honed on Luke. His insistence on marriage acted like an irresistible drug.

A smile broke across her face. "He's a romantic. I can tell."

But romanticism didn't change that he was essentially a stranger.

Tara blew into hands clamped over her mouth. Was marrying Luke God's direction for her life?

Her friends bemoaned the idea, believing Luke hid ulterior motives. Any man who proposed to a practical stranger would bother them. Until last night, unpredictable behavior would've bothered Tara. Only, her personal involvement changed her perspective.

A car door closing had her rushing to the window.

Too much daydreaming. Instead of waving, she sprinted down the stairs, grabbed her purse, and held the door open.

When Luke drew her into his arms, she melted against him. Her knees knocked as their lips touched. Numb arms hung useless. She slowly broke away.

Skin at the corners of Luke's eyes crinkled. "Perfect. We're both elated. Ready?"

At least he was besotted, even though his outward demeanor withheld proof. The curtain-raiser for her brand-new life rose higher. She hooked her fingers on his arm.

Did one kiss win me over to marrying him so quickly? Hmm ...

Inside the car, Tara sat with her hands folded on her lap. "Where are we headed? There aren't many restaurants that serve breakfast in my neighborhood."

"Actually, Kenny's Diner is just four miles down the road. It serves home-cooked meals. Cassidy Roofing is across the street."

I'm minutes away from seeing his office complex and business. Out loud she said, "That's very close. I haven't heard of Kenny's."

"It's a well-known trucker stop near the highway. Terrific food. Fair prices. Plus, I love the owner and his family. I eat breakfast there most mornings during the week. But never on weekends, until today."

Three miles from her house, Luke turned right on an access road Tara had never used. As their destination neared, she no longer wanted to act subdued. Obtaining pertinent information about Luke's business and usual haunts buoyed her spirit. She'd get to know him better and conquer her doubts.

He hooked a left into a large parking lot where seven other cars were parked out front. Two eighteen-wheelers and three semi-trucks were parked behind the circular building. Its structure reminded Tara of an old-fashioned drive-in with carhops.

"Here we are." His hands rubbed together eagerly. "You'll thank me later."

Luke's transparent expression oozed boyish charm and guilelessness. Vulnerability served him better than the laidback air he usually projected. Tara liked his unguarded side more.

Something about the diner disarmed Luke. He has special memories tied here. Keepsake moments. I can't wait to go inside.

Tara's cheek brushed the hand that curled around a wisp of her hair.

Luke was a hands-on person, and Tara enjoyed his softer side.

A glance across the road broke tentacles drawing her deeper into Luke. A modern three-story building stood directly across the street. Der-Jenca Place was etched above the door of the office complex.

Tara gazed at Luke. "Yours?" Smiling as he nodded, she looked again. "Der-Jenca Place is a curious name. What does it mean?"

His grin subdued. "A derivative of Derrick and Jenny. My parents. It was

Steffi's idea for the office complex. Cassidy Roofing is in the rear parking lot. How about a tour after breakfast?"

With a fervent nod, Tara clasped Luke's hand as he led her inside the diner. At once, she appreciated the homey atmosphere. Its mixture of wood and warm colors set an informal tone. Twelve customers occupied separate booths and round tables. People were doing various things apart from eating their meals. One woman typed on a tablet beside her plate. Three people watched a Christian program from a giant television screen. Two men read the newspaper while eating. One woman read a hardcover book in what appeared to be a rest area. Tara's gaze settled onto an elderly woman, who hummed until she chewed deep-red watermelon cubes from an oversized bowl.

Her mouth watered. She loved the delicious summer treat. How much would her favorite fruit set Luke back?

Luke didn't sweat the expense and ordered a large bowl comparable to the woman's. After the server brought their sampler platters, Tara munched on generous portions of hash browns, pancakes, sausage, and eggs. They talked about various topics and shared the same viewpoints on issues: conservative opinions on social themes and liberal views on financial matters.

Luke lifted the check once Tara pushed her plate aside. "So what did you think?" He stacked their discarded dishware and utensils into a pile.

"You called it. Tasty food and a down-home atmosphere. It gives off a homey, 'we're all family' vibe." She wiped her mouth with a napkin.

"I think that's what most attracts people to Kenny's. Diners feel at home."

Tara retrieved the bill Luke laid down, taking a look before placing it into Luke's outstretched hand. "The meal was top-notch. And the watermelon was sweet, even though it's out of season for Missouri."

A middle-aged man with grey hair sprinkled in his beard and mustache appeared at their table. He clasped his hands in front of his white apron.

"My family and I have waited ten years for this momentous day," he said. "I rocked baby Luke. Bringing a woman with him on a Sunday morning can only mean one thing."

Chapter Six

Luke studied Kenny. "What if it doesn't? That mistake could embarrass this lovely lady." He grinned then chuckled. "Meet Tara Simpkins. Tara, this is Kenny Junior. His father owns the joint."

Kenny covered Tara's hand with his. "Was I right?"

Tara knew her blush disappeared into her hairline. She parted her lips then snapped them shut.

"Blushing tells me all I need to know." Kenny paused. "Luke's father, Derrick, and I were closer than brothers."

"Luke told me the diner holds precious memories for him," Tara said.

Grinning, Kenny pointed to Luke. "You're here to meet the family. We oldsters work Sunday mornings."

As Kenny stepped aside, three women joined him.

"Our schedules vary during the week, but we're the breakfast crew on Sundays." He turned to a woman with stylish salt-and-pepper hair. "Meet Connie, my better half. On her right is my mother, Regine. On my left, my mother-in-law, Flora."

The smiling women shook hands with Tara.

"Did you enjoy breakfast?" Connie asked. "Watermelon's my favorite fruit."

Tara smiled. "I just devoured the first home-cooked meal I've eaten in five months. My parents would've loved it here. I can't wait to try your lunch and dinner platters, too."

"Thank you." Connie gave Luke a thumbs-up. "Our cooks may change at various points in the day, but the food quality won't."

Kenny's palm covered Tara's hand again. "Luke's parents were regulars of ours. They worked together at the roofing company and often ate lunch here. Luke has said he hopes to do the same thing in the future."

She was noticing a pattern. Luke craved the life his parents had enjoyed.

But she knew her and Luke's personalities wouldn't allow the two of them to have either of the parents' lifestyles. They needed to have their own unique relationship.

Luke eyed her like he'd read her mind. "You all keep chatting while I pay the check."

Once the women and Kenny Junior returned to the kitchen, Tara studied Luke gabbing with a gray-haired man behind the checkout counter. The fifth time they glanced her way, Tara waved. Laughing, Luke hurried to her side then ushered her to the man perched on a cushioned stool. Awards and trophies filled the display case in front of him. Shrewd eyes accessed Tara from head to toe.

Luke tucked her in his arm while performing introductions. "Tara, Kenny Hamilton. Kenny Senior to everyone."

Tara laughed the whole time they talked to the older man. Once they left the diner, she glanced at Luke. "Mr. Hamilton should write a book on humor. He has a teasing view on life that's on target."

"That he does. Which is why I went ahead and paid while you talked with everyone else. You never know what that man might say."

Luke walked Tara across the street to the office complex. Quiet efficiency effused the place. Fully occupied, the grounds were magnificently landscaped with ample parking. Plus, the utility structures behind the building blended with the scenery. Once inside the building, Tara peered into every nook and cranny. Luke answered detailed questions throughout the tour. Behind the office complex, a warehouse and workshop connected Cassidy Roofing and Expert Plumbing. His brother's company was the last stop.

"So you and Benton share the warehouse and shop."

Nodding, Luke locked the door and escorted Tara across the parking lot. "The work relationship saves money. Coming aboard? I want you to work here."

Not yet. More information was needed before planning her future. Marriage was debatable, as was changing her career. Her wanting to quit didn't matter. Luke would steamroll over her concerns if allowed.

"Tell me about who works here. Is Jackie the office manager?"

Luke nodded. "She'll leave soon. I mentioned you as the likely replacement, and she agreed. Besides the men, we staff a receptionist, supply clerk, and a service coordinator. I hope you'll like it."

Why does Jackie want me to work here? How close are Luke and his office manager? Tara slowed her steps. "What did you tell Jackie about me? About us?"

"That I might propose on our first date. And God would make it so."

Tara studied him with squinted eyes. "Don't use God's name to have your way."

Although Luke appeared annoyed, he tried to hide it.

"I don't play games, Tara. I come without surprise."

"Neither do I. I'm trying to figure you out."

A smile won out over irritation. "Our future offers a promise we'll both accept." He hesitated when she frowned. "Enough of that. Back to talking about the staff."

At the car, Tara pressed further about his office manager. "Is Jackie a personal friend?"

"Grand Aunt Jackie is my Granddad's only living relative. She's single and childless. Hence her avid interest in her niece's and nephews' lives."

"To me, her agreement to a two-week engagement doesn't seem aunt-like."

Luke tucked Tara inside the car, hurrying to his side. He shut the door, immediately facing Tara. "Aunt Jackie recognizes genuine love. Will you find it hard to quit your job?"

Tara laughed. "In one word, no. I dream of quitting. It's a joke," she said as Luke fastened his seat belt, grinning. "But I don't make snappy decisions."

Luke eyed Tara while backing the car out of the parking spot. "What do you do for fun? Tell me your hobbies."

Thanks for the subject change. All diversions help me remain calm. Keep them coming.

Luke was worse than Abby, who was another relentless person. *Lighten up. Enjoy the journey.*

"Don't laugh. Do you promise?" she asked, smiling. "I enjoy attending open houses and visiting furniture stores."

"Likewise. Except the furniture store part. We have a lot in common. I plan to acquire more rental property soon." He glanced at her. "Will you consider working at Cassidy's?"

Evidently, marrying Luke, working for Cassidy's, and acquiring real estate are non-negotiable. It must be sibling-payoff time.

Tara donned what she hoped was a no-nonsense expression. "No more pressure. I mean it." She shifted in her seat as she regrouped her thoughts. "Um ... how does real estate fit into your plans?"

Luke chuckled at the deflection. "Aunt Jackie manages the property our parents left. If you had her role, that would be one of your jobs after learning the ropes."

Tara reconsidered the job offer. The position seemed doable in the foreseeable future. As for marriage, that would happen later rather than sooner. Even though the praise at Kenny's Diner validated Luke's good character.

The couple talked like lifelong friends on the drive to her church. Six blocks from her house, The Gathering Place was the only church she'd ever attended.

While walking across the parking lot, old friends and well-wishers welcomed Tara back. Most of the congregation had attended her parents' funerals. The ones who hadn't had sent condolences and flowers. Today, she would've preferred their silence over sympathy. Reminiscing about her parents' deaths brought pain.

Tara shivered as she stepped inside the lobby. Inquisitive glances followed her and Luke into the sanctuary.

After she stopped beside her favorite seat, Luke continued down the aisle until reaching the fourth row. Once there, he stepped aside so Tara could enter the pew first. Next, he draped an arm around her shoulder while Tara ignored stares, even though she felt each one.

She nudged Luke. "Stop drawing attention. Everyone will gossip about me if you don't come back."

Luke's lips brushed across her forehead. "We're both involved for the long haul. Participate."

Luke always went back to his main goal of marriage. Sensibility warred against prudence. Awareness of Luke conflicted with Tara's self-discipline.

"You're moving too fast. It's a marathon, remember? Not a sprint. Let's move slower."

"Kenny Senior and the family understood that I love you." Lowering his voice, Luke matched her tone, pausing as Abby's aunt and uncle spoke to Tara. "They loved you. Kenny Senior told me not to screw up."

Tara's eyebrows met her hairline. "He told you that?"

"And a whole lot more."

Turning away, she surveyed the choir streaming onto the platform. People lingering in aisles found seats once Deacon Perez reached the podium. "Pastor Victor's preaching. His son, Carl, took over as senior pastor after his father's retirement. Carl and Annie must be out of town."

Elated to sit beside Luke, Tara sneaked peeks at him and sung loudly with the choir.

Pastor Victor's sermon doused her like a refreshing shower. Enlightened words resonated within her heart. Especially, "Guard the parameters of your life. God allows believers to buy back lost seasons. Trust the Father. Christians miss their God-given destiny with neutralized thinking."

Moments later, Luke repeated those exact words in Tara's ear. Was that God's wisdom for the fledgling couple? Had He dropped a private message into the sermon for her and Luke?

The message touched Luke enough to share the revelation. Can we both be wrong? I don't want to follow my heart down a dead-end road. And neither does he.

Tara glanced at him. Far from nonplussed, Luke appeared confident. Life with him would be totally different from her previous pursuits.

Her nineteenth-birthday blind date came to mind. That awful experience would pale against mistakes made with Luke. Marriage to the wrong man would surpass every idiotic act she'd ever committed. Tara tossed the idea from her mind. Thought food rarely whetted the appetite for more.

After the service ended, the couple headed outside, but congregation members surrounded Tara and Luke in the lobby, blocking their escape. Luke shook hands with each person that approached. He handled interactions with self-confidence Tara wished she possessed, and all the while he edged a route toward the door.

"The Gathering Place becomes my church home as it is Tara's," Luke told everyone he met.

At the door, Pastor Victor and his wife, Petra, stopped the couple before they escaped.

"Hello, young man. I'm Victor, and this is my wife, Petra. We're glad you came. Our congregation enjoys visitors fellowshipping with us."

"Tara's the link to my new church home." Luke's hand found hers. "You delivered a stimulating message I needed to hear."

"Tara's presence energized our celebration. Petra and I officially retired twelve years ago. The congregation dusts off us relics from time to time. My son, Carl, is senior pastor."

"Tara thought he and his wife were probably out of town."

"On retreat until Thursday. He'll be back in the office Friday."

Luke observed Pastor Victor's pointed look at Tara and held out his hand. "Luke Cassidy. I plan to marry Tara in two weeks. Can you perform the ceremony?"

Congregants swarmed in seconds. "Congratulations, Tara," sprang from everyone's lips. "You too, Luke."

Men patted his arm while Tara waited for the retraction that never came. Where was Luke's hypothetical question explanation? The broad grin cast further false impressions.

Neither Petra nor Pastor Victor acknowledged his request until the older man switched his gaze from Tara to Luke. "Was Derrick Cassidy your father? You're the spitting image. Petra and I have a longtime friendship with your grandparents."

"I will tell The Grands we met. And the wedding?" Luke asked, nodding.

"At The Gathering Place, pre-marital counseling comes first. Do you still work, Tara?" Pastor Victor asked.

"Yes, sir," she said out loud, though her mind was wrestling with Luke's display. *I said no to the marriage.* Although Tara wanted to correct Luke's fabrication, she couldn't without refuting his comment. First impressions counted.

Pastor Victor glanced at his wife. "Pre-marital counseling with Tara and Luke on Tuesday after service, dear?"

"That works." Petra gazed at Tara. "Are you okay, hon? You seem confused, and that's unlike you."

"I'm fine. Just listening to Luke's plans." Tara hoped her smiled eased Petra's disquiet. "We're spending our first day together," she whispered in Petra's ear.

Pastor Victor eyed the couple when his wife frowned. "Seven, Tuesday evening? Additional sessions are available if needed."

Luke agreed while backing Tara out the door.

Neither one spoke on their short walk to the car. Instead, Tara made small talk with church members headed their way. The lobby scene played over and over through her mind.

Luke has control issues. Overbearing behavior might make me balk.

There wasn't an upside to using manipulative tactics. Winning at all costs negated his laidback persona.

"Where to?" Tara had steadied her breathing long enough to ask.

"Breakfast's been over awhile. Hungry?"

Tara silently nodded.

Her back turned to Luke, she observed the scenery outside the passenger window. The crooked angle strained her neck, causing a slight headache.

Before long, the car entered the I-40 ramp. Last night, Luke said he had a thirty-minute drive home. How close are we to his house?

Is the house visit on? Is Luke ticked off? I'm the one who deserves to be upset.

His silence indicated displeasure. Tara almost demanded he take her home.

Luke was quiet until pulling in front of a small café on a tree-lined street. The quaint building was tucked away in a tranquil neighborhood near Washington University.

Absentmindedly unsnapping the seat belt, he watched a slender woman being walked by a rottweiler. Gazing at Tara, he sighed. "I don't eat here often, but here's the other restaurant I visit solo."

Compassion diminished what was almost a snappy retort. "You grew up eating at Kenny's. Why come here alone? People share places where they enjoy eating with others."

"Not if they plan to keep the joyful memories alive." Snorting flared his nostrils. "Why ruin success by bringing the wrong person?"

Tara's heart melted. There wasn't a way to ignore the haunted look he tried to hide.

"Oh, Luke. You took me to Kenny's and brought me to Nouveau Départ Bistro. You're building on pleasant memories that now include me. I'm touched."

Luke cupped her face in his hands. "Speaking to Pastor Victor without first consulting you was wrong." Hesitating, he looked repentant. "I won't railroad you into marriage. My M. O. is to cover all bases. I don't want any unturned stones causing problems."

"Good. That's an explanation I can accept." Tara lay her palms on his hands, searching for wise words that weren't off-putting. Misconceptions could doom the relationship prematurely. "Sometimes excitement overrules caution. Even if I say yes, two weeks isn't long enough to plan our wedding."

Luke tweaked her nose, and her spirit felt lighter.

"Who'll help with the wedding once the date's official? I refuse to accept no. We will marry."

Did the man ever relinquish an idea? It seemed his wishes were engraved in stone.

"Perhaps. But that issue can't be settled until we're comfortable together." She shrugged when he stared. "My four close friends want to meet you. One day next week?"

The finger stroking her cheek stopped. His hand fell to his side. "Perfect. Set something up. Are they longtime friends?"

"Uh-huh. And that's the problem. The wedding ceremony requires coordination between five people. They're married with families."

"Four close friends," he repeated. "Which friend is closest?"

Tara smiled. "You must have a best friend as well. It's Abby. I've known her since before starting kindergarten. She's more like a sister than a friend."

Luke's gaze pierced hers. He opened his mouth, but apparently changed his mind about what to say. "In what way?"

"We're both only children and basically lived at each other's houses. People considered our homes interchangeable."

"That close, huh? Were your parents friends too?"

"Friendly. Fifteen years separated their ages. Their ideas were light-years apart." Her thoughts flitted to the past. "Abby's family loved camping. Especially in the Ozarks. I went on all their family vacations. Abby stayed at my house when her parents traveled alone."

"It appears you and Abby share an unbreakable bond."

"We do and always will. Which explains why two weeks isn't long enough to pull off a simple ceremony. I hate unnecessary stress. Besides, the best memories are made without regrets." She hesitated when Luke grinned. "Okay ... why are you smiling?"

His grin grew wider. "I heard a yes in your explanation."

"Luke ..."

"Shh ..." His lips skimmed hers. "Events unfold on their own accord." He unsnapped her seat belt then left the car and slid an arm around Tara's waist once she stood beside him. They chatted until they reached the door.

Inside the restaurant, subdued lights created a cozy, romantic setting. The bistro bore little resemblance to the family atmosphere of Kenny's. Instead, there was a seductive quality in Nouveau Départ's layout. No wonder Luke had never brought a woman here. From the muted lights, to the fresh bouquets on each table, the ambiance whispered, I love you!

A man and woman dressed in white oxford shirts and black chinos greeted Tara and Luke.

"Tara, Brielle and Adrien LeFevre. Old friends. Their parents own the bistro."

Instead of holding out their hands, both brother and sister hugged Tara. Pleasantly surprised, she returned the hugs, unable to stop smiling. The conversation centered on Brielle's upcoming marriage until they reached a table across the room.

Tara sat in the chair Adrien pulled out for her. "What does *nouveau* départ mean?" she asked.

"At the beginning." He handed Tara a flower from the table's bouquet. "Your fiancé called us Friday, explaining he hoped to bring his fiancée here today."

Luke really was incorrigible and dead set on having his way.

Brielle wiggled her nose at Luke then smiled at Tara. "Congratulations. Your meal is on us. Father insists." Once Luke conceded, Brielle hugged Tara, and the siblings left the table.

Tara turned to Luke as soon as the pair strolled off.

"You brought me here as your fiancée, even though I haven't accepted."

"I've never desired to devote my life to any woman but you. That's why I seldom eat here."

Words stuck in Tara's throat. She struggled to answer in kind, but endearments evaded her mind.

"Um, how did you find this amazing bistro?"

Luke chuckled. "Car trouble. It broke down outside the restaurant door on the way home. One look was all it took. The bistro was a keeper. Need I continue?"

"No. I understand."

Tara chose her meal from the colorful photos on the two-page menu. They had made their food decisions when a server approached the table. She blushed when her stomach growled before he left with their orders.

I can't be hungry. I ate more food at breakfast than I usually eat all day.

Luke watched her closely, covering her hand with his while they waited.

With the first bite, Tara knew that Nouveau Départ Bistro was a keeper. The food was superb. Stuffed, Tara lay her fork aside.

So did Luke. "Dessert?"

"No thank you. I can't eat another bite. The delicious food and efficient staff won me over. When are we coming back?"

"The groom pays for the rehearsal dinner. Either here or Kenny's would work well for that."

Tara shook her head. "Do you ever get discouraged?"

"Not since meeting you. Pastor Victor's message hit hard. Those life-filled words confirmed my belief. Destiny. Our lives intertwine. Why wreak unnecessary havoc." Luke wiped his mouth, laying the napkin on top of the plate. "What's bothering you? List the pros and cons of marrying sooner rather than later."

Tara shook her head without looking up. "Repeatedly, I've voiced my opposition, yet you downplay it."

"Your views are realistically respected." Luke scooted within inches of her. "But playing it safe produces missed opportunities. Our time is now." He captured her hand in his. "Consider me a secure harbor you can dock inside. What we feel for each other doesn't happen often."

Beautifully stated. I love the way Luke talks. He identifies and pursues whatever he wants.

"I believe you. But—"

"No buts. My grandparents weren't in love when they married. Yet they're sincerely blissful today. We're blessed. At the first moment, you and I discovered true love."

Luke squeezed her hand after the server removed their plates. "The people dearest to your heart have passed on. My obligations to my family have finally ended. Don't squander our time together. Make the happiness we've found last. Forever."

Tara steeled her heart against the passionate request. "Is that what you think? That I thumb my nose at what's meant to be?" His nod filled her with sadness. *Empathize with me. I understand you.* "I want our relationship to move slowly to ensure we don't make a terrible mistake."

"Look, we both want four children. We'll build our family. Create a long-lasting bond with me and our future children."

"I refuse to play connect the dots to reveal my life." Her lips pressed together as her resolve vacillated. "Our futures are on the line."

"Meaning we should travel the conventional route. But neither of us are typical people."

"Luke—"

"Don't sleepwalk through life. You can't live by default. Why hold out?"

"For the reason I stated last night, plus a new one I need to add."

Luke pushed his chair from the table, standing with his gaze on Tara.

Without a blink, she met the gaze head-on. "You're bossy."

Luke shook his head, laughing.

"What's funny? What did you expect me to say?"

"Nothing as benign as that statement. Believe me."

"Hmm." Tara grabbed the hand he held out. "Where to?"

"My house. It's time you saw the real me." Luke chuckled when Tara smiled.

Chapter Seven

Sometime later, Luke turned into a quiet cul-de-sac, stopping in the circular drive of a ranch-style house.

Tara checked the manicured landscapes. Luke lived in a serene cookie-cutter neighborhood. If she preferred suburban life, Tara could make this house her home. She opened the door before Luke shifted gears into park, hopping out and tapping her foot on the pavement until he reached her.

"I can't wait to get inside." Tara beamed her widest smile ever. "Hurry."

Luke grabbed her around the waist. "Are you eager to expose my secrets?"

"More like uncover. But for my eyes only, sir."

Laughter lit his eyes. "So, you believe in keeping secret things private."

"As long as we both understand the truth, it isn't anyone else's business." The corners of her mouth dimpled. "I once heard my father tell my mother that very thing. Of course, he advocated keeping me out of the loop about something or other." Tara joined Luke's laughter. "I knew all their secrets that pertained to me."

"As it should be." Luke urged her through the front door. "I would've loved to meet your parents. Were they like you?"

"In some ways they were. Pastor Victor's son, Carl, claims I'm a mixture of both their personalities, which could be good or bad, depending on whom you ask."

"Point taken. When will I see your negative persona?" Luke led her into the kitchen, stepping aside. "Mother's favorite room."

Tara had seen every inch of the house by the time she entered the laundry room. She lingered in front of shirts hanging on a rack. Thirty shirts with assorted names were on display.

"Pathetic! No wonder you wore Andy's shirts three days in a row. None of these shirts has your name on the pocket."

"This is my 'go to' stash. I grab a clean shirt from the rack if I'm running late. Let's check out the garage."

Tara frowned. "I didn't see a garage."

"Although it's attached to the laundry room, you reach it from behind the house." He opened the door then stepped aside.

Tara entered the cleanest garage she'd ever seen. It was nearly empty and reminded her of her own home with its sparse furnishing. "Are you a declutter bug?"

"Is that a catchphrase for a neat freak? I live by the motto 'each item has its proper place'." He retraced his steps into the kitchen. "And so do you. I stood in the doorway while you prepared dessert."

Tara sniggered before he finished speaking.

"You took out a tray from your platter cabinet and sundae dishes from the dessert cabinet. You didn't use any old spoon. You used an ice cream scooper. Our cookies were placed on a cookie-specific platter."

Tara fell over, laughing. "You spied on me."

His eyebrows arched. "Expect me when you least suppose you will."

Stifling giggles, she broke into laughter again.

Luke placed two saucers and napkins on the table and peered inside the refrigerator. "Do you like all melon or watermelon only? Honeydew? Cantaloupe?"

Tara noticed beer on the bottom shelf. *A six-pack? Luke drinks?* Her mind was consumed by the beer she saw. Tara was a nondrinker. Neither of her parents drank alcohol. Marriage to a man who indulged presented something serious to discuss. "I do," she said when Luke repeated the question. "Especially watermelon, as you know. The bowl at Kenny's was unusually sweet for the early season." *I must tiptoe through the minefield without declaring war.* "So, I saw beer. You drink?" she asked in a soft voice.

"Beer." He sat two bowls of fruit on the table. "I might pop a can open if I'm watching a game with friends. That six-pack has sat in the refrigerator for three months."

"Then I can skip the 'drinking isn't a good idea' talk. Ooh. These melons are sweet." She took a bite while seeking a subject change. "Nice wall decor. Your house has a definite woman's touch. Your mom's or Steffi's?"

"Little has changed since my parents died, although Steffi has made some updates."

"Your sister did a superb job. This home is comfortable."

"As is your home. May I move in?"

He has a one-track mind. It's nonstop marriage bombs.

Tara licked melon juice off her sticky fingers. "It needs many updates. It's a big job. The high ceilings and cavernous rooms would kill my budget. Plus, the basement needs an overhaul."

"May I suggest we live here while the work gets done?"

Tara scooted back the chair. "You have such tunnel vision. Your single-mindedness squashes opposition. Have you received that *compliment* before?"

"Compliment, huh? It was more like a put-down."

Luke relaxed on the kitchen's cushioned chair.

Tara couldn't think of what to say next.

Well, might as well clean up.

She rinsed dishes and utensils before stacking the pile neatly inside the dishwasher—an appliance Tara never used at home. Luke made small talk as she worked.

Back at the table, she covered the melon and then moved across the floor.

"You feel at home enough to tidy up. Terrific."

Half-filled fruit bowls wobbled in wet hands. Tara felt like a klutz after Luke's remark.

His stare is heating my back. I shouldn't get nervous with a man I'm considering marrying.

"We're a great team," he began. "And sorry I can't control my tunnel vision. Is it bothersome?"

"Who's at the end of the tunnel?" Tara reclaimed her chair, studying Luke. "My mother believed Jesus demands that spot Himself."

Grabbing Tara's fingers, Luke rubbed their hands together. "Grandma spoke similar words. Speaking of The Grands, they requested to meet you today. Grandma and Granddad have digested Tara news for two weeks without an introduction."

Tara's hand went limp in his. "For real? Um ... what did you say?"

"That I love you was all they needed to hear. The Grands are aware I proposed last night. And they know you left me hanging."

"You mean declined. That's what I did. Remember?"

"I heard yes with restrictions. No cause for concern." He scooted his chair closer to the table.

Luke threw too many curveballs. She became even more determined not to give in.

"Well ... do your grandparents live close by?"

"Next door. But don't let their proximity decide for you."

Simmering in silence, Tara sought a befitting comeback. Nothing. Still, she couldn't dismiss his slyness. "Thanks for the textbook example of why not to make hasty decisions. Necessary information gets lost in conversations. If told at all."

Waiting for Luke's reply, Tara easily deciphered the inner battle raging within him. She'd spent too much time caring for dying parents to miss a sad heart. Should she speak up or wait?

Luke's chuckle revealed a man seeking an advantage. "Steffi's car is parked in their driveway. If she spotted my car, the troops were alerted. Anyone without plans is already there or on their way."

"You told your entire family about me?"

"I love you. It would've been strange not to tell them."

She lay her face in her palm. Her mouth filled with negative replies. It took willpower to keep from lashing out. Left to his own devices, Luke would run roughshod over everyone. It was a character deficiency requiring immediate attention. Raising her head, she combed fingers through her hair.

Tara slid back the chair but didn't stand.

Luke hurried around the table and sat beside her.

"We can spend a quiet evening here or at your house. The choice is yours. I wanted you to see my house. That's it. Just promise me you'll meet my family before our wedding."

He sounds like a broken record.

Tara rose, knocking away his hand, and moved toward the bathroom. As she entered the next room, she spun around when his chair scraped the tile floor. "I don't require an escort to your bathroom."

Luke's family's expectations were a done deal. She would meet his family as a friend, nothing more yet. It was on him that he had muddied the waters.

In the bathroom, Tara focused on a towel rack next to the shower. She hated no-win situations, and Luke had dropped her into one. The disadvantage could seal her fate with his family. Tara already had difficulty meeting new people.

What do they think? What did Luke say? Would they think less of her because of the proposal? Did their opinion even matter? *It does. His family would be a part of our lives.*

Indecision proved inadequate in a crisis. His grandparents and Steffi waited to meet her. Did Steffi's husband make the trip? Luke's brothers? Their wives? Did they bring their children?

Oh Luke! How could you dangle me in front of your family? You know it looks terrible if we don't visit. Everyone knows I'm here. With a deep sigh, Tara glanced at the ceiling. *Lord, it's been a while since I've come to you. Please. Help me.*

Tara frowned at her reflection in the tri-fold mirror, then added a splash of color to her face. The image staring back proved less than pleasing.

Something else is needed. Got it!

Taking off her sweater, she tied it around her waist. Next, she sat on the tub's edge, untied her sandal laces from around her ankles, then wrapped each one over her jeans just below the knees. Ruby earrings were swapped with dangling gold hoops she carried in her purse. Verdict?

That ought to do it. Who cares if it doesn't?

When she opened the door, Luke almost toppled into the bathroom. He righted himself, pointing at the doorknob.

"There's no peephole. I couldn't peek if I wanted to."

"Your sad eyes don't sway me." Her hip butted him out the way. "It's too late to show remorse. You set me up."

Luke raised three fingers. "Scout's honor. I had no expectations either way. The choice was always yours." His voice softened as his gaze caressed her face. "Beautiful as always."

Tara steeled herself against the compliment. Real facts deserved more than a passing remark that missed the point. "Just admit the truth. You wanted to achieve your objective. And since your grandparents live next door, you lured me in with the house visit. You should've told me you're neighbors with them. Level with me. Is your family expecting us?"

"I promise they don't expect a visit. But one can hope, and they probably do. We're a close-knit family. They know I wanted to bring you by today, but you refused."

Tara mouth draped open. "What were you thinking? Your grandparents think I snubbed them." Her hands massaged her cheeks.

"You're accustomed to family life and understand how loving families work. Meeting them today isn't a requirement."

Tara forced herself to relax while imaginary static clung to her body. Even the hair on her arms bristled. She unclenched her fingers.

"Okay. You want to marry me in two weeks. They're curious. I get it." Tara turned away, then spun around. Making a good first impression required fast action. Her hands dropped to her side. "You win. Let's go."

As they exited Luke's house, Tara studied his grandparents' house. Luke locked the front door.

Three other vehicles had joined the lone car parked in their driveway.

She eyed Luke. "Is everyone accounted for?" At least he had the decency to look contrite.

Luke nodded. "The gang's all here. They recognize the seriousness." Luke slid his arm around her waist. "Together we conquer every obstacle we face." A light twinkled in his eyes. "I love you. If that comment helps at a time like this."

I can't let Luke always have his way as if my preference doesn't count.

Tara stopped beside his car. Her feet refused to carry her farther. "Take me home. Something is off. Timing. Nerves. Whatever. It ... doesn't feel right to meet your family today." She studied his empty facial expression. "No one's expecting us to trot over there. Right?"

Luke drew her into his arms, brushing his lips across her mouth. "Someone's standing at the window. My siblings came hoping to see you." He stroked her cheek then lowered his hand. "You admitted your friends are curious about me. I'm willing to meet them right now."

Tara barely listened. She needed a soft ear and sound mind. Carl and Annie were out of town. "Yes. They are, and ..." *Abby.* "My best friend asked to meet you. I'll call her."

Tara slid inside the car.

* * *

"Where to?" Luke asked as he turned the car key.

"Abby lives across the street from my father's parents' house. Four blocks away from where I live. I'll direct you."

Thirty minutes later, Luke inched the car down a heavily treed street. "Last year, Cassidy's replaced a roof in this neighborhood."

Tara smiled. Historic houses there contrasted with the ranch-style houses in Luke's subdivision. Mature trees and sculptured landscapes rivaled stately pictures in any museum. Once they turned onto Abby's street, they neared a house with a porch swing. "We're here. The house with the porch swing belongs to Abby. It was my housewarming gift." She then pointed across the street to the only fenced house on the block. "My grandparents lived there for forty years. It's a two-family flat, and both houses are vacant."

"A duplex." Luke parked the car in their driveway. "Given the neighborhood, I expected single-family dwellings. Can we take a tour of both sides?"

While Tara studied the two-family flat, her lips broke into a smile. "Sure. You'll love it. The structure was altered after my great-grandfather became ill. One side has been vacant since Great-Granny passed away fourteen years ago."

A screen door closed across the street. Abby and Craig waited on the porch.

Clasping Tara's hand, Luke led them over.

Abby stared the entire time.

As they crossed the street, Luke whispered, "A firing squad couldn't be more daunting than those two. Is your friend as fiery as her hair suggests?"

"She's a harmless and protective longtime friend."

"Is her husband a body builder?"

"He's giving it a valiant try."

Abby spoke when they reached the bottom step. "Glad you stopped by. Your call was a welcomed surprise."

"Sorry about the last-minute visit. Luke, Abby is my best friend since forever. Her husband, Craig. Abby, Craig, this is Luke Cassidy."

Abby said hello, and Craig held out his hand.

"Playoffs? Into the game?" Craig asked Luke.

Luke checked his watch. "The pregame show begins in ten minutes." He glanced at Tara. "Are you a basketball fan?"

"No. Neither is Abby." Tara followed her friend into the house and stopped outside the family room. "Go with Craig. I'll keep Abby company in the kitchen."

Luke kissed her mouth then whispered in her ear, "Your lips are delectable. Seconds?"

Her cheeks turned pink. Tara laughed and hid her face in his shirt.

Abby watched Luke until the men disappeared into the den. The expression on her friend's face kept Tara silent. But she made small talk while the women headed down the hallway.

Once in the kitchen, Abby closed the door. "Okay. Spill it."

Tara's voice dropped an octave lower. "No way. Luke might overhear what we say."

Mashing her lips together, Abby opened the back door. She led Tara outside and sat on a deck swing, pulling Tara beside her.

"Okay. It's private. So talk. Did you agree to marry him? That kiss says yes."

Tara almost floated off the swing. "Oh, Abby. Luke upset me earlier, yet it's been mostly idyllic since yesterday. I love Luke despite his faults." She hesitated. "I've discovered a few."

"Only a few? Tara—"

"It isn't an act. Luke loves me. Somehow the impossible has happened despite the reason why we're here. I was a little perturbed with him earlier."

Abby massaged her temples, executing the perfect eye roll. "You agreed to marry Luke knowing he's baggage-laden?"

"I didn't commit to anything. Besides, who doesn't have flaws? We've spent a well-rounded day despite the pressure."

Tara brought Abby up to speed without glossing over trouble spots.

"That's too much information to digest in one sitting. Especially since you want my honest opinion." Abby eyed her. "You do, right?"

"Your opinion matters more than anyone else's."

Abby's fingers flexed. It was a nervous tick she hadn't outgrown. "My skepticisms haven't changed. Luke's a stranger who sends mixed signals. We're in day two. Take the time to develop a relationship." Her fingers flexed again.

That unconscious quirk tempered Tara's response. Abby was her closest friend and confidant. A sister couldn't love Tara any more than Abby did. "Are you suggesting our instant rapport is commonplace and isn't God's plan?"

"The Holy Spirit will direct your steps that way if it is. You asking my opinion means He hasn't told you to marry Luke."

Tara laid her head on the swing's back cushion. "Marriage to Luke seems impossible to resist."

"All the more reason why you should. Why rush? Neither of you are going anywhere." She shook her head when Tara frowned. "Marry if your feelings mature after dating for twelve months. Craig and I will support your decision."

Tara studied Abby. "And if I walk down the aisle Saturday after next?"

"I'll purchase my matron of honor dress."

"Would your father walk me down the aisle? Pastor Victor would be performing the ceremony."

"Says who? He only agreed to give pre-marital counseling. God knows it's needed. Carl's coming home Thursday. I can't wait till he weighs in."

"How did you know Carl's out of town and Pastor Victor agreed to counseling? Oh. I forgot your aunt attends the church. She and your uncle stopped beside our row and greeted me this morning. But I didn't introduce Luke. She called you?"

"Mother did."

"Ooh ... well, at least that means your father knows I might get married soon. Anyway, Bossy Carl will play the heavy and won't walk me down the aisle. Mr. Benson is the only person left."

"He'll walk with you without sanctioning your wedding. Expect Mom to stand by you after her shock recovery. The way this conversation is going tells me you've basically said yes to Luke. You've given in."

"Only inside my head. It just feels like happiness is within my grasp."

"It isn't found in people. Slow down. Headlong dashes down the aisle seldom work. Date Luke for a while." She paused. "Skip work tomorrow. Hang out with me. The twins are having their school picnic at Forest Park."

Tara grimaced. "I've already missed three consecutive days of work."

"In pursuit of a man you didn't know. Yet you won't take a day off to attend your godchildren's school picnic."

I wish you'd just accept no. You're making me seem like a bad person. Guess I better give in.

"Yes, under duress. If the twins were home I could introduce them to Luke."

Abby planted her chin on Tara's shoulder. "Who are you texting?"

"Group texting Marcie, Suze, and Mindy."

"Hoping to get them on your side won't mean your decision is right. Validate your own convictions."

Tara lay the cell phone beside her. "Are the children coming home tonight or tomorrow morning?"

"In the morning. What are you planning? Craig and Luke are watching playoffs. You'll never drag my husband out of the den. Hone up on your basketball knowledge. Clearly Luke's a fan too."

Tara picked up her cell phone. "Points pile up in his favor."

"Here we go again."

"Stop trashing Luke. He opted to spend time with me instead of watching a game he obviously wanted to see." Tara gave her customary curtsy at the kitchen door. It was a practice she'd adopted in first grade when trying to make amends. "Let's pick up dinner and then join them in the den." She hesitated, struggling to find the right words. "Do—do you know how many years I've prayed to have a man who loves me?"

"Don't tell me." Tears swarmed Abby's eyes. "The answer will break my heart."

And mine. I can finally admit how unhappy I've been without romantic love.

Tara reflected on distant memories while Abby secured the kitchen door to the back yard.

Chapter Eight

After they left Abby and Craig, Tara and Luke toured both grandparents' houses: the two-family flat and the single-family dwelling that was three blocks away. Despite her tiredness, she wanted to keep Luke with her and thought of excuses to make him stay longer. Was she just lonely like Mindy had suggested? A perplexed Tara stepped inside her home.

Luke walked close behind her. "Remarkable. I love old homes. Give me a house tour of your home. Did Abby grow up in the same neighborhood?"

"Her parents still live across the street." Tara turned the deadbolt lock. Her mind was on his family. "Any thoughts on the missed meeting with your grandparents?"

One eyebrow rose. *Hmm ... did the question seem strange?*

"Can't imagine any particular reaction since they didn't expect a visit. Because you walked right to the car, no one suspected we were headed their way."

"That makes me feel better. I'd hate to start off on the wrong foot with your family." She opened the basement door. "We'll start at the ground floor and work our way upstairs."

Tara's second-floor, street-side bedroom was the last tour stop. Luke sprawled across the bed with his back on the headboard, patting the space beside him. "You look exhausted. Take a rest."

Hovering in the doorway, she gingerly stepped forward. "Is it safe? Or should we talk on the sunporch? How about a snack?"

"Our Mexican meal hit the spot." He grinned and patted the bed again. "Join me so we can talk houses."

Grow up, Tara. You're old enough to converse with a man in your bedroom.

Tara untied her sandal laces, kicked off her shoes, and scooted beside Luke.

"Cute sandals. Casual chic suits you. I noticed you made two subtle changes in my bathroom, and it revamped your outfit."

"Thank fashion expert Abby. My trendy friend invented a few tricks herself."

"You were well taught." A low whistle voiced pleasure.

Luke appreciates me and my houses. Somewhat saddened, Tara smiled. "Glad you appreciate old houses."

"They normally depict good bones and character." He eyed the wainscoting on her lower walls. "Your grandparents' houses appeared structurally sound. Although some updates would increase market value."

"My parents kept regular maintenance schedules."

"It shows. Both houses are located in prime residential areas. Front and back yards look fantastic. No one would think those houses were empty. Do you own all three?"

"Um-hum. My father deeded the houses when the first symptom occurred."

"Three vacant houses. Were your parents against leasing?"

"Never got around to it." Operating on reserved energy, Tara shrugged. "Perhaps they preferred just knowing the houses were there."

Luke's eyes narrowed. "That game plan teamed with those houses will rob you blind. Each year, homeowners pay insurance premiums and property taxes, while maintenance and repairs continue mounting. Especially with the age of those houses. Don't forget, manicured lawns add an extra expense. Those lawns were well kept. Only neighbors realize they're vacant houses."

"I hadn't thought that far ahead. Each week I go by both places to stagger lights, declutter mailboxes, and scout trouble spots. Does your frown mean you don't like my answer?"

"Wavering isn't an acceptable option at any time. Stop living life by default and participate in the outcome. It works better. It was an effortless lesson I learned well."

"I don't twiddle my thumbs."

"I've noticed a pattern in your lifestyle. Live. Don't exist. Embrace life."

Luke is worse than Suze and Abby.

"What if I enjoy how I live?"

"Step it up a notch. Branch out. Embrace new experiences. Playing it safe stymies progress."

Maybe he does know me. I understand him. Can you misinterpret facts? Each conversation brings new questions.

Tara sighed. "Sometimes I punt the ball into tomorrow. Okay. A renovation or an overhaul?"

"A sell rehab is different from a lease rehab."

"I won't sell. Lease."

"An excellent choice. Retain the property your family left. Of course, you can request a tidy sum for each house. Attached garages are practically unheard of in those neighborhoods."

"No one on my street has a garage. Which is why I don't have a garage, even though there's space to add one. My grandparents on both sides split an adjoining lot with a neighbor to install garages." Looking around the room Tara strummed fingers on her thighs. "Who to do the work."

"Easy fix. My best bud, Pete, is a licensed contractor. New roofs, a repiping, and rewiring will bring the buildings up to code. Each foundation appeared solid and should pass inspection. The lawns at both houses provide excellent curb appeal. Bank on the two-family flat bringing a hefty monthly return. Each side leases slightly less than a single-family dwelling. And I suggest removing the fence." He paused as Tara yawned. "Sleepy?"

"Very. Yesterday was a long day and late night."

"Point taken." Luke gently pulled her into his arms. "Let's rest before I leave."

I enjoy being cared for. This man loves me because he wants to. No one chooses who they fall in love with. Who can control natural occurrences?

"You know, lying on you makes me feel protected."

Luke kissed the top of her head when Tara cuddled closer.

Stirring within his arms, she stared at Luke through squinted eyes. "You better leave before I lose the strength to lock the door behind you."

"I can always stay overnight."

Laughing, Tara sat upright. "Give me a goodnight peck. See you tomorrow."

The light peck deepened into a lengthy kiss. Tara murmured against his lips. "Loosen the grip. Ever hear that sex without marriage is wrong?"

Luke stroked Tara's cheek. "Heard it somewhere. Care to explain why?"

"No. Why elaborate on the obvious?" Disliking where the conversation was headed, Tara sat on the bed's edge. She hated asking obvious questions. Still ... "You indulge in sensuous habits?"

Luke sat beside her. "Not as often as I would like." A low chuckle rumbled from his chest.

Tara felt foolish. Had she overreacted to his kiss?

"Stop teasing. I raised a serious issue." Laughter trickled from the lip she bit. "I won't sleep with you." She paused when his avid gaze stroked her face like a caress. That one look reminded her of what had come before. "Honestly ... I welcomed the sensations. Which explains why teenagers get into trouble."

"Teenagers get into trouble because they fail to practice birth control and safe sex."

"Which their unmarried status doesn't require. These are lifelong beliefs." Tara sighed. Would Luke criticize beliefs he knew she held?

Reflective lights twinkled in laughter-filled eyes. "Certain people behave themselves better than others. It's too bad that exemplary behavior isn't catching. One can only extract what they put in."

"Get serious. Self-indulgence is problematic for every person. Why add bad habits you have to break later?"

"Bad habits? You mean intimacy between us?"

"Thirty-two is too old to indulge in known sins."

Luke grabbed her hands. "Make me an honest man. Marry me, Tara. The sooner the better for both of us."

This final assault has torpedoed me. Luke is the trustworthy man I've always desired. And he won't make vows he doesn't plan to keep. We're good together.

If Tara helped Luke settle his parents' estate, he could buy out his brothers and sister, divide the proceeds, and be done. *A life can be built that benefits the entire Cassidy family, which includes me, if we marry. Tara Michelle Cassidy. A perfect name.*

She brushed teardrops off her eyelids. "I fell in love the first day you smiled at me. You're kind, thoughtful, and honest. Your parents trusted you to honor their wishes. You did." *Tara, slow down the train.* She closed her eyes and bowed her head. "I need to think."

Her chin rested on her chest. What would bring the most satisfaction?

Luke was giving her time to sort her thoughts, which showed patience. Still, she knew he had other faults, including manipulation. Probably acquired from raising siblings while he was still young. His single-mindedness was worth remembering.

Her smiling gaze locked with Luke's.

"Well?" A grin belied his wrinkled forehead. Luke was far from certain she would accept his offer. No one fancied rejection. Especially after they had placed their heart on the line for a second time.

Operation reciprocate kindness gained control.

Tara jumped into Luke's arms before she thought otherwise.

Whispering endearments, he hugged her to his chest.

Tara marveled at both of their reactions; specifically, her own.

How can saying yes become acceptable a day later?

Yanking her body away from Luke's, she splayed her hands on his cheeks. "I, Tara Michelle Simpkins, fell in love with Lucas Michael Cassidy at first glance. A dark veil lifted off my life when you smiled." Teardrops rolled from her eyes. "We're a matched set. You no longer work on roofs but spent three days replacing my roof to date me. I skipped work three days to hear your voice."

"Pastor Victor will provide pre-marital counseling on Tuesday. Ring shopping Wednesday?"

"Yes for Tuesday. I just need to let my friends know we won't meet here this week; we usually meet every Tuesday at six. Um ... Wednesday works. Will I meet your family next Sunday?"

"Sooner." Luke brushed his lips across her mouth. "They'll love you, Tara."

"I'm glad. God's giving me a family I can wrap my arms around."

When Tara's head pressed against his chest, Luke's sigh undid her. The couple reveled in the silence of their love. Peace prevailed until a terrible thought had Tara shivering within his arms.

Luke lifted her face. Keen eyes probed hers until she turned away.

He massaged her wrist. "What happened?"

Unable to reply, Tara looked down. "How did you know something changed?"

"Each nuance affecting you impacts me."

"Mom and Dad expected to travel worldwide after retiring. Yet they would be alive today had they remained home."

Luke snuggled Tara closer. "More than likely. Tell me more."

"Fulfilling their dream brought them home with an unpronounceable disease and death within three months. Obtaining their long-standing desire proved fatal."

"Years ago, your parents placed theirs dreams on the backburner." He tipped her face toward his. "They aimed to travel the world, but they waited too long."

Tara winced at the reminder. "It was heartbreaking to know their lifelong dreams ended as they did."

"A devastation, *but* pursuing life still works. Those consequences should press us forward. Action trumps waiting."

"Surely it depends on why you're waiting."

"Unrequited dreams die with the people who dream them."

"No one relegated your dreams to a backburner. Washington University accepted you into its medical school. The tragedy that stole your parents' lives negated the offer. You chose an alternate path to follow."

Luke shook his head. "The decision to become a doctor happened at age eight. A better choice was made after my parents died. That night, I fell onto my knees and rose with new convictions. I followed my heart." Luke kissed the tip of her nose. "They left me a lifetime of cherished memories."

Love for Luke oozed from every pore. The man kept amazing Tara. She couldn't stop smiling while he appeared spellbound.

"I'm in repentant mode. Although I lived a normal life, the effects of previous, awful choices may linger. I pray they don't." Luke lay a finger on her lips as they parted to ask the obvious question. "I love you." As his lips replaced the finger, he secured Tara against him. "Agony is living a single day without you near."

"Aw. Wooed by a romantic."

"I've never been described that way before. Women use other descriptions."

Tara whispered through his kiss. "Oh-oh! Is a shock coming down the line?"

"Tara makes Luke a better him. Remember our conversation on the drive to Shelli and Rick's?"

"We discussed multiple topics. Which one?"

"Where we surmised strong friendship can equal deep love. You gave your parents as an example."

"Both agreed they'd shared a loyal friendship before marriage."

"You said they were two lonely people who dedicated their lives to each other and lived happily for many years. We love one another now. Thanks for saying yes."

"Thanks for asking me to join your family." Remembering her thought about settling the rental property with his siblings, Tara bounced on the mattress. "Begin marriage with a clean slate. I'll help settle your parents' estate."

Luke looked elated until his head shook. "Unable to accept the perfect offer."

"How come? I won't charge interest," she said, smiling.

"In a traditional courtship I would agree in a heartbeat. Our shortened courtship obliges I decline."

"Lack of a traditional courtship didn't stop a marriage proposal." Tara bit down hard. "You can propose, but I can't help secure our future?"

"It's a hefty loan. We own several properties."

"Marriage is a lifetime commitment. Besides, who said loan? Didn't we fall into the impossible? Love at first sight."

"Saying no doesn't negate facts. My goal is your protection."

My marrying you is wise, but my generosity is misguided? I made both decisions.

Speeding from the room, Tara rushed down the stairs. Ignoring Luke when he called after her, she waited at the front door.

Luke's breathing steadied when he reached her. He loosely held her upper arms. "What did I say wrong? How were you offended?" His eyes searched her face for answers. "Tell me so I can avoid similar missteps in the future."

Tara's tear-filled eyes studied the floor. Her father had often said that her stubbornness mimicked determination.

Go home so I can reassess everything that's happened. Did I overreact? Up and down. Down and up. Oh! Go home.

"Level with me if you want me to leave. Until then ..."

Unhappy eyes stared into his. "I said yes. Who could resist your beautifully painted picture?"

"My ladylove, you exceed expectations. Neither money nor anything else can ruin what we have. Details will sort themselves out. Let's start over. Agreed?"

Tara remembered a different remark he'd made. "Earlier you shot down leaving decisions until tomorrow. Is this the way you'll end our disputes?"

"Living in peace with you will receive my best shot every time. When can I expect you home tomorrow?"

Luke changes subjects better than I do. Only I let him get away with dupes.

"Around four twenty. Tomorrow is my godchildren's school picnic."

"Can you take days off from work at will?"

"Everyone receives five personal days per year, and I have some left. Eat dinner here. Five-ish?"

Luke nodded. "Beautiful and an accomplished cook. I'm looking forward to sampling a meal." He trailed a finger over her cheek. "Are we okay? I won't leave unless we are."

"My feelings haven't changed." She opened the door, stepping onto the porch. "Leave in peace and break bread over dinner tomorrow." Tara smiled at Luke when he lingered at the door. "I promise. We're all right."

"It's difficult to walk away. Sure?"

"It's been an eventful day. I'm drained, and my emotions are a tinge erratic. Your reasons for refusing my offer are sound, even though I disagree with them. Kiss me. Have a safe drive home."

"Those are two commands worth obeying." Luke kissed her laughing lips. "Go back inside and wave from the locked storm door."

"Goodnight, Luke."

* * *

Luke made a U-turn then waved at Tara, who was watching his progress from the window.

I'm walking on eggshells with Tara and still messing up.

Building a healthy relationship required skill sets he hadn't previously employed, but visions of success pumped his spirit. Of utmost priority was introducing his fiancée to his family. Monday was too soon after Tara had rejected the idea so recently. Tuesday was pre-marital counseling and on Wednesday, Tara and he would purchase rings. Thursday? Perhaps.

Would bringing up the subject on his goodnight call keep Tara awake?

"I found the woman I've always wanted. Tara loves me without any other considerations."

After ten years of missteps, life in the family lane proved closer than ever. His lifetime destination lay ahead.

Contentment surrounded Luke the entire drive home. He parked in the driveway instead of driving behind the house to the garage. A nightlight lit his grandparents' porch and front yard.

The Grands must hear the good news first thing in the morning. That'll jolt them out of bed.

Luke walked into his living room but stopped inside the doorway, glaring at the composed man stretched out on his sofa. Tossing keys on the end table, Luke sat on the recliner near the window.

About to break the news regarding Tara, Andy's polite grin prompted Luke's anger. He'd better strike first since the first punch frequently told the story.

"Did you park your car inside the garage so I couldn't detect my home invasion?"

"Of course." Andy raised to his elbow. "Would you expect anything less? You would've driven off had you spotted my car. If I'd missed you tonight, I would've wasted two trips." He yawned, covering his mouth. "Home is a thirty-minute return trip. I abhor wasted energy."

"I didn't invite you either time." Luke resigned himself to what was coming. His brother could agitate the meekest person, which Luke was not. "State your case, then leave. Do you realize what time it is?"

"It's late." Andy's grin broadened. "I could be asleep now had you showed up at a decent hour."

"Then leave. Your sister woke me up at seven." Luke massaged the bridge of his nose.

"Yeah, well, Benton woke me up at six because of you. Man, you've turned into a regular sleep disturber."

"Look." Luke paused. *These guys won't relent until meeting my fiancée. Sorry, Tara. You're the sacrificial lamb. I can't bear any more sleepless nights.* "I texted with Benton until two. What else was there to say?"

"He couldn't stay asleep, so he badgered me instead of calling you. Apparently, Ben didn't appreciate your answers." Andy's smirk was irritating. "Sorry, man. You're cursed with a family that loves you."

Luke almost caved to Andy's concerns until his brother chuckled. "Your caring is welcome on most subjects. My relationship with Tara isn't one. Give me a second. I promised Tara a good-night call." He dialed Tara, who was halfway asleep. The call ended with a smile until Andy grunted. Luke laid the cell phone on the armrest.

"It's late. Come back next week."

"That marriage idea hasn't left. Cooperate. It's too late to bandy words."

"Exactly. Butt into my business at a decent hour."

"Tell me what's happening so I can leave. What's the endgame? My mind says there isn't one."

Enough psychoanalyzing. "Congratulate me. Tara accepted. Jot Saturday after next on your calendar."

Absentmindedly stroking his chin, Andy's analytical brain worked overtime.

Uninclined to decode his personal agenda, Luke bided time until his brother spoke.

"Why doesn't that answer surprise me? Leah?"

This family has a fixation with that woman. "I'm a free man. I can date whomever I choose."

"The grapevine says she'll arrive in St. Louis on Friday. A month earlier than planned. Guess she didn't accept your answer."

Luke chuckled. "Now she knows that proposing to a disinterested man has consequences. Besides, holding false expectations is a character flaw I hate."

"Really? Expecting marriage after a five-year relationship is holding false expectations? No wonder her dagger is out."

"That's a low blow," Luke said through laughter. "Association, not relationship, is a better description."

"Stop parsing words." Andy sat on the sofa's edge. "You were an item with her. Even if no one liked her."

"I didn't like her either. So there you go."

"Five years is a long time to sleep with a woman you detested. Her proposal shouldn't surprise you."

"As my declining shouldn't surprise you. Or would you condemn your brother to marriage with a con artist due to prior bad judgment?"

"Heartless, bro." Andy sighed. "Explain why Tara's a keeper after two weeks."

Luke eyed the clock on the wall unit. "How much time do we have?"

Andy made up his mind quickly. "Plenty. I wish to hear whatever you want to say."

Shifting position, Andy maneuvered three throw pillows beneath his head.

Chapter Nine

While at the park the next day, Tara, Abby, and their other three friends planned the wedding ceremony by text and phone. Between visits to the zoo, a lengthy debate had consumed the friends throughout the morning. The unusual circumstances had brought Marcie to the park for lunch. Even though Marcie had employed every tactic she could think of, Tara had refused to postpone the wedding. She'd called the church and secured Saturday after next for the ceremony. Mrs. Pruett, the church secretary, promised to contact her organ-player sister. Marcie had left thirty minutes later armed with details for her friend's special day.

Then Suze took charge and supplied Tara with choices for everything from flowers to decorations. Tara laid her cell phone on the picnic table and turned to Abby. "What's your opinion? Suze thinks lilies are funeral blooms."

"They are unless you chose lilies for your wedding. Daisies?" she asked in a teasing tone.

"As in pushing up daisies? What's with you and Suze? No more funeral jargon."

While Abby sent the children to join the volleyball game in progress, Tara pored over her choices, then asked Mindy to secure the deals.

The cell phone pealed. "It's Luke." Tara listened for a moment then mouthed the words "I made a big mistake" to her friend.

Engrossed in the one-sided conversation, Abby glanced at the twins and scooted closer.

"Oops. I forgot to tell you Grandpa Burt restored old cars ... He loved classic vehicles, and worked full-time on his hobby after he retired ... Well, it was too dark to show you his toys last night ... No, Luke. I plan to keep everything as is ... No way. I don't want to sell my cars. They're keepsakes ..." She sighed deeply. "Okay. I apologize for not telling you about them yesterday. See you later."

Her heart broke. "Oh, Ab. I didn't tell Luke about the cars. He discovered the vehicles in the utility shed while checking Grandpa Burt's roof."

"The roof is on the house. Why was he snooping in the back yard?"

I should've told Luke about the cars. Better defend him as best I can.

"He wasn't prying. You can see the utility building from the roof."

"And he decided to look inside? You forgot to mention the cars. No one can tell their life history in two days."

"I agree. But I don't think he'll accept that logic."

"Then don't offer him an explanation he doesn't deserve."

Down from the high of wedding plans, Tara watched the children play while Abby cleaned up. Her thoughts tittered until Sonya and Tad begged for another zoo trip. The twins loved riding on the zoo's train. Instead of sweltering in the heat, Abby and Tara rode with the kids throughout the zoo.

While waiting in line, she began feeling overwhelmed. Too many important decisions weighed her down that day. A short time later, Mindy had confirmed each order. Their legwork was finalized in less than six hours. Back at the picnic table, Tara paid the bills. A synchronized launch had achieved enormous results. Her dream wedding was bought and paid for while at the park. Engagement finality sank in.

* * *

Descending the ladder, Luke saw Colton pull into the driveway. He'd planned to call his brother that evening. The inspection of the single-family dwelling was completed. He'd checked the roof at the two-family flat an hour ago. Both houses had undergone several patch jobs and weren't up to code. On solid ground again, he waited until Colton reached him.

"I'm surprised you're here. How did you find me?"

"Aunt Jackie. I tried the two-family flat first. Stop screening your calls and I won't have to track you down in person."

"Did you stop over to buy me lunch?"

"Sure, if that means you'll fill me in."

Luke snuffed rising anger and punched Colton lightly on the shoulder. "Congratulate me. The ceremony is scheduled for Saturday after next. Pre-marital counseling is tomorrow at Tara's church."

Colton eyed Luke then shook his head. "You worked on her roof for three days, took her out twice, and planned a wedding in two weeks? She's after your money."

"Tara owns this house, plus the two-family flat you left."

"Three empty houses. She needs a contractor. Hook her up with Pete."

"Four houses. Tara owns the house she lives in." Luke retrieved the ladder and headed toward the truck.

Colton fell into step beside him. "I still think she's a gold digger."

Luke attached the ladder to the truck and retrieved a toolbox from the floorboard. "Tara isn't greedy. She hasn't even considered the houses' value. Follow me."

The two men rounded the house and trudged along the stone walkway. Luke stopped in front of an old utility building situated at the edge of the yard. He switched on the light then beckoned his brother inside.

Three fully restored vintage automobiles filled the space like a showroom.

"Whoa boy!" Colton walked around the vehicles until he stared at Luke. "There's real money here."

"Tara's grandfather restored old cars."

Luke stood to the side as Colton opened doors, closed doors, and sat inside each car. He did everything except toot the horn, shift the gears, and turn the steering wheel. Then he whipped out his cell phone. Colton's friend's uncle owned an auction house in the Chicago area. Mark scouted antique cars in three states. Waiting for his friend to answer, Colton drummed his fingers against a wall. "Hey, Mark. I found three classics: a 966 Porsche 911, Sunroof Coupe, a 1965 Jaguar XKE Coupe. Here's the clincher, there's also a 1937 Cord 810, Phaeton Convertible. Luke's friend owns the lot." His finger and thumb formed the okay sign. "I'm with you, Mark. Check it out." Colton stuffed the phone into his pocket. "Certain she owns these beauties?"

"Each one. I called her after peeking inside. She hadn't mentioned owning vintage vehicles." Luke swore underneath his breath when Colton grunted. "Don't say it."

"You mean don't verbalize the apparent? That you can't digest details of someone's life in two days? People have slept in the same bed for thirty years and still don't have a clue."

Another unwelcomed lecture. People who seldom took advice offered plenty.

Luke cleared his throat several times. "What are they worth? Probably an insane amount of cash."

"Mark claimed that in mint condition they'll easily sell for one hundred K a piece. Which means they're worth more. And man, her grandfather did an excellent restoration job."

"Whew! That much?" Luke ran his hand over the nearest bumper. "Whoa boy is right."

"A 1937 Cord 810's a rare find. What is Tara going to do with them?"

"I imagine leave them here."

Colton resembled a deer in headlights. "This house. Selling or leasing?"

"Hopefully she'll lease, because she's already rejected selling. Their vacant status is fine with her."

"That idea doesn't concern you?"

"I'll offer input and support. Tara's keeping the houses for our children. We want four."

"If her house is in the same neighborhood, I know you'll vote for living there. That leaves a single-family and a two-family flat. Three down and one left." Colton frowned. "Your house? These houses will sit vacant for twenty years? You're that gone?"

"Neither one of us is delusional. Still, her parents loved routine and kept these houses empty. Tara wants to keep to their wishes."

"Is the plan to lease everything but this building?" Colton surveyed the cars.

Luke's fiancée was a creature of habit. "Afraid so. Unless, I persuade her otherwise."

Colton pulled out his cell phone then shoved it back into his pocket. "Thank God no one broke in and stole the lot." He stuck his head outside the door. "The yard is well kept. Someone landscapes it weekly. What was her father thinking?"

"Apparently the workers are honest people. Mature trees obscured the view from neighbors' windows. No one realized these treasures were hidden inside. The Simpkins lived a simple lifestyle."

"Someone will discover these cars during renovations." Colton glowered at the lockless door. "Nobody even secured the building."

"I'll talk to Tara tonight and see what she says." Luke pushed away from the wall. "Tara dislikes change."

"Yet she accepted the proposal of a man she met two weeks ago."

Colton guffawed as Luke's eyes narrowed.

"Where can we store a classic car collection? Sort out a location."

Colton nodded and ran his hand over the Cord's bumper. "Suggest she sells. Collectors benefit from a classic paradise. These autos won't make it onto an auction floor."

"It isn't a slam dunk. The cars belonged to her grandfather. Each one's a keepsake."

"Yeah. To squirrelly people like you and Tara. 'I can't sell the houses. Mom and Dad bought these properties.' You sold the stock fast enough."

"The stock market fluctuates. Real estate values increase." Luke's hand raised in the air. "How can you reject kindred spirits? Tara and I fell in love at the same exact moment."

"That doesn't exonerate your marriage proposal." His cell phone rang. "Mark. Meet you at Kenny's." Colton headed toward the door. "Please secure the place as best you can."

"I'll do that, then meet you in thirty minutes," he said as he grabbed his toolbox. "Oh, and hey, Tara needs an attorney."

Luke spent fifteen minutes attaching padlocks to the door and side window. With one last look at the cars, he switched off the light and closed the door.

* * *

Two hours later, Luke took out his cell phone in the truck. He'd just inspected a roof job in the midtown area. His work day had finally wound down. It took planning to take ten days off work at short notice. He had to dot the I's and cross the T's with work and family.

"Hey, Benton, it's Luke. Do me a favor."

"Finishing up a job. Buy me lunch?"

"I ate with Colton earlier. Hey, Tara said yes. Our wedding's in two weeks. Before you ask, the plan is bringing Tara to The Grands' house at six. Give everyone a heads-up for me. Siblings only this trip."

"Hailee wants to meet her, too. You could bring her by our house tonight."

"We'll host a meet and greet before the wedding."

"Make sure that happens. About this evening ... You seem unsure whether Tara's prepared to come."

"She has a trace of shyness. Go easy on my ladylove."

"When will you tell her about meeting us?"

"After three appointments, I'll head her way. You'll love your new sister in-law. Promise."

"I hope so. I'll text everyone."

"Thanks for helping me out of a jam, Ben. I'm well behind schedule. Colton is long winded."

"I'll relay that message too. Later."

Tara joined the line of cars headed from the park. Her haggard brain was ready for a nap. Approximately fifty buses stood between her car and the road home. She drummed her fingers on the steering wheel, instead of succumbing to what she really desired to do. Her mind hankered to blow the horn until reaching Kingshighway. Sort of a celebration cheer and "get out of the way" rant combined in one.

The relaxing evening she imagined with Luke fueled her determination to hurry home. Next on the agenda was a marvelous dinner. The legwork was prepared that morning. She only had to pop the casserole into the oven and prepare a salad.

The traffic moved at a tortoise's pace, but Tara eventually rounded the corner to her house. With his hands behind his head and his legs crossed at the ankle, Luke sat on the porch's top step.

She sprang from the car and dashed toward him.

He met her on the sidewalk.

"Heavy traffic? I almost drove to the park." He kissed her lips then hauled Tara to his car. "Get in. We're late."

Her brain exploded with possible things that could've gone wrong. "Get in? Where to?"

"A mercy mission regarding important stuff." After tucking her into the passenger seat, Luke headed to his side.

"To do what, go where?" Tara fastened her seat belt while he buckled his.

"The Grands expect an introduction since our engagement is official."

Tara gasped while checking her face in the mirror. "I look like my day was spent at a school picnic."

"Pastor Victor confirmed our appointment tomorrow." Leaning over, Luke brushed her lips with his, then drove off.

"Ooh. Turn this car around. My face is shiny. I only have lipstick with me. My earrings are on the nightstand." Her fist clenched when Luke kept driving.

"Your natural skin is flawless like the rest of you. Recognize that you're a beautiful lady."

"Uh! Are you certain ... I mean ... did you tell them—Luke, what's their opinion of our engagement?"

"That they need to meet the woman who stole my heart with one look.

You're the prize they've always prayed I would receive. Grandma wants more women in our family. They'll love you. Wait and see."

So say you. Yet she also knew her parents would've expected to meet Luke by now.

"I'm at least taking some treats. Stop by Keller's Bakery."

"Which way?"

Minutes later, Luke pulled into the parking lot, and Tara hurried into the bakery. Back inside the car, she placed her packages on her lap.

"I still look tacky, but taking a peace offering helps."

Keeping up a steady stream of conversation about his family calmed Tara. Then Luke developed a laughing fit as she complained about road construction.

Tara glanced at him when he continued laughing. "What's funny?"

"Stop badmouthing construction sites when we pass by. Didn't you read the last sign? They're plastered everywhere. It's progress you voted for."

She was glad it wasn't more problems and released the breath she'd held.

"Well, I didn't vote for ruts, nails, and deadlocked traffic," Tara said, happy to change to a non-stressful topic. "What else is on the agenda?"

Hopefully, I'll meet your family and leave. She couldn't handle more than introductions.

Luke's eyebrows furrowed. "Why do you ask?"

Tara eyed him briefly then shrugged him off. *Why is he keeping secrets?*

She understood his grandparents' expectations. His meeting her parents would've been an up-front requirement. She understood reciprocation. Luke didn't have to result to schemes. She would've agreed to meet his family on her own accord.

Luke shifted lanes. "Talk to me. What's bothering you?"

"You keep secrets. I need a special line of defense to protect myself."

"What do you mean?" He turned on the cruise control, then eyed her. "I'm all ears."

"My meeting your grandparents is half of the story. Explain the half you refuse to reveal."

"Was that the politically correct way of calling me a liar?"

Tara mused over his reaction. "Give me the entire itinerary in understandable language."

"Trust that I'm an honest man." His Boy Scout grin returned. "We're headed to my grandparents' house."

"Luke—"

"I invited my sister and brothers over to meet you too."

Tara gazed at her grass-stained jeans and T-shirt. A shower would've helped as well.

Set up again. No way was this a spur-of-the-moment idea.

I should've showered and changed clothes. Luke's placed me at a disadvantage with his family.

Luke pulled into his circular drive while Tara counted vehicles parked next door.

Four cars. The gang's all here. Whoopee! The cross-examinations begins.

Once Luke left the car, Tara refused to move an inch but sat quietly until he opened the passenger door. She alighted from the cushion, smoothing her hands over her jeans, then retrieved the bakery boxes.

The front door opened before Tara and Luke crossed the property line. A bubbly young woman stepped onto the porch.

"Hi. Steffi. Luke's younger sister." She moved forward with outstretched hands.

"Hi, Steffi." Tara shook her hand, then passed the bakery boxes. "I brought a little snack."

"Keller's Bakery. I hear they serve the best pastries in the city. Now I get to taste if what I hear is true."

Luke made small talk while Steffi discreetly checked out Tara.

Tara noticed that Steffi's lips parted several times, but Luke hogged the dialog.

A muscular guy sporting a crew cut greeted Tara and Luke inside the living room.

"Benton." He held out his hand. "Happy you guys finally arrived. The Grands are anxious to meet you. Quickie wedding and all of that."

"Hi, Benton. Nice to meet you," she said, wondering why she came.

Hoping the artificial smile conveyed warmth she didn't feel, Tara nodded in case it didn't. Her gazed focused on an elderly couple across the room. Lively eyes and a steely gaze revealed an indomitable pair.

The two remaining brothers rose.

Tara strolled forward.

These two men looked like Luke, but Benton favored Steffi. The handsome family was made of good-looking people.

Being in a room filled with strangers was difficult for Tara. She thought about an earlier invitation she'd accepted for her and Luke.

The Bensons, Abby's parents, were in an uproar about the forthcoming marriage. Alicia Benson called Tara, demanding she and Luke attend Sunday dinner. Tara agreed straightaway, refusing to antagonize the snippy couple.

Luke stood beside Tara. Pride-filled eyes gazed at her face.

"Grandma, Granddad, meet the lady who changed my life's direction. Tara Simpkins. I've never been happier." His lips brushed her temple. "An agreeable partner has taken a rare chance on me." A fingertip followed the blush up her cheek. "Once we say, 'I do,' we're married for life."

Tara's courage escalated when Luke publicly declared his hopes. Perhaps she'd erred by rejecting making the visit yesterday.

"Tara, meet the most generous people alive. Edna and Bruce Cassidy, soon to become Grandma and Granddad."

Tara cleared her throat, smiling. "Pleased and nervous to meet everyone." She gasped. His siblings had surrounded her and Luke. Steffi still held the bakery boxes.

Edna lifted her arms.

Tara stooped to hug her.

His grandmother whispered in her ear. "We'll have a private discussion. First, mingle with the family."

Bruce stood, crushing her fingers in his. "Welcome to the family, Tara. Victor and Petra Hilliard dropped over after lunch, providing a heads-up about Tuesday's meeting. So, you're Ralph and Kitty's granddaughter. I met Ralph and Victor one week after moving to St. Louis. Victor's father married Edna and me at The Gathering Place. Edna and I attended your grandparents' and Maggie's and Lenny's weddings and funerals."

Tears sprang into Tara's eyes. Reality bored deeper. "Pastor Victor and Grandfather were school friends. Your knowing my parents makes me happy."

Luke led her to the loveseat.

Tara's keen gaze ogled the room.

The place was decorated in the same oldies style both her grandmothers had adored. Whatnots and ceramic animals were grouped together on shelves. Comfy chairs and ottomans were everywhere. A card table held an unfinished thousand-piece puzzle. Yet the room wasn't overcrowded.

Luke winked at her.

She giggled under her breath.

Preliminaries completed without a scratch. Yay, team Tara!

Steffi left the room, returning with a pastry tray. She placed the snacks on the cocktail table. "Gifts from Tara. Dig in."

Benton beelined to the treats. Bruce followed behind him at a sedate pace.

Then Luke's siblings began the interrogation. Their cleverly masked inquiries perplexed Tara. Interest centered around her parents' deaths and family connections. She fielded queries without playing the sympathy angle.

Luke draped an arm around her shoulder while she fielded questions. The quiet support illustrated teamwork. He recognized she could manage difficulties without assistance.

Inquiries over, Steffi moved her chair beside the loveseat. "By the way, you look my age. Sure you're thirty-two?" She giggled when Tara nodded. "Let's plan the wedding."

Chapter Ten

Tara hadn't anticipated instant success. She beamed a warm smile.

"Thanks to my resourceful friends, wedding plans were completed while I was at the park." She glanced at Luke. "Sorry. I didn't think to tell you on the drive over. We had so many other topics going."

Andy wiped his hand on a napkin. "That would've been a conversation to hear."

Steffi frowned. "If you'd been there, they would've chosen a different topic. What's the plan, Tara? Let me help."

"Thanks, but everything's finished. We want a simple yet intimate ceremony."

Colton scarfed down his cream cheese brownie amid disbelief. "Imagine a wedding being finalized in one afternoon at the zoo."

"My friends acted like an ant army and got the job done." She turned to Luke. "We need to talk about the guest list. My list has forty names."

"My names were whittled to ninety-five folks." His pointed glance took in each sibling.

"Really? You know lots of people."

Luke chuckled. "I left off a bunch of folks. Nasty messages will spew, but we want an intimate affair."

"I have people to invite," Steffi said.

Uh-oh. We messed up. Tara nibbled a finger. "Sorry, guys. Excluding others input is the downside of being an only child. Please, invite whomever you wish."

Luke shook his head. "Add your husband's parents and no one else."

Steffi rolled her eyes, refocusing on Tara. "Is the reception at your church?"

"Uh-huh. In the fellowship hall. My friend's aunt caters banquets, weddings, and large gatherings," Tara said. "She's onboard and ready. Luke, the wedding's at ten, with the reception right after." She leaned her back against

Luke's chest. "I decided on a brunch menu. Do you like that idea?"

"You're a godsend. I'm happy with whatever you decide."

Everyone was watching. Tara felt her cheeks blushing. "Steffi, er ... Steffi, I want two attendants in my wedding. One is my best friend, Abby. I'd also like Luke's sister. Please?" It felt weird issuing an invitation to a woman she had only recently met.

"Woo-hoo!" Steffi's gaze darted to her grandmother then back to Tara. "Shopping Saturday?"

Tara nodded. "Early morning? All expenses paid. I'll update Abby if you agree."

"An excellent time. My husband sleeps in on Saturdays."

Breathing deeply, her heartrate slowed. "Perfect. Abby has fraternal twins. Sonya's a flower girl and Tad's an usher." She tilted her head at the man who stared. "Andy, can your two daughters be flower girls?"

Tara released an audible breath after he agreed.

Andy's brows drew together. "Should Rachel call you?"

"Yes. Thank you. We'll exchange numbers." Tara grasped the hand Luke draped over her shoulder. "Colton, another flower girl is needed, and of course a ring bearer."

Colton nodded. "Delighted. Include my wife, Megan, in the mix. Thanks for asking."

Tara's gaze switched to Benton. "As a toddler, little Bennie is too young. When is Hailee's due date?"

Benton swallowed, washing down pecan tart with bottled water. "Next month. And before that and the ceremony, she expects to meet you."

Nice. Everyone accepted.

"Let's see," said Tara. "Dinner? Um ... maybe ... next week?"

Luke kissed her brow. "The to-do list continually grows. Earlier, Benton and I discussed a meet and greet for the family. Now I think meeting the others at the rehearsal dinner is better."

Everyone's gazes fixed on Tara as if saying, your turn.

Better nip the extra entertainment in the bud. "My bridal shower's next Tuesday. Hopefully, I can meet Hailee then."

"Sweet," said Steffi. "Leave your phone number so I can text everyone's information. Who's standing with you, Luke?"

"Pete and Andy. Pete will hear from me tonight."

"I don't recall you asking me to stand up with you," Andy said.

The brothers' gazes locked until Edna rose.

"Those miniature cakes are calling. I haven't eaten anything from Keller's Bakery in years." Edna picked up a vanilla cupcake with sprinkles and continued walking. "Tara, we'll have our chat in the kitchen now."

Edna left the room.

Tara licked her lips and looked at Luke. "Mrs. Cassidy said she wanted us to talk later. Guess later is now."

"Welcome to the family, love." Luke released her hand.

"Don't sweat the dungeon," Benton said, and he licked goo from his fingers.

* * *

When Tara entered the kitchen, Edna was nibbling a cupcake at the table. The room had that homey, lived-in feel Tara loved most. The kitchen had been her mother's personal haven. A radio on the refrigerator had played throughout the day on weekends.

"Take a seat, dear. Luke has been giving me frequent updates. The discussion in the living room eased my mind somewhat."

Edna's smile was comforting. Her kind eyes melted Tara's shoulder tension. His grandmother reminded Tara of Petra. Yesterday, Pastor Victor's wife had worn that same expression. Empathy. Maybe a private meeting with his grandmother worked best.

"What did Luke say? We both realize he didn't know much about me."

"Luke astonished us by falling hard. A two-week courtship indicates you did as well." Edna pushed the saucer aside. She appeared earnest about whatever was coming. "You answered many of my questions earlier. Those kids have inquisitive spirits. They grew dependent on each other once their parents died. Each one adapted to their new reality and found supporting one another beneficial. Luke and Andy shouldered many parental responsibilities."

Feeling a little like her old self, Tara nodded. "Their deep affection for each other was evident. Luke enjoys family life. You all top his conversations."

It appeared her comment caught Edna off guard.

"*You* dominate his conversations with us." She studied her fingers. "You're a family girl who enjoyed unconditional support. It's problematic that you recently lost that foundation. You've lived life cocooned inside a remarkable family unit giving love and having it returned."

Eyes wide, Tara gasped into her hands. *How did she know?*

"What's wrong, dear?"

"I ... Mrs. Cassidy, you nailed it. I live to love someone who'll love me back. Life is brief. Rebuilding what I lost is my reality. It's Luke's too." Tara scooted her chair closer to the table. "I ... practically shunned God after my mother died. I'm realizing that He didn't forget me." Her voice barely rose above a whisper.

"No person can supply what you lost. Only He bridges gaps between past and future. Life with the Father replenishes everything taken. To follow up on my previous comment, did losing your family prod you into accepting Luke's proposal?"

Moisture entered Tara's eyes, yet the tears remained unshed. Her inner battle finally became evident to herself. Loneliness swept through her. Their conversation unleashed lost memories of feeling cherished. Abby and her friends loved her, but their own familial responsibilities weighed heavy upon each one. She refused to intrude on any of their lives.

"I love Luke. He's thoughtful, *and* he understands me. I've always known affection would run deep if—" Tara glanced away. *Luke grasps aspects of me I hadn't figured out myself. His discernment is uncanny.* "Luke possesses the best of everything I've ever wanted."

Edna's composure shifted into neutral. "Surely you don't expect a perfect life with Luke."

"Oh, no. No—no. Luke sometimes behaves like a control addict, manipulating events for his own end. Did his parents' deaths and sibling responsibilities produce those characteristics? He and Andy had quite a large mountain to climb." Sadness rose as she glanced at the docile face observing her. "Does he always get what he wants?"

"No person does. Real life doesn't work that way. In a short time, you've gained insight into my grandson's personality. Does perception work in reverse? Carefully consider the question without replying." She paused. "Has Luke disappointed you any?"

"More than a little after our latest roadblock regarding his rental property." Tara slumped onto the cushion. *Should I tell a doting grandmother that her grandson deceived me about coming over here? Nah. Too candid. Stick to the houses.* "Luke refused my offer to pay his siblings for the rental property."

Edna softly laughed. "Thank God. Your parents would've agreed with Luke's refusal."

His grandmother knew that Luke spent his own money from Cassidy Roofing, plus proceeds from the rental properties to help pay his siblings' college tuition. Why would she disagree to Tara helping him? "Paying for their education depleted Luke's funds."

"As you know, the rental properties are shared assets. But the children could've footed the bill with their own inheritance. They didn't require his assistance."

Tara understood Luke's accepting responsibility. She would've too. "Then they would've missed the experience Luke and Andy shared."

"Choices have consequences we deal with."

She shook her head. "Generosity made the rental property an issue. Settling his parents' estate is a priority. I chose to help him."

"Why? Other options exist. Luke can sell the rental property and divide proceeds."

"But selling property his parents valued isn't ideal."

Edna savored pieces of cupcake she'd pushed aside. "Dear, this lady has talked long enough. You're a lovely addition to our family. But is marrying my grandson *now* beneficial *to you*?" Edna rounded the table and embraced Tara in strong arms. "Think about it. The wedding is twelve days away."

Tears filled Tara's eyes as she hugged the lady who gently patted her back.

"Mrs. Cassidy, you offered sound advice I can't follow. Thank you for caring." Tara turned away, then swung around and kissed Edna's cheek. *I find it difficult to leave her.* She fought back tears. *Tears. Again. My parents died, and I didn't cry. I hate any show of weakness.* She clasped her hands behind her back. "Your treating me like a granddaughter is kindness I won't forget."

How can I feel connected to a woman advising me not to do what I feel I must? God bless my relationship with Luke.

She sighed loudly in the doorway. "Our discussion reminded me of my parents. I'm grateful we talked."

"Tara, turn around, dear." Edna waited until Tara faced her. "Many decisions have lasting effects. Futures hang in the balance. Choose wisely."

A nod was all Tara could manage. Shuffling down the hall, she struggled to retain poise. A straight line to the car was her fervent desire, but Luke waited inside the living room door.

One look at Tara's tear-filled eyes propelled Luke to draw her near. "We're out of here," he called over his shoulders.

"Wait until I say goodbye." Inhaling deeply, Tara poked her head inside the room. "Thanks, guys, for making my evening." She waved to Bruce. "I'll be back."

Bruce stood. "So much like your mother. You had better visit us again. You're a keeper."

When Tara felt a light touch on her waist, she smiled at Edna.

"Bruce and I have a few mementoes to pass on. Stop by our house on Saturday after you finish shopping."

"Sure thing." Tara clapped her hands together. "Like a kid at Christmas. Should I bring lunch?"

"We'll eat a home-cooked meal."

"Eat light," said Andy. "Rachel's inviting the family to a barbecue that evening. Is six a good time?"

"Works for me and Hailee. I'll bring The Grands," Benton said.

"Tara, do you have prior plans?" Steffi asked.

"Not to my knowledge." She glanced at Luke.

"Did you forget our planetarium date night?"

"How about after our honeymoon? I can meet the rest of the family at Andy's. Agreed?" She faced Andy when Luke nodded. "We're free. Can't wait to meet everyone's spouses." Tara rubbed her hands together. "The children?"

"Dessert at my house Sunday?" Colton slid his cell phone into his shirt pocket. "Four?"

Tara turned to Luke. "We were invited, and I accepted, to eat dinner at Abby's parents' house at one. The Bensons eat an early Sunday dinner."

"Four it is," Luke said. "Dessert will help me recover after being scrutinized. Are the parents anything like their daughter?" He grinned at the others. "Yesterday Tara's best friend gave me the evil eye all evening. We watched the game with her and her husband, Craig."

Everyone laughed except Steffi. Her gaze went from Tara to Luke.

After glancing at his sister, Luke backed Tara from the room.

Colton called after Tara before they reached the door. "My brother said you need an attorney. Fill me in on Saturday."

Tara's mind was fuzzy. Her thoughts centered on Steffi's frown. Everyone else wore smiles. At last, Colton's words soaked through.

"Bringing the packet my father left might help. It hasn't been touched yet. These days I ignore anything business-related."

"Which is understandable under the circumstances," Andy said.

"I agree. Later." Luke tugged Tara into the hallway. Outside, he passed by the car and led her to his front door. "Eat here, and then I'll take you home."

Tara lagged back. "No way. I prepped an excellent meal for dinner."

"It's late. Tomorrow after church might work better. I'll make you a deluxe sandwich."

"Works for me. This sandwich lover had a long day. My culinary skills can wow you tomorrow."

* * *

The warm night found Tara shivering underneath a quilt. Edna's advice disrupted her peace all evening. Luke's departure switched her brain into daydream mode. Tara wanted to marry Luke, but having the right timing mattered. Glitter lost its glamour with wedding debates and diverse views. However, Edna's opinion that they should postpone the wedding backed Tara into a corner.

To marry Luke now or marry Luke later is the question. What happened to her perfect solution? Get married and leave the consequences to God. Had she miscalculated? Outcomes revealed truth. But reaching a verdict could take years, and by then the damage could've ruined her life. Could she wait that long?

Our marriage is either doomed or it's a miracle.

* * *

A conflicted Tara slinked into work Tuesday morning. If there was ever a day to blend in with the scenery, this was it. Somehow the engagement euphoria had worn off during the night. Would ring shopping Wednesday rekindle her previous fervor? She slung her purse and satchel onto the desk, staring at the computer. All morning she hadn't comprehended anything she'd seen.

Sit down and start the day so you can leave.

Oh no. A frowning Olivia is headed my way. Evidently Luke told Rick, and he told Olivia. She's a blabber. Dang it. News spreads around this building quickly. No wonder the guard congratulated me.

First lesson learned today: Ask questions when someone makes a comment that you don't comprehend.

Tara had simply thanked the pleasant man and moved on.

Second lesson learned: Ignore people whose opinions don't matter.

With the headset over her ears, Tara powered on the computer.

* * *

Well-wishers came out of the woodwork that morning. Congratulations rang across the work space. Tara attempted to shrink in stature. She'd talked to more people in one hour than she had in fourteen years.

Before her first break, a middle-aged woman aimed for her desk. Yet Tara took another call, hoping the woman would move on. She turned to face her when she didn't.

"So, you're getting married in two weeks," old lady Matthews said with a toothy smirk. "That's funny," the woman continued. "I never knew you had a boyfriend."

"I keep personal business private." Tara leaned against the chair's back cushion, awaiting a response.

The woman's mouth hung open until she sneered. "Don't get snippy with me. You engaged yourself to a roofer who made the repairs just last week."

Oh—no—you—don't. Even fifty-year-old gossipy women don't get a pass.

"Refrain from insults, Mrs. Matthews. Goodbye."

Tara took the next call.

* * *

When her break arrived, Tara rolled her shoulders in forward circles, giggling as her bones cracked. "Too much sitting. Tea time." She dropped a ginger tea bag into her coffee cup and headed to the hot water dispenser. Topmost on her mind was Friday dinner. Luke's best friend, Pete, and his wife, Molli, had issued the invitation via Luke last night.

A bearded man fell into step beside her. "Gossip says you'll marry in two weeks." His bleary eyes leered. "I suppose it's too late to request a date?"

Tara sighed. Some days were longer than others. She wouldn't answer imbecilic questions. All morning unwanted attention sapped her strength. As she walked back to her desk, she began the countdown to lunch.

* * *

Two hours later, Tara fled the building. Kenny's Diner came to mind right along with Tuesday's lunch special. If she remembered correctly, today was roast beef au jus, mashed potatoes, sautéed green beans, and scratch-made biscuits. Her mouth watered.

The lunch I brought today will return home.

"Mmm. I can't wait to get there. Maybe I'll run into Luke."

Proximity to her neighborhood acted like a magnet that drew her home. Tara made an unnecessary turn onto her street, tooted at her house, and drove on. The parking lot at the office complex teemed with cars. Successful businesses must occupy the building. She jumped when someone tapped her passenger window.

"Steffi!" She bounded from the car.

The younger woman hurried to her side. "Hello again. Today's filled with surprises. You are another one. Eat here often?"

"Luke brought me for breakfast on Sunday. Are you coming or going?"

"Going. Andy has a potential client coming in twenty minutes." Curiosity entered her eyes. She scratched her ear and giggled. "Aunt Jackie said you're joining Cassidy Roofing soon. I would hate working with Scott. But then, I've known him forever."

Tara tried to keep from frowning. *Where's Steffi headed with the disjointed barb?*

"Yes! My morning at work offered a prime example of why I'm leaving."

"That bad? Glad I work for my brothers. Aunt Jackie wants you there this week."

"Seriously? I thought Luke was joking." *That's food for thought. Were there internal problems within the company?*

"Thanksgiving Eve is my aunt's last day. Reorganize the office as you wish. I did."

"Good advice." Tara checked her watch and backed away. "I know you're in a hurry. I won't keep you."

"Wait." Steffi touched Tara's arm. "You were in la-la land as I walked up. You seemed ... distracted. Is everything okay?"

"It's difficult not to think about Luke every second. Is everything okay with you?"

Steffi's eyes clouded over.

Tara reconsidered his sister's subdued behavior at Edna and Bruce's house before Tara left. She'd become low-key then *and* now. It seemed she was debating her response.

"What do you think about our wedding?"

"That it's too soon. Luke met you two weeks ago. Saturday was your first date." A car driving into the parking lot caught her attention. Steffi hung her head then glanced at Tara. "I'll support you guys marrying at a later date if you postpone the wedding."

Tara flinched but hoped Steffi didn't notice. *I just had to ask.* "Candor serves a purpose even if the truth hurts."

"Please—don't get the wrong idea. You and Luke belong together." Her tone softened even more. "Take whatever time you need before tying the knot. My brother loves you. He'll wait."

Tara's arms wrapped around her body then dropped to her side. "So, you want us to postpone the wedding—because we barely know each other? The depth of our relationship defies time."

If Luke had a Boy Scout grin, Steffi had a Girl Scout smile and beamed Tara with it.

"It's catch-up time. You and Luke should spend more time together before getting married." She walked Tara to the door. "Did Luke tell you our grandparents married three weeks after they met?"

"Sure did." They stopped outside the diner. "Luke hammered home that point on our first date."

"He's relentless over everything he values." Steffi moved closer. "Our family likes you."

Fighting back tears, Tara accepted the olive branch. Must she lose two steps with each one gained? "I appreciate Luke's gracious family."

"Which you'll soon join." Steffi's arms opened wide. "Welcome."

Tara returned the hug. "Now I'll have the younger sister I've always wanted. Thanks, sis."

Surprise entered Steffi's eyes. "Sis. Saying that says love. I can't get over how young you look. Hardly thirty anything. See you later."

Tara stepped inside the diner and watched Steffi's progress through the window. Twenty minutes later, she stacked discarded dishes into a pile and studied the clock over the exit door. Somewhat deflated by Steffi's honesty, she reassessed recent decisions. She'd committed herself to a life with Luke. What about her job?

Quitting my job's a done deal—but now? I'm sweating over my entire life while my fiancé acts stress-free.

Chapter Eleven

Luke's cell phone vibrated while he discussed prices with a potential customer.

Grandma. She seldom calls during the day.

"Our earliest available appointment is Monday," he continued. "It's a three-day job." He nodded at the paperwork the receptionist handed him and returned the file. "Beth will fax the contract early this afternoon. It must be signed and in our office by close tomorrow. The crew arrives at seven sharp Monday." Luke ended the call.

Sean, the service coordinator, waited beside his desk. "Both patch jobs confirmed for Thursday. A two-man crew on each job?"

"One man on the garage. Two men on the house." Luke headed toward the door. "Heard anything from the partial roof?"

"They chose to pay weekend rates. The contract was signed and delivered before lunch."

"Slot the same three men for Friday and Saturday. I'm out of here, guys."

Luke listened to the voicemail on his way out the door. The cryptic message stopped him short.

"Stop by as soon as possible, dear. Call me if you can't come."

Luke had never received an ASAP message from either grandparent. His grandmother had called from the landline. Luke returned the call on the spot. No one picked up. He called her cell phone. No answer. His grandfather's cell phone was next.

Where are they? Someone always answers one of those phones.

Luke spun around, rushing back inside the office. He hadn't received an emergency summons, but taking a proactive approach wouldn't hurt. Especially since no one answered nor returned his calls. Better to treat the situation as a crisis and pray that it wasn't.

"Beth. Where's Aunt Jackie hiding?"

A spry lady with white hair stumbled into the room from the storage closet. "I don't like that tone. Anything wrong? I thought you left to inspect the roof in Brentwood."

"Grandma left a message to come by the house ASAP. My return calls went unanswered."

"Although it's strange, don't be concerned. Everything's probably fine."

Luke dialed the house phone again, tapping his fingers on the desktop while he waited. When no one answered, he eyed his aunt. "Have you spoken to either one of them today?"

"I spoke with Bruce twenty minutes ago. He was headed to the barbershop."

"That's his routine every Tuesday. I'm headed to their house. Beth, if possible, reschedule the appointment until tomorrow morning." He left once the woman nodded.

Jackie walked Luke to the truck. "Drive carefully. I'll keep calling. No worrying if you don't hear from me."

Twenty minutes later, Luke rang the doorbell, even though the spare key was poised and ready.

The door sprang open. Grey eyes twinkled before Edna turned away.

"Glad you're here. We needed this talk before Bruce returns from the barbershop. Your grandfather relishes chitchats with the few friends he has left."

"Grandma, stop talking about death." Luke stepped inside the house. "Steffi's married. I'm engaged. Benton's awaiting his second child. Colton's law practice is booming, and Andy just hired another accountant. This family is full of life."

"Pooh. No one lives forever. Even the people you love. Life is cyclical. The old die off and the new are born." Edna left Luke to secure the door and ambled toward her favorite seat in the house.

Luke followed behind her. "Why didn't you answer my calls? I dialed all three numbers several times."

"The two phones here didn't ring. Bruce was probably in the barber's seat." She set the rocking chair into motion. "Hope my call didn't worry you. That's why I added, call if you can't come."

"Which only works if you answer the phone." Luke removed his cell phone from his pocket, sent a text message, then chuckled at the swift reply. "I texted Aunt Jackie to tell her it wasn't an emergency. She's bringing dinner. Now, why did you call?"

"Tara. Derrick and Jenny would've welcomed her. They knew her parents well in their younger years."

That was high praise, but an axe would fall. Luke positioned a seat beside the rocking chair. "Good marriages on both bloodlines. All the grandchildren were blessed with perfect mates. It's been nine years since Andy married the girl who lived around the corner. Colton just celebrated his seven-year anniversary to his high school sweetheart. Benton married his best friend's cousin on his twenty-second birthday. And Steffi married Benton's best friend. A man she's known her entire life."

"Yes. And our eldest grandson is engaged to a lady his grandfather adores."

Luke chuckled. "That's a first. Granddad's a hard sell. Especially on the first visit."

"Finding out she was Ralph and Kitty's granddaughter didn't hurt. Plus, Tara brought goodies from Keller's Bakery. Of course, Bruce is an excellent character judge and a man of few words. He said, 'Tara is a precious girl, just like her mother. I like her.' "

Those were comments Luke expected to hear. Accolades for his lovely lady. However, his grandmother was shooting the breeze instead of explaining her summons. "Tara likes you all back. She enjoys family events. We'll share many. But why the ASAP message? You've never sent any when you should have, so I thought it might be an actual emergency."

"Oh that. Hope you weren't alarmed. There are many topics for us to touch on."

"Concerning Tara? I cancelled an appointment and came right over. Fill me in."

"On Saturday, we'll fulfill familial obligations with gifts to Tara. Traditionally, the oldest grandson's wife gets the family photo album. It's been passed down for many years. After your parents died, I removed the album from their house and kept it safe here."

Luke's jaw muscles slacked. "The photo album. I never missed it." His eyes narrowed. "What else did you swipe?"

Edna couldn't stop laughing. Each time she tried, she giggled again. "Just the photo album. Steffi would've placed the photos into picture frames." She placed a hand over her mouth. "Wait a minute, Luke. I can't stop laughing. Do a house search if you like."

"Nah, I believe you. Now ... the call."

"You mean, what else besides the legitimate reason of giving gifts? As you know, our mothers kept tokens intended for the wife of the eldest son. Since

Jenny didn't receive the gifts before she died, those rings come to Tara." Her face saddened. She started to speak, then shut down.

"What's wrong, Grandma?"

"Visions of my son and daughter in-law crop up close to wedding celebrations."

"Same with me." *Time to liven things up.* "Which fond memories caught you?"

"Wedding rings disrupted my morning. Jenny's rings were lost in the explosion. She expected to pass her engagement and wedding rings to your oldest son." Edna smoothed her hair with trembling hands. "I dreaded burying empty coffins. Well, such is life. Time moves on."

"I hated that part too. It would've been better to see Mom and Dad again, even if they were dead. I'm glad we've finally turned the page on that ordeal." Those haunting visions couldn't tarnish his life with Tara. Painful memories deserved a burial. "Quite often it appeared my life was over. That was the hardest part about losing Mom and Dad. Pieces of me perished with them."

Edna captured his hands with her fingers. "Those circumstances were difficult to overcome, yet God brought us through each one." Her head tilted slightly to the side. "In less than two weeks all their kids will be married. An accomplishment they'd hoped to witness for themselves."

"Snapshots of their happy faces at my congratulations bash and Andy's engagement celebration are heartwarming." Luke wore a wide grin when he secured Edna's fingers to his chest. "Our entire family has tons of joyous memories. Grandma, I can't wait to say my vows to an incredible lady." Luke hesitated until Edna nodded. "The Cassidys weren't a perfect family, but I cherish the life we led. Mom and Dad taught us values." Luke paused as Edna lifted her feet onto an ottoman. "Is there more to the purpose behind this visit? The reason for calling."

"To offer a personal perspective. Derrick and Jenny were godly people. Remember each principle they advocated."

Luke hitched a leg beside Edna's on the ottoman. "Here we go. The real reason you called."

"You kids were raised in a godly home with structure." Edna slipped her fingers out of his hand and stilled the rocking chair. "There isn't one excuse for wayward lifestyles."

Definitely not the conversation Luke imagined. It seemed his grandmother had a grievance to bare. He would need to approach with caution. "Grandma, your grandchildren are imperfect individuals striving to remain on the right side of wrong living. Our stable upbringing was advantageous."

"Then explain your previous pursuits. Before Tara, your lifestyle wasn't exemplary. Those past choices didn't denote stability. Family-minded men date like-minded women. They search for wives in Sunday school rather than at bars."

"I met Leah at a sporting fundraiser in an upscale pub."

"You say pub. I say bar. The women you dated lacked morals. From what I've heard, no one pretended they were anything other than what they were."

Luke's eyebrows knitted together. "How can you judge women you haven't met?"

"That Bruce and I didn't meet those women says it all. Tara is the only woman you've brought next door since Jenny and Derrick died. Why date women you wouldn't consider marrying?"

"Female companionship offers simple enjoyment."

"Does companionship involve sex without restraint? You dated women you wanted to bed."

Luke gripped the chair's edge to keep from falling off. Edna Cassidy seldom pulled punches. "You condemned the women I dated along with me."

"I retain full knowledge of what I do, say, and think."

Luke instantly backtracked. "I was passing time until my love match appeared. Only Tara is in my life these days."

"Tara's unpretentious and possesses desirable qualities for your wife. But are you the man her parents hoped for her?"

Jaw muscles slacked involuntarily. "Please ... explain."

"Simple enough. Uncontrollable events devastated Tara's life. She's struggling to stem the pain of losing both parents, and she views you as a lifeline to happiness. Money isn't her objective; you are. Tara will eagerly share her resources with you."

"Her words?" *What else was said? Perhaps you spent too much time alone in the kitchen.*

Edna studied his face a long moment.

Luke wished he could read her thoughts.

"Rejecting her assistance is her lone disappointment about the courtship. She truthfully answered after I asked if you'd disappointed her in any way," Edna added as Luke's eyebrow rose.

"As she would. Grandma, you understand why I can't accept her money, even though I suspect Tara inherited a hefty sum." Luke's expression became bland once relief relaxed Edna's features.

"Of course, I do. Thank God this family isn't self-seeking and money hungry."

"You consider me selfish in other ways?"

"Those words were spoken by you. Tara seeks love. Stability. Family. Your fiancée plays for keeps."

The insult that he was whimsical found Luke picking his face up off the floor. What a low opinion his grandmother must have of him. "You doubt my love for Tara?"

"Successful marriages require more than love. Equal portions of dedication, humility, and patience, to name a few, are essential attributes. How do Leah's visits affect these marriage plans?"

Moving to the sofa, Luke planted bare feet on the coffee table. "Leah again. Steffi, Andy, and today, you. Granddad and you never met the woman because meaningless associations don't count."

"Neither one of us is fooled by that remark. You acted as if a boomerang circled you back to Leah. What bound you to her? Was the sex too good to walk away from?"

Luke coughed into his hand. "Whoa, Grandma ... please." He sputtered then coughed some more. He massaged the bridge of his nose. Grasping for control, he practiced deep breathing. "How can you ask such a question?"

"Marriage in eleven days. That's how. Leah wasn't a love match. What else did you have in common? No one raised you to use women or vice versa. Listen to me. An untimely death and related responsibilities overwhelmed you and Andy. Everyone was blindsided, Luke."

"Although equally affected, we all reached adulthood without disaster."

"Getting on the correct path requires insight as to how you got off course. Confessions aren't necessary. Pray. Our grandchildren mean the world to Bruce and me. Don't wreak havoc with your life. We want a legacy of secure relationships left behind."

Luke abandoned the sofa and stooped beside his grandmother. The wise woman had the kindest eyes he'd ever seen. "No worries. Leah was a game I played and lost with great cost. The experiment failed."

"You wanted a permanent relationship with her?" Concern creased wrinkles around her brow.

"It's complicated, so I won't trouble you with details. Recently, a non-effective bomb dropped. Leah proposed."

The wrinkles deepened. "She's serious about you?"

"No, ma'am. Whatever set her off, affection wasn't it. Look. She lives in Los Angeles and visits family in St. Louis. Last fall, I ended our association. When she tried to make a comeback, I advised her not to contact me. Backward looks never amount to anything more than wasting time. I choose to live without future worries or past regrets. I no longer accept her calls."

Edna's face flushed. "A harsh reaction. You shared a relationship with this woman for five years."

"She called on her arrival and said goodbye whenever she left. Except for a few texts, there was no in-between-visit communication."

"Sometimes explanations unload more confusion." Edna's hand repeatedly brushed her forehead as if the gesture improved thinking. "The concept befuddles me. Right or wrong, you and Leah shared a five-year relationship. At the very least, conversation is due."

"I disagree. The boy took care of business, now let him be." Bruce made his way from the hallway to the recliner next to Edna's rocking chair.

A timely intervention. "Thanks, Granddad. Sometimes it's difficult correcting past mistakes."

"Cutting the wrong ties is more productive than acting polite. An association—" he glanced at Edna, "ended that never should've begun. Take free advice. Devote your life to Tara and the children you hope to raise." Once Luke nodded, Bruce faced his wife. "He's engaged. Don't regurgitate past sins. Our grandson is paying attention to his life these days. I'm proud."

Edna sighed. "Perhaps my ideas stem from a feminine viewpoint."

We need a subject change before Grandma changes her mind about accepting Granddad's opinion.

"Granddad, you knew Tara's grandfather on her father's side. Do you have information on her mother's father?"

"A good man who kept to himself. Burt Williams restored classic vehicles. After he retired, Burt turned a hobby into a lucrative business. The shop wasn't far from his house. You can glimpse the building behind Victor's church. His name is still on the sign above the door."

Luke observed the alert expression on his grandmother's face. Had he asked the correct question to obtain needed answers? If not, then what? "Did he own the building?" He studied his grandfather once Edna relaxed her grip on the armrest.

"He did." Bruce eyed Luke. "The property probably belongs to Tara."

More property, Tara. Ignoring facts won't negate making proper decisions. Life brings changes we learn to deal with.

His fiancée's cooperation on important matters would benefit both their lives. Had the entire Simpkins family lived inside their own reality?

And my family accuses me of withholding pertinent information.

* * *

Back at work, Tara mumbled under her breath. "If one more person says, 'So happy you're getting married,' I will scream." Too bad the crew that clocked in after lunch hadn't received the word that morning. Once again, the congratulatory game began in full swing. Same story, different players. After the fifth, "I didn't think you had a boyfriend," she spent the rest of the afternoon pining for evening.

I'm quitting this job after the honeymoon.

The hands of the clock inched along. *Quitting after the honeymoon won't work. The wedding is two weeks away.* Fed up, Tara scripted her resignation letter between calls. It was a well-worded last-minute effort. Next, she ticked off pros and cons and was staggered by the results. The nays outweighed the yeas, uncovering numerous reasons to stay put. *This isn't the moment for second thoughts.* After pressing print on her letter, she darted to the printer and grabbed the copy, hiding the single page inside a folder. Shelli walked in on Tara's way out. One look proved the woman was in chat mode.

"Too many nosey people hung around your desk all day." Shelli's elbow dug into Tara's side. "Is Luke on the agenda this evening? Lonely nights are over."

"Lonely nights?" Her eyes grew wider. "What do you mean?"

Satisfaction fled Shelli's face. "Nothing. Forget it." She sat on the copy table. "Will Rick and I receive a wedding invitation?"

Tara's hand covered her mouth. "Oops. Luke didn't say. I'll check his list tonight."

Surprise crossed Shelli's features. "Meaning our names didn't make the bride's list."

"No one at work was invited," she said quickly. "It's my break time. Gotta run." She left without a backward glance. No doubt Rick's and Shelli's names were on Luke's list.

Tara's steps slowed just before reaching the manager's office. The folder weighed heavily in her hand. Sauntering into the empty room, she laid her

112

letter on the desk seat's cushion, scooted the chair under the desk, and sped away.

Within minutes Tara went back and retrieved the resignation letter.

Am I crazy? Handing in my two-week notice today is foolish. Countdown time to quit my job after the honeymoon begins now.

* * *

The work day ended once Tara signed off the last call. She'd waited all day for freedom and couldn't reach her car fast enough. There were multiple things to do and precious little time to do them. Beginning next Monday, she would surprise Luke with unexpected tokens of love until their dress rehearsal.

The first shop would close in forty minutes. Luke had enthused over her grandfather's car collection. Earlier, Suze located a company able to build 1:12 scale models of each car. Due to the short time frame, a hefty price had been quoted. Luke had five pre-wedding gifts coming. Eight classic car models were one.

The craftsman's shop was stuck on the backside of a rundown lot. Tara broke into a sprint near the door. What smelled like tar assaulted her nose once she walked inside. The messy interior almost prompted a retreat until she sighted the classic automobile display. The models showcased underneath a magnificent glass dome were larger than any miniatures Tara had ever viewed. Her body popped with excitement as she handed the mustached man with lively eyes a picture-filled folder.

"I'd like to get 1:12 scale miniatures of the first eight photos. How much for the dome case display?"

Her lips formed a circle at the figure quoted, and then she smiled. "These models are huge. Do you sell domes large enough to showcase eight cars within the same one?"

If eyes could dance, the owner's did. "I have two such glass enclosure tubes in stock." The man glanced through the folder. "Awesome pictures. Are any of the actual cars for sale?"

"Afraid not. They were my grandfather's private collection."

"Let me know if they become available." Whistling, the congenial man printed eight copies on a color copier, replacing the folder into her hands. "The molds will get casted tonight. They will be ready for pick up Wednesday afternoon. Bring plenty of man power to move them. The cost to replace the lot before the wedding will be expensive."

"Gotcha. The miniatures are a surprise for my fiancé. Thanks for taking my order on short notice."

"Suze is quite a talker. She had me agreeing to help you before I knew it. Congratulations on your engagement."

Tara smiled her way out of the shop and jumped into the car, breathing hard. She had four additional stops before the drive home to prep for the meeting with Pastor Victor. Hopefully he would handle the new couple gently at the meeting that evening. None of her friends had provided credible ideas of what to expect. Each one had undergone a different experience altogether.

Her mind returned to the first purchase. Eight miniature cars would initiate Luke's private collection. Those were models of the automobiles currently in her possession. *Luke will hear about the other vehicles after he opens his present. Then he can view the actual models at the shop. Won't he be surprised that there are five other cars he hasn't seen.* Thank God her grandfather had photos of each car restoration. She could add to Luke's collection throughout the years.

Five days of wedding gifts for Luke was officially underway. Humming about her planned surprise to the tune of "The Twelve Days of Christmas," Tara backed out of the parking space. In eleven days, she would marry the man refusing to divulge the honeymoon destination. Secretive people vexed her. Luke was one. Heading toward the highway, she set up GPS.

One down, four to go. How should I rollout the presents?

Gifts two and three forced Tara to drive downtown during rush-hour traffic. The cars on the busy street were backed up two blocks.

An hour later, Tara sped down the road in the opposite direction. Two presents lay hidden inside her purse. One was a gift card that covered four dinners for two at an exclusive downtown restaurant. The other was four weekend reservations at a hotel overlooking the riverfront. For the first four months of their marriage, they would stay in the same suite and dine at the same restaurant the last weekend of each of those months. Only two gifts were left to buy. Creating memories was great fun.

Chapter Twelve

At the fourth stop, Tara found a lot across the street from the store. She should've taken off work early instead of competing for parking spots. This next gift would catch her fiancé off guard. The sideboard in Luke's dining room teemed with handbells. He rang a few during her visits. His mother had collected an amazing assortment from countries around the world. Suze had located an antique gift shop boasting a sizable bell collection. Over time, Tara hoped to find handbells from places she and Luke would visit.

Eager to shop, she zoomed into an empty space vacated by a minibike. Once inside, she found a polished store void of dusty scents associated with such places. Tara fingered a rack of Tiffany lamps and merchandise displayed nearby. Each item was categorized and displayed with honor.

"Hello. My name's Barbara." A wispy voice spoke from behind.

Tara turned around, smiling. "Hi. Tara. Earlier, my friend called to inquire about handbells. I raced to get here before closing time."

"The lady implied you would come after work. I'd planned to remain open an extra hour in case you ran late. The handbells are kept inside the precious memoir room."

Five entryways led to separate designated spaces. Barbara entered a side room left of the main showroom. Handbells in different shapes, various sizes, and multiple colors decorated one of eight sideboards on display. Other cabinets showcased fine china, handheld fans, glassware, vases, scrolls, ceramic and glass owls and birds, plus carved-wood animals.

She hadn't expected such exquisite treasures inside a nondescript store. "Splendid replicas. Some are quite fragile." She stopped at each showcase and picked up several items. "What an exceptional exhibition." She smiled at the woman striding beside her. "Handbells are on the agenda today. But I'll definitely be back to see more."

An appreciative light shone in the woman's eyes. "Tell family and friends about us. My mother opened our store when I was ten. Some of our oldest customers no longer visit. We need younger generations to know we're here."

"My friend who contacted you is a blogger. She and her husband own a marketing firm." Tara pulled a business card from her purse.

"Thank you." The smiling woman scanned the information. "I'll call her tonight. Perhaps we can set up a visit sometime this week."

Before leaving, Tara purchased four delicate handbells. Christmas in July sales teased her mind while walking to the car. After renovations, she could decorate her house with items from this shop.

She placed the gift-wrapped box on the back seat. Once settled, she sped from the curb, needing to reach the next appointment on time.

Luke's fifth gift was a collage of their first weekend together. Each day she and Luke had taken numerous shots on their camera phones. The photos began with dinner at Rick and Shelli's. Every aspect of their weekend had been captured. Some showed Tara engrossed in the beautiful sunset and layering cookies on a tray. Others had Luke talking to Rick and Kenny Senior. There were pictures of the office complex, grounds, and her grandparents' houses.

Other people had also joined the fun. An usher from The Gathering Place had texted Tara two photos, and Brielle had sent Luke three shots from their lunch at Nouveau Départ. Abby captured them coming, leaving, and watching the playoffs in her den. Even Steffi had sent a few along. Thirty-two pictures. Tara wanted those special memories chronicled forever.

She arrived at the upscale store, and Suze was right. The affable attention proved first-rate. A smartly dressed woman collected Tara at the door and led her to a cubicle across the room.

Thirty minutes later, Tara exited the shop, colossal receipt in hand. Besides the collage, she had ordered two matted and framed eight-by-ten pictures—one of herself and one of Luke, plus two key chains with photos of her and Luke at the bistro, and a photo album. Of course, it required printouts, which she purchased. Things she hadn't known she needed. And the price of it all added up.

* * *

At home, she showered and changed clothes. With no time to spare, she opened the door to greet Luke with a kiss.

He stepped inside the foyer then pulled her into his arms. "How was work?" He kissed her lips again. "Miss me?" His mouth stalled the answer.

Tara licked the lips he'd kissed. She laughed and pointed toward the door. "Wow! Walk out and come in again."

"I can give a repeat performance without leaving."

Tara evaded his arms, but Luke pulled her closer. She hugged him with one arm, then grabbed her purse from the banister post.

"I bet you could, Mr. Cassidy. We'll arrive at church late if I let you prove it. Hungry?"

Fine lines crinkled around his eyes. "Starved for you."

"How should I take that remark? Don't answer. Ready?" Tara opened the front door, glancing over her shoulder. "We could have the masterpiece I prepared yesterday for dinner. After our meeting?"

With the back of his hand, Luke brushed hair from her face. "You've been on my mind all day. Let's get these marriage instructions behind us."

"You fill my thoughts as well." Tara tingled deep inside her body. "What can I say but thank God we share the same feelings."

* * *

Four chairs were pulled up to the round table in the conference room. Luke stepped aside so Tara could take the seat next to Petra. Uneasy thoughts battered his mind when the women hugged. *Have I erred in taking marital instructions from Tara's pastor and the pastor's wife? They've known Tara her entire life; they don't know me at all.*

Pastor Victor shuffled papers then winked at Tara. "There are many methods to marriage counseling. No procedure is written in stone or better than other methods used. What actually matters is why Petra and I invited you to come. Marriage counseling brings up topics that engaged couples don't often consider. Age and life experiences dictate our approach to marriage." He eyed Tara and Luke. "Any questions? Then we'll begin."

Tara smiled at Luke. "That's a speak now or forever hold your peace statement."

Pastor Victor and Petra grinned at one another.

Luke relaxed. Tension in his shoulders lessened. The teasing words had the desired effect. Had his amazing fiancée sensed his discomfort?

Pastor Victor continued. "You both being over thirty simplifies our task in some ways but escalates challenges in others."

Luke touched Tara's hand. *We're at the starting line. Almost there.*

The older man turned to his wife. "Do you have anything to add before we begin?"

"Only one thing." Petra's eyes turned reflective as she studied the couple. Her attention focused onto Luke. "I've known Tara her entire life. She comes from a small, close-knit family. Her parents held old-fashioned ideas that Tara retains in most areas." She glanced at Tara, who played with her fingers and then studied Luke. "You lost parents in a horrendous auto wreck. You understand Tara's pain. Yet her healing may differ from what you've experienced."

Luke was on solid ground. He'd lived through the aftermath of a loved one's sudden death. "I realize we all utilize various coping mechanisms. Tara faces numerous unknown difficulties in moving forward. I'll stand beside her through each one."

"Support may be insufficient to pull her through. Everyone yearns for comfort after severe losses. What if Tara regards you as an anchor in her storm?"

Insufficient? He'd pegged Petra as a member of the "love never fails" brigade. "Tara recognizes a safe harbor she can dock her life in." Luke turned to Tara. "We'll work as a team."

Tara beamed at his answer. "I want that, too."

"Marriage represents significant lifestyle changes that can overwhelm couples." Pastor Victor took up where Petra left off. "Success in married life won't come by osmosis. Hard work forges lasting alliances. How long ago did you meet?"

"A little over two weeks ago," said Tara. "A short but adequate time frame."

Pastor Victor drew a line on a sheet of paper. "Challenges will either strengthen love or destroy the relationship. No marriage is exempt. Realistic goals beforehand will generate positive responses during conflicts. Despite provocation, divorce shouldn't be viewed as an escape route. Adultery is the only biblical exception. Of course, abuse is another allowance." He glanced at his wife. "Anything you want to contribute?"

"Perhaps later." Petra clasped Tara's hand and gently squeezed her fingers.

Pastor Victor glanced at the couple. "On to the lightning round. First question: Why do you want to get married? And why now?"

"Me first," said Tara. "I've never believed in fairy tales nor love at first sight. That is, until I opened the front door and Luke stood there."

"What does love at first sight mean?" the pastor asked.

"Luke is the future I've dreamed of having." She smiled at the man observing her in open admiration.

Unable to tear his gaze away, Luke secured her other hand in his. Somehow her answer had exceeded his expectations.

"How did you interpret the reaction of seeing Luke and falling for him?" the pastor asked. "With calm or agitation?"

"A little of both. Because he's been involved in multiple relationships, Luke was out of my depth." She smiled. "He's helping me catch up."

"Tara ..." Pastor Victor paused then pressed forward. "Why do you think this marriage will work?"

"History is repeating itself. My parents' marriage provided a living example of faith in action." Her eyes misted over. "They were longtime friends who married because of loneliness. *And,* they made the correct choice." She hesitated before laughing. "By the way, I want a hasty wedding because that's what Luke wants, but he isn't railroading me. I'm satisfied with the date he chose."

Luke squeezed her fingers then released her hand. *Marrying now is the ideal choice. I won't backtrack or lay low. Passivity wrecks lives.*

Pastor Victor gazed at Luke as if he'd read his mind. "Here's a similar question. What makes Luke the right man to build a life with?"

"It's simple. Luke answers the vision inside my heart." Tears welled in her eyes. "He possesses embraceable family values."

"You can make that assertion after two weeks?" Pastor Victor glanced at Luke then back at Tara.

"The quality of our relationship bears out those facts. We were created to be together." She hesitated, gnawing her bottom lip.

Luke stroked her fingers. "My turn. Fourteen years of waiting for the right woman produced Tara. She answered my heart's question."

"Here's a follow-up query. Why marry Tara vs. other women you dated?"

Luke paused. "Tara is my first and only love. It took awhile until she manifested."

"Shouldn't that revelation increase desire to become better acquainted?"

Luke shook his head. "I understand her now. Data has poured in from all sides. My heart. Our time together. We share similar core values."

"Core values," Pastor Victor repeated. "Spiritual life matters more than the physical life does. That is the true test of how you spend eternity. Are there any disagreements in general?"

"I don't think so," said Tara.

"I'm unaware of any differences," Luke replied.

"You both replied without reflection. What views do you have concerning God? In-laws?"

"We're both Christians who believe in godly values." She looked at the man who grinned her way. "Luke won't have in-law problems on my side."

"Tara won't on the Cassidy end. The family loves her." He leaned closer to Tara, covering her hand with his palm. "Obeying God matters. I've chosen wrong in multiple areas too many times. But, I recognize the mistakes I made."

Pastor Victor nodded. "People are flawed, as you both well know. Problems increase without adequate attention and positive adjustments. Tara, what changes might improve your and Luke's characters?"

"My fiancé relishes living his own plan." A crooked smile touched her lips. "I want him to stop manipulating situations for his own advantage. Me. Hmm ... friends say I'm stubborn. Don't believe them."

"Has anyone labeled you a control addict?" Pastor Victor asked.

"They've only said that I don't let go."

He studied Luke. "What behavior improvements benefit Tara and yourself?"

"Tara should live instead of watching life happen." One eyebrow rose. "I don't have control issues. Other problems? Perhaps. People management isn't one."

Laughing, Pastor Victor and Petra glanced at each other.

The pastor laid down his pen. "How do you each envision married life?"

"That's easy. I want us to live a simple and quiet lifestyle. We'll nurture our children and grandchildren. I foresee a happy family." Tara smiled at Luke.

The pastor turned to the silent man who stared at a spot on the wall. "Luke?"

"We'll follow our dreams wherever they lead us. What counts is we'll be together wherever we are. I didn't release a travel blurb for the future; I'm talking in the here and now."

Petra smiled. "Although Luke's response was very broad, there's disparity in your aspirations. You must reach a consensus regarding lifestyles before the wedding. Give and take is inevitable in marriage."

"It's the reason why we're here." Pastor Victor paused. "Now, on to finances. How will you handle money? Share expenses and income? Or keep separate accounts?"

"I'll pay all expenses even though Tara plans to join me in the business."

Tara rested her chin on his shoulder. "And the money I earn?"

"Save it for the rainy day we won't have."

Pastor Victor noted Tara's non-response. "Speaking of finances, Tara, have you shown Luke the cars behind the house and in the shop? Have you and he discussed that issue?"

"A little." Tara offered Luke a sheepish smile. "There are five fully restored cars you haven't seen. They're related to my pre-wedding surprise."

A surprise, huh? I'm bowled over.

Tara winced when he didn't speak, then she shrugged at Pastor Victor. "My parents never mentioned selling."

"Tara, we're seeking an attorney and CPA for our family and the church." Pastor Victor cleared his throat. "Lenny gave you explicit instructions to do the same, and he placed details in the safe deposit box. Have you read them?"

"I haven't checked the box. *Yet.*"

"You can't put off such things. Take care of business, young lady."

Luke's gaze focused on Pastor Victor. "My brother Colton is an attorney, and my brother Andy is a CPA. They'll assist Tara, you guys, and the church. I'll leave their cards."

Pastor Victor nodded while Tara spoke.

"No one mentioned selling." She eyed Luke. "That means—"

"You won't change a thing."

Tara started to speak then hesitated. "My father loved those cars. Selling wasn't an option for him."

"That doesn't mean they can't be sold." A sigh seeped from deep within Luke's chest. "We'll talk about it later."

Pastor Victor and Petra silently observed the couple's interaction. Both Tara and Luke remained quiet.

"Questions and honest answers mitigate false ideals and intentions. Financial secrets devastate marriages yearly. Luke, what are Tara's assets?"

"Tara owns four houses and three—make that eight—classic automobiles. I was shown the houses and stumbled upon three vehicles. Grandfather scooped me on the shop earlier, but he thought the building was vacant. I figured her parents left retirement funds and savings accounts."

Tara's sad eyes begged forgiveness. "In my defense, I forgot about the cars inside the utility building." Tara splayed fingers on her chest. "The other cars were kept secret because ... well ... they're related to a surprise for Luke." She dug papers from her purse, passed Luke the proof, slid closer, and read over his shoulder.

Luke read a description of the purchase and handed it back to Tara.

"Every two weeks," she began, "I let the cars run at both locations without driving them around. And ... I—"

"Don't plan to change a thing." Luke chuckled. What else could he do but laugh? Her aversion to change went deeper than he'd imagined.

Pastor Victor turned to Tara. "List Luke's assets."

"Luke inherited the business and family home outright. Everything else was split between the siblings. Only the rental property is left to divide."

"You grasp each other's finances more than most thirtysomething couples," Pastor Victor noted. "Let's finish up. What are your thoughts on dealing with friction? Luke, how will you negotiate conflicts without imploring manipulative tactics?" His gaze switched to Tara. "Will you address issues instead of ignoring problems?"

"Of course. My husband will tell me the entire story upfront, and I'll make intelligent decisions. As for the car dispute, we keep all eight." Tara batted her eyelashes at Luke.

Right. "My wife will tackle problems, so our challenges don't defeat us. That remedy ends any manipulation on my part."

"That exchange establishes why we're here," said Pastor Victor. "Marriage counseling should spark vital discussions between engaged couples. It's too late after the wedding. Is there anything that compels either of you to postpone the date?"

"No," said Luke.

Tara shook her head then smiled. "I agree with him. I don't want to change anything. Pastor Victor, I've attended The Gathering Place my entire life. Please say we passed the test and that you'll marry us."

Petra grinned at Tara. "You're so much like your mother in the way you deal with people." Her voice softened as if she spoke only to Tara. "A sound marriage is made of many components. Love, patience, shared ambition, and realistic expectations are a few. It's okay to disagree on minor points. You both must give and take on all issues."

Pastor Victor pushed his writing pad aside when Tara nodded. "Based on the responses to the last query, we're done." When he stood, the others stood with him.

Petra handed a list of talking points to Luke. "Discuss these questions later. The answers might surprise you." She led the way to the door.

"Forgiveness is crucial in marriage, as it is in any relationship. Remember, God alone determines people's value. Judge situations by His standards and not your own." Pastor Victor paused in the hallway. "The ceremony is set for next Saturday. And remember, our door is always open."

Luke passed Pastor Victor, his brothers' business cards, and waited while Tara hugged the couple, then he led her to the water dispenser.

Tara waved at Petra and Victor until Luke placed a cup of water into her hand.

"It was an unconventional meeting. Any thoughts?"

Swallowing the last drops, Tara discarded the cup into the wastebasket. "I keep getting a lot to think about. And you?"

"Likewise. I learned about the extra cars."

Tara's almond eyes resembled circles. "Luke!"

"Finally. The exasperated look I'd hoped to witness. We can attack Petra's list over dinner." Luke wrapped an arm around Tara's waist. Heading toward the parking lot, his mind overran with the latest revelations. *More cars. Eight classic vehicles instead of three.* He glanced at Tara. "Name the cars."

Her eyes glowed in the dwindling light. "There's a 1934 Rolls Royce Phantom II Drophead. A 1928 Packard 443 Runabout. A 1961 Ferrari 250 GT California. A 1967 Ford Mustang Shelby GT 500 Coupe. And a 1976 Porsche 911 Turbo Carrera." She hugged him closer. "You appreciate old cars, I can tell."

"Fully restored antiques are irresistible, although Colton is the real classic car lover. His friend's uncle owns an auction house in the Chicago area."

Tara stopped in her tracks. "Wilkens Auctions? Grandpa Burt only dealt with their company."

"Prior dealings should expedite matters ... if you decide to sell." Luke paused as Tara eyed him.

Instead of replying, she swung his hand. "We live in a small world. Remember that children's song 'It's a Small World'?" Tara sang a few lines. "Stop me before I take a sentimental journey."

Kissing the top of her head, he hugged her to his side. He'd never met a woman like her.

Despite her simple lifestyle, our lives won't be dull.

Chapter Thirteen

As Luke drove to her house, Tara analyzed each mistake she'd made. Hindsight exposed a flawed plan regarding the cars. In spite of her desire to give Luke a surprise gift, no justification existed for withholding information. Especially after he'd discovered the cars inside the utility building. Having the particulars at the meeting lent credence to her gift story.

It would be time to let the cars run next week. Luke could tag along.

Once home, Tara took extra care with dinner and sat across from Luke at the kitchen table.

Why wait till later to have a discussion? If he's riled, it'll get worse.

"Are you angry over the cars?"

Luke's soft gaze caressed sore spots within her. The grin matched the love in his eyes. "No way. Listen. You held back with purpose." His head shook at their new reality. "Eight cars. May I view the other five?"

"After receiving your gift."

"Why? I can't get any more surprised." He laid his fork across the plate.

"Is that good or bad?"

"A little of both." Luke picked up his glass then set it down. "You throw more curveballs than a seasoned pitcher."

On Sunday, Tara had had almost identical thoughts about him. "Your curveball analogy dripped with sarcasm but acted like sweet nothings."

Luke rounded the table and pulled Tara to her feet, crushing her chest to his.

"Don't fight against us," he whispered against her cheek.

What? Where is he headed? Tara's lips settled on Luke's neck. "My love isn't namby-pamby. You won't get rid of me that easily." Her joke missed its mark. Luke looked through her. His mind appeared elsewhere. "Our food is getting cold. Let's eat."

While eating, Luke pulled Petra's list from his pocket, scanning the paper in between bites. "Name marriage deal-breakers. State unforgivable offenses."

He re-read the last directive. "List any non-negotiable beliefs." Alert eyes fastened on Tara. "Do you have any? I know. Dumb question."

Luke's off-kilter. Somehow the list disturbed him. We're at another crossroads.

"I have one answer for all three. An affair ends our special relationship. No second chances allowed." Her cool gaze never left his.

The straightforward answer clearly troubled Luke. He sputtered a few unintelligible words then resumed eating. His lack of response said it all. Luke had expected Tara to babble trivialities, not a life-changing serious point. His silence sparked a desire in her to hear his thoughts. Important questions required answers before standing at the altar. Courage was needed to do what must be done.

When she cleared her throat, his forehead wrinkled.

As Luke continued eating, Tara hesitated.

Meaningful relationships weren't built with faint hearts. Her throat cleared, but her voice remained obstructed. *Help me out, Luke. You know what I'm thinking.*

"Don't leave me hanging. Answers, please."

Luke continued eating. Then he finally said, "Right. Petra's queries." He scanned the paper beside his plate. "Technically, your answer underlined what I already know about your beliefs."

"Then why the meltdown? You haven't spoken in five minutes."

Eventually, Luke chuckled. "I didn't foresee a one-answer response for all three questions. Then again, the revelation's distinctly you. So, I'll follow your example and do the same. It's over; for good, if you leave me for any reason."

Luke's threat to walk away trumped Tara's promise to leave him if he cheated. His comment on her sunporch after their first date came to mind. "We don't play by the same rules," he'd said. He was right. They didn't. But instead of challenging the statement, she'd let it slip right by. Now she understood its meaning. Her fiancé considered turnabout fair play.

His winsome grin depicted a man in control. "I think we understand each other. Am I right?"

"Totally. I can read between lines as well as anyone."

He started to speak but hesitated. "Tara, I won't be unfaithful, and you won't kick me out."

"Then after the ceremony we're bound for life. That's what marriage means."

His right hand saluted her comment. "Lifetime commitments work best."

Although they were seemingly in agreement, something about the discussion felt off center.

Tara sighed. "Tidy-up time."

While drying dishes, Tara jumped as soap suds hit her face. She spun around when Luke laughed, right before lobbing another soap ball at her. She ducked. Only trickles of water dusted her hair.

Her reflexes immediately kicked in. The water pitcher was in her hand before thinking better of her next move. The shock on Luke's face stilled her hand. He was soaked. Water slid from his hair, and over his body, until it streamed across the floor.

"Oops! Blame yourself and not me," she yelled, charging past him.

Lunging for her, Luke slipped on the wet floor, bringing them both down with a thud.

With a tight grip, he held her on his lap as Tara swiped at his hands.

"Why are you trying to get away?" he asked with a chuckle. "*I'm* sitting in water."

Tara peeped up at him. "Do you promise we won't trade places?"

"Hmm. Now that's a thought. Relax," he said when her struggles resumed. "That was a spirited trouncing, Ms. Simpkins. You won."

"Yeah, I did. No payback?"

"Do you think I'm a spoilsport? Don't answer. You're safe for the moment."

Tara leapt to her feet when Luke released his hold. Smiling sweetly, she held out a hand to help him up.

"Ah! You got soaked. Sorry. It was all my fault."

Luke joined in her laughter. "Of course, that cockiness deserves retribution."

Too late, she saw mischief in his eyes. Luke yanked her back onto his lap, layering her sputtering lips with kisses.

Their silliness prevailed until the last dish was dried and put away. After Luke changed into the extra work clothes he kept inside his car trunk, they cuddled on the sofa watching old sitcoms until the cuckoo clock chimed eleven.

Tara reached for the remote control. "Goodnight."

At the door, Luke pulled her into his arms. "Rings tomorrow. Come prepared to shop. Six?"

Tara nodded.

"Perfect. See you tomorrow evening. Love you."

Tara melted against him. "Aw! Love you more. See you tomorrow."

"In less than two weeks I stay put all night." He rubbed his forehead on hers. "Looking forward to living here, unless … we stake out at my house until renovations are completed."

"Either way works for me." She yawned and covered her mouth. "Excuse me. Drive carefully."

"Count on it." Luke kissed her, broke away, and opened the door. "Stay inside. Watch me walk to my car from the window."

"Thanks for taking care of me. Call me."

Tara closed the blinds once the vehicle pulled from the curb, then she headed toward the stairs. She'd found love with an impossible man.

No dwelling on our dinner discussion. We're okay. I'd better tidy up.

The landline chimed as Tara slid underneath the cover. Only Abby, Annie, and Petra called the home phone. She checked the caller ID. "Hi, Abby. Are the children asleep?"

"It's after eleven. Why are you awake?"

Tara frowned at the telephone receiver. "You called. I'll fall asleep in an instant if we hang up."

"Sorry. I can't oblige. Power up the laptop. It's shopping time."

"It's bedtime. We'll talk tomorrow."

"You're the reason I'm awake. Laptop, please."

"Hold on. Luke's calling."

Moments later, Tara dangled her legs over the bed's edge, her laptop poised on a tray.

Normal people are asleep. Abby wants to window shop online.

"Stop sighing and follow the links in the email I sent. Ready?"

Tara searched her emails until finding the one from Abby. "Yeah. But why now? We haven't window shopped online before. It's ridiculous."

"Quit complaining and shop. You go first."

Abby had chosen clothing websites Tara hadn't heard of. Two irretrievable hours were spent selecting outfits she wouldn't purchase. Especially the wispy little nothings Luke would never see.

"Now you," she said when Abby named the last website.

"I shopped earlier. Look at those knockout shoes. Select something dressy, casual, and sporty; two pairs of each category. Don't forget boots."

"Okay, bossy." Each item selected was found on the first two pages. "All done. I just emailed my choices. Can I hang up now?"

"Wait until I check your selections. Two-inch spike heels. How shocking," Abby said with a giggle. "Okay, you've deprived me of sleep long enough. Nighty-night."

"Goodnight, Ab."

As Tara hung up, she thought about calling Abby back to give her a taste of her own medicine. She slid into bed and turned off the light.

Nighty-night, indeed.

* * *

A disoriented Tara crawled out of bed the next morning. Abby had kept her shopping much too long. Fantasy wardrobes couldn't replace lost sleep, even though they were the clothes she'd always planned to purchase. Was she destined to live a lifestyle of wishful thinking? That thought reminded her of the desire to quit her job. Halfway down the steps, she decided to resign. Exhaustion hadn't robbed her "time to quit" spirit. Her job was toast. Fourteen years of discontent would end. Her only regret was that without giving two-week notice, "no rehire" would be stamped on her personnel file.

* * *

Tara glanced at the closed door in the middle of the room. Quality support team members had hunkered in their manager's office all morning. As soon as the team left, Tara poked her head through the cracked door, resignation letter in hand.

Jillian's pursed lips deepened the grooves around her mouth. It must have been a real doozy of a meeting. Her manager was moody. Abruptness was evident on peaceful days and if Jillian was put upon—everyone else took cover. Only Tara and a chosen few received kind treatment.

The woman's tilted head beckoned Tara into the room. "I hear congratulations are due. I'd planned to seek you out after lunch."

Tara closed the door behind her. "If it's regarding my engagement, thank you. But, if it's concerning the training class, I'd better hand over my letter." She sat in the opposite chair and extended the envelope across the desk.

"Our new team members need a senior agent on support detail for six weeks." Jillian took the letter from Tara's outstretched hand. Frown lines creased around her eyes. Her chair squeaked when she stood. Curious eyes studied Tara. "Two major moves in one week?"

129

Tara and Jillian had developed a beneficial work relationship. Jillian was a considerate boss, and Tara was a dependable worker. Until her parents became ill, she'd only used sick leave once in fourteen years. "I'll work for my fiancé after the honeymoon." She held her breath. Sighing had become a regular part of conversations.

"Take three months of personal leave without resigning. Talk with human resources. A leave of absence is available when immediate family members pass away." Jillian leaned on the desk's edge.

Tara rose, shaking her head. "The resignation stands, although the offer makes leaving harder."

"Call if you reconsider. Gems like you aren't commonplace in business." Jillian peered at Tara over her glasses. "Human resources will conduct an exit interview this afternoon. Call me if your plans change."

"Phew! I'm glad I'm rehireable."

Laughter shone in Jillian's eyes. "All valuable employees are. I hate losing you."

"Thanks. I feel wanted." Tara paused at the door. "Could you please do one thing for me? Please wait until tomorrow to announce my resignation."

"Understood."

"You made the job worthwhile. Tell Lance and the children hello and so long. Take care."

That conversation proved harder than Tara had imagined. Most simple things weren't easy.

After leaving Jillian's office, she took her break on the patio she'd termed butterfly alley. The gorgeous insects flew all over the place.

"I should tell Luke." Retrieving her cell phone, she texted a message. *Good news! Used my get-out-of-jail-free card. Handed in my resignation. Today equals last day.* She hit the send button and immediately texted her friends.

Luke called as she sent the message. "You called fast. Taking a break?"

"Headed to a roof inspection. When did you decide to quit?"

"This morning. Yesterday, I was primed and ready until my feet froze."

"Have you set a date to join us at Cassidy Roofing?"

"Sure have. A week after we return from our honeymoon."

"Perfect. I'll give Aunt Jackie a heads-up. You'll meet her at Andy's house Saturday."

Tara frowned at the cell phone. "Think she'll like me?"

"The rest of the family adores you. Why should she be an exception?"

"Hope she isn't."

"Stress not. Live longer. Oh, and forget cooking tonight. Dinner's on me."

Abby was the next caller. "Are you insane? Stop with these impulsive acts. Enough."

"Calm down. Meet me for lunch at Kenny's. My treat. I'll text you the address."

* * *

Tara arrived at Kenny's ten minutes early and found a table. As her friend entered the restaurant, Tara shoved her e-reader into her purse. *Abby doesn't look happy. It's cheer-up time.* "You'll love the food," she said once Abby reached the table. "It's Luke's favorite diner. Grab a seat."

"So why did you quit?" With a stern eye cast on Tara, Abby dropped her clutch onto the table.

I guess we're cutting to the chase.

"I feel the love." Tara beamed a bright smile. "You know I wanted to quit the day I started."

"But now you're suddenly engaged and quitting your job within a few days of meeting someone. You've disrupted your life over some man."

"*You* advised me to quit."

"Don't be a pain." Abby paused while the hostess set menus on the table, continuing when she left. "Okay. You needed to make a few adjustments. *But*, stay Tara. Luke isn't worth a reinvention."

I detest micromanaging.

"I'm marrying Luke in ten days because I want to. My resignation was given because *I* wanted the job to end. *Today*. Blame me if everything blows up."

"You should be depending on yourself instead of on Luke. God is your lifeline and not him."

"Can we at least agree that I've been in a slump too long?"

Abby ran fingers through her hair, nodding. "Just tread lightly. Slow down the pace. Does that advice sound familiar?"

"Uh-hum. I remember the day I told you that. My self-destruction isn't on the itinerary."

Tara observed her friend's surrender, but would it last? Her shoulder muscles relaxed when Abby pointed at the building looming in the glass window.

131

"His?"

"And his sister is walking through the door."

"Luke and Steffi look nothing alike. Are they a family of mismatched people? Invite her over."

"That comment sounded derogatory. Steffi's a sweetheart. Behave yourself."

Tara waved, and the younger woman scurried across the floor.

"Back for more? Me too. The food's delish." Her gaze settled onto Abby.

"Steffi, Abby. Abby, Steffi." Tara pointed to an empty seat. "Join us."

"Hi, Abby. I finally meet the matron of honor." Steffi sat on the seat's edge.

Tara held her breath until Abby smiled.

"Bridal shopping is bright and early Saturday morning," Abby said. "Tara's an early riser."

"I sleep in whenever possible." Steffi's eyes sparkled like diamonds when she giggled.

"So does Abby. But starting at nine beats the crowd."

"Fine with me," said Abby. "Craig can bond with the kids that day."

Steffi signaled the waiter. He balanced a tray with three full glasses of water and an ice-filled pitcher. "Hi, Tony. A deluxe burger and fries. Heavy on the lettuce, tomatoes, and onions." She grinned at Tara. "The extra veggies give me delusions of healthy eating. What are you two having?"

"The same for me. I enjoy eating healthy." Abby faced the waiter. "Burger and fries, heavy on veggies. Mustn't forget dairy. Do you have pepper jack cheese?"

Grinning, Tony nodded at the women.

"Two slices, please." She glanced at Tara. "And you?"

Tara handed the menus to Tony. "Make my burger extra healthy, with provolone cheese, jalapeño peppers, and avocado on the side." She held up her glass when Tony walked off. "We're on a roll, ladies. Here's to longevity."

Steffi laughed as their glasses clinked mid-air. "Awesome. We'll get our exercise at the mall."

* * *

Luke lay the cell phone on the passenger seat and made a U-turn at the corner. Another summons. Steffi. She must've left work early. Maybe *she* could leave her job at will. Whatever the purpose, it had better be important. He wouldn't put up with any more nonsense.

132

I won't shuffle my schedule at someone else's whim.

Steffi's husband, Scott, was on his way out the door when Luke arrived.

Scott held the door open wide. "She's in the living room. Good luck."

"Yeah. Appreciate the pep talk," Luke told the empty space. He watched his brother in-law lope across the driveway.

Luke scratched his head as he stood just inside the door. Had the architect been drunk when he designed the house? Their kitchen was off the small foyer while the living room looked out on the back yard. Steffi hated the place.

Prepared to shut her down, adrenaline flushed from his body at the doorway to the living room. His usual effervescent, life-of-the-party sister wasn't herself. Steffi paced in front of the coffee table, engaged in conversation. Luke listened as she playacted an imaginary talk between the two of them. Seconds later, he knocked on the doorframe.

There wasn't a dash across the floor to greet him. Instead, her feet appeared anchored to the floor. Steffi's grimace troubled Luke.

This attitude isn't because of my engagement. Something else upset her. "I came while on my way to appointments. Let's hear it."

Steffi shoved the blanket to one side of the sofa and sat down with her legs tucked beneath her. "Sit down. Our talk might take a while. But first off, I like Tara. I ate lunch at Kenny's with Tara and Abby. Tara is sweet *and* feisty. A rare combination in any person. Why do you laugh?"

"I hear a *but* coming. What's next?"

"Leah will arrive in St. Louis unannounced. Hope you're ready."

His abdominal muscles jerked. "May I ask ... for what?"

"You're wearing a target, Luke. Stop pretending I'm wrong." A loud sigh escaped her lips. "Has the relationship ended?"

"Absolutely."

"FYI, her sister was at the cashier counter on my way out. Tara and Abby were still talking at the table."

Those last remarks grabbed his attention. Now Luke understood Steffi's distress.

"Her sister said Leah is flying in on Friday to discuss marriage."

"Did you forget two people are required for marriage?"

"Her sister said that Leah talked to you recently. You didn't say anything about that conversation when we talked on Sunday morning."

"This evening, Tara and I will purchase rings and share a candlelit dinner.

No other woman is worth my mentioning."

"Kenny Senior blurted that out at the counter. Since her sister heard, Leah probably knows by now." Her searching gaze sought his as she fidgeted.

Luke hated that twiddling finger thing she did.

Fire lit Steffi's eyes. "I've thought about this mess all afternoon." On her feet, she paced the room then faced him. "For five years you've dropped women every time Leah came back."

"I won't discuss my personal life. Is that all you want?"

Steffi's hand raised like a traffic cop. "Then why come over? It's your fault I met Leah and her sister by accident last year. Don't date woman you're ashamed to bring home."

Invisible steam escaped Luke's ears as he stifled a barb through clenched teeth.

"I like Tara and her best friend," Steffi said. "We're choosing wedding gowns on Saturday. You've dropped women for Leah before. How does this time differ from your previous lapse in judgment?"

"I love Tara. There's the difference, sweetie."

Steffi glanced away, sighing. "I don't buy that answer. Is Leah blackmailing you?"

Luke stuffed his hands into his pockets when he stood.

I may as well leave; I'm halfway gone anyway. One look at Steffi's crushed spirit kept him there. He peered out the window at the apple tree in the back yard. "I love Tara, and I won't cheat on her. Got it?"

"Leah won't accept no." Steffi snuggled into the cushion, glaring.

I've had enough. I'm out of here. Grandma can check on Stef.

"I have an appointment in the city. Remember where we left off."

"Count on it." Steffi walked outside behind Luke and opened her car door. "Where are you going?"

"Grandma's. Remember to stop by later."

Luke watched her drive away as his self-assurance ebbed.

Chapter Fourteen

Tara found a vacant parking spot in front of Marcie's condo. Yesterday, Marcie and Mindy volunteered to address the wedding and shower invitations. Luke's family had discovered extra folks they couldn't leave out of the wedding, so the final tally was one hundred sixty people. Tara had allotted one hour to visit. The twins would drown her in questions until she left. She trooped up the steps, her mind on early-departure excuses.

Mindy opened the door before Tara reached the porch. "Come on in. The invitations for the bridal shower and wedding are ready for pickup, and envelopes are addressed and stamped. Just drop the bundle into the mailbox."

"Stamped, too! Thanks. How much did the stamps cost?"

"Don't worry about it. It's time for an uninterrupted gabfest." A critical eye passed over Tara. "You've worn that blouse too many times. We need a shopping expedition."

"Bite your tongue." Tara glanced at the shirt she'd been happy to wear. "Shame on you. Now I'm self-conscious. We're choosing our rings this evening."

What else should I wear?

"Don't worry. Luke hasn't seen the entire wardrobe. I have. Too many times." Mindy snapped the lock and pointed to a closed door. "Head to the guest bedroom."

Identical twins Mindy and Marcie looked exactly alike, yet their personalities held little in common. They got along famously, however. The two sisters married two brothers, and the couples and their children spent most of their spare time together. Suze believed that was too much togetherness for any sane family.

Tara glided across the floor. After a peek inside the room, she ventured inside.

"Give us the full story," Marcie said, walking out of the closet.

Tara jumped, holding her chest. "Hiding in closets now?"

"Abby met Luke and his sister. Plus the pseudo family at the diner." Marcie plopped onto the bed. "Abby three. Marcie and Mindy zero."

"News travels fast." Tara laid her purse on the nightstand. *There's nothing like an aggravated Marcie.* "Sunday's visit was impromptu. I treated Abby to lunch to calm her down. Steffi showed up coincidentally. Suze hasn't met anyone either."

"I see a pattern. The Bensons will meet Luke on Sunday. Abby, again. Consider the three rejects doing the work."

"Thanks, guys. I appreciate the help. Truly. Pastor Victor and Petra let us off easy during counseling. But so much for the miniature car collection surprise. Pastor Victor told Luke about the cars in the shop. Can you believe he did that?"

Mindy nodded. "Yes, I can. The man knows you well enough not to trust you to tell Luke before the wedding. But what's the problem? Those cars are insignificant."

"Pastor Victor didn't think so. Neither did Luke. I didn't divulge real property. It was an oversight."

"Big deal," said Marcie. "He'd found the collection behind the house. What's five more cars?"

"An extra four hundred thousand dollars," the man holding a gym bag at the door replied. His finger wagged at Tara. "Marriage requires honesty."

Tara laughed. "Hello, Stan. Having a faulty memory isn't an excuse?"

"Not in marriage. Ask my wife. That's her everyday position since we married." He grinned at Marcie. "I'll be home by six."

"Dinner will be piping hot. Pick up a case of ginger ale. Bye-bye." She faced Tara after Stan left. "When do we meet the fiancé?"

"Hmm ... tomorrow's out. We're having dinner at his best friend's house this Friday. Can't do Saturday morning either. That's when we're choosing the bridal outfits."

"Abby, you, and his sister. Left out again."

"You and Mindy should come with us." Tara paused, tugging her lip. "Hmm ... Oh! Do you think it's appropriate to wear a wedding gown at my age?"

"Thirty-two is hardly ancient." Mindy dropped a bridal magazine onto Tara's lap. "Women older than you wear typical wedding apparel. Unlike you, some don't deserve to wear white. I didn't." She sat on a window seat.

"Suze dropped off the magazine. She and hubby have a date night."

Tara paged through the magazine. "These gowns are striking."

"Focus. Fiancé?"

"I'm thinking, Marcie. There's a late lunch with his grandparents on Saturday. Barbecue at his brother's house in the evening. An early dinner with the Bensons on Sunday. And dessert at his other brother's house. Next week?"

"Mark the date on your calendar," said Mindy. "Fish fry at Marcie's house Wednesday."

"Living in interchangeable homes now?" Tara snapped her fingers. "Right. Mindy's house is getting renovated."

"Her house is messy. Mayhem in every inch of the place." Marcie untied the ribbon holding her hair. Curls cascaded around her shoulders. She tucked a lock behind her ear. "She and Woody and the kids are staying here until renovations are completed. Mindy is welcome to use my kitchen. She fries fish better than I do."

Mindy laughed and bunched her hair into a ponytail using Marcie's discarded ribbon. "It's like we're sixteen. Only, you, Suze, and Abby are missing the fun."

"The good ole days were less complicated." Tara removed the cell phone from her purse. "I'll run the date by Luke."

She texted Luke while Marcie messaged Suze.

"Luke promised to clear his schedule."

"Suze's bringing dessert."

"Did you text Abby?"

"I don't recall Abby texting me about lunch or watching the playoffs."

Tara immediately texted Abby. The good ole days had had their sour moments too.

* * *

Luke pulled to the curb to read Colton's text message.

ASAP. My office.

His brother refused to placate anyone's whims, yet he expected an instant response when he needed something. An important matter must have cropped up. They could've discussed car storage facilities over the phone. There was still time before going back by Steffi's, so he could go see what Colton wanted.

Forty minutes later, Luke turned into the complex and spotted Colton's car backing out of a parking space. Luke floored the gas.

Colton braked inches from Luke's truck.

Don't summon me then think you're getting away.

The brothers departed their vehicles at the same exact moment.

Luke leaned on the hood until Colton reached him. "What gives? You're leaving after demanding I drive over thirty-five miles to get here?"

"Am I a mind reader? I waited thirty minutes for a reply that never came. Next time, answer the text. How would I know you planned to show?"

"Which do I despise more: miscommunication or false blame? I always honor your requests. That's how."

"I wouldn't be leaving if you did. I thought you were still blocking my calls."

"Vetting calls doesn't constitute a block. What do you want?"

Colton leaned on his car trunk. "OK, testy. Here's the crux. I've been thinking about your statement at The Grands' house."

Luke frowned. "I drove over thirty-five miles when you could've phoned?"

"I have other matters to discuss, but this point first. You told Tara, 'Once we say, 'I do,' we're married for life.' When did you stop believing in divorce?"

Patience isn't a lengthy visitor. Mine fled. Make the point so I can drop by Stef's.

"Since I said it, Colton. So there you go."

His brother pushed from the car. "Man, you advocate separation more often than a divorce attorney would. Have you ever heard of marital counseling? Talks with mediators help."

Luke quietly studied the car bumper. Colton normally sought his advice. Did his brother fancy himself a sage with Luke the pupil? "Every couple deserves workable solutions. In marriage, I prefer longevity." Even though the character bashing incensed Luke, his brother championing Tara made it bearable.

"A person's recommendations highlight their belief system. Divorce is a safety net for most couples."

"Look, I went to church Sunday and don't require additional sermons."

"Listen anyway. Permanence is Tara's goal. Her parents' death left her fragile. Tread lightly. Ensure she isn't hurt."

Luke staggered. "That's your estimation of my character?"

"It's personal for you. You're an emotionally involved straight shooter who's improvising. Slow it down, Luke. That's all I ask. Will you at least consider taking my advice?"

"No. You should've stated your case before I proposed. What else do you want to discuss?"

Colton retrieved his briefcase from the back seat. "Burt Williams was Tara's grandfather. In multiple states he'd earned a creditable reputation for car restoration. Wilkens, his only client, offered three hundred K. Mark asked to view the cars today."

Luke welcomed the subject change. "Low three figures. What's his uncle's profit?"

"Wilkens will make that amount selling the Cord."

"Then three hundred K won't work."

"I hear you. There were buyers lined up to purchase each vehicle before her grandfather's death. Those collectors were alerted the cars might be available."

"Tara's grandfather died a few years back. But that info is game-changing. There are more cars in the collection." He raised his hand with spread fingers. "Five more. Fully restored."

"What?" The briefcase hit the pavement. Shaking his head, Colton retrieved it.

"Continue negotiations, but don't inform Tara until you receive an acceptable offer."

Colton stared at him. "What about client privilege?"

"There's nothing official between you and Tara. The two of you have only met once in a social setting."

"That fine point could get me disbarred." Colton passed Luke a folder from his briefcase. "This is the contract Mark faxed over. I'll condense it to one page later. Of course, the new vehicles must be included. This contract is for the three vehicles in the utility building. Ole man Wilkens is committed. He thought the family had sold the cars elsewhere. Wait until he hears they're all available. He'll contact the other five collectors. Where are the cars stored?"

"Her grandfather owned a shop off Lindell."

"That's what Mark said. I figured her grandfather had sold the building."

"It's situated behind Tara's church. I drove by there last night. The door is locked, but the building is unsecured other than that. No outdoor lights. Darkness surrounded the place."

Colton eyed him. "The three cars I saw were in mint condition. What do you know about these vehicles? Did Tara tell you? Or did you discover the cars some other way?"

I have too many questions without adequate answers. What else had Tara kept hidden?

Luke glanced at a diesel truck that turned into the Kenny's parking lot. "Granddad mentioned the building. Her pastor revealed the cars were stored inside."

Raised eyebrows revealed Colton's thoughts. "What's the inventory? It's close by."

"No access." Luke removed a list of the automobiles from his wallet. "Check it out."

"Fweeeeh." Colton's whistle pierced the air. "Selling is vital. She can't leave these cars unsecured. Tara owns the building?"

"She does. Her parents never discussed their plans regarding the property. Keepsakes, she thinks. Tara won't upset convention. The pastor indicated pertinent information is in her safe deposit box."

"Maybe I should look over the information before we meet on Saturday. What's on your agenda for later?"

"Ring shopping. Then a romantic dinner for four. We'll stop by afterwards."

Colton laughed. "Isn't four, two too many? I'll hold Mark off until tomorrow. Won't he be surprised."

Not as much as I was.

* * *

While checking the time, Tara listened to Luke's latest request. "Sure thing. The credit union is my next stop." She shoved her cell phone into her purse then glanced at Mindy and Marcie. *Here we go, more questions and advice I can't follow.* "That was Luke. Gotta go. His brother requested the packet Dad placed inside the safe deposit box. Colton's into classic automobiles. Big time."

The sisters glanced at each other but neither spoke until Marcie sighed.

"The noose tightens. Here's free advice. Sell the building, cars, and houses. And don't let his family browbeat you into submission. Make the decisions!"

"Pay strict attention to their mannerisms. Don't overlook anything," Mindy added. "Yet resignations from jobs bring consequences. Leasing the houses and selling the cars will supply income."

"Hmm ... Colton appeared honest to me. I think he's okay. Anyway, I trust Luke." Tara gnawed her fingernails. "I'm having second thoughts about handing in my resignation. It took five minutes to end a fourteen-year job."

"Will you be working for Luke?"

"Yeah, Marcie. One week after we return from our honeymoon." Moving toward the door, Tara held up the box containing the invitations for the bridal shower and wedding. "Thanks again. I appreciate everything my friends have done."

Marcie opened the front door and stepped onto the porch behind Tara. "Stop making snappy decisions that transform your life. You've undergone a sea of change in three days."

"Marcie—"

"Don't blow us off. Your security matters to us. We want you blessed." Sincerity filled Marcie's eyes.

Mindy squeezed Tara's hands. "Who knows if marrying Luke accomplishes either goal?"

Once Tara stepped onto the bottom step, Marcie called, "Tara, wait. Yawn and touch your right ear if you reconsider marrying Luke at any time during the wedding ceremony. I'll object to the marriage."

Tara dashed back up the steps and hugged her friends. She'd lost family, but she still had lifelong friendships. Those bonds would never break nor fade away.

"No more quick decisions, *please*," they both said together.

Their parting words stayed in Tara's mind after she rounded the corner. Quick decisions? *Are there any more left to make?* "Probably so. Life with Luke won't be dull."

* * *

Luke lifted a peppermint from the candy dish on Steffi's sofa table. Could he pacify her anxieties before leaving?

"Don't worry about Leah," he said. "Trust that I know myself better than you do."

Steffi shook her head. "I can't, um, watch while you wreck your life. Her sister said you devoted your time to Leah three months a year."

"Do you consider her sister a reliable source?"

"I don't know her well, but when we talked at that ball game that one time, I didn't have any reason to dismiss her. During the game, Leah told me you only dated her. Meaning you ditched everyone else when she arrived. Leah's sister said Leah had originally planned to marry you this year. She's coming to St. Louis in May instead of in June because you blocked her calls."

The audacity. Luke grinned until remembering Steffi's presence. "Her schedule concerns you because ..."

"It's Tara. Did you overreact to Leah's call by proposing to my new friend?"

In a perfect world, Luke could squash Steffi's fears and retain independence. But relinquishing his preferred way to handle matters now might start tsunamis in other areas.

"Even after five years, no one forges meaningful relationships three months out of twelve."

"But you can in two weeks with Tara? Get real."

Her rebuttal struck Luke where he lived. Five years hadn't been long enough for him to solidify anything with Leah, yet Tara stole his heart with a smile. He wasn't an instant-fall-in-love type of guy. Luke had ridiculed fantasy seekers with their hopped-up dreams. "Our unspoken agreement worked until I pulled the plug. Why did Leah propose? Who knows." Luke hesitated. Of course he knew.

"Leah was your exclusive date whenever she came to the city."

Luke reached for Steffi's hand. "You thought I loved her?"

"What was the attraction if her character fell flat? You couldn't resist the woman."

Luke dropped her hand as if it scorched his fingers. "Couldn't or didn't?"

"It's even worse if you could've walked away but chose to stay. Example: You encouraged my remaining pure until I married. Scott scoffed at the idea, but you were right. My honeymoon was fabulous." Steffi twiddled her thumbs then looked up. "Scales fell off my eyes last year. My faultless brother sold me on an idea he didn't practice. I stayed on course. And Andy reinforced godly advice, confirming he and Rachel waited until marriage."

With his head on a cushion, Luke massaged the bridge of his nose. "I guess Andy forgot to tell me."

"Andy promised to keep our first secret."

First secret. Had there been others since? Somewhat offended by Steffi's lack of confidence in him, Luke almost missed her next remark.

"Our brother taught me a vital truth. Remain on track even if the instructor fails the test."

Luke reeled as if the floor sucked him into a void. Without his knowledge, he'd fallen in how Steffi viewed him. His betrayal threatened their relationship. *Thank God she had Andy. I must apologize.* He stilled his finger from touching her hand. "Virginity on the wedding bed is the best way to begin marriage. At least my sins didn't tarnish your belief system."

When Steffi's gaze lowered, perspiration dotted Luke's upper lip. His lungs demanded more oxygen than he inhaled. Foggy brain syndrome set in quickly. An image of himself at seven invaded his mind. An expensive vase had been broken while he was the only child home. Then and now, Luke was without a hiding place. His bid for control failed. His entire system rebelled against him.

Steffi touched his arm. "Level with me. Why are you rushing into marriage?"

My track record on strong finishes isn't great. I don't want to lose Tara.

"Listen. I want my favorite dream to succeed. Regardless of my past sins, I envision a different lifestyle now. Priorities shift. Tara's my ladylove."

His concentration snapped while an inner voice droned on, and then sobs thrust him to the present.

Teardrops trickled over Steffi's cheeks.

Luke laid a handkerchief on her lap.

Steffi wiped her eyes and blew her nose, but tears freely flowed. Her hand raised. "Wait a minute. You know I'm not the weepy type." A tense silence followed. Her facial expression underwent several transformations.

As Steffi fought for composure, Luke struggled in a similar fight. There were three significant women in his life: his grandmother, sister, and fiancée. Although two of those relationships hadn't suffered irretrievable losses, his failures were palpable. The strength of his and Tara's relationship hinged on humility. Luke wasn't a humble man.

Regrouping, Steffi tossed the handkerchief aside. Sadness peeked through her brave smile. "I love you, big brother, romantic man that you are. Let this talk be the first of many more."

Luke draped an arm around her shoulder. "That's the plan. We're rebuilding. For now, I should go. Walk me to the door."

He turned to Steffi in the foyer. "Did you and Grandma discuss Leah?"

"A little bit. We mostly listened to Granddad talk about letting past events stay there. He's gung-ho on you and Tara. Luke, Tara deserves happiness. Protect her."

Luke nodded while his heartfelt sigh remained silent.

* * *

Ring shopping that evening took just twenty minutes. Tara saw the perfect engagement ring and wedding band set, with a matching groom's ring, the moment she approached the display case. Its intricate design stole her heart in an instant. Love at first sight, second edition. Her eyes teared as Luke pointed to the silver and gold knotted rings without knowing her choice. They were on the same page even regarding their wedding rings.

"A perfect fit," the jeweler assured while he held her hand.

Tara agreed. She watched Luke slip on his wedding band. Perfect. They would take the rings home.

Moments later, the jeweler handed over a folded gift bag to Tara. She began to pull up the flap.

Luke removed the opened bag from her fingers. He shook his head when she swatted his hand.

"Why can't I wear the ring home? My finger is lonely for it." Her eyelashes batted. "Please. Pretty please." A grin broke across her face as Luke took her left hand in his.

"I'll acquiesce *if* you don't mind onlookers. I've rehearsed this very scene since the day we met." His irises darkened to a deeper hue. "Ready?" The back of his hand caressed her cheek. His lips hovered over her mouth.

"That's okay." Tara snatched her hand from his grasp. "Patience is a virtue. I'll wait it out."

They both laughed as Luke led her out of the shop.

Tara scooted into the car. "Where to?"

Luke winked at her.

"I don't know where we're eating dinner or our honeymoon destination. So, Mr. Secret Keeper, I have the portfolio. Are we headed to Colton's house?"

Luke's lips stretched into a sly grin. "Later. Much later."

Tara's heartbeat accelerated.

Luke meandered through sparse traffic.

The Nouveau Départ Bistro came into view.

Chapter Fifteen

Once inside, Tara veered right while Luke cut left and gently pulled her into a private alcove off the lobby. The hideaway had gone unnoticed on her first visit. In the smallish room, soft gray, billowy curtains hung ceiling to floor. Light, classical strains piped in from an unknown source. Muted wall lights and ruby-red peonies in vases created a romantic atmosphere. An appetizing scent wafted from a food bar filled with treats. As she got further into the room, Tara's pupils adjusted to the low lights and smoky haze. Suze and her husband, Josh, sat at the only table inside the room.

"What are you guys doing here?" She studied Luke. "It happened again. I'm underdressed."

Pleasure-filled eyes fastened on her. "Nah. You look perfect, as usual. Do you like my surprise?" Luke pulled out Tara's chair and sat beside her. "Josh I know. Please, introduce his wife."

"I'll do it, Tara. Hi, I'm Suze." Ambivalence dotted her features. "Tara has been a bestie of mine since ninth grade."

"That's right." Tara blinked at Josh. "I can't believe you guys are here. How did you and Luke connect?"

"In passing. Sporting events in high school and the usual social occasions. His brother, Andy, and I go to the same barbershop. Suze filled me in on the Luke and Andy mix-up, but I hadn't connected the dots."

"Oh—oh. How much of my personal business is public knowledge?"

"Relax. We compared notes while we waited for a chair at the barber. I told him my wife was having conniptions about her friend marrying a man she'd just met. After I stated that you were an otherwise sensible person, Andy asked, 'Tara Simpkins?' Luke contacted me and set up tonight."

"Thank God you and Andy had a private discussion. I'm shocked to see you two because Suze claimed you had a date night."

"We did until Josh promised that dinner here tonight would supersede our time together." Suze brushed her cheek on his shoulder. "As right as ever."

"That's her story. Now. The dinner was intended as a surprise for both of you. Suze's threat to bail on our date forced my hand to tell her. The surprise dinner with you and Luke leaked after she cancelled our date." He grinned at Suze. "Didn't you, love? She said, 'Tara's headed to Marcie's after work. Luke keeps her too occupied for her friends. I'll never see her without going to Marcie's house. We'll go out Friday, Josh.' "

He'd mimicked Suze's voice perfectly. Everyone laughed. Suze included.

She turned to Tara. "You expected a private dinner, but I'm glad you're pleased to see us." Her elbow nudged Josh. "Be thankful you married someone who's a loyal friend. That character trait benefits *our* relationship." She smiled, then pointed to the buffet. "I'm starved. Let's talk while we fix our plates. The waitstaff brought the food in just before you arrived. Josh released our server from duty."

The others stood back, allowing Tara to go first. She glanced over her shoulder at Josh. "Consider doing voiceovers. That mimic was spot-on." Her mouth hung open in front of the buffet. *Luke remembered.* Tara lay her cheek on his chest and wrapped her arms around his waist. "It's the exact menu from lunch Sunday sans dessert. Your attention to detail is astounding. Guys, my fiancé is a romantic man."

Luke chuckled. "No other woman seconds that claim."

"Believe him," Josh said. "I'd considered Luke a confirmed bachelor."

"He hadn't met the right woman," Tara said. Before her gaze swept the buffet, she spotted exchanged glances between Suze and Josh and moved down the food line.

Back at the table, the couples maintained a lively discussion.

"Yum ... delicious food. We'll return." Suze wiped her mouth with a linen napkin. "It's our first time eating French cuisine."

"Sunday was the first time for me. You should try Kenny's Diner next. You'll love the place."

During dessert, Tara touched Suze's arm. "Marcie and Mindy won't treat our dinner as a coincidence."

"They've already blasted Abby about meeting Luke and his sister." Suze's grin exposed two hidden dimples. "That's why I signed up for dessert detail for Wednesday's get-together when Marcie texted me earlier. I don't want to receive the Marcie freeze."

"Wise move. Abby passed on coming. Isn't she sweet to clear the field for everyone else?"

"She's lying low until daggers vanish from Marcie's eyes." Suze shook her head, laughing. "We're taking the children to a kiddie carnival tomorrow. I'll tell Abby you called her sweet. That'll make her laugh."

After two men cleared the table and removed the food bar, a pigtailed woman rolled in a small table covered with gift boxes.

Luke pointed to the space between Tara and him. "Right here. Thank you." He waited until the woman left the room. "These are a few mementoes I've saved throughout the years." He scooted closer when she smiled, picking up the first box.

Tara's hands shook as she untied the ribbon until she glanced at Luke. "I didn't bring a present for you."

"You are the only present I want." Luke gazed into her eyes. "Open your gifts, Tara."

What a way with words. Careful. I don't want to weep in front of Suze and Josh.

Tara removed four high school yearbooks from the largest box. The women slid their chairs together, peering through the first book. "Ah! Doesn't he look adorable. All smiles. Luke was a cute freshman." Tara lay the yearbook aside and opened the next one. "And an endearing sophomore." She laid the second book on top of the first. "Suze, look at Luke's engaging smile. He's quite charming and only a junior."

Josh laughed. "Charming? I remember things differently."

"Maybe the opinion that he looks charming is a female thing." Tara and Suze discussed Luke's sophomore and junior pictures until Tara opened the senior yearbook. "I knew this year would be my favorite picture." Both she and Suze stared at Luke. "Years added maturity," Tara continued while flipping pages. "How many people signed these yearbooks? There's hardly an empty space. Ah, superlatives make good bedtime reading." Reluctantly, she lay the books aside.

Inside the second box, three photo albums crammed with pictures presented a montage of Luke's life from his college days until recently. She studied a few, thinking any woman he'd dated for five years should've stood out from the crowd. Yet no one did. After five days of constantly seeing each other, Luke hadn't mentioned the woman Olivia said he'd dated for five years.

No closer to finding out the woman's identity, disappointment increased as she opened the next box. Inside was a framed eight-by-ten picture of her and

Luke. Someone had snapped a shot of the couple, with their gazes locked, in his grandparents' foyer. "Beautiful. I don't recall us standing in that position."

A smaller box held a double miniature frame of the couple exiting the car on Sunday. The final gift was a silver locket with their picture. The shot was taken in his grandparents' living room.

Tara's smile quivered as she turned to Luke. "Steffi?"

"She snapped more pictures than I sent you."

"Steffi will be a younger sister and a friend."

As her finger dotted over her eyelids, Luke placed his hand into his pocket. He pulled it out with Tara's engagement ring on his finger. Her mind filtered through the ride from the jewelry store. *When did he remove the ring box from the bag?*

Luke held the ring over her left hand's *fourth finger.* "I love you, Tara Michelle Simpkins. Most of the people closest to you haven't met me. That's why Suze and Josh are here. I wanted someone you love and who loved you to share tonight with us. My knowing Josh made my wish possible." His head bowed, Luke kissed teardrops on her cheeks, brushing them off with his thumbs. His head gradually lifted until their gazes met. Anticipation highlighted his eyes. "Marry me, Tara. I've never wanted to live happily ever after with anyone but you."

He slipped the ring on her finger and kissed her trembling lips. Tara melted into his arms as Suze and Josh surrounded the couple.

"I love you. Talk to you tomorrow," Suze whispered, pressing a small package into Tara's hand.

"Congratulations," Josh added. "We'll leave you two alone."

After they left, Tara and Luke unwrapped the present together. The gift was a wooden plaque engraved with gold letters.

Tara Michelle Simpkins and Luke Cassidy
Love at first sight
From the first day they met
Until forever

"It's beautiful." Tara couldn't stop smiling. She'd seen the exact plaque two days ago at the gift shop. Evidently, the owner's daughter, Barbara, had contacted Suze to promote their business, and Suze had made a trip there. Had they come to terms?

On the ride to Luke's brother's house, Tara replayed Luke's proposal over and over. Suze and Josh's presence lent credence to the occasion. She focused on her surroundings after Luke pulled into Colton's driveway. When nervousness overtook her, Tara offered Luke the portfolio taken from the safe deposit box.

"Here. It's been a long day. I'll wait for you inside the car."

"You're sure?" Luke took the folder from her hand. "Megan wants to meet you."

"I'm too tired. I hope it's okay to meet her Tuesday at the bridal shower."

Wimp. Get used to meeting new people.

The garage door raised two minutes later. A brunette with a pixie haircut strolled toward the car.

Tara glanced at the ignition. No keys. Unable to lower the window, she stepped outside.

"Hi. I'm Colton's wife, Megan," the grinning woman said. "Luke explained you're tired. Come rest inside. The children want to meet Uncle Luke's girlfriend. For my little ones, saying girlfriend is easier than saying fiancée."

"Hi, Megan. Sure. I would love to meet the children." She realized she had shallow breathing. As her lungs filled with air, tension eased.

"If you haven't chosen their wedding outfits, Rachel, Andy's wife, and I might tag along Saturday."

"An excellent idea. We can color coordinate to the smallest detail. Are the children coming?"

"Unlikely. Rachel can make alterations if needed."

The women discussed the wedding until they entered the kitchen, where the men sat at the table.

Luke pulled out a chair for Tara, scooting it close to his. "I was on my way out to bring you inside. Colton's quick overview raised many questions. Were you aware—"

Noise at the door caught their attention. Two children scurried into the kitchen, followed by a dachshund. Megan stopped the dog in the middle of the room. "Sorry. These are our little ones. Patrick is six, and Kim is four. Tara is Uncle Luke's fiancée and your soon-to-be auntie. Call her Miss Tara until after their wedding."

Tara's spirit lifted. She loved children. "Hello, Kim, Patrick. Play-doh fingers. What are you making?"

The girl peeped around her brother. "A basket."

"I'm making a fire truck." The boy slipped into a chair beside his father.

Megan scooped her daughter into her arms and beckoned her son. "Adults are talking business. Patrick, back to the family room."

The child jumped to the floor, running full speed out the door.

"You, too, Ranger. Get." She turned to Tara as the barking dog scampered from the room. "We'll chat before you leave." Megan shut the door behind her.

Tara eased into the chair. "You look tense, Colton. Something wrong?"

Colton held up a swath of papers. The top one was embossed with the credit union's logo. Instead of handing her the paperwork, he pushed an envelope across the table.

Tara blinked as she read her name on the envelope. "My father's handwriting. Okay. Guess I better read the letter." She tore open the envelope, scanned the page, then glanced at Luke. "Excuse me."

Tara stood at the counter with her back to the men. Tears blurred the words written on the page.

Dearest Tara, safeguarding you is our top priority. That you're reading this letter means Maggie and I didn't make it. Rely on God. He loves you more than we ever could. The Father will carry us home and protect our daughter.

Finances were placed in order before the trip. Those were the papers you signed. Pertinent information is in this safe deposit box. Every deed was transferred to you, plus you were added to all CDs and savings accounts. Every penny received from Maggie's mother's car accident was saved. You own six CDs and four savings accounts in four credit unions and six banks. Your grandparents wanted their homes passed through generations.

Don't run back and forth to the shop alone. Unscrupulous people are everywhere. We want you safe. The auction house information is inside the packet, along with authenticity certificates for the vehicles. Deal with Wilkens Auctions. The owner is an honest man. Those cars were slated for him. Leave the delivery method to the buyer. Further obligation ends after signing contracts.

Unfortunately, parental selfishness stunted your growth in social areas, backfiring in spades. Family members are no longer available. Maggie and I enjoyed life with one regret: The injustice we fostered upon our daughter by not allowing you to mingle more with your peers when younger. Learn from those mistakes, but keep things simple. Live, Tara. Don't save life for a rainy day. Experience proved those days may not come.

Our attorney and accountant team plan to retire in March. Seek a reputable replacement. Neither Victor nor I trust the men set to buy their practice. He and Petra and the church seek other alternatives as well. Victor and Petra are a phone call away. Let them help you. My parents' closest friends will stand by you. Remember, trust the advice of Carl and Annie and Petra and Victor.

Uppermost in our hearts is leaving you alone. God will provide the perfect man. He's out there, Tara. Don't launch a search. Let the right man find you.

We love you, baby!

Both of her parents had signed the letter. The squiggly writing brought tears to her eyes.

Tara slumped against the refrigerator and stuffed the letter back into the envelope.

A distant voice called.

Luke stood behind her.

She leaned into him.

"How's Tara?" He kissed the top of her head.

"Fine. Wish I'd read those encouraging instructions after Mom's burial. It supplied insight." Clearing her throat, Tara sat at the table. "What's on the agenda?" Her gaze went from Luke to his brother, and then the doorbell rang.

Colton stood. "Andy. I called him after I looked the packet over."

Sometime later, Andy pushed back his chair and stood. "Let me recap. Tara isn't interested in purchasing stocks and bonds. Only savings accounts and CDs in credit unions and banks. Savings bonds remain untouched unless necessary. No one should pay needless taxes. Tara's selling the shop after the auction house removes the cars from there and behind the house." He studied Tara. "Is each item on point?"

Tara squirmed in the chair without answering.

"Did I surmise incorrectly?" Andy asked.

"Prematurely. The letter said sell the autos in the shop. The ones behind their home weren't mentioned."

Andy and Colton looked at Luke who turned to Tara.

"Do you mind if I read the letter?"

It was intended for my eyes only. Yet Luke is the man they prayed would find me. How can it hurt him reading what they wrote?

Tara pressed the envelope into his hand. Her eyes closed while he read.

"Wish I'd met the parents who wrote such a positive missive." Luke passed her the envelope. "Their thoughts were on you despite the debilitating disease. You were well loved by two terrific people. Their sentiments revealed strong character and convictions. Did reading their perspective alter your plans?"

Tara tilted her head slightly to the side. "How can we rent houses they expected their grandchildren to occupy? Your eyebrows rose. Did I say something foolish?"

Luke chuckled. "It was just a strange question."

"You raise an eyebrow whenever you hear something *you* consider non-sensical. I *know* we can lease the houses. *But,* what if some careless person set a fire or otherwise damages them?" She lifted her hand. "Of course, each building is insured and can be rebuilt—"

"But they won't be the same buildings your grandparents loved."

In sync again. Thank God the man understands me. "Whew. Thanks for understanding, even in disagreements."

Luke enfolded Tara within his arms with her back pressed against his chest. Tara liked it that way. She clasped her hands behind his neck, rifling fingers through the hair above his collar.

"Tara, I have a proposition. Ahem ..." The words appeared stuck inside his throat. "In fact, I have an offer to make my brothers and sister. I'll update Benton and Steffi."

The brothers' gazes switched to Luke. Both men leaned into their chair cushions while Tara sat up straight.

"Project 'release the past' is underway," said Luke. "If my family agrees, we'll set up an LLC, and then the LLC owns the rental property."

Colton grinned. "Great idea. I'll draw up the paperwork tomorrow. Stop by the office."

"Finito," said Andy. "I'll inform Steffi and Benton on the drive home."

"Sweet. You field their questions." Luke turned a wary eye on Tara.

Tara looped loose hair stands behind her ear. "I'm glad your brothers agreed with your marvelous idea. Hopefully, so will Steffi and Benton."

"That's good to hear you agree with moving forward. It's your turn."

"Lay whatever it is on me after our honeymoon."

"That's the wrong response. Try again."

"Is it something I won't want to hear?" Tara paused when Luke chuckled. "Okay. What's my part in the project?"

"Why not guess? You'll object to a spoon feed."

"Perhaps. But please—enlighten me anyway."

"Sell the vehicles and building; lease the houses. We're approximately twenty-two years from having our children leave the roost." He clasped her hands in his, squeezing her fingers.

"Agreeing with you will make three snappy decisions on major issues in four days." She smiled at him when he frowned. "My friends are keeping count. What sounds reasonable today might not suit tomorrow."

"Procrastination won't work either. Colton's and Andy's suggestions achieve your parents' wishes."

"In theory: in reality is debatable. Will ... will the shop sell within one week?"

"It's a prime location. Although commercial property often stays on the market longer than houses. But does the building really have only one week to sell?"

Tara nodded. "A rapid sale would lessen the heartbreak of selling."

"Gotcha. Megan and Rachel are real estate brokers. Ask Megan about it on the way out."

* * *

After Luke drove off, Tara closed the blinds and plunked onto her sofa. Her day had been extremely long, although talking with Megan proved productive. Last year, the sisters-in-law went into partnership. Rachel specialized in commercial property while Megan managed the residential side. She gushed about the prospects when Tara told her about the business cards shoved through the mail slot. Multiple investors wanted to purchase the building. The cards were stacked on the counter inside the small lobby. Tara was glad she'd kept the information handy.

Resourceful individuals hindered her natural instinct to dawdle. Besides her friends, the Cassidys were prime examples. Their family existed on competency steroids. Attorney. CPA. Plumber. Roofer. Real estate brokers. They were like a one-call shop that covered all bases. Too well. Like her mother, Tara believed slow walks replenished souls.

Grandpa Burt kept the automobiles he and Grandma cherished inside the utility building, even though he eventually sold each one. Keeping one car as a keepsake won't hurt anyone. Grandpa favored the Cord. I like the Jaguar.

"The Jag stays. So there."

Tara tapped a lone finger on her lips. Should she break the news when Luke called for their nightly chat?

"Uh-uh. I'm exhausted. Never do today what you can put off until tomorrow."

Chapter Sixteen

"What the ... A privacy invasion. Again." Luke parked behind the car in his driveway.

Long days and even longer nights. No one leaves me alone. It had better be a necessary visit.

Benton met him at the front door. "Lucky I ran into you. We need to talk."

"Yeah, well, a stakeout outside my house doesn't constitute running into me. It's late. What do you want?" He glanced at his brother's expressive gaze while unlocking the door. "Did Andy call you?"

"On the way over here. Hailee and I think rental property's a fantastic investment. No upfront money required."

Luke locked the front door behind him and led the way into the living room. "You approve of the plan?"

"I do. We're strapped for cash."

"How? You were given ample money last week." He banged his fist on the fireplace mantle. "Did you blow it all? What happened?"

"Geez. I deposited the money into the bank like you requested. What else would I do?"

Luke's eyes narrowed. "In both names?"

"No, sir. Cut out my wife like you requested. Satisfied?"

"Immensely. Missouri's an equitable distribution state. Hailee's a spendthrift." Luke tossed his keys onto the cocktail table and lay the ring bag on the mantle top. "Now. Why did you come?" He turned around to an empty space.

Luke followed the light illuminating the hallway into the kitchen. Benton was fixing a sandwich at the butcherblock counter.

Luke lingered in the doorway. "Grab a doggie bag and scat."

"Can't. I came to talk." He licked spicy mustard from his finger, glancing at the container. "Tasty. I should pick up a jar."

"Fess up. You stopped by here to eat." Luke tried hard to keep from laughing.

"Is Hailee still scorching water?"

"Hilarious." Benton sat at the table with an overloaded sandwich and a huge glass of milk. "Next time, buy pastrami and cheddar cheese."

"I prefer provolone and cotto salami. Do you ever get tired of eating?"

Benton shook his head. "Only chewing. I stay hungry. Maybe I'm still growing."

"Eat the sandwich and scram."

"Dictator." Benton gulped milk and wiped the white mustache with a paper towel. "Can't a brother visit the old homestead and eat a meal in peace?"

"It's eleven thirty. Buy me breakfast in nine hours."

"That response is cruel. I always listen to *you.*" He licked surplus mustard from his lips.

"You wouldn't be here if you did." Luke sighed through clenched teeth. "Let's hear what you have to say." He pressed his back onto the chair cushion, stretching out his legs.

"I'll keep it simple." Benton wiped his mouth, tapped his fingertips on the table, and balanced the chair on its two back legs. Finally, he gazed at Luke. "Doubt surfaced concerning the proposed quickie marriage."

"Proposed?"

"Hey man, you nailed it with Tara. She's the sassy, laidback woman you've searched for. But, she's operating on stress overload. What happens when she wakes up inside a life she hadn't foreseen?"

Luke's abdominal muscles tightened. Tension assaulting his shoulders spread across his back. *Go home, Ben, and take the doubt-infested conversation with you.* "Tara loves me."

"But losing both parents affected her emotional state."

"Leave." Luke glared until his eyes felt stuck in place.

"Tara's lonely and desires a family."

"She found me. After the wedding, she'll have us. We'll all fill the void her parents' deaths created."

"Tara was dealt a harsh blow. A surrogate family can't replace the one she lost. One day she'll discover that reality."

Glacier eyes fixed on Benton. "We're accustomed to the grief process."

"Those experiences pale against what she went through. Tara's alone. The Cassidy family had each other. Our grandparents lived next door, and Aunt Jackie lived in the city. And Mom's family is alive, but they live in other states."

"Tara has four special longtime friends." Luke strolled to the door and propped his back on the doorframe. "Their relationship is solid. And don't forget her church. Petra and Victor are surrogate grandparents. Their son, Carl, his wife, and their children act as family."

"I bet Tara spends most of her time alone. Yes. She loves you. But the woman I met Monday wouldn't marry a stranger unless she suffered from duress."

Benton followed Luke from the kitchen and playfully swiped Luke's shoulder at the door. "Ease up on her. Just slow things down. Before meeting you, Tara kept herself company."

Luke grimaced. "Now she has me. So there you go."

"Tara is a low-pressure woman." Benton hesitated, popping his knuckles. "One day she'll recognize her husband isn't a laidback man. You won't compromise."

"So that's the problem?" Relief replaced tension in his limbs. "I won't tell Tara my way or the highway. I love her too much to lose her."

"That's the point. You're in for the long haul. You'll change Tara instead of exchanging her for someone else. She'll be unrecognizable once you're done."

"Benton—"

"The idea is to improve each other's lives. What if she wakes up inside a life she hadn't envisioned? The wrong move might leave her whirling."

"Give and take is a marriage requirement. I plan to do both."

"I'm rooting for you. Know that." Benton hugged Luke then gripped Luke's shoulders. "Thanks for listening."

Luke stared at the sky long after his youngest brother drove off. The moon wasn't showing itself that night. He thought of Tara's love of sky shows. Their honeymoon projected the best time to watch the first of many. Together.

Women he'd dated in the past paraded across his mind. Tara applauded his character where his previous dates wouldn't. He'd never mistreated any woman. Still, his refusal to dangle false marriage hopes had angered some. Luke refused to berate himself regarding non-issues. Sparring with oneself often failed, as it would now.

Keeping those associations honest had been the honorable thing to do.

* * *

The next day was a busy one for Tara. The faint smell of disinfectant permeated every room. Especially in the kitchen. She took a walk-through inspection. Hardwood floors glistened with a finished sheen. Decorative tiles produced a brilliant white gloss, and laminate countertops glinted to perfection. Sun rays filtering through kitchen windows created a homey ambiance. Her first morning off the job had been productive. The spotless house was ready for the bridal shower.

Tara scratched cleaning off the to-do list, contemplating her next task. Luke's gourmet dinner was next. She specialized in one-dish meals. Stir-fry or casserole was the question. Which would Luke prefer? She fingered the dated packages stored inside the freezer.

"Hmm ... which would whet Luke's appetite most?"

Casserole won hands down.

In no time, tantalizing aromas wafted throughout the house. Now Tara roamed through the rooms with a designer's eye. She and Luke loved old homes and desired to keep the charm intact. A gut job wasn't necessary in any of the houses. Repairs had always been ongoing. The bad roof occurred from a judgment error. Tara allowed the neighbor's handyman to patch the roof when the neighbor's tree hit their house. Faulty thinking at its worst. Her parents, who had just gotten home from the hospital, had consumed every thought. Everything else was an afterthought. Unfortunately, the third-rate patch job covered half of the roof and took its toll during the rough winter. Water seeped beneath the top layer and ruined the entire roof.

Glad I took Pastor Victor's advice and called Cassidy Roofing.

When the home phone rang, the caller ID revealed a Hilliard cell phone number: Annie, three calls and Carl, two. Pastor Victor had said the couple would come home today. She hated ignoring them but wasn't inclined to defend her wedding plans. Especially to her old babysitter and surrogate brother. She did think it odd that neither had called her cell phone. Why did they assume she wasn't at work?

The cell phone. Sprinting upstairs, Tara retrieved the cell phone from the nightstand. Seven missed calls. Four calls were from the duo she hoped to avoid. Neither had left a voicemail or text message. Tara returned the other three calls, then lolled around the kitchen.

They'll drop by if they don't hear from me soon. What if they ran into Luke?

The doorbell pealed twenty minutes later. Definitely not Luke. No signature ring. Besides, he had a heavy workload that afternoon.

"Oops! I should've taken the calls."

Tara peered into the hallway, hoping to see an image through the door's peekaboo window. Daylight eliminated the chance to see a silhouette from a distance. She set the Dutch oven on the stovetop and hurried to the door. The shadow took shape.

"Suze!" Tara swung open the door then stepped aside. "Two days in one week. We're on a roll."

Suze sniffed the air as she entered the house. "Something smells delicious. What's for dinner?"

"Italian-style pot roast stew. Eat dinner with us."

"Sorry. On a drive-by visit. I can't stay long." Suze pointed down the hallway. "Shall we go to the sunporch?"

"Not if you plan to tell me bad news." Tara crossed her arms on her chest. "Only light conversations are allowed in my favorite place."

Suze hooked Tara's arm, propelling her down the hallway into the sunporch. "Friends don't ask the impossible. We haven't held a more serious discussion."

Tara beelined to her favorite chair before the floor opened and swallowed her whole.

Suze faced her cross-legged on the loveseat.

Sighing, she hugged a throw pillow to her chest. "Glad you and Josh attended our engagement celebration."

"Thank Luke for inviting us. I liked him, Tara. Josh thinks he's a straight fellow. Here's the problem. I don't doubt you and Luke did that instant fall in love kind of thing. *However,* love doesn't strip us of common sense to make appropriate decisions. Hope my bluntness didn't offend you."

"Honesty serves me best." Tara hugged the pillow tighter and briefly closed her eyes. "Anything else?"

"Josh admitted Luke's outgoing but keeps his personal life private. His chatter reveals nothing. He's dated women still wondering who he is."

"Does Josh know any of the women he's dated? Please say yes."

"These are rumors he's heard in passing. If the women Luke dates can't figure out the man, can you?"

Suze. Quit. My brain went numb. I can't think straight. Blinking back tears, Tara lay aside the pillow and picked up the gift from Suze and Josh. "Look at our scroll. *Tara Michelle Simpkins and Luke Cassidy. Love at first sight. From the first day they met—Until forever.* That's my reality. Those words depict our relationship."

"I pray they come true." Hesitating, Suze stroked a fingertip across her eyebrow. "You went on a stupid blind date at nineteen. Otherwise, you've cold-shouldered every man since high school. Why him? How did Luke break through defenses?"

"Luke kept trying and wouldn't quit."

"That one statement sums up the engagement. For years you've claimed you wanted to date but ignored every man who noticed you."

"Don't revise history. No guy ever asked me to dance at parties. I was shunned in high school and after I graduated. I finally wised up and stayed home."

"Why did you always glance away when a man spoke to you if you wanted to dance? It was an unconscious reaction that happened every time. I think your parents made you wary of men."

"Well, look what happened when I took a chance at nineteen."

"Please. You can't base all dates and relationships on one bad experience."

"After what happened, can you blame me?"

"I grant you it was a terrifying encounter. I'll give you an out about high school, but as an adult you even refused to visit our homes when other guests were invited."

Tara sighed into her hands. "How does this old news relate to Luke?"

"He's like you. Stubborn and expects his way despite cost." Suze sadly shook her head. "Luke didn't give up because he has zero flexibility. He wants what he wants, when he wants it."

"An invalid argument. Luke's compromised so far."

"So far you want the same things. What happens when that situation alters? Family had been your everything, especially after your friends married. Test the waters. Enjoying life while single will prove you and Luke share genuine love."

"Please. Stop." Tara brushed teardrops off her cheek. "Only the timing might be off."

"Okay, I don't have any more to say. But as your friend, I had to say something." Suze unraveled her legs then rose.

Crossing the room, Tara lay her head on Suze's shoulder. "Your visit is appreciated. You guys don't think I should marry Luke now, yet you planned my wedding." Her laugh fell flat. "If I'm wrong about Luke, I won't dump my troubles on any of you."

"That's one promise you'd better renege on. I'm invested in whatever concerns Tara."

"Thanks. Oh, how was the kiddie carnival? Glad I wasn't there." Tara led the way down the hall.

"Can't claim it was an awesome trip. Too much Tara on my mind." Suze pressed her back on the door. "For the record, Josh doesn't share my concerns. He thinks you and Luke will face headwinds, but after that it will be smooth sailing."

"Ooh. Encouragement. Pray for us. Suze, I would reverse course if I thought God wanted me to."

"I accept your decision. Talk to you later, friend."

* * *

That evening, Luke surveyed the landscape at Tara's house with a fine eye. There was enough side yard to add a two-car attached garage. St. Louis's harsh winters demanded heat and adequate vehicle protection. Since Tara was edgy on certain topics, the word "change" wouldn't cross his lip. Besides, adding a garage was an improvement.

In one hand, he carried a single red rose in a fluted glass vase. His other hand held a black box with *Dulce Tratar* embossed on the velvet cover. The treats marked the first official gifts he'd bought her. He already had most of the gifts he gave Tara at their dinner with Suze and Josh.

When the door opened, Tara's drawn features caused concern. He placed the vase beneath her nose, rubbing his face on her smooth cheek. His grin broadened. "To you, with love. What smells delicious, besides my lady?" Luke's lips forestalled the reply.

Tara leaned into the kiss then sniffed the bloom. "Hey, sweet talker, you're the first man to bring me flowers, but you're late. I almost wrote you off."

"A flood of calls came in at the last minute." Luke strolled past her, booting the door closed. "Heavy rains are hard on flat roofs. Most people forget the yearly mop down. That is, until—"

"Right. Been there. We're having a rainy spring. Is business booming?"

"And then some." He swooped in for another kiss.

Tara evaded his arms. "Hungry? And do not say for me."

"Cuddle with me. I enjoy enfolding you in my arms just to hold you."

The vase received a place of honor above the fireplace while the open chocolate box tempted them on the cocktail table. A faint disinfectant scent lingered in the air. Luke always found a faultless house when he visited. It was the perfect backdrop for his prim and proper miss. "Are you a true neat freak, or will stuff drop on my head if I open a closet door? I vote neat freak."

"We're simpatico. Guests can eat off your floors." Tara nestled into the arm Luke draped around her shoulder. "Mmm. I like sitting close to you. How was your day?"

"It's over. I'd rather discuss us."

"Choose a topic."

"The garage—"

"What garage? I don't have … ah! I've learned how your mind works. You want a garage. Why? Park in front of the house like I do."

"Garages protect cars from inclement weather and auto thieves. Test the premise. Build the garage. See if I'm on point."

"You mean give in to you to prove you're right. Fine. Tell Pete I agree."

Luke's head cocked to the side, gauging her reaction. Too easy. Tara was usually a hard sell. He braced himself for what would come next. But Tara kissed his cheek and snuggled closer.

Luke broke the hold. "You didn't debate the issue with me. Tell me why."

Tara's eyebrows rose up and down.

What was she doing?

She laughed as his eyebrow rose.

"I've practiced that one eyebrow lift all week," she said. "Both of mine raise. Together. How do you raise one?"

"You're just trying to change the subject. The garage. Explain the speedy change of heart."

"You and the Jag can share the garage. It's my favorite car." Tara laughed when Luke slumped against the cushion. "I'll park at the curb."

"Colton told Mark you agreed to sell all the cars." Luke pushed speed dial on his cell phone. "Change of plans," he spoke into the phone. "Tara wants the Jag … Well, now he'll purchase seven. So there you go." He glanced at Tara with furrowed brows. "In the morning? They've lined up five of the eight original buyers?" The slow burn set in while he listened. His brothers had approached Tara about business without permission. "I'll ask her." Luke muted the call. "Did you open three savings accounts at different banks today?"

"Sure did. Andy called after Suze left. I went to do it straightaway." She nibbled her fingertip. "You seem annoyed. Anything wrong?"

His answer was a smack on her lips with his. "I was left out the loop. We'll talk." Luke brought the cell phone to his ear. "What time tomorrow? … How do we move the Jag to my garage? … Okay. Rent a hotshot at the same time …

Right … Tell Megan and Rachel to meet us there … Leave that part to Andy. Wrap it all up tomorrow … Colton, tell Andy to always check with me first … Yeah. I understand client privilege, but nothing formal has been signed … According to you … Take care of that, too … Tomorrow at nine."

Luke maneuvered Tara across his lap. "Selling those cars took on a life of its own. Two eighteen wheelers left Oak Park at four. They'll transport the cars to Illinois tomorrow morning. Colton believes a hotshot, that's a truck, should carry the Jag to my garage. We'll move it here once we build our own." His lip brushed across her brow. *It's past time to end the car saga. However, those vehicles represent life as Tara lived it.* "Don't be sad. Those cars will acquire owners who cherish classics like Grandpa Burt did."

Luke's use of her grandfather's name brought a smile to Tara's lips. "Grandpa achieved an excellent relationship with Wilkens Auctions." Her mouth drooped at the corners before she smiled. "Luke, I'm experiencing empty nest syndrome over automobiles. Our children can live with us until they're thirty."

"That old, huh?" Luke cupped her cheeks in his hands. "Think I'll pass."

* * *

Later that evening, Tara lounged across the loveseat on the sunporch with her feet up. Her plans for the evening had gone kaput. At least she hadn't toiled over a dessert Luke would've left uneaten. She'd expected a cozy evening with her fiancé. Instead, he left after dinner to head to Pete's house. Yesterday Luke had walked his friend through the houses she owned. Tentative restoration plans had been drawn on his visit. A walk-through at each house with Tara was scheduled for Monday.

Laughter in the next yard grabbed her attention. Tara balanced on her elbow then plopped onto her back. *Luke left too early. After Suze's stopover, I needed a longer visit. It's easier to forget we just met when we're together.* Their wedding would take place next Saturday. Shouldn't every nonworking hour be spent with her?

Tara jumped off the loveseat, bolted upstairs, and settled onto the exact spot where she and her mother had watched amazing sky shows. It marked the second time she'd ventured inside her parents' bedroom since her mom's death.

Guilt set in as pinkish light rays streaked across the horizon. Had she lost herself in Luke? Abby thought so. Or did loving him bring out her best parts? Luke insisted Tara had secured the soothing role in his life. Was she becoming a better version of herself? With Luke, Tara truly felt as if her life mattered for something more than being alive. Fog diminished. Clarity of mind and renewed hope gained strength, along with forging new territory and being open to reason. Life was no longer a question mark. She was now unafraid to fight for what and whom she wanted.

"Luke is the only man I'll ever love. The Simpkins family dynamics change with me. Tara Michelle. Trailblazer."

Luke chose to love me.

Chose to. She had had that same thought the night Luke proposed.

How could a person choose to love someone? Our connection was instant because I required encouragement to leave the cocoon. Did Luke suffer from the same lack of happiness?

A slammed car door disrupted her thoughts. Had Luke made a turnaround trip? Tara scuttled to the window, peering down the street in both directions. A neighbor hauled two shopping bags filled with groceries across the walk. Her body sagged onto the window ledge.

Luke won't come back tonight. The chiming of her cell phone interrupted her doldrums. Carl. Again. Did the man ever give up? Tara thumbed through the messages she'd missed. "Ah! Annie doesn't give up either."

Luke may be missing in action, but she was greatly loved.

Hmm ... I must call my surrogate family sometime. Tomorrow.

Chapter Seventeen

The door to Pete's house opened to the homey aroma of Molli's delicious icebox rolls. Without a glance at Luke, Molli's head jerked toward the back of the house. "He's on the deck. I'd hoped you would bring Tara for a visit."

Luke's face lit with a megawatt grin. "Tomorrow's soon enough. Pete and I worked out a renovation strategy for her houses."

"While the homeowner is strangely left out. Imagine that."

Luke looked her up and down. Molli and Tara had a lot in common. They were both only children and, like Tara had been, Molli was devoted to her parents. The two ladies would get along fine. Luke picked up two rolls off the cookie sheet on his romp through the kitchen, consuming one as he exited onto the deck.

"Scrumptious as usual, Mol," he called over his shoulder. "Make me a batch next week."

He eyed his friend, then slid onto the deck chair. Pete looked like Luke felt. Exhausted. There weren't enough hours in a day to tie up loose business ends before the wedding.

Molli stuck her head outside the door. "Mr. Sticky Fingers, I'm removing two rolls from your package."

"They're delectable as usual. Switch careers and open a bakery. Give Tara the recipe." He stuck the last bite into his mouth.

"It takes ten hours to make the rolls you scarfed down in three minutes. Does she even like baking?"

"She does, if I go by the delightful Italian pot roast stew she cooked for dinner. These rolls would've complemented the meal." His eyes turned serious. "How's your dad? Making progress?"

"On his way to a speedy recovery. Thanks for asking." Molli glanced at Pete. "Want anything, honey? If no, I'll skedaddle."

After she left, Pete set his beer can on a coaster and offered one to Luke.

"Can't. Drank my last can last January."

"You're totally done? Does abstaining come with marriage?"

"It does with mine. Tara set me straight on Sunday. Drinking shortens your life. She'd hate it if I died an early death."

Fine lines around Pete's eyes crinkled as he tried not to laugh. "You sure? It's free."

"Few things are these days. But no. Tara doesn't drink, so neither do I."

"Remember, you can love Tara and still keep your voice."

"I've decided to become a teetotaler like my ladylove."

Pete burst into laughter. "Come out here, Molli! Quick. You have to hear this rot, but you won't believe it." He waited until his wife appeared at the screen door. "Repeat that statement for Molli."

With raised eyebrows, Molli stepped onto the deck. "What did you say that my husband found so hilarious?"

"He called you out here. Ask him."

Two pair of eyes studied Pete as he guffawed.

"Ahem … Funny stuff. His fiancée forbade Luke to drink. Says it's bad for his health."

"*I* appreciate her common sense. Finally, a friend's marrying someone I can hang with. Who needs a can of beer to end their day?"

"I don't *need* a drink. Beer helps the heart and brain in moderate amounts."

"Moderate? Except for Luke, your friends drink heavily. That's why liquor isn't served here." She sat on Pete's lap and extended her legs across Luke. "Tara's friends sent me a quirky bridal shower invitation. Based on that, and the way she wowed Luke, I see friendship for her and me."

"Bridal showers seem unnecessary," said Pete. "Can't women just show up at the church without preliminaries?"

"My thoughts exactly," agreed Luke. "I advised Tara to forego needless expenses."

"We'll watch a game while they revise your life," snickered Pete. "Ouch!" Pete rubbed the leg Molli kicked. "I hate violence."

"Then clamp the lethal weapon you call a mouth."

Luke watched as Molli snuggled into Pete's arms. They'd all started kindergarten together. He never suspected the two might someday marry. Nine years and counting. The only missing ingredient was the children they hoped to have.

Pete pulled his wife closer. "Speaking of getting physical, where's the honeymoon?"

"Due to the way her parents died, a cruise is out. I decided on Kissimmee, Florida. Don't tell her the secret."

Pete picked up his beer can, blowing kisses at Molli as she got up to go back inside. "May I finish this can?"

"No."

Chuckling, he turned to Luke. "Learn from my mistakes. Don't ask questions you don't want an answer for." He handed over the beer can. "When is Tara set to start work at Cassidy's? My mother thought November is Aunt Jackie's last month."

"One week after the honeymoon. Thanksgiving Eve is Aunt Jackie's last day." He paused when Molli sat back down and whispered into Pete's ear. "You're going to pass secrets in front of me?"

Pete elbowed Molli's side. "May as well tell him. You've told me enough times."

"Lay whatever it is on me while I'm in a good mood."

"Well, anyway, Pete loved the idea. Lighten Tara's load and take rental property off her plate. Rachel and Megan can branch into property management, hiring me as the overseer. Their company will manage the rental houses."

Molli's suggestion would streamline Tara's job. Also, it'll make retiring easier for Aunt Jackie since she manages the rental property. "I'm not sure what I expected you to say. That wasn't it."

"Molli proficiently handled the job at Briggs and Wabash for seven years." Pete draped an arm around her shoulder.

"Adding a new division will require tedious planning," Luke said. "Although adding rental property should be profitable, making eight to twelve percent of rental fees plus expenses might not be a big enough hook. What will you bring to the table besides your lovely self?"

"Bringing your seven houses, and two four-plex apartments, and office complex, plus Tara's single-family dwelling and two-family flat with me should give me an advantage."

"It's more than feasible. Even though the fees will shrink our profit margin, Tara should agree in a heartbeat."

Molli picked up beer cans as her foot nudged Pete. She tipped a can at Luke. "I'd planned to plead my case with you and Tara after you ate a marvelous dinner."

Molli headed inside, and Pete waited until she moved away from the door before he spoke. "Benton was at the gas station yesterday. Tell me the short version of the family's reaction."

"Everyone loves Tara, but I've been chastised and scolded since proposing."

"Which was expected. That's the way you all roll."

"True. Now, let's talk some business before I regret leaving Tara." His fiancée was someone worth going home to, but business called. "She's the first honest woman I've dated. Reliable too."

Pete did a double take while opening a design pad. "You eliminated anyone worth taking out before choosing a date."

"Stop maligning my character. I've wanted a love match since my fourteenth birthday." Luke had the grace to laugh as Pete did. Oftentimes, longstanding friendships could work against you. Pete knew Luke had never dated a woman he could fall for.

"That comment was false and deceptive, man." Pete wiped his eyes with a napkin. He grinned each time he glanced at Luke.

Luke chuckled. "Cynics should attend a positive language training course instead of slandering."

"Only if the reviewer drops the history revision class. Here's your dating life until meeting Tara: You traveled rough roads onto a dead end."

"I hope your true opinion is better than that lambaste indicated."

"You weren't a positive influence on the women you dated, nor were they on you." Pete hesitated until Luke eyed him. "I still don't get how destroying Leah would vindicate Paul. Wrong decisions can't work out right."

Remorse entered Luke's eyes. "I was afield, pure and simple; and I won't justify bad actions."

"I'm glad it's over. Your conscience would've condemned you had you succeeded."

It took three years to admit I lacked the guts to follow through. And two years battling guilt to end the madness. Vivid reminders of his discussion with Steffi assaulted his memory. An occasional lapse in judgment had been made at times. But not the egregious errors that family and friends implied. His objectives were as honorable as those of the women he'd dated. No harm had been done to anyone. Especially Leah. Luke had emerged from the fire into Tara's tender embrace.

"Leah. You're telling Tara—when?" Pete's brow furrowed. "You don't plan to."

"Righto. Why should I?"

"You had a five-year relationship that ended last year. Tell Tara."

"Leah was a woman I occasionally dated."

"Then tell Tara and let her decide if it matters."

Luke's heart sank. Would confessing to Tara push her away?

* * *

Tara whispered to Luke inside the shop while Mark inspected the cars. The door buzzed Megan and a tallish woman in stylish apparel into the shop. Both women stopped at the counter where Tara had placed business cards left by potential buyers.

The taller woman scooped up the pile. "Twenty-two cards. Four duplicates. This is a good start to knowing people are interested."

Both women looked up as Tara approached the counter.

"Hi, Tara. What a squeaky-clean place. Meet Rachel, Andy's wife."

Tara stretched out her hand, but Rachel hugged her.

"Expect a fast sale." Rachel glanced at the business cards she held. "I recognize some of these names. Have you set a list price?"

Tara glanced at Luke, who stood beside her. She hadn't a clue about the building's worth.

"Did you check the comps?" he asked Rachel. "What's fair market value?"

"The second-floor layout helps determine its full worth. What's up there?"

"A three-bedroom flat in mint condition. Tara took me on a tour first thing. Take the stairs at the end of the hallway."

Clicks sounded on the tile floor as the women walked off. Then the door buzzed in two more visitors. Andy strolled into the building with a bearded man Tara had never met although he appeared vaguely familiar. Footsteps sounded in the background. Colton and Mark stood in the service bay doorway. Mark's haggard expression signaled tension. He stared warily at the stranger.

"I told Kirk the cars were available." Andy approached the counter with sure steps. "Collectors are salivating over the Cord and both Porsches."

"Also for the Mustang and Rolls," the older man spoke up. "The Jaguar, too. If the lady sees fit to sell."

"Burt Williams sold his vehicles to Wilkens Auctions," Mark told him. His position next to Tara boxed out Kirk.

But the man sidestepped him and faced Tara. "Burt promised to sell me the Cord if it became available."

Burt? Was Kirk Grandpa's friend? Should I know him? Perhaps my father did.

Until that comment, Tara's gaze had swept back and forth between the men.

"He promised to sell you the Cord? Were you friends?"

"Longtime acquaintances. I often dropped by the shop to see the latest car Burt had restored. Sorry your parents passed on. I often encountered Lenny here. The sixty-six Porsche was his favorite."

Tara immediately pulled Luke's sleeve. He nodded his head then glanced at the men. "Excuse us." He walked Tara into the service bay, placing a hand on each shoulder. "Your father's instructions were to sell the cars, including his favorite."

Tara whispered back, "Only the cars in the shop. Those vehicles were slated for the auction house."

"Same as the autos behind the house. Keeping the Jag makes sense. You want it. Sell the Cord and Porsche." He lay his forehead against hers. "We don't have enough land to build a four-car garage."

"Am I off on another tangent that doesn't matter?"

"Afraid so."

The sparkle in her eyes matched his.

Luke hooked his arm with hers. "Continue with the plan as agreed."

When they returned to the lobby area, the conversation hadn't stagnated in their absence.

"I imagine industry people dropped by on a regular basis." Stepping to the counter, Colton's gaze pinpointed Tara. "Wilkens was the intended destination. Paperwork validates it was your grandfather's go-to auction house. Mark's uncle had thought the family sold the autos at cost."

Mark pointed to the office. "Tara, Luke, we'll finalize the deal and move on."

"That contract is up for grabs," Kirk said. "I'll top whatever offer Wilkens makes."

Mark eyed the man, refusing to back down. "The price was settled."

Not with me, Tara thought. So far, neither Andy nor Colton had mentioned money. Andy only requested she open savings accounts. About to speak, she clamped her jaws shut, not sure if she should say anything.

"You haven't even seen the cars. How can you make an offer?" Mark moved to the office door.

Kirk's narrowed eyes didn't match his smiling lips. "I saw each auto after restoration was completed. How much did Wilkens offer?"

"I conduct business in private with the principals involved. The contracts are ready to sign."

Kirk turned to Tara. "One hundred eighty-five thousand for the Cord today. Seven fifty for the lot, including the Jag." His business card hit the counter. "My offer stands firm." The man exited the building without a backwards glance. There was silence until the door shut behind him.

Mark immediately faced Andy. "Why bring Kirk here? He's trying to buy the cars out from under me."

Andy did that one eyebrow raise like his brother. "My allegiance belongs to Tara, my client and future sister in-law. She deserves the best possible deal. We want those cars sold today. Kirk's offer included the Jag. Both of you guys' offers fall short of my own research for high-caliber classic auto restorations. Tara's keeping the Jag. State Wilkens's final offer."

Cagey eyes stared at each other until Mark glanced at Tara. "Seven K without the Jag. We'll clear out both buildings this morning."

"Sweet. Is it a deal?" Luke asked Tara.

She hooked his arm. "I'll confer with Luke in private." Inside the office, she leaned her back on the closed door. "Did Grandpa Burt promise Kirk the Cord? That's my quandary."

"Is Kirk an honest broker? Who knows. I won't take his word on anything, and neither should you. At least he didn't realize the cars were here."

Her mouth gaped. *Was Kirk a thief? Surely Grandpa would've distanced himself.* "You suspect he might've broken in?"

"I rule out nothing. Kirk answers to himself."

"Then why did Andy bring him by if he's a disreputable client?"

"Kirk isn't seedy, but he is a freelancer. From Andy's perspective, driving up the price means a better deal from Wilkens. Individually sold, the cars would net a greater profit. However, the auction house has multiple connections and deal-wrangling inclinations. Besides, four of those autos are already sold to the collectors who expected to buy them."

"Oh Luke, at my house you said five of the previous collectors were on board. The Jag."

"Belongs to you. Other Jaguars will become available. I'm sure they'll be first in line."

"What if I sell the remaining cars to Mark, and sell Kirk the Cord? It'll cover Grandpa if a promise was made." Her head dropped. "I hate disappointing Colton's friend. Sell Mark the Jag."

Luke's eyebrow rose. "Honesty rules with you." His eyes softened as Tara nipped her lip between her teeth. "Kirk's claims that Grandpa Burt promised him the Cord can't be substantiated. Mark gets the lot. And the Jag stays with you."

"Um, doing the right thing counts."

"Right along with making appropriate decisions. Kirk wasn't mentioned in your parents' letter. Keep the Jag and allow Andy and Colton to protect your interests."

With closed eyes, Tara blew into her hands, but surrender-filled eyes reopened. "Is this the best option?"

"Actually, I prefer selling the lot for eight twenty-five, netting a greater profit."

"Ah! So that's the way your mind works. Grandpa Burt would've loved you."

"What's the verdict?" Andy asked as they exited the office.

"We decided ..."

"To stick with the original plan," Luke said after Tara hesitated.

Mark immediately extracted his cell phone. "Thanks, Tara. My uncle swore Burt promised Wilkens these cars plus the autos behind the house. Kirk wasn't in the picture."

Tara nodded. "What's the next step?"

"Depositing funds," replied Mark. "I have signing authorization on Wilkens's contracts. My part was finished earlier in Colton's office. The purchase price was amended and initialed." Mark tipped an imaginary hat. "You're a lifesaver." Without delay, he walked into the office with his cell phone in hand.

Andy jerked his head at Mark's departing back. "Mark's uncle sends the wire, I verify funds were deposited, and Mark dispatches their trucks. Then Colton takes over. A hotshot truck delivers the Jag to Luke's garage."

"Thanks for negotiating more money and less wait time," said Tara. "I would've sold at cost and accepted a check through the mail."

Mark called Colton from the doorway. "Funds are on their way. Contract?"

"I'll verify criteria was met." Andy stepped into the office Mark vacated.

Colton repositioned three sheets of papers on the counter. "Sign three, one-page contracts."

Tara read the contract. "Impressive. I expected lawyerese."

"The contract was redrawn Thursday. The Wilkens version proved complicated."

Tara held out a contract to Luke. "Read before I sign?"

Luke gently squeezed her arms and whispered into her ear. "I read the contract over breakfast at Kenny's." He stood behind Tara while she signed.

"Wilkens's bank faxed a medallion guarantee on Thursday. Funds are irretrievable by Wilkens. They can't back out." Colton notarized the signatures, trifolded the contracts, and handed Tara one.

When she passed her copy to Mark, thinking she would take the next one, Colton removed the contract from her hand.

Luke accepted it from his brother. "Place the contract into the safe deposit box before tomorrow."

Colton stashed one contract into his briefcase and slid the other one into an inside jacket pocket.

Mark chuckled while shaking Tara's hand. "Unnecessary antics. My uncle and I are honest men. Enjoyed doing business with you."

"It's been insightful. Even though I hate selling the cars."

"You held on to your favorite auto. Congrats on the engagement."

"Thanks, Mark. I appreciate your well wishes."

"Notify Colton if the Jag becomes available. Cars in the service bay will occupy me until the trucks arrive."

Colton followed behind Mark. "Her brother-in-law gets first dibs on the Jag."

Heels clicked across the tile floor. The women appeared within seconds.

"What's the verdict?" Luke asked.

"We're pretty sure this was a single-family dwelling at one time," Rachel said. She glanced at Tara. "A previous owner or perhaps your grandparents turned the first floor into a shop."

"It's the cleanest garage I've ever seen," Megan added when Tara nodded. "The upper level was equally well maintained. Someone still cleans here. It's dust-free."

"Thank Lois Padgett. She cleans the two empty houses and tidies up the shop and upstairs flat. She's cleaned my grandparents' homes since I was ten. Her husband does the landscaping."

"Could you give me their number?" Megan set her purse on the counter. "While upstairs, I noticed a separate entrance on the side."

"Which to us changes things somewhat," said Rachel. "One option is to sell as-is. List price two hundred fifty. Or you can restore it back to a single-family dwelling and list it for four twenty-five. The final possibility would be to renovate the shop into a family flat. List each floor at three hundred thousand."

In a split-second Tara's heart made the decision on her behalf. The building would remain with her and Luke. Their children would occupy the space someday. With sparkling eyes, she turned to Luke. "We'll renovate this building into single flats. Right now we only have four houses for our four children. The single-family dwelling, the two-family flat, and your house. What if we have five or six kids? It doesn't seem fair for our children to buy houses when we didn't."

Luke's chest puffed out. "We might indeed. Yet, adult children need to make their own way. Andy and Colton purchased their own homes. Benton and Steffi rent." He grinned at his sisters-in-law and pulled Tara against his side. "I'll pull together a renovation team while you shop tomorrow."

"I thought Pete was handling the updates. Is he busy?"

"Keeping the building changes the time frame." He glanced at his sisters-in-law. "Sorry you won't get a commission."

"No problem. Keep us posted so we can view renovations. Tell my husband I said goodbye," Megan said at the door.

"Wait a minute, Rachel." Andy left the office while talking on his cell phone. Ending the call, he approached her. "A client is interested in flipping houses. Can you and Megan meet him in my office at two?"

"I'm free." Rachel looked at Megan.

"Me too. Which location is he considering?"

"North County. Florissant area." He turned to Tara after the women left. "Funds were deposited." He pushed a button on his cell phone. "Have at it, Colton."

Tara gazed into the service bay area just as Colton passed the contract to Mark. Then the men continued play driving cars. She touched Luke's arm. "Look at those two acting like children. They're having real fun, though. I can't believe they love cars that much."

"Car buffs are everywhere," Andy said.

Rachel stuck her head back inside the door.

Andy paused. "You need me?"

"Question. Is he looking at fixer-uppers or move-in ready property?"

"Show him examples of both. But hold up." His attention turned to Tara. "You're all set. Let's look over the portfolio on Monday. See you tomorrow, guys."

Luke walked to the door with Andy. "Brilliant move bringing Kirk. Thanks, bro. Tara, Andy wanted to get you a higher price. Mark had initially offered five fifty. I didn't mention an amount because Andy hoped to net you a greater profit."

Everything fell into place after Andy left. Minutes later, two eighteen wheelers pulled up to the service bay entrance. Tara and Luke watched the men's progress from outside the building. Despite having separate trucks, the four-man crew exemplified teamwork.

Colton looked at Tara. "Hang in there. Almost done."

After twenty minutes all the cars were safely stored inside the trailers. As one truck departed for Illinois, Colton and the other truck left for Tara's grandparents' house to get the other two cars. The Cord and Porsche would soon join the Mustang in that trailer. Afterwards, Colton would trail the hotshot truck delivering the Jag to Luke's garage.

Her grandfather's car collection was now little more than a fond memory.

Grandpa Burt's hard work vanished in one morning. Tying up loose ends propels life forward. It's a new era. Bless our marriage, Lord. Help us make our relationship work.

Luke gathered her into his arms, and Tara relaxed against him.

Although safety nets diminished, her confidence gained traction daily.

"You made a wise decision. A roof and plumbing check for this building is high priority for leasing. Pete and Benton can look things over sometime today. All in all, we're faced with a major overhaul inside and out. Even landscapes don't come cheap."

"Use brick. I dislike siding. Justin Padgett, Lois's husband, does the landscaping. I'll give you his phone number. Can't you inspect the roof on Monday?"

"It's better to meet Colton at the house then head back here. What's today's agenda?"

"I'd thought about clothes shopping. Now, who knows."

Luke led the way to their separate cars, stopping short of his own. "Visit Abby. But ignore her when she warns you to stay away from me."

His suggestion surprised Tara. Luke seldom mentioned her friends, which was odd since she didn't have family. How would she bring everyone closer? Hmm ... Nothing effective came to mind. "Stop speaking nonsense. My friend suggests I wait, not that I should quit you."

"That's because she hopes you'll send me packing if you wait." His grin evaded watchful eyes. "Too bad she doesn't think that your happiness includes me."

"You might believe that drivel if it's spouted long enough."

"Voicing my beliefs while others disagree is a character flaw I accept. Abby won't attempt to split us, yet she won't weep if I'm ditched."

Tara shook her head. "Wrong assumption."

"It isn't. I'll lock up."

Minutes later, Luke waited until Tara started her car and, with a wave, executed a perfect U-turn and drove away.

Undecided over her destination, Tara glanced sharply across the street at the church parking lot. Had Carl and Annie continued calling? A scroll through her messages revealed they both had.

Plank-walking time.

Tara drove around the corner.

Pastor Victor and Petra lived in a duplex next door to The Gathering Place. Carl, Annie, and their three teenagers occupied the other side. Tara parked in front of the annex attached to the church. Offices and meeting rooms, plus a large banquet room, were housed inside the building.

Talking to Annie and Carl wouldn't be easy. She should've called them back.

Chapter Eighteen

Tara edged around Carl's desk. She yearned to leave, but she couldn't.

"Hastiness is out of character for you," he told her. "A mad dash into matrimony concerns us."

"How come? Each detail lined up like clockwork. Timing is the one issue I've wavered on. That might be a little off. The date. Not the man." Instead of throwing a temper tantrum, Tara consoled her bruised ego by slouching onto a chair. Carl had spent the last hour questioning the engagement. Numerous objections were raised since her arrival.

Support me. Take my side. His opinions had always figured into her decisions. *Well, I've always at least listened.*

"Tara—"

"Luke believes it's better to live in action instead of delay. Tiptoeing through life doesn't work." She paused a second, frowning. "Experience proves that postponing for the perfect time often backfires. Even the best-laid plans can spell disaster. My parents died without living. Luke's parents' lives ended instantly."

"Accidents happen, as one did with Luke's parents. But that other statement implies that Maggie's and Lenny's existence was insignificant. They were blessed people who savored the simple life they'd chosen."

Tara reassessed her previous remarks. Carl was right. Her parents had been two of the happiest people in the world. Life had thrown many curves throughout the years. Her parents had weathered each one without losing hope. Each setback had found them on their knees. Even though their lives had offered numerous challenges, her parents overcame every problem that arose.

That is, until they died.

"I wish they'd traveled more. Traveling had been their fervid desire." Pensive eyes fastened on Carl. "My parents didn't start living until retirement, and I won't follow suit."

Carl sat on the desk's edge. "Their death defied odds, Tara. Cashing in on long-lived dreams seldom ends in heartbreak. Life presents numerous trials. Trust in God brings us through each one."

"My parents died. Too early. Their letter encouraged me to live fearlessly."

"For Christians, absence from the body means our spirit lives in God's presence. Sometimes the truth can hurt loved ones left behind. Maggie and Lenny are happier than they ever were in life."

"Hope saved me from losing my mind." Her fingers twiddled as she stared at Carl. "Like old times, I'm back to talking to God, even though I never blamed Him for their deaths. Yet, He could've healed Mom and Dad if He'd wanted." Bright eyes shone through tears. "Mom and Dad's last letter empowered me. Despite physical pain and certain death, they regretted leaving me alone. Their trust in God never wavered."

"Your parents had multiple reasons to wait to travel after retirement. Caring for elderly relatives was tradition in both families. As only children, full responsibility for parents and grandparents fell on their shoulders. Travel time lacked priority."

Same facts. Different view.

"Are you listening? Even though they lacked free time, Maggie and Lenny enjoyed life. Tara, you made sacrifices to take care of your grandparents." Carl held her hand in his palms. "Were *you* dissatisfied?"

Numerous happy occasions sprang to mind. "That's impossible when you're surrounded by love on every front. I did despise my social life. No guys asked me out or to dance at parties." She wagged her finger. "Do not mention the blind date."

"Wouldn't think of doing so. Still, I refute that assessment of your social life."

"Haven't you always? Okay. I'm ready to listen."

Carl offered his classic "too little too late" look. "Here's a synopsis. Tara Simpkins rebuffed advances from all admirers. Males were drawn to the pretty, standoffish teenager/young adult/adult woman who ignored them."

Tara laughed. "I get the picture."

"Each time, you walked away without a second glance."

Suze had voiced that same opinion. I would accuse them of comparing notes if they were friendly.

Tara shook her head. "I never knew a guy was interested in me."

"Correction. You never cared that they were. Luke broke defenses. How?"

"Luke loves me." Her hand raised then dropped onto her lap. "He didn't give up."

"Back there again." He paused. "Make sure I meet Luke. Soon."

Tara sprang from the chair and hugged him. "Thanks, Carl." She sat beside him on the desk. "The wedding's at ten. Expect Luke bright and early next Saturday."

"Bright and early Sunday at church."

"We're coming. But after the sermon, I'd planned to sneak out the back door. Nosey people might ask questions if we hang around."

"Inquisitive is a softer word."

"If you give a sermon on intrusion, Luke and I will congregate in the lobby."

"Nice try. My message was prepared last Tuesday."

"Who's officiating the wedding? You or Pastor Victor?"

"We'll share the honor. I knew Luke's parents. Derrick was ten years older than I."

Finally. Inside information. Tara had waited days to hear some news. "How well did you know his parents? What were they like?"

"Derrick and Jenny were wonderful people who married straight out of high school. Luke was born within ten months. His brother came along eleven months later."

"Luke often mentions his parents. From all accounts, they were a close family."

Carl stood, tugging Tara off the desk. "About the wedding ... during the ceremony, wink if your mind changes. I'll play the heavy."

Tara measured the abrupt suggestion. "Are you joking? Please say yes."

"A mere wink pushes me into intervening." He paused. "Why do you laugh?"

"Marcie basically said that same thing." She patted her stomach to still the rumbling.

"That just means many people love you." Affection-laden eyes studied Tara. "And in the future, answer my calls."

"Sure thing. Tell Annie I ... oops, there you are."

A brunette with smiling eyes stood inside the doorway. Tara hurried to her side. The two women hugged then stood apart, staring at each other.

"I was instructing Carl to tell you hi."

"Thanks for showing up. We were going to drop by later otherwise. Did you forget about us?"

"My only babysitter and big brother? Of course not."

Annie flicked a questioning glance at Tara. "Why did you ignore my calls and texts?"

Tara's head hung for a few seconds. "I realized you and Carl would disapprove regardless."

"When I passed by the house yesterday, another car was parked out front. Luke's?"

"Um-hum." Tara's heart warmed at Annie's compassionate expression. "Next time, stop by. I love it when you drop in."

"Does Carl have the pertinent information regarding Luke?"

"Yes." Tara beamed an angelic smile. "And, he said everything you told him to."

Annie laughed hard. "Stop causing trouble. I won't rake you further over the coals. Carl will bring me up to speed. Have dinner with us, and bring Luke."

"His best friend tapped us for dinner." Tara sucked her bottom lip, thinking. "Church Sunday?"

"We'll hound you if you don't show. And my bridal shower invitation arrived yesterday. I'll do the honors and pay for everything."

Backing out the door, Tara stepped back inside. "Thanks, Annie. Is your mom and my only niece coming?"

"Yes. Kylie begged to invite two friends. I told her no."

"She could've. What more can I ask? Tell Mrs. Kennedy I missed her at church last Sunday. I mailed the wedding invitations this morning." Tara pointed to an empty chair beside the desk. "Discuss me at will while I let myself out. Carl knows the juiciest parts."

"Ring me if you wish," Annie reluctantly answered. "As always, it's never too late nor too early. Call."

Tara blinked away tears as love lured her back inside the office. It took her another thirty minutes to tell them about her re-emerged dreams and high hopes.

* * *

Around two, Tara was applying finishing touches to Luke's dessert. Pineapple upside down cake was his favorite. When the doorbell chimed his signature ring, she set the cake plate on the counter. Licking sticky fingers, she swung open the door and stepped outside.

Luke kissed her lightly on the lips. "Mmm. You taste sweet. I want seconds."

Tara accepted the kiss with a smile. Her face glowed with pleasant thoughts while hoping neighbors weren't watching. A quick glance across the street confirmed neither of Abby's parents were home.

"You're my second visitor today. Come on in."

"You go first." The bag Luke held rustled as he stepped into the house after Tara re-entered. "Who stopped by? Anyone I know?"

"Hailee and little Eric paid a visit. They were a welcome surprise. She promised they'll come again."

Tara had been astounded by a silhouette of a woman and small child in the peekaboo window. Strangely enough, she'd figured the duo was Benton's wife and son. As she opened the door, a very pregnant Hailee had given her a timid smile.

"They didn't stay long, but I'm pleased they came. They were in the neighborhood."

"Right. Any excuse works since the visit pleased you." He sniffed the air, grinning. "Smells terrific. Pineapples. Are you baking my number one cake?"

"Baked and ready to eat. Either now or when we get back tonight." Her gaze darted to the take-out sack he carried. "What's in the bag? I smell Chinese food. General Tso's chicken?" Her face glowed when he nodded. "Mmm." *In sync again. Our relationship gets better and better.* "We'll both eat our favorite dish for lunch. How did you know I was home?"

"I passed by the house on the way to the building. Pete scoped out the shop."

"What's his opinion on the rehab?"

"It's a total overhaul on the first floor and outside."

"Well ... okay. Have a seat while I grab you some cake."

Back in the living room, Tara tossed throw pillows on an end table. "How can you play hooky from work with a busy schedule?"

Luke paused while placing their food on the cocktail table. "You and I come first. Today my workload shifted to Manuel until the honeymoon ends. He's worked for the company for twenty years and fills in on my vacations. Aunt Jackie knows the business inside and out. She'll price the jobs."

Luke's contented expression increased Tara's confidence. *Kindred spirits. The strength of our love will pull us through bad timing if the timing is off. Love conquers all, as the Bible says.*

Jesus's love conquers all, her mind replied.

Tara rubbed her forehead on Luke's chest. "Good reasoning. That attitude bodes well for our future." Her thoughts conjured images of the workers on her porch. "Did I meet Manuel?"

"He was on a different job when I was doing yours. We usually have four to five crews working simultaneously. I visit each site daily and after the job ends. About last night. I left early because Pete has a hectic schedule, and it was the only time I could go. I horned in on his and Molli's evening." Luke squeezed her closer. "My family has seen me more than you have. I'm not taking any more SOS calls from anyone except The Grands."

Tara's heart settled somewhere around her toes. "Emergency calls? Is everything all right?" The words barely squeaked past her quivering lips.

"Nothing was a major problem." Luke hooked an errant curl behind her ear. "I don't require their help solving personal business."

A light-bulb moment. Tara's heart lay bare.

Luke's grandfather welcomed me into the family, and his grandmother supplied motherly advice. Steffi was friendly in both instances at Kenny's. Andy and Colton went above and beyond duty to help me with the cars. Even Benton sent his wife over to meet me. Could there be a problem?

"Does our marriage plan present problems? Was I mistaken that everyone now approves?" Tara knew the flat tone revealed her angst as she unhooked her arms from around Luke's waist.

Luke drew her back into his arms. "Don't jump to wrong conclusions. My family loves you like I do."

Tara recalled her self-made rules: Remain positive against all odds. Keep the conversation light and basic. Yet, a sigh seemed to form within her feet. "Now, I only have to meet Scott and Aunt Jackie." Her attempt to smile failed miserably. "Steffi implied her husband is laidback about everything."

Luke sniggered. "Laidback? Try a different 'L' word. Scott is beyond lackadaisical. But he has an adequate work ethic, so he's saved from being called lazy. But back to us—"

"Tell me their concerns about us marrying."

Luke kissed her lips then hesitated.

His kiss told the story. They must totally hate the idea of our marriage taking place. I figured all parties were equally invested, just with a few reservations. What obstacle derailed her hopes?

"Tell me their frank assessment."

"Some believe you reached a crucial decision before you were emotionally ready. They well remember how our own loved ones dying disrupted their lives. They also think I took an unfair advantage of you and your emotional state."

Luke's smooth tone soothed apprehensions Tara never thought she'd have. *These people hardly know me. How can they form an opinion regarding my emotional stability either way?*

"I'm at a loss. How could they reach any conclusion?"

"Experience. Vivid memories of their own losses resurfaced. Other people's opinions are unmanageable. Let's get back to us. Starting Monday, we'll spend each day together. Except for the bridal shower, of course."

Tara laughed, even though his siblings' views bothered her. "Us against the world. Glad we're on the same team."

"Enough to cancel dinner at Andy's and dessert at Colton's. Throw in Sunday with the Bensons as well."

"Blow off my future in-laws and renege on Abby's parents' offer? No way! Why increase the Bensons' angst and the Cassidys' misgivings? Come up with alternative plan, please."

"Then we take advantage of the little time left. What's on the itinerary?"

"Let's see. Dinner tonight at Pete's. Bridal shopping in the morning. Lunch with The Grands, and dinner at Rachel and Andy's." She hesitated then rushed into speech. "I spoke with Carl and Annie in his office earlier. If you value my life I *must* introduce you guys before the wedding."

Luke opened his mouth, paused, averted his eyes, and then he eyed Tara. "Why is it important to meet those two?"

They're family. Accommodate Carl, Annie, and their children right along with Petra and Pastor Victor. Forever a mainstay in Tara's life, the Hilliards kept her sane during and after her parents' illnesses. "They're the brother and sister I never had. Annie was my babysitter until I turned thirteen. Even after that we spent loads of time together. Still do. Their children call me Auntie."

"We'll be under the microscope again. Bet Carl and his wife take up where his parents left off, paving the way for Abby's parents. The Bensons."

Tara beamed her brightest smile. "Exactly. Where was I? Oh, yeah. Also, there's Sunday's early dinner with the Bensons and dessert at Colton's. Then there's the bridal shower Tuesday evening, and dinner with the twins and their spouses Wednesday. Our rehearsal dinner is Friday." She wiped her brow. "We're booked. A cleared schedule sounds great after that rollout."

"We'll do those things together except shopping and the bridal shower. That gives us most days alone, from sun up until nightfall. We'll make the hours count. For us."

"Well. Um. We'll see. You're addicting. I might have to forgo my daily fix."

Color fled his face. "Well that's a wake-up call. Time was allotted for a fiancée who won't acquiesce."

Tara opened her mouth to speak, but then she pushed Luke away.

As Luke's fingers captured her chin, Tara evaded looking at him.

"Weddings don't just happen," she finally said. "Did you forget preparations must be made?"

"I apologize, Tara. Three sisters-in-law prepped Steffi's wedding. I footed the bill. Look, other than the wedding prep, may we spend every available moment together?"

I overreacted and must regroup. "I love that plan. I'm looking forward to having Luke-filled days. Until then, are you hungry?"

Luke checked his watch then opened the food sack. "Let's eat. We have five hours until dinner at Pete's. I came here directly from the site. A change of clothes is in the car."

Sometime later, Tara smacked her lips and swallowed the last bite. Luke's company surpassed the yummy food. Spending time together made the waiting game to meet his closest friends bearable. After this evening, his Aunt Jackie would be the last pivotal introduction. And she mustn't forget Scott.

"You make the best pineapple upside down cake I've ever had." Luke hitched a leg onto the sofa.

"Baking is a favorite pastime. You ate two slices and brought lunch. A well-orchestrated afternoon. What's next on the timeline?"

"A nap." He yawned and covered his mouth. "It's been a hectic day, but holding you close improves it."

"Aw. I'm what the doctor ordered?" Tara eyed the empty containers on the table then bolted to her feet. "Must tidy up." With blur-type action, she jammed discarded cartons into a trash bag. Luke laughed as she made kissy faces at him while she worked.

Tara dropped onto the sofa beside him. "Spit spat. All done."

Luke had watched the practiced movements until she put the cloth aside. "My turn. Sit tight."

Luke hauled the trash to a large receptacle in the alley. Tara tracked his progress across the yard from the back door.

It's nice to have someone to help with housework. Dad never helped Mom with hers.

Unwanted memories resurfaced. Her father disappeared whenever her mother lifted a broom. That wouldn't happen with her fiancé. Tara smiled when Luke opened the door, studying the sunporch as he entered.

"I'll contact two contractors to help with renovations at the other houses."

"I thought Pete was doing the renos."

"Remember, adding the building changes things. It'll take too long for Pete's company to do all the rehabs."

Tara removed two bottled waters from the refrigerator before heading to the living room. This time the couple settled onto the sofa.

"We'll update this place, the single-family dwelling, and the two-family flat first. The shop and upstairs flat might take three months."

She fidgeted against him. "How long will the entire process take?"

"I think we should do more than the standard updates at all locations, especially here, so, approximately eight weeks at our home, and ten weeks at the vacant houses. Every house should be completed by late-August. Pete will renovate our house and the shop."

"Isn't he the go-to man on every job?"

"When he doesn't have prior obligations, yes. Time constraints keep me from using Pete at all four locations. Do we stay in the city or suburb during reno?"

"Suburb. Planning to rent your place after we move out?"

"Steffi and Scott asked to buy it. Benton and Hailee want The Grands' house. Since Andy handles the family's finances, he's coming to lunch tomorrow. We'll discuss particulars and give everyone possible scenarios."

"Luke! We're keeping all houses for our children. Do The Grands want to sell their home?"

"In time it'll come to us grandchildren. Listen. We'll have two flats once the building is rehabbed. That makes two two-family flats and a single-family dwelling. Five houses for our children to live in."

"Five homes. What if we have six children?"

Luke's eyebrow immediately rose.

Uh. Over the top. Reel it in, Tara. Luke's house will still be in the family if Steffi and Scott buy it. The same with his grandparents' house if Benton and Hailee do the same. Besides, he only wants to leave our eldest son a house.

"Got it!" She beamed a bright smile. "Give the houses to the LLC. And then the LLC can sell them to Benton and Steffi. Put in a clause that neither of them can sell to anyone other than the LLC. Will that proposition satisfy everyone?"

Luke's lips lingered on Tara's cheek. "If legal, it's the perfect proposition. However, their spouses may have legitimate claim. Although I don't imagine we can give the LLC property. There may be a nominal cost involved."

Chapter Nineteen

"We're here, Tara. Do we welcome Molli's assistance if Rachel and Megan agree to branch out into rental property?" Luke asked the question as he turned the car onto his friends' street. He parked in front of a craftsman-style house with a wraparound porch. "Moll's a hard worker who knows her job. Wait until you two meet. Molli grows on you."

"Surely we'll get along fine. I like the idea as well as their house. A wraparound porch. I haven't seen one in years. Was Pete the builder?"

"And the designer. Pete has a BS in architecture."

"Let her manage our properties regardless of Megan's and Rachel's choice." Luke's astonished expression confounded Tara. When hadn't she followed his lead? *I'd better keep track. Don't want to become his "mini me."* The thought stayed with her after she left the car.

Molli opened the door before the bell rang. "Hello, Tara. I've wanted to meet you since you met Luke. You're what he talks about most." The auburn-haired woman's hearty greeting proved she welcomed the visit.

Molli's hair was redder than Abby's. Shyness fled Tara. "Hi, Molli. Thanks for the dinner invite."

With his hand on her elbow, Luke ushered Tara into the house. Once inside, Tara offered a plant purchased for the occasion.

"Hope you like philodendrons."

"Thank you." Molli quickly grabbed the plant, placing it on the dining room table. "Wait until Pete sees this superb gift. I've boasted about having a green thumb. Watch him say, prove it." Molli wagged a finger at Luke as she passed him. "I've waited years to meet Luke's fiancée. Dinner's ready. Follow me." Stopping in the kitchen, her hand indicated the connecting family room. "Let's hang out here until Pete comes inside."

French doors opened as Tara settled beside Luke on the loveseat. She took one look at Pete and couldn't stop smiling. The man was the direct opposite of her fiancée. Both men were medium height. Pete's muscular build contrasted with Luke's angular frame.

Their host washed his hands in the kitchen, then joined his wife on the sofa. His piercing gaze appeared friendly. "We finally rated high enough to get a visit from you. Luke said going to visit you was off-limits."

"Although we were tempted to ignore the warning," said Molli. "I almost stopped several times after work."

"Next time, stop by. Today, Hailee made an unannounced visit."

"Pete told me you had met Megan and Rachel. Hailee hates being left out. Pregnancy intensifies self-pity."

"That was Hailee's exact explanation except for the self-pity part. Benton encouraged her to visit after a crying session."

Molli laughed. "Touching. Dutiful husband bailed her out. Again." Her elbow nudged Pete. "Kowtow to me sometime."

"Surrender's my middle name. Marriage to Moll's a balancing act I often lose."

Both comments and subsequent laughter successfully broke the ice.

Talking to Molli and Pete is similar to chatting with Abby and Craig. They're a nice fit as friends.

While they ate spaghetti and meatballs with all the trimmings, Luke confirmed Molli would manage their rental property.

Clink. Molli's and Pete's glasses clicked.

Pete lowered his fruit punch goblet. "We expect additional leads for my company from Molli's new position. She couldn't procure work for my business at her last job. She quit today."

Does he need more work? Pete should renovate all the houses.

Tara tapped Luke's shoulder. "Let Pete renovate all the houses. Don't approach anyone else."

Luke considered the idea. "It's a time frame issue. Those houses have sat empty long enough." He eyed Pete. "Can you complete renovations on Tara's properties within three months?"

Pete nodded. "The hair salon wraps up next week. Three months is an adequate approximation to complete all locations. Of course, all updates depend on what's found behind the walls. A walk-through starts us off running." His expression lost its seriousness when a smile appeared. "Thank you, Tara. We'll renovate your house first yet work simultaneously at each location. The vacant houses should be available within four weeks of finishing your house. The shop and flat will wind us up.”

“Sounds like a plan,” said Tara. “No rush. We’re staying at Luke’s until the reno is completed.”

“Thanks, Tara,” Molli added.

Pete whistled. “The two of you are a perfectly matched set. Tara’s a friend, buddy.”

* * *

Tara lay in bed with her ankles crossed. Her day was a tremendous success story. She sold her grandfather’s cars and teased with Luke’s closest friends. Her future took shape before her eyes. It was a vision she could champion. Friendship with Molli proved easy enough. Both women welcomed a relationship. At the bridal shower the new and old would mix.

Only reasonable people had been invited. She couldn’t fathom any of those folks not getting along. Even Abby’s mother usually behaved herself at social gatherings outside of her house.

Tara yawned.

Tomorrow is bridal shopping day. I can’t wait.

* * *

“Gee, ivory looks exquisite on you. And that dress! The slim cut accentuates your body shape.” Abby stood behind Tara, peering into the trifold mirror. Their gazes met. “Next Saturday’s coming. Ready for the grand finale?”

Tara flopped forward, covering her mouth. “Purchasing a wedding gown cements the engagement.” *I’m getting married next week. Thank you, Lord.* Her gaze sought Abby’s. “It’s amazing that Luke brings out my best side. My train-wreck days are over. Strangers actually like me.”

“Thinking that Luke is the reason for your success with his family and friends is another hindrance to actually living.”

So says Abby. Luke plus children equals future.

Tara sashayed a side view. “Remember our vow the day we graduated high school? Marriage for you to Craig that year, and me soon after.”

Abby nodded. “Fired up to marry at eighteen. Waiting would’ve served me better.”

“Do you have regrets?” Tara eyed her through the mirror.

“Only not waiting two years as my parents advised. Maturity lessens growing pains. We had a bumpy ride out the gate.”

189

"Is that why you guys kept children on the back burner for six years?"

Stooping, Abby smoothed Tara's gown. "No one should invest children into a dying marriage. It makes the situation dicier, plus hinders growth."

When a knock sounded at the door, Tara and Abby stared across the space.

"Coming in," Steffi announced. Inside the dressing room, Steffi mouthed a silent scream. "Tara! Luke will pass out. Promise. Come in, guys. Everyone look at our beautiful bride-to-be. Dazzling."

With oohing and aahing, Rachel and Megan crowded around Tara.

"This gown is definitely the one," Rachel said.

* * *

A lively debate swarmed around Tara as she devoured the home-cooked meal Edna had prepared. Fried chicken, jalapeño cornbread, and cabbage stuffed with tomatoes. Simply delicious. It was the same recipe Tara's grandmother had used except for the missing fried yellow onions.

"Are you on board?" Luke asked.

"Sorry, wasn't listening. Too busy enjoying nostalgia food. Granny used a similar recipe, only she added fried yellow onions. Did you and Granny share recipes?" An engaging smile tugged her lips.

Edna laughed. "We did. Bruce's digestive system balks at onions these days."

Tara joined the general laughter. "So, what did I miss?" she asked once the others settled down.

"The Grands lean toward relocating to the city. Andy suggested the lower level of the flat behind their old church. Sound familiar?" He paused a little, grinning. "Making the move in the summer allows an easier transition."

Tara silently worked out the details. "What happens to their house?"

"Everyone agreed with the proposal," said Andy. "The Grands sell their house to the LLC for one dollar, and Luke sells his property at half value. Steffi and Benton will purchase their homes from the LLC with your suggested stipulation."

"What's the verdict?" Luke asked. "The Grands want their old stomping grounds back."

Bruce grinned at Tara. "Those delectable treats you supplied from Keller's Bakery made Edna and me homesick. Keller's should've opened a west county location."

Both Edna and Bruce wore cheery faces while waiting for her reply.

As Tara surveyed Luke and Andy, blank expressions veiled their thoughts. Desiring her response to match Luke's intent, Tara delayed. *Come on. Intentions, please.* Tara winged it once Luke winked. "I'd love you living close by. Expect frequent visits from Petra and Pastor Victor." Her gaze focused on Bruce. "Luke said you go to the barbershop every Tuesday. Will you miss going?"

Edna patted his knee, then lifted a box off the floor and placed it upon her lap. "Attending The Gathering Place will mitigate our losses. Tara, I've awaited this moment since meeting you on Monday. I skipped our family rituals with Jenny. At the time, I felt her too young to appreciate familial traditions. And then I thought I would have time to remedy my mistake. That experience alleviates making the same mistake with you. All that said, these are for you, dear."

Tara left her seat and kneeled between the elderly couple. The gravity of the situation humbled her. Even if they were unconvinced the wedding should take place, his grandparents still honored her and Luke's relationship. Her eyes blinked away tears.

Edna removed her engagement ring from her finger. "Jenny wanted her engagement ring passed to Luke's eldest son. It was destroyed in the explosion." She placed the jewelry on Tara's palm, closing Tara's hand over the ring. "Take mine. And I'll hope that our great-grandson will someday present the first gift I received from Bruce to his fiancée."

Tara's eyes closed as her emotions flittered into overdrive. Whatever control she had had fled. Never had she felt so vulnerable. Not even the day she discovered her blind date was the man she loved, and he proposed. Her gaze darted to the others but centered on her fiancée. The glimmer of tears in his eyes unleashed the floodgates in her own. Drops flowed, refusing to stop. Bowing her head and covering her eyelids failed to work.

I'm a goner. Luke's family consumes me.

When strong arms gathered her close, Tara dissolved into its protective cocoon until her sobbing ebbed. As she opened her eyes, she found that she and Luke were alone. Clearly affected by what had transpired, he passed Tara a tissue box.

"Crying clears rooms." Tara blinked back more tears. "I'm surrounded by kind people. These gifts are unprecedented."

"Grandma's a remarkable lady. What other treasures do we have?"

Luke peered inside the box. Together he and Tara poured over each picture in four photo albums. Pictures of his great-great grandparents were in fantastic condition. Both of his great-grandmothers' wedding bands and solitaire engagement rings were part of the collection.

"Personal keepsakes for the next generation. Surely our oldest son shouldn't receive everything. I say follow tradition with the photo albums and your grandmother's engagement ring." Her head tilted as she contemplated the other rings. Tara smiled at Luke's frown. His skeptical expression was priceless. Luke suffered from oldest-child syndrome. He wanted their eldest son to receive it all. "Our daughters will inherit the wedding rings."

"And leave out our other son? That's why the oldest son inherits. Period. Tradition eliminates unnecessary feuds."

Tara's head shook fervently. "Neither of us is starting from scratch and both have accumulated property. How can one child get everything and leave the other siblings with nothing? You received the business and their home, but other assets were equally split."

"Perks come with age," Andy spoke from the doorway. "That's been his argument since forever. Rachel called. I'm on my way to the store. Tara, The Grands don't expect to live free. The LLC will pay their rent each month. And, of course, your houses will be kept separate from the LLC's rental property. See you two later." He called down the hallway. "Leaving, Grandma. See you guys tonight."

* * *

At the barbecue Luke's aunt prompted Tara to call her Aunt Jackie. She appeared fifteen years younger than her brother and sister-in-law. Close-cropped salt and pepper hair hung long down her back. She dressed in white pedal pushers and a lilac top. Purple Reign was embroidered with purple thread on the front.

"Meet the afterthought, or should I say surprise," Bruce had joked as he made introductions.

The memory caused a chuckle to rumble in Tara's chest. Aunt Jackie was the life of the Cassidy family. She was probably a live wire in her younger years. Luke had revealed his grandparents basically married sight unseen. But he omitted that his great-grandparents had raised their son-in-law's sister.

Tara sat on Luke's lap while they talked with Jackie. Working with the dynamo even a short time would be great. She enjoyed listening to Aunt Jackie's viewpoints. Seconds later, her stomach quivered when a scowling

Megan sat beside Luke. And then Rachel sat next to Megan, obviously upset.

"Molli called to proffer the rental property idea," said Megan. "Although she played it off, she was surprised to learn she'll have that same job at Cassidy's with you. That's what you just told us in the kitchen. You never mentioned Molli wanted to work for us."

That comment yanked Tara's attention from the conversation with his aunt. *Working for Luke at Cassidy's. When did that development occur?* Both women appeared livid as her heart dipped. Something here was way off the mark. Luke seemed unperturbed about whatever had transpired.

"Evidently, Pete hasn't given her his new idea." When the cell phone pealed, Luke eyed the caller ID. "Hang on. It's Pete. I'll see what's up." He listened a moment, then scooted Tara off his lap and grabbed her hand. "We'll be back."

Luke rounded the house, explaining the change of plans until he reached his car. His hurried explanation skimmed over pertinent facts. Tara had a tiny inkling of what had occurred. Still, the drastic shift in direction disturbed her.

"Okay, Pete ... Hey, man. I understand. Things can fall through the cracks even if you live inside the same house ... I just informed Tara ... The plan is solid. My sisters-in-law will regroup ... Exactly. Teamwork is essential to achieve success. Is Molli on board? Put her on." He winked at Tara, then returned his attention to the conversation. "Thanks. Glad you agree, Mol ... Stop bragging on the man. But yes, Pete nailed it. Now to convince my future wife." Luke held out his cell phone, wearing a wide grin. "Molli."

Tara closed her eyes before speaking, "Hi, Molli ... It seems practical ... Megan and Rachel dropped the bombshell. I played catch-up ... Hmm. Luke indicated the same thing ... Really? ... If the new arrangement works, count me in."

A tinkling gurgle wafted from her throat. She eyed Luke's pensive stare. Something was up. His apprehension didn't fit the crime. What was he hiding?

"Okay, Molli. See you Tuesday ... Oh yeah. The walk-through at the houses on Monday. Bye-bye."

Tara hesitated when Luke refused to meet her gaze. What now? *Either some other problem exists, or there's more to this situation than you've admitted. Fess up. Don't make me dig for answers.* She wanted the truth. Now. Tara waited on Luke to confide in her and sighed when he didn't. *Trust me. I trust you.*

"Luke, Molli said Pete wanted her to work with you and manage the rentals from Cassidy's office. He thinks her working there might bring him more business. Molli likes the new arrangement better."

"It's a win-win deal for everyone involved. My sisters-in-law included. Let's get back."

The couple silently retraced their steps to the back deck. Tara hoped Luke would confide in her, but he didn't. Instead, he swung their arms and teased her with a grin until they rejoined the others.

"Explain who hijacked Molli's original plan. And why?" asked Colton once they entered the yard.

"It was her husband's decision. Tara."

Tara jumped right in. "Molli said Pete wanted her to work at Cassidy's but forgot to tell her after Luke agreed. He believes her working there will bring in more clients. Megan and Rachel deal with home buyers, while Luke's customers are established homeowners probably needing renovations."

"That's a believable scenario," said Andy. "I accept Luke's version."

Luke glanced at Andy then turned away. The brothers knew each other better than anyone else. They had overcome many obstacles together. Rachel's features relaxed after her husband weighed in. How long would it take Tara to be in tune with everything Luke?

"What's Pete's number?" asked Scott. "A different line of work is required for my sanity." He blew a kiss to his laughing wife. "Office work is too restricting. Stef and I agree that physical labor is my forte."

"Join Benton's plumbing business," Aunt Jackie said.

That suggestion brought a demonstrative head shake. "No way. Ben went to plumbing school, plus he worked for four years as an apprentice. Besides, classwork is too confining. Practical experience trumps formal instruction every time."

"Oh really. How so?" asked Megan.

"Ben knew how to perform the tasks better than his instructors."

"How would you know?" Hailee asked. "You didn't attend his classes. You've never seen him work, either."

While Tara joined the laughter, her mind sought ways to approach Luke. All wasn't as it appeared to be. What were his Molli plans, or was Tara creating problems? Something bothered Luke during her Molli conversation. If not the new arrangement, then what?

* * *

Luke intercepted another mystified glance from Tara. She sneaked peeks when she thought he wasn't looking. He realized that time alone with his fiancée proved more important than ever. Tara resembled a caged animal seeking freedom. From whom? Him? Never. Their future was sealed when she opened her front door. A vision of their afternoon in The Grands' living room bolstered Luke's determination.

Neither of us can turn back. Our honeymoon begins next week.

Luke snagged Rachel's attention. "As usual, the marvelous food hit the spot. But the company was better." He squeezed Tara's hand without a glance. "Yesterday, Tara and I promised to devote every possible waking hour with each other. Yet we were separated most of today."

"Let me make a suggestion before we leave," Tara said. She hesitated when everyone looked at her. "Maybe ... maybe it's better for Molli to work for the LLC instead of Luke. If you all agree, will it be possible for her to manage my property as well as others? And, since Megan and Rachel probably sell rental property to investors on a regular basis, there are potential clients there too."

"We can set up the LLC accordingly," Colton said.

Tara released a big breath. "I know the office complex is full, but on my tour of the warehouse, I saw an empty office Molli can use. That'll give her greater access to Luke's customers, which is Pete's preference." She turned to Luke. "What do you think?"

"That it's an excellent idea. In time, receiving eight to twelve percent of each rental property plus expenses will net a tidy sum and pay for Mollie's salary and more. Thanks, love. You guys kick it around and let us know if it's a go when you decide."

Tara practically raised her hand. "If I can make two more suggestions. Don't forget Lois and Justin Padgett have maintained my grandparents' properties for over twenty years. Those jewels run an excellent housekeeping and landscaping business. Once I lease the houses, cleaning and lawncare becomes the leaser's responsibility. So please, keep them in mind. *And* I bet acquiring additional rentals will produce a hidden job for Scott somewhere."

"I agree," said Steffi, laughing. "A tailor-made job will serve my husband better."

"I know the best position," Benton added.

Good. Tara's still in the mix. So far, she isn't leaving me.

Luke kissed her cheek. "You are a caring and thoughtful person who continues to surprise me. Let's go home."

Tara sprang from the lounge chair as Luke stood. The arm he wrapped around her waist bound her to him. Their searching gazes met then focused on the group at large until Tara smiled at Rachel.

"Thanks for the welcoming party. I truly enjoyed my evening, plus I finally met Aunt Jackie and Scott. You and Andy lay out quite a spread. I hope we can come back again soon."

"Definitely. Andy loves grilling, and I enjoy eating it! Saturday after the honeymoon ends?"

"Works for me," Tara said without consulting Luke. "Count us in."

"Sounds like a plan." Luke's lips brushed her brow. Hearing her agree confirmed they were still engaged. Tara would've disagreed if she was planning to cancel the wedding. He could trust her word. If she thinks she's made a mistake about getting married Saturday, will she comply with existing plans or cut losses?

Pete's haranguing Luke on Thursday prompted Luke to reassess discussing Leah with Tara. Why guess what his ladylove would say? He should just find out. She wouldn't string him along. But would she terminate their engagement if she learned he had a past misstep?

Walking Tara and Luke to the end of the yard, Bruce hugged Tara, and then patted Luke's shoulder. With his mouth close to Luke's ear, he said, "Your ladylove is capable and sweet. Toe the line."

The sober look advised his grandson not to blow it.

* * *

Thoughts hit Tara as she studied Luke on the ride home. Even though neither of them typically talked nonstop, on this trip, quiet weighted the air. The couple needed a diversion. Anything that would keep the relationship on track.

Hmm. Concentrate on someone other than ourselves. Someone fair and balanced like ... got it!

"Carl and Annie live in the duplex next-door to the church. Stop by Keller's Bakery. Their teenagers love Keller's key lime pie. We'll drop it off on the way home."

Luke's hands lightly tapped the steering wheel. "Home. Us. There's an optimistic lilt when you say that word. Say it again, Tara."

Tara promptly complied. Sentiments appeased aching hearts. Her eyes blinked rapidly as warmth suffused her body. Luke's unguarded emotions and longing gaze increased her faith in their relationship. Thinking "Luke plus Tara equals boundless love" strengthened her whenever doubt ascended. Yet maintaining comfort remained impossible without knowledge.

"Home is wherever we are. That security in our relationship assures neither of us will walk away. Luke, real love is determined, committed, and loyal. It can't be swayed."

"I know you love family life. We're surrounded by family and friends. Our core will increase once our children arrive." He veered the car into the exit lane. "Let's also pick up a chocolate cake at Keller's. I'm craving something sweet, and Rachel didn't serve dessert because Megan's saturating everybody in sweets tomorrow."

"You have a pineapple upside down cake."

"Right. The men told me to thank you. I dropped off the cake when we stopped by the worksites on the way to Pete's."

How had she missed the package? "You're not only a thoughtful man but also kind." Tara beamed at the raised eyebrow. "Did I lay it on too thick?"

"You definitely want something. Let's hear it."

"If I can stop laughing long enough to speak."

Joshing ensured no contention remained on either side. *If Luke is honest, we move forward. If not, back to square one.*

"Annie and Carl would enjoy meeting you. Could we have a slice of pie with their family instead of cake at home?"

Several expressions altered Luke's features. The cagey man usually hid his emotions well. That had ended with Pete's phone call. Tara thought about Luke's bringing Chinese food the day before. No-no. It started with his unexpected visit yesterday.

Luke's silence was a symptom of inner conflict. *What were we saying? Oh, yeah.*

"Annie and Carl and their kids are harmless. Carl knew your parents and saw you and Andy as toddlers. Would stopping by be okay?"

"When have I denied you anything?" Luke's mouth curved into an alluring grin.

Luke is in control again. Chameleons changed less than Luke.

* * *

When they arrived at her house, Tara accepted Luke's kiss inside the foyer. Her fiancée had acquitted himself well at the Hilliard homestead. Although the duo wasn't won over, that Carl and Annie liked Luke was evident in their conversation. Before long, momentum had swung into Tara's and Luke's favor. Now Abby's parents were the issue. Prickly people added untold complications in inopportune circumstances. The Bensons could vex a saint.

Tara tugged Luke's arm when he released her. "Stay until we settle an earlier issue." Even though she could see his defenses kick in, Tara forged ahead. "What happened while I spoke with Molli? You acted like a man facing a battle he might lose."

Luke groaned under his breath. "Don't remind me. Visions of getting jilted rocked me. Blame Pete."

His best friend? "What did Pete say or do?"

"On Thursday he took me on an unwanted trip down memory lane." His hesitation depicted a man cherry-picking what to say. "While you and Molli spoke, I was doing a quick self-analysis. I despise the man I once was. You would too if you knew him."

"The past is over. Move on."

"Here's the problem. I pray you never discover that man."

"Isn't the ultimate test, my loving you despite revelations?"

"I planned to tell you on our honeymoon, but will today if you insist."

Tara tapped fingers on her forehead. She needed to think. Alone.

"I ... guess the life story divulged on my sunporch Saturday was a synopsis. How far back are we talking?"

"Last year I altered course after a reality check." Luke touched her arm when she turned away. "Look at me. Please. I was a better man than my actions showed. While not proud of my past, I should tell you my mission remains unfinished."

Unsteady hands rubbed her arms as her brain revolted. Luke had handed her a loaded gun without the firing pin. Tara wanted the full story yet believed his assertion.

His family's love and respect prove he's trustworthy. It must be related to the woman.

Should Tara wait to hear the story he didn't disclose when he proposed? Saturday on her sunporch, he had claimed he'd told her everything. Her gaze flickered across Luke's face. Blind faith was reserved for God.

"Tara, look at me as if you see I'm standing here." His hands reached out to her.

"Conclude the mission. You won with gained wisdom and reaffirmed integrity."

When Luke moved closer, Tara backed away.

"Will I walk once I hear the news?"

A vehement headshake followed a wounded expression. "It's shamefully disappointing but isn't off-putting. I would tell you in an instant if I thought it might cause you to."

"Then why not tell me? You said you would do so if you thought I would leave. Why not tell me now since you think I won't?"

"My revelation will kill your belief in me."

"Do you think I might potentially walk away? Trust that I won't."

Luke's closed expression indicated a man fighting for control. Now Tara found herself mired inside a quandary. Their wedding ceremony was paid for. The box filled with mementoes from Luke's grandparents set atop the end table. No person can move forward while looking backwards. Instinct must guide the correct path.

Father, I pray I'm right about waiting until the honeymoon to hear Luke's confession.

Tara focused on Luke. "I'll flex and meet you where you are. I don't believe in blind faith, yet I do trust the man I plan to marry. *But,* I expect the full story once we check into our hotel. All of it, from beginning to end. Everything, Luke. I don't want additional snippets passed on later."

Relief filled Luke's eyes as if Tara's agreement boosted trust in her love. The tight embrace constricted her breathing. His words from the night they sat on her sunporch consumed her thoughts: *My life is an open book I want you to read. Ask questions, if you like, at any time.*

Really?

The stakes raised each day they got closer to the wedding day. Tara's lips moved as she silently prayed for wisdom.

Chapter Twenty

The eloquent sermon Carl had delivered that morning still inspired Tara on the drive to the Benson home. A portion of the message inferred she'd jumped the gun on her wedding plans. Moments later, she fidgeted in her seat counting down until Saturday. Carl's voice had been firm and crisp.

"God's grace mitigates troubles. That's the reality when Christians live in His presence. Is a constant awareness of the Father easy to maintain? It's impossible without Jesus and the empowering Holy Spirit. We must stay in His word to know Him."

Tara had eagerly listened while Luke's chin had jutted forward as he spot-checked his watch. Regardless of how the talk had affected Luke, Tara found comfort. But how would living in God's presence work?

"That's my problem," she mumbled under her breath. "Not spending time with God yet expecting His help."

Luke turned off the car radio. "I missed that. Repeat what you said."

"Um, talking to myself. I wonder what we're having for dinner."

Tara looked out the window. *That was Luke's deepest sigh yet. Too bad I can't read minds. What was he thinking and why? Kept any secrets lately? Tara, don't think negative thoughts. Play nice.*

"I will if he does," she murmured softly.

Luke glanced at Tara, and she smiled.

Another close call. Get a grip. Please.

Minute by minute, the ability to change course grew slimmer. The nuptials would take place on Saturday. Radical circumstances demanded drastic measures. Tara's mindset resembled a tipsy drinker. Plucking petals from make-believe flowers ignited the should she or should she not debate. Luke's holding something back changed her attitude from yesterday. Whatever bothered Tara wasn't enough to call off the wedding. That dream had etched itself upon her soul.

Shared futures hung in the balance while she worried.

Then her gaze shifted to Luke. His set jaw bore little resemblance to the joking man she'd first met. Curt nods at church revealed a tension she hadn't expected. However, Tara glimpsed his heart within his eyes. *I don't have issues with his lapse in judgment. That part is over. It's his implying the cards were on the table. It irks me that they weren't. And then, after he admitted he'd been less than honest, I let him off the hook.* No more surprises. Period. And if he sprang another one … then what? Hmm …

"Abby and Craig are here. His SUV is parked out front. You won't meet my godchildren at dinner. They're spending the day with Craig's parents."

Luke parked in front of Tara's house. "I can't believe that I agreed to this dinner. Out of the hot seat at Abby's house and into the fire at her parents' home. Are the parents anything like the daughter?"

Tara brushed off the offense. "That's a naughty statement. Shame on you. Abby is a sweetheart."

"Suze already shot down that misnomer."

* * *

"Young man, let me complete my sentence. You keep butting in."

Alicia Benson's bosom heaved. She'd interrupted Luke for the umpteenth time. A rational person wouldn't classify their one-sided conversation as a discussion.

It wasn't the woman's clashing with everyone's ideas nor the sarcasm dripping off her tongue that bothered Luke. Based on Tara's honest assessment, the snarky attitude had been expected. Beads of water sloshing over the glass Mrs. Benson pushed aside to harangue Luke had set him off. Enough.

Tara squeezed his finger when his arm muscles flexed.

He hesitated. "Please, excuse me." *What I wanted to say was*—"Let me rephrase my comment."

"Thanks for making my point. Rudeness around this table is rampant. Don't interrupt."

Luke resumed eating when Tara leaned her head on his shoulder.

Mrs. Benson droned on. "Tara isn't used to men like yourself. She's lived a sheltered life, despite her age."

"Her friends didn't," said Craig. He glanced at Abby when she offered him a basket of rolls, shook his head, and then faced his mother-in-law. "And Tara lived vicariously through each one. She was right in the mix and isn't naïve

202

by a long shot."

"That's true," Tara agreed. "I chose a quiet lifestyle on purpose. Truthfully, my parents would've welcomed Luke. He has godly convictions, loves his family, plus he's a great provider. With him, I'm cherished and protected." She paused, facing Abby's father. "Mr. Benson, please walk me down the aisle. Carl and Pastor Victor are performing the ceremony."

Calvin Benson sipped coffee while everyone awaited the verdict. His wife's curled lip drooped on one side.

Luke stroked Tara's upper arm while he waited. *Forget me. Consider Tara. Ignore your wife's inuendoes. She'll make others.*

"Your parents would've liked Luke while disapproving of Saturday's wedding." Mr. Benson set his cup on the saucer. "I would expect Lenny and Maggie to give Abby wise counsel *and* support her decision. It's an honor to walk you down the aisle in Lenny's place. However, an arbitrary date picked out of nowhere isn't an authoritative command to marry on Saturday."

Tara and Abby left their chairs and hugged him, Craig resumed eating, and Alicia Benson appeared resigned to his decision. However, Calvin Benson choosing to support Tara failed to appease Luke. Only his regard for Tara kept him seated.

* * *

Later that evening, four children and Ranger raced around the yard until Megan called every child to come inside with the adults.

"Come along, Patrick and Kim. Bedtime. No baths tonight." She beckoned Kizzie and Candy, Rachel and Andy's daughters, along. "You two sleep in my bedroom until your mom wakes you. Tell everyone night-night, kids. Come on, Ranger."

Everyone obeyed immediately, except Kim. "Nighty-night," she said around the thumb stuck between her lips.

Tara's hands clutched on her lap as her future loomed before her. In time, she and Luke would enact similar scenes with their children. Fun days and quiet evenings. Luke blew out a long breath. His arm crooked around her shoulder. She cooed, nuzzling closer. In sync once again.

As the room turned quiet, everyone listened to the kids' waning voices.

Lights in the back of the house switched off. Filtered light rays streaked into the hallway. Multiple giggles tittered. A whiny voice questioned why Eric wasn't placed in a bed.

Eric snored on Benton's lap. Hailee curled within Benton's arms.

"He's already asleep," Megan said to the kids. "Sleep tight. No playing in bed."

"We aren't sleepy," a voice that sounded like Kizzie's replied.

Rachel joined Megan in the hallway. "Lie down anyway. We'll leave after watching Aunt Jackie's movie."

"That's my cue. Movie time." Aunt Jackie dangled the remote between her thumb and finger. "Here, Steffi. You figure out the TV."

"Which movie?"

"*Bright Side of Tomorrow.* It's an action-packed mystery thriller that received rave reviews."

"Never heard of it." Scott scratched his head. Then his gaze settled on the surprisingly silent elderly couple. "Bet you two have."

Edna laughed. "We've heard nonstop commentary. From Jackie."

"Here we go," said Steffi. "Lights. Camera. Action."

"Hold onto your seats," Aunt Jackie added. "The geriatrics loved the concept behind the storyline so I'm told. Now if only the lovebirds can stop smooching."

Mystified by the inaccurate statement, Tara joined in the friendly laughter.

Her happiness soared when Luke kissed her. And then her grin widened when Steffi winked at her.

"Why are you smiling?" Luke whispered.

"This night validates sixteen agonized years without a real date. Your family's love for each other justified the wait," she whispered back.

Luke settled her in his arms. "Tara's my forever lady. My life is jelling."

Everyone's gaze sought Tara's reaction at the self-proclaimed achievement.

"Luke is my dream man. Hope I never wake up."

His thumb tilted her face toward his. "You'll find my arms around you whenever you do."

Steffi's thumbs rose.

Scott snickered.

Tara beamed. Caring gazes lifted her spirit.

I fit right into the mix. If only my parents could enjoy the festivities with us tonight, then my life would be complete. Today, I'm an unofficial family member. After Friday, it's official. Wait till Abby hears what happened.

"We're in for a wild ride," Colton said. "Seconds on dessert, anyone?"

Everyone's hands rose.

Andy followed behind him. "Dibs on the apple crumb cake."

* * *

Tara's eyes popped open to sunrays streaking through lacey curtains. Birds twittered nosily in the trees. Monday morning and still in bed; today she didn't have the day-after-Sunday grind. She would soon be working for her husband. Aunt Jackie was ready to resign. Tara was primed to take over.

Aunt Jackie had fashioned the office to her liking over forty years. Luke sought innovative methods to sell their service to new consumers. Tara had chosen Cassidy's for her own roofing needs based on Pastor Victor's recommendation. Word of mouth was an ideal form of advertising, with built-in limitations. Utilizing the internet should enhance their exposure to homeowners under fifty.

Suze! How had she not thought of this before? Suze and Josh's marketing firm placed businesses on the map daily. And Tara wouldn't even need to talk them into helping or Luke into accepting. Josh's association with Luke would cut through red tape.

An hour later, a fully clothed Tara placed a warming tray on the table. Grilled onions scented the house. A tempting aroma wafted up her nose. Her stomach gurgled as the doorbell rang.

Luke greeted her with a kiss. "Morning, fiancée. How are you?"

"Thankful. At home at nine o'clock on a Monday morning. Freedom's my lot every day until after our honeymoon." She brushed a finger across his cheek. "Like the stubble. Wedding-day look?"

"Nah. I'll be clean shaven. Don't want to send Grandma into a tizzy." He sniffed the air then headed down the hallway. "Whatever is cooking smells delicious." Luke studied the traditionally set table. His gaze drifted over Tara. "Thanks, love. You and everything you do in the house personify everything I've always desired inside my home."

Tara sucked in a deep breath. The compliment provided more than the thank you she'd expected. Did Luke's appreciation project a preview of their mornings? It boded well for their marriage if it was a prelude.

"And your favorite breakfast foods are ..."

Luke lifted the warmer top, exposing a stir-fry of grilled potatoes, portobello mushrooms, onions, and red peppers. Crisp bacon complemented the meal. Fresh-squeezed orange juice filled the glasses. Diced fruit filled bowls set beside each plate.

"Wow! It can't get any better. Let's eat this feast."

While they ate, Tara explained her marketing plan for Cassidy Roofing.

"I'll ask Suze to present a business plan after our honeymoon. Should we add Expert Plumbing into the mix? I vote yes."

"Don't forget Andy and Colton, plus the LLC."

"Talk to Pete too." Tara grabbed her cell phone to text Suze.

There could be five more parties involved than she had originally envisioned. Maybe we could get a group rate.

Tara hesitated as Luke's eyes glowed. His lips curved into a lazy grin.

"What? Do you approve of the plan?"

"It's you, Tara. You're a helper. I believe that description sums up your family philosophy. The Simpkins are nice people."

Warmth coursed through her body. Her parents were thoughtful and so was Luke. Yet, there was a hardness beneath his veneer that she had still failed to decipher.

* * *

After waiting twenty minutes, Luke secured the first available table at Kenny's. The diner overflowed with customers scarfing their meals and vacating seats in rhythmic motion. However busy, the waitstaff whizzed between tables, balancing trays on fingers without mishap. It was a skill Tara was pleased she'd never learned.

"Do you approve of Pete's plans regarding the houses?" Luke asked Tara. "You appeared onboard for the other houses, but what's the verdict on our home?" He clutched her hand in his.

Floodgates of memories had presented a kaleidoscope of life in each place. They were silent images of the way things had been for people no longer alive.

Tara blinked away tears. "I approve Pete's designs for the most part. Knowing we are renovating the houses for our children made the exercise bearable. Hold on." She dotted her eyes with a napkin. "I'm suddenly coming to grips with my parents' deaths *and* getting married on Saturday."

Luke's pointed gaze intensified. "I should've asked you earlier. Is it too soon to get married? Talk to me."

How do I articulate feelings I can't define? A walk-through of the houses with Molli and Pete proved we're no longer dealing with abstracts. Luke and I are getting married.

"Tara ..."

206

"It's crazy, but I'm ecstatic we're in love and also bewildered that we are."

Luke's hand crushed her fingers. "Does moving the wedding date help? I'll acquiesce in a heartbeat."

Tara eased sore fingers from his grip.

"I don't think so," she spoke through tented hands, confused about his willingness to postpone the wedding.

Nodding, Luke read an incoming text on his cell phone then gazed at Tara. "Andy requested an immediate visit. I told those guys emergencies only."

"Annie too. She called while you were talking with Kenny Junior. We'll make our visits separately, then meet at my house." She held up two fingers. "Two o'clock?"

Luke pulled out Tara's chair. "We can make the rounds together."

"Perhaps we should make our visit alone. Annie didn't provide a heads-up. Did Andy tell you what he wanted?"

"Right. Going by ourselves might be best. What's the plan for later?"

"A home-cooked meal and a movie. I dug out Mom's cookbook. No casserole or stir-fry tonight."

Kenny Senior engaged the couple in small talk at the cashier counter. They continued the trend on the drive to her house.

Luke parked behind Tara's car. "What types of movies do you watch?"

"Whodunits. British style. Poirot and Agatha Christie are my favorites."

"Something else we have in common. I can watch those all day."

"Let's have a movie marathon. I'll stop by The Corner Market for popcorn." Tara whipped open her car door and trudged to her car. Spinning around, she waved. Her hand dropped at Luke's pained stare.

"Two sharp, Tara. Don't be late."

Luke's eyebrows knitted into a single line.

Tara's teasing reply died on her lips.

Confide in me. I need knowledge in order to stand by you.

Back at Luke's car, Tara stooped, brushing her lips across his mouth.

"Hurry back."

* * *

Luke's self-confidence faltered when he bustled into Andy's office. He sought to control the conversation.

"More SOS calls? What gives?"

Alarm bells rang in Luke's ears as his brother leaned into the chair cushion.

Something urgent had taken place.

"Leah's back. Now what?"

It wasn't something he wanted to hear, but Luke's knotted muscles relaxed. "We discussed that probability last week. You saw her in passing?"

"Her sister accosted me in the parking lot."

"And the significance is ...?"

"Leah sent a scout who targeted me. Forethought isn't a characteristic she's known for."

"Uproar over a woman who lives in another state." Luke forced a low chuckle from closed lips. "I won't defend myself over sporadic dates that ended last year."

"Check the definition. You hooked up whenever she visited." Andy frowned at the ceiling. "In April, Leah proposed marriage and arrived a month early to stake her claim. And hey, I won't judge why you proposed to Tara."

Score one Andy. His brother just threw a weak moment confession into Luke's face.

"How does showing up a month early accomplish her marrying goal? And as for Tara, I don't require a buffer to thwart Leah. Did you forget our conversation on my engagement night?"

"Concentrate. Focus on you and Leah. Tara—"

"You brought Tara up—"

"Leah came back early so you could permanently clear the field of other women. Last year, you kept her waiting a few days before meeting with her. I doubt that she welcomed chasing you while her friends watched."

Luke could banter these remarks all day. Anything was better than delving deeper into the how and why of a hated woman. *Reflection can wait until my honeymoon. My past died after meeting the lady I've ached for.* Luke was a new man.

He eyed Andy. "You think I ticked her off, huh?"

"The master manipulator thought she'd lost her prey. Last year, your time delay in seeing her probably sparked the idea to her that her charm had worn thin. Closing the door last September confirmed it."

"Leah has something." Luke frowned as he contemplated the last remarks. "Charm? Nah."

"Leah sensed she was losing you and sprung a trap to hold on." Andy unscrewed the cap on his bottled water. "Need I continue?"

"Please. So far you're providing adequate entertainment."

"Try this one on. You changed the rules on this go-round, proposing to a stranger. Extreme behavior, big brother. Next time decline the marriage offer without involving a third party."

"So, I'm marrying Tara because I fear booting Leah? That's your position?"

"Fear is the wrong word. You used her, Luke. We both know why you took up with Leah."

Andy rose when Luke stood. "Leaving while we discuss you means we won't discuss me in the future."

In other words, grin and bear it. My brother often did and so did I. Disagreements concerning Leah can't taint our relationship.

Luke retook his seat. Andy never made idle threats.

"Accommodating you won't strengthen me. Play by my rules and not your own."

"Got it." Andy studied Luke with a lopsided grin. "Bear with me a moment while I set the scene. For five years you never desired any more from Leah than you received."

Granted. Leah should've been ditched once I figured out who she was.

"A regretful miscalculation. Even worse would be marrying Tara just to disengage Leah. Why ruin three lives instead of trashing one?"

"You tell me, Machiavelli. You wrote the script."

One eyebrow rose as Luke stood. "Machiavelli would kill the relationship and then move on."

"You prefer a little civility in victories." When Luke headed toward the door, Andy followed behind him. "The return volley's coming. Ensure Tara's unscathed."

Luke's searching eyes turned serious. "No worries there. Leah understands her limits. She won't approach Tara, or me, if we're together."

"Then Leah's seen a side of you I can't fathom."

"Nothing as stark as that ominous remark implied." Luke put a hand on Andy's shoulder. "Trust me."

Two choices battered Luke's mind on the walk to his car: inform Tara today or stick with his original plan. Withholding information until their honeymoon was practical. Confiding in her after the wedding wouldn't be catastrophic. Tara would comprehend his dark season. She'd promised her love would withstand each querulous test. Taking up with Leah had been the worst mistake of his life. Hating Leah had overruled conviction until his unwillingness to destroy her had ensnared him.

Luke's stomach roiled as moisture dampened his forehead. He lowered the window, ushering in fresh air. Should he alter plans that safeguarded Tara's rejection over his murky past? *Murky?* No crime had been committed. His only fault had been strategizing. One false step led to five years of mismanagement. Until Leah, Luke had no inkling his dark side existed.

He had two choices. Either tell Tara now or wait until later. The latter choice won hands down. He was too close to marrying her to chance a setback on any level. What had transpired over the last five years fashioned him into the man he was today. He loathed to compromise the values he was raised with for any reason. Did his silence now dispute that claim of decency?

It's a dilemma, Lord. Instead of consulting You, I sought revenge. And then jockeyed to extricate myself.

His head laid on the steering wheel. He felt sunk.

* * *

"Chocolate icing with yellow cake. Thanks for baking my favorite flavor." Tara licked frosting off her fingers. "May I take Luke a slice?"

Annie slid the cake plate across the table, along with aluminum foil, laughing as Tara cut a hefty piece.

"Luke loves pineapple upside down, but he'll appreciate any sweet treat." Tara's spirit crashed when Annie remained silent.

Chitchat is nice, but why delay the inevitable? Annie clearly invited me over for a reason.

Tara scooted back her chair. "Terrific cake. Now. Why the sudden summons? I've seen you three times recently. I dropped by Friday, surprised you with a visit on Saturday, plus you saw me at church yesterday."

"Your demeanor on all occasions sparked the call."

My confusion was noticeable? If Annie saw it, has anyone else paid attention?

"Truthfully, my life is unsettled, but I don't know why." Answers had evaded Tara for days. "Everything dear was lost in March and April. Then May arrived. I rebounded. Even though no person can replace my parents, time with Luke fortifies new hope. And then, I waver back and forth and forth and back."

Annie unhurriedly studied Tara as if dissecting Tara's reply. "Stress. Too much pressure. Since January you've battled through tremendous upheavals. Maggie's and Lenny's debilitating illnesses. Lenny's dying in March, and Maggie passing away in April. You suffered through their misery with them and survived."

As Tara wept, Annie knelt beside her. "May brought Luke and instant rapport. Unusual circumstances ended in an extraordinary proposal and a startling acceptance. Stress overload produced negative results, because now you realize Luke isn't a faultless human being. That revelation ended the fairy tale."

"I don't view Luke through rose-colored glasses. Yet there's an affinity between us I can't explain." Tara wiped her face with napkins. "I'm reading my Bible and talking to God again. I didn't completely end communication after my parents died, but my fervor had lessened. Our fellowship suffered a great loss."

Annie claimed the seat next to Tara. "Why are you distanced? Confide in me."

Tara's hands raised then flopped onto her lap. Bright eyes fixed on Annie. "Too many issues large and small. Mom and Dad. Luke. My friends. His family. Resigning from my job. Beginning a new one. Selling the cars. Keeping the Jag. Renovating the houses. Converting the shop and flat into a two-family dwelling. And the topper, marrying a man I met three weeks ago in five days. Whew!" Her head brushed the cushion. She glanced at Annie and sat upright. "I'm certain Luke's the one. I just struggle with when to marry him."

"Yet not enough to change dates? That's quite a list you ran down. You're going through a lot."

"I wouldn't have chosen Saturday, but Luke's wishes matter too. God always tugs my spirit when I misstep. I've only ignored it once. That tug hasn't manifested this time. Annie, can I tell you something in confidence?"

"Carl won't hear unless you require protection."

Tara made up her mind in seconds. "OK." She took a breath. "Luke has a secret he'll reveal on our honeymoon. He said I won't like what I hear, yet the revelation wouldn't impact our wedding if he tells me now."

"That's an assumption Luke doesn't know you well enough to make. No one does."

"Annie, I'm a happy adult for the first time ever. Did you know Luke plows through issues my parents procrastinated for years about? Even though Mom lived a prudent life, if alive, she would support my marriage."

"That's a stretch. We'll agree Maggie would stand by you through it all."

"Your version is accurate." Tara scooped up Luke's cake and headed toward the door. "Thanks for the invite. This talk was necessary."

"Stay until the kids come home."

"Can't. I'm meeting Luke at two and need to stop at the store. The bridal shower's tomorrow. See ya there."

While hugging Tara, Annie spoke softly in her ear. "You need rest, and Luke keeps you occupied. Busyness can make you disoriented and bring confusion."

Curious remark. "I'll unscramble that brain teaser later."

Jumping inside the car, Tara raced to The Corner Market, bought lemons, honey, and popcorn, then sped home where she made lemonade and popped the corn. Her enthusiasm plummeted while she watched a blue jay frolic in the birdbath. He seemed carefree while Tara wasn't. Where was the simple life she loved?

Blind trust offered a passport to destruction. She knew that Luke's secret would be neither a favorable admission nor a heinous crime, but rather a potentially serious character flaw. And it seemed as if his previous girlfriend somehow figured into the story. Infidelity was the one offense that would doom their marriage.

Is it possible for Luke to divulge material that changes my mind?

Wavering doesn't suit me. I'm stronger than Luke's problems.

* * *

That night, Tara lay across her parents' bed, disappointed she'd missed the sky show again that evening. Like Tara, her parents had been a product of their upbringings. Had they truly enjoyed living simple lifestyles? Had fear mandated their choices? Was it a little bit of both?

I crave simplicity and put off stuff that should be dealt with. Choices define us.

Can these personal idiosyncrasies determine my relationship with Luke?

With Luke's assistance, Tara had accomplished more in one week than in the month following her mom's death. It emboldened Tara to dream again.

A picture of her parents celebrating their fortieth wedding anniversary sat atop the dresser. Lively gazes were filled with laughter while blowing out forty candles Tara had placed upon the cake. She glanced at other photos taken throughout the years. Rolling onto her back, Tara wiped away teardrops that cascaded down her cheeks.

Carl got it right. My parents lived successful lives. When will their daughter relinquish the loss?

She sprawled across the stripped mattress. "Happy thoughts heal wounds. Think I'll sleep in here tonight."

Tara turned onto her side, sobbing.

Chapter Twenty-One

Luke hopped into the car, carrying a Keller's Bakery box filled with apple fritters. Last night, Tara told him that she craved the fruity treat. From her mouth to his ear. Keller's had been the first morning stop. Back inside the car, he marked the visit off a mental checklist. Complete.

After the last stop, he attached scripture cards to strings tied to ten helium-filled balloons. Tara had accepted his marriage proposal ten days ago. Faith-filled scriptures highlighted their time together. He'd dropped by a Christian bookstore last week to purchase a Bible. Scripture cards had been selected at the checkout counter. They would come in handy at breakfast. Friendly reminders never hurt righteous causes.

* * *

Fully dressed, Tara labored over cooking Luke's tasty breakfast. Last night's crying spell had ended on a high note. Tuesday morning offered a fresh start. Minutes earlier, neighbors had probably taken cover when rambunctious cheers rang down the hallway.

"Bridal shower day. I'm running in the fast lane."

Propriety minimized high jumps and kicking feet.

Her eager gaze fastened on a maroon gift bag placed beside Luke's plate. So much for five days of wedding gifts. Yesterday she'd overlooked presenting the first one. The forgotten present dictated how she would distribute the others. Four weekends at a riverfront hotel and dinner at a nearby restaurant sparked the spree.

When the doorbell pealed, Tara opened the door, gaping at the balloons and bakery box Luke carried. On another roll. In sync again.

Luke extended the box of secret treats. "Just a little something I picked up." His teasing grin held promise.

Tara's peek inside almost dislodged the box. "Luke. You remembered.

Apple fritters!"

"Admit I dote on your every word," he said, grinning.

Their latched gazes re-established the camaraderie hallmarking their cozy relationship. Whatever contributed to Luke's restraint yesterday wasn't evident today. He appeared his laidback, contented self.

Tara reached for the balloons. "Ten balloons match our tenth day of being engaged." She hesitated at his knowing grin. "I scratch a day out on the calendar each morning."

Luke chuckled as Tara read each scripture card out loud.

"Thank you, fiancé. Honoring our relationship keeps us close."

Luke sniffed the air while allowing Tara to enter the kitchen first.

"Breakfast smells tempting. What's cooking?"

Tara set the weighted balloons on the countertop. Peeking at Luke, she silently removed saucers from the cabinet.

Luke removed two envelopes from the gift bag beside his plate. He studied the gift cards, quietly reading each note. Instead of facing Tara, he turned away. Shoulder muscles flexed beneath his T-shirt.

Tara placed an apple fritter on saucers beside their plates while studying the man staring into space.

"Luke?"

"Yeah."

She wrapped her arms around his waist from behind. Her cheek pressed against his back.

"Closer, please." Turning, he hauled Tara into his arms.

They stood there, leisurely rocking side to side.

"Hungry?" Dropping her arms, she broke away. Affording Luke time to regroup, she removed the warmer top and sat at the table, glancing up once his steady gaze penetrated her thoughts.

"When did you purchase these gifts?"

"Last Tuesday. For four months we'll spend the last weekend in the same suite facing the Arch. And we'll dine in the private alcove of a nearby restaurant." Shiny eyes latched onto him. "We're building memories. Just like we did at Kenny's and Nouveau Départ Bistro."

"I'm speechless." Luke hooded his eyes when his voice cracked.

"Oh, Luke. I feel special whenever we're together."

Luke sat and unfolded his napkin. "So do I. I gave myself a talking to after visiting Andy."

Tara inhaled deeply. Was it secret-revealing time?

Luke scooped up an omelet. His mouth switched from grinning to chewing.

Silence. Eating sounded good right now.

Luke polished off the last bite of apple fritter while Tara washed dishes. She blinked after noticing the camera phone aimed her way.

"Are you videoing me washing dishes?"

His hand shook trying to contain laughter. "No one will believe you're washing dishes with a dishwasher in the kitchen. You're even wearing plastic gloves." His free hand pointed at the appliance. "I thought last Tuesday was an anomaly, but you truly handwash dishes. Why not use that contraption like you did at my house?"

"Because there I followed my host's example." Tara shrugged, considering his input. "Mom never used it, and neither did I."

Sometimes learned behavior stifled my branching out in different areas. Mom wouldn't have cared if I used the dishwasher. Why didn't I break the mold on that one?

Tara dried her hands on a paper towel then swept the kitchen, finishing on the sunporch.

Luke stood in the doorway. "What's the agenda?"

"Heavy lifting. Move the loveseat and two chairs from here to the living room. I'll grab the dining room chairs."

Tara followed Luke through the kitchen where he sat on the love seat in the living room, patting the cushion beside him. "Luke, I'm concerned about the renovations. Adding a deck outside is a great idea, *but*, why replace the single door with French doors we won't need?"

"Practicality and aesthetics. Let's see what's available tomorrow. Any objections at the other houses?"

"I'm good with those, but leave the laundry room in the basement here. I've always washed clothes there and prefer having two bedrooms on the first floor."

"You'll change that tune once you wash clothes for me and our children. Convert half of the space in one bedroom into the laundry room. Then you won't have to run up and down the stairs. The other half could contain a three-piece bath, which creates an en suite guest bedroom."

Tara weighed the advantages. The suggestion made sense.

"I'll give you that one. *But*, I dislike open-concept houses."

Luke chuckled. "You prefer defined spaces. Check. On the first floor we're changing the full bath to a powder room, gutting the kitchen, and bringing the laundry upstairs. And adding an en suite to the guest bedroom. Plus, enlarging the sunporch into a screened room, adding a deck, and updating the living and dining rooms and den. Separate rooms. Satisfied?"

Tara shook her head. "The basement. Why can't it just remain a basement? Again. French doors. We never entered or exited the house from downstairs."

"A revamp there creates living space for guests. Pete will reconfigure the steps leading to all three floors in compliance with safety codes. And we'll allocate space alongside the garage, leading to the back yard. Then guests can enter the family room in the basement from outside. What's wrong?"

"One big family room is too much space to waste."

"Name the alternative."

Tara kneeled beside him. "Making an in-law suite in one half."

"Why?" His eyes narrowed. "Or need I ask?"

"What's wrong with The Grands moving in downstairs? It's still close to church."

"Tara—"

"Pure economics. Their living here for free eliminates the LLC disbursing rent. Then Molli could pursue getting paying tenants for both flats."

Luke massaged the bridge of his nose. "A spontaneous suggestion?"

"Um-hum. Just thought it up while we talked."

"Sure you did. Any objections concerning the second and third floors?"

Need he ask? "Of course. You expect changes upstairs."

"Trying hard. Well, let's hear it."

"There are five bedrooms and one bathroom on the second floor. Adding an en suite to our bedroom and widening closets eliminates two bedrooms, placing two children onto the third floor."

"Right. Smaller children can share rooms. My brothers and I did. Only Steffi had her own bedroom. We'll move the oldest two kids upstairs at the appropriate time."

"There's too much space for two bedrooms and a bathroom on the third floor. Besides, you recommended updates and now claim the entire second floor needs reconfiguring. Why should we remove the back staircase?"

"If everyone coming upstairs at night passes our bedroom, we'll know everyone's whereabouts. The third-floor stairway needs to be seen from our bed."

Luke's family's safety concerns him. Love it.

"Is that why you're removing the door from the stairway?"

"Exactly. Visibility is better on stairways."

"*And* the extra space upstairs?" Tara beamed her brightest smile.

Luke's eyes narrowed. "There won't be space for our children if anyone else moves in here."

Tara couldn't help laughing. Her fiancé truly knew his fiancée. "Only The Grands inside this house. However, creating a family room on the third floor would eliminate kids and guest disturbances for them in the basement."

"As would soundproofing The Grand's apartment if they accept. They won't intrude when friends visit. Otherwise, they can join in basement family gatherings. As you wish, our private family room moves to the third floor."

Tara gnawed a fingernail, staring at Luke.

"Now what's wrong?"

Aunt Jackie is downsizing ... "We could build an apartment over the garage for Aunt Jackie. And then she can sell her condo to the LLC for one dollar, which means more money for everyone."

Squinted eyes twinkled with mischief. "A family affair, huh?" With a side head tilt, Luke glided a finger across Tara's mouth, smiling when her lips trembled.

Ooh. Stop it. Wait until Saturday.

Tara frowned as he repeated the gesture with slow strokes that made her entire body quiver.

Grinning, Luke lowered his hand. "I'll run it by her and should have everyone's answer at dinner. Happy?" He checked his watch. "Who's picking you up for shopping, and where are you going?"

Tara glanced at the clock on the counter. "Oops! I'm running late. I'm shopping with Mindy and Marcie, who should arrive within an hour."

"After furniture from the sunporch is moved into the living room, I'll take the roofing crews some surplus apple fritters."

* * *

Early that evening, before reaching his house, Luke spotted a lone vehicle parked in his circular drive and maneuvered the car in the opposite direction. Making his escape undetected, he parked inside the garage behind the house.

Unexpected ambushes wouldn't work with Luke.

What did work was permanently axing Leah.

Inside his house, Luke peeped out a side window.

Still chattering on her cell phone, expecting to surprise me.

He stretched achy muscles, yawning.

Would Leah's willpower to confront him outlast his nap? Or would she surprise Luke and leave?

After dropping his keys into the empty candy dish, Luke headed to his bedroom. Shirt stripped, shoes discarded, and alarm set, he plunked onto the mattress. Tara's bridal shower should end by eight. Then the couple would dine at a private supper club featuring candlelit meals.

Luke considered his past dates. After previous disasters, he'd refused to go anywhere he'd considered to be family friendly places. He didn't want any more chance meetings with members of his family.

One windy summer evening, Luke and Leah had run into Andy and his family at the zoo. Next they collided with Colton's and Benton's families on a lark arcade visit one rainy Saturday. His biggest blunder found them at the ballpark with Steffi and Scott. Empty seats within their row kept Leah glued to Steffi's side.

An engine started.

Luke chuckled but skipped checking the window. Whether she left now or later was of no consequence to him. *If* she left before he got up and needed to leave. Saturday he'd dodged a bullet with Tara and wouldn't squander the relationship God provided.

Lord, I am irreversibly onboard with marrying Tara.

He was receiving the gift of marriage to an amazing lady from the God he'd virtually ignored. No one could claim that victory but Him. Her confidence grew daily and so did his. Yet he knew that sadness filled Tara's eyes in unguarded moments. Wounds from losing her parents in the previous months weighed heavy. Whatever it took and as long as it was within his power, Luke would fill the void their passing left.

He lay on his back, fingers entwined behind his head.

Pete's lecture on Thursday spooked me. I can't let that happen again. Tara notices everything.

* * *

At seven o'clock, Luke left the house and strolled toward Leah's car. His body plastered against the door, he tapped the window.

Leah jumped, clutching her chest. Air blew layered blond hair off her temples.

"An unofficial stakeout? Why don't you just knock on the door."

Flinty eyes glared at him. "Why, when you obviously weren't home. I didn't see your car." Her eyes narrowed. "Is the garage behind the house?"

"You seem desperate when you stalk. How did you learn my address?"

"Hold up. I waited three hours on a man who was already home?" Leah pushed her weight on the door, but Luke wouldn't budge. Swearing, her nostrils flared. "Let. Me. Out."

"We're not talking now. I'm sharing a candlelit dinner with my fiancée soon."

Luke observed the rhythmic rise and fall of Leah's chest. If eyes shot daggers, Luke would be a dead man.

"What about this Tara person? You're marrying a woman on Saturday that you only recently met?"

Luke grinned. "The day I met her was a marvelous day all around. I spotted my dream house, in my dream neighborhood, and my dream lady opened the door."

Leah threw her cell phone on the passenger seat. "Ugh! Let me out, Luke." She pounded her fist on the dashboard. "Move!"

Luke had Leah where he'd wanted her. Groveling. Yet her downfall left him flat. What had he expected? Fireworks? Exhilaration? Disappointment mounted. Five wasted years of plots and regrets made him appreciate Tara even more. Now to end his self-orchestrated fiasco. Luke wasn't interested in making Leah feel better, but in keeping himself from feeling worse.

Talk of Tara calmed Luke. She was the quiet within his storm. "Tara and I are on a lifelong journey through our forever years."

"And what we had was a jaunt through hell by comparison?"

"You provided a well-learned lesson on how to avoid the fast track to death."

Leah pushed the door then kicked it. "We've been together for five years. You were on my mind each time I left St. Louis."

"You contacted me whenever you came back to town."

"Stop fooling yourself. We were a couple. Ask anyone. People saw the way you looked at me, and they knew you dropped every woman when I visited. You couldn't get enough of me."

Fascinating. Leah was in love with herself. "I certify my own facts. Learn when to cut losses."

"If spending time with me was so bad, why did you stick around?"

She asked. Here you go, swift and direct.

"You're a mediocre teacher, and I learn slowly. So there you go."

Leah's face transformed through three distinct phases: Fury. Disbelief. Defeat. Luke and Leah equally disliked each other. Luke checked his watch. He had limited time to waste.

"Why deny truth?" she asked in a tinny voice. "I gave you ample heads-up that I was coming home to marry you. I even showed up one month earlier than I'd said."

"It was wasted effort. Our playtime ended last September."

As Leah's stature shrunk, trembling hands touched her downturned mouth. "My leaving angered you. Admit it."

"Did that fairy-tale version of what happened fester for eight months? Have I ever asked you to prolong your visit or suggest I visit you? Self-deception is worse than fooling others."

Leah's head hung as Luke's words sank in, but her teeth were bared when she looked up. "Any woman thinks she's special when a man drops everyone for her."

"Special is a woman dating only me. If there's love, it doesn't matter how far apart you are."

"Jerk. I invented the game you're trying to learn."

Luke's eyes resembled slits. "Ever been dumped? Welcome to the first-time club. You were an occasional date, nothing more."

"Don't rewrite history. We talked throughout the year."

"An occasional reply to a few texts was it. Forget about me and don't come back."

Leah lifted one leg over the console.

Luke's hand rose instantly, with the camera phone poised and ready.

"Want that image plastered over social media? So-called friends will light it up."

Her foot hit the floor mat beside the other one. "You'd never do that. Why make idle threats?"

"Why chance it?" He pulled a second cell phone from his pocket. "The recorder's running. A friendly reminder, I don't want to see you again. Don't make me use it."

"You win. Erase the recording and video. Today bad boy Luke showed. Has the fiancée witnessed this ruthless side?" Leah's chin rested on her chest.

What a drama queen. *Nine, eight, seven ...* He stepped back once Leah turned the key.

"She's welcome to you. I can do better." Her hands raised then smoothed windblown hair. "Tell me why you dated me so long. Something held you captive. I stuck around to find out."

Luke hesitated as moisture appeared above her lip, and then he tried to keep himself from grinning. "Some things are better left unsaid; this is one."

Leah's hands covered her face until she looked up, smiling. "Never count me out, Luke. Are we still friends? Departing as enemies won't work."

"Friendship is reserved for friends. My fiancée's bridal shower is winding down. I need to go."

Unfocused eyes stared at him. "That's it? You aren't curious why I attempted marriage?"

Luke eyed trembling hands gripping the steering wheel. Culpability kept him there. *Listening is the least I can do. Under different circumstances, Tara would be proud.*

"Who dates a person they dislike for five years? Were our romps in bed that satisfying?"

He held up two of his fingers. "You're running out of time."

"Here's the deal. I dated my boss before meeting you. Still am. Can you believe the man is also getting married on Saturday? If I continue warming his bed, I'll retain my position. I won't accept second place from any man. You seemed a suitable replacement."

"Cut your losses. Make a clean break and find a new job."

"There're other options. You failed miserably as a standby. It's shameful that you didn't stand by me."

"You just gave a less than stellar performance: if you have a next time with someone else, beg harder. Here's more free advice: God is the hope every person needs. Remember that."

Tears? Nah. Luke went inside the house as Leah sped off.

Chapter Twenty-Two

Typically, as a matter of etiquette, brides wouldn't host their own bridal shower at their house. But when the bride-to-be insisted, Annie gave in. And the invitees brought gifts befitting Tara's current life. Cutlery, linen, china, and the usual newlywed staples weren't needed. Family-minded individuals enjoyed family-oriented pursuits. Original gift ideas lined the cocktail table.

"To Tara, from Mindy and Woody and Marcie and Stan." Annie's daughter, Kylie, handed Tara the first gift. It was a smallish gold box with a white bow.

Tara's almond eyes widened into circles after she ripped open the envelope that accompanied the gift. "Oh my goodness! Two weekend season tickets for the Cardinals at Busch Stadium." Her gaze went from Marcie to Mindy. "Thanks, guys. I'll thank Stan and Woody at dinner tomorrow."

"Tara is big on memories," said Marcie. "She and Luke will be able to create some with the tickets."

"And we purchased season tickets for ourselves in the same row," Mindy added. "See you there."

"Wow!" said Steffi. "Luke loves baseball. I'll text him."

"Wait, Steffi," Rachel said. "Let Tara tell Luke later."

"Our card. The Hilliard and Kennedy families." After nodding toward her mother and grandmothers, Kylie passed the card to Tara.

Tara read it aloud. "Ah! Thank you." She held up stapled papers. "An expense-paid marriage retreat in Denver next spring. Luke and I will be able to celebrate our first wedding anniversary in Colorado."

Kylie picked up two presents, passing Tara a floral-wrapped box. "To Tara, from your neighbors: The Watkins, Perez, Lennard, and Price families."

Unwrapping the box, Tara extracted a card. "To our favorite bride-to-be. Aw ... yes! A skyline dinner cruise for two on *Tom Sawyer*." She eyed each neighbor. "I've never stepped foot onto a boat. Much thanks. Glad we're neighbors."

Without a pause, Kylie passed Tara a gift wrapped in neon-pink paper. "Your friendly diner crew: Flora, Regine, and Connie."

"The girls wanted to come, but they're needed at the diner," Connie told them. "However, our entire family will attend the wedding."

Tara tore open the box and read the card aloud. "Welcome to the family. How sweet." Waving the card in the air, she faced the other guests. "Woo-hoo! Passes for three movies and three free dinners at Kenny's Diner. Plus, free breakfast on weekdays in June." Teary eyed, Tara smiled at the beaming women. "We love Kenny's food. Thank you much."

The next gift was a blue card with blue and white curling ribbons. Kylie straightened the ribbons, giggling when they sprang back in place, and tried detaching them from the card. "Cute. These ribbons will look awesome in my hair."

"Just pass the gift, Kylie," Annie said.

"Mom! Here, Auntie. From Lois, your friendly cleaner, and Sami and Rhonda Padgett."

Tara handed the ribbons to Kylie then gazed at the family sitting on the loveseat. "Sami, did these ribbons come from your and Rhonda's hair salon? If not, you'll have to tell Kylie where to buy them." She read the verse out loud before removing the gift certificate. "An interactive murder-mystery dinner show. Interactive? As in, requiring participation?"

"We promise you'll appreciate the experience," Lois said.

Lois and her daughters laughed at Tara's squinted eyes as Kylie scooted five cards and two remaining gifts closer.

"To our future sister-in-law, from Hailee, Megan, and Rachel."

Tara read the card to the others and the note to herself. "Two season passes to The Playhouse. I love plays, but I've only been there once." She hesitated, eyeing the group. "Has Luke been talking?"

Megan laughed. "Not to me; we barely speak." Moaning, she touched her mouth. "Ouch. Bit my tongue."

"Lies are punished," said Steffi.

Smiling, Kylie passed Tara an envelope. "All yours. Open."

Tara blinked rapidly as she mouthed the message to herself. Written sentiments matched Steffi's expression, offering unconditional welcome into her life. Steffi expected more than a sister-in-law. She desired love and friendship.

"Thank you, Steffi. From my heart to yours." Sniffling, Tara raised the gift higher. "Two season passes to *The West End Repertoire*. Everyone here is on the same page. Who's been talking?"

Kylie waved a card underneath Tara's nose. "From Edna and Bruce with love. Read it."

Tears welled in Tara's eyes as the message landed home. "After renovations, my new grandparents are moving into the in-law suite." Still dabbing away tears, Tara frowned when Kylie nudged her. "Oh—yeah. Gift." Tara quickly opened a money holder and then stared at Edna. "Seriously? My parents died after taking a cruise. I'm thankful, but I don't understand the gift."

Edna's compassionate gaze remained steady. "Enjoy the trip and return home safely."

"But ..."

"Maggie's emails confirmed she and Lenny had a marvelous vacation until the return voyage," Petra reminded Tara. Pausing, she cleared her throat. "Traveling topped lifelong adventures they'd envisioned during retirement. Travel, Tara. Enjoy the experiences in their stead."

Six people had died out of thirty-eight hundred passengers. Somehow their immune systems had been compromised beyond repair. Tara had battled numerous fears throughout life and refused to live in bondage anymore. Luke would welcome the vacation, and in a strange way, so would she.

"Three more cards and then these two large presents," said Kylie.

When Tara pulled out the first card, keys fell onto her lap. Dangling keys on her pinky finger she read the card out loud. "Free use of a condo in Florida from Aunt Jackie." She looked up at Jackie. "Thank you. Can we go any time?"

"Vacation in Naples, Florida, after the cruise. You kids enjoy the condo. Rachel's and Megan's families visit Florida more than I do. Bruce and Edna haven't visited in ten years. And thank you for my new apartment over the garage."

"Yay!" Tara said with a tinkling laugh. "Thanks for moving close by."

The envelope Kylie passed Tara was embossed with two lovebirds. "From Molli."

Tara scanned the message then relayed it to the others. "Luke's and Pete's college buddy has an exhibition at an art gallery in Colombia, Missouri." She nodded at Molli. "Luke won't go without you guys, and I know Pete will be tied up."

Molli laughed. "It's in July. Pete untied himself to make it happen. Traveling together will be fun."

"My first art gallery plus a free trip. Looking forward to it."

"Here's the last card." Kylie lay her chin on Tara's shoulder while Tara opened the card. "That couple looks like you and Luke. It's a silhouette of you guys!"

Kylie grabbed for it, but Tara maneuvered the card out of Kylie's reach. "You cannot have my card. It's a keepsake. You got the ribbon I'd planned to keep."

"Don't cast your niece aside," Kylie retorted. "Until Saturday, I'm the only one you have."

Annie laughed. "Stop guilt-tripping Tara. Respect her bridal shower."

"Yeah. Let me read my card in peace." She lightly swatted Kylie with it. "Teenagers. Ahem—May love grow in joy and expectation. Brielle, Lisette, and the LeFevre family. Ooh! An overnight stay at a winery an hour drive from St. Louis." Walking on her knees, Tara hugged Brielle and Adrien's wife, Lisette. "Thanks a lot, you guys."

"Come back here." Kylie stared at the remaining presents. "Um … these two gifts are together but have different name tags." She picked up one large box and read the tag. "Open them together. To our dear friend, from Abby and Suze. The second tag says, best friends' families. Bensons, Garzas, and Gibsons."

Smiling, Tara glanced at her friends' mothers. Each woman had accompanied their daughter to the bridal shower. Suze's mom, Angelica Garza, waved.

Glad that even Alicia Benson appeared happy, Tara unwrapped both presents, then she and Kylie opened the boxes together.

Six apparel boxes filled with clothes were in the first box, and three clothes boxes and a box filled with shoes were stacked inside the second one. Her online window shopping spree with Abby hadn't been a lark. Tara's sift through top boxes revealed a brand-new wardrobe.

"Abby, I played along to make you fall asleep that night." Her eyes grew incredibly wide. "Expensive clothes and undies are items I would never buy. I thought we were playing a game."

"Which is why you felt freedom to indulge," said Suze. "These clothes will look gorgeous on you. Wear the first outfit at dinner tonight with Luke. Heels and flats are in the last box."

Glancing at her friends' mothers, Tara sucked in a quick breath. "I—I'm having difficulty speaking. Lifelong dreams lie on the table." Fighting back tears, she gestured toward the presents. Her hands rose then fell onto her lap.

"How could you guess my dreams? Only a few people knew."

Tara's youngest neighbor spoke up. "The invitation to the bridal shower read, 'Tara adores keepsakes and fond memories. Let's create a few for her and Luke.' Each summer you've told me you want to take a dinner cruise."

"Likewise," said Hailee. "You talked plays while we ate dessert at Megan's house."

Mindy nodded. "And Tara's always wanted to attend a ballgame. But she's never gone."

Marcie pointed toward the large boxes. "Those are clothes you drooled over but wouldn't purchase."

Aunt Jackie grinned. "Although you were quiet at Rachel's, traveling spouted whenever you spoke."

"While a teenager you sold me on braving a murder-mystery theater," said Lois.

Wiping away tears, Tara read the text when the cell phone pinged. "Luke's on his way and wants to see everyone."

"Wait." The oldest neighbor sorted through boxes. "Choose an outfit and shoes, then hop upstairs. We'll entertain the fiancé when he gets here."

Abby grabbed a black cap-sleeve midi dress, while Suze produced a pair of black slingback pumps.

Tara stopped in the doorway. "My hair. Rhonda, Sami?"

"We'll come upstairs in fifteen minutes," Sami said.

* * *

Forty minutes later, Tara slipped into the living room, eyeing Luke hunched by the cocktail table, fingering condo keys for Naples. A quick peruse confirmed the living room had been restored to its previous pristine state. Even sunporch furniture was missing.

Tara observed her image in the mirror hanging over the fireplace. A wispy hairdo and expertly done makeup highlighted the stunning appearance. Luke glanced up, freezing. Keys dropped onto the table as he stood.

"I ... never imagined using such words, but, you're enchanting, Tara."

Tara's shy smile understood his reluctance. Luke stumbled toward her like a tranced man. Fumbling hands jerked while his thumb traced a pattern across her cheek until he kissed the spot, instead of offered lips.

Warmth gradually reached each nerve point in her body from the gentle touch.

Luke wrapped her in his arms, squeezing her close. "The guests' generosity is humbling. No toasters, can openers, coffee pots, and other things we don't need."

"I expected lingerie."

"No lingerie?"

"Oh. Yes. Some."

Wiggling his eyebrows, Luke pulled on his stubble. "That admission has potential. Can I get a fashion show?"

"Every day beginning Saturday."

"You're making me a patient man. Ready, beautiful?"

* * *

The next morning, cinnamon spiced the kitchen and spiraled throughout the first floor. When Tara opened the front door, Luke blew her a kiss.

She stepped aside. "Hope you're hungry."

"Starved. I smell two scents battling for dominance." He noisily sniffed the air. "Fish?"

"Yes, sir. Breakfast is something of a posh brunch. Grilled salmon over sautéed baby spinach, sliced avocadoes, and diced tomatoes with a dash of fresh dill and garlic, served beside homemade cinnamon buns."

"What time did you wake up and fall asleep last night?"

"Before midnight and up by six. My head hit the pillow after you called. I almost woke you up at seven."

"You should have, because I crawled out of bed after eight." Luke glanced at Tara then squinted at the present beside his plate. "A gift?" He removed a box from the gift bag as Tara clutched a spatula to her chest. "I see it says fragile. Thanks for the warning. Any hints before I lift the lid?"

"Nope. The hotel and restaurant visits were gifts one and two. Now, open the third surprise."

"Third? Are there more coming? Is this gift the miniature cars you mentioned?"

Tara smiled. "I can't disclose my secrets. Open the present—don't keep me waiting."

Luke wordlessly placed four distinct handbells in a lineup beside his plate. Each one was exquisite: a frosted bell with gold leaf and a thin handle, a hand-cut crystal bell etched with rose petals, a glass porcelain bell trimmed with gold, and a stained-glass bell with a silver handle. No handbell duplicated any in his mother's collection.

An awkward silence followed what should have been a joyous moment.

Tasteless food slid down Tara's throat. She shifted on the cushion, awaiting his response.

What's the verdict? Does he like his gift? Learn to communicate, Luke.

* * *

Luke gulped his food with minimum chews. Grape juice slid each morsel past the lump inside his throat. Just as he had mastered his emotions, Tara struck again. No shadowboxing with her. His fiancée came out swinging and landed him a TKO.

Tara demanded every inch of him, leaving nothing for himself. What should've been a good thing came across bad. Luke felt like he was suffocating. He hadn't foreseen permanent submission to anyone. Even with his siblings, he knew one day each one would acquire families of their own. His forever lady was there to stay.

She's the companion I've always desired. Honest. Sincere. Someone I can love and embrace.

Authentic individuals were daunting, and Luke accepted that his ladylove completed him. Yet he knew his lack of response was a rebuff. Against what? Accepting his love and loving him back? Making him feel like a man for the first time ever?

God had blessed Luke with the perfect woman. And he kept nearly blowing it. Tara wilted before his eyes. One hand was clenched in a fist while the other hand rubbed the back of her neck. Luke's silence created obstacles for a woman deserving better treatment. He knew he had to make amends. At once.

He kneeled beside Tara, taking her hand in his. "Gift and giver are unique. On just your few house visits you honed in on what I hold dear. Everything my mother loved gratifies me like nothing else. Your thoughtfulness enlarged the collection. These handbells are flawless." Luke paused.

"But ... what else is coming?"

"Listen. I've never dated any woman I loved and respected. I'm getting lost inside such love."

Wistful eyes sought his. "Tell me what's going on so I can help."

"We're so alike, yet very different. You fix problems. I walk away. Tara, relationship building is unknown terrain for me." Luke returned to his chair, staring at her. "I won my family and friends by default. I'm forging a different lifestyle, but perhaps my previous choices are fighting back. I'll take a hit and compromise for you, my family, and Mol and Pete. There aren't many people on my 'take a hit' list. Bear with me as I muddle through my self-made maze."

"We're kindred spirits who found each other. Can't you assume I have positive intent regarding us?"

"I trust we belong together. Our relationship proves it."

Once Luke spread his arms, Tara nestled onto his lap, laying her cheek against his chest.

* * *

Early that evening, Tara taped up the last box and pushed it to the landing outside her bedroom. Every item needed during the renovations was stored in these boxes and heading to Luke's house. Anything else was slated for storage tomorrow. She spot-checked the spartan house. Tonight, Luke would drop her off at Annie's and Carl's, where she would stay until the wedding.

As Luke stood behind her, Tara leaned into him.

"Did you remember the jewelry and pictures in the upstairs dresser?"

"Um-hum."

"Is the honeymoon luggage packed?"

"Carl picked everything up earlier."

"That's it, then. It's dinnertime."

Yeah. Marcie's. Hobnobbing with the gang will help me relax.

* * *

Abby, Craig, Suze, and Josh arrived at the same time as Tara and Luke.

Tara stopped by Craig's car. "Glad you came, Ab. I figured you couldn't stay away."

"Marcie stopped the rampage about me meeting Luke and Steffi before she did. No more death threats."

Luke's eyebrows rose.

"She's joking," Tara said, grinning at his doubtful expression. Luke was reticent tonight.

"You guys need help emptying Tara's house?" Craig asked.

Luke shook his head. "Thanks for asking. The boxes are packed, and movers come in the morning."

Suze hugged Tara. "Your parents' foresight streamlined the work. It's

232

good they stripped the house of everything you didn't want or need."

"Since I cleared out the first time, I've been packing what's left a little bit each day since Luke proposed."

It's just three days until my walk down the aisle to Luke. We're getting married. Whew.

The couples gathered on the porch, and Mindy opened the door.

"Welcome. Your timing's spot-on."

"Mmm, I smell rosemary. Did you cook my favorite potato dish?" Tara asked Mindy.

"A pre-wedding present. Curtsy when you say thank you."

Laughing, Tara did her customary knee dip.

Luke held her upright.

Marcie hovered in the background, her eyes lighting up as she saw Abby. "Abby. Thought you weren't coming."

"I relented once Craig insisted."

"Admit you wanted to visit me."

"Of course. Pretty outfit. Where did you buy it?"

"At an out-of-the-way boutique close to downtown. We'll check it out next week."

Marcie sidled beside Abby as everyone drifted into the living room, where Stan and Woody stood, waiting. Only their hazel eyes bore resemblance.

Extrovert Stan kept the conversation moving. "Marcie's husband, Stan," he greeted Luke. "My wife relaxed after meeting you yesterday." He shook Luke's hand then pointed across the room. "Woody. Mindy's husband, my brother."

"I've waited years to meet Tara's fiancé." Woody sat, making room for Mindy. "The twins were in an uproar until Suze revealed the Josh connection."

"An uproar. Over me." Luke brought his and Tara's locked fingers to his lips. His eyes gleamed with mischief. "Didn't you tell everyone I'm harmless? Or did they think you were lying?" His lips brushed hers in a light kiss.

Tara smiled timidly and slipped her hand from his grip. *Stop teasing. Behave.* She beamed at the brothers. "Thanks for the season tickets. I've always wanted to watch the Cardinals play live."

"A grand gift," Luke added. "Tara and I will host tailgate parties before each game."

"You're on," said Stan.

Woody nodded. "I put four other tickets on hold next to our seats."

Craig touched Abby, who nodded. "My wife's on it."

Suze hugged Josh as he settled her onto his lap. "It'll be so much fun to hang out at the games. Go Cardinals!"

Standing, Abby headed for the door. "Stay seated, Marcie. I'll set the table for dinner." She paused in the doorway. "Are we really having rosemary potatoes at a fish fry?"

* * *

Tara turned off the stove timer and headed to the door. It must be Luke, even without his signature ring. She swung open the door, wearing a ridiculously happy smile. "Hello. Where are my love notes? You didn't do your signature ring."

"You call it my signature ring?"

"Um-hum. Look at you. Refreshed. See, the twins are nontoxic."

"They gave me the once-over the previous night, so they didn't need to make an uproar." Luke sniffed. "Breakfast. I'd planned for us to drop in Kenny's."

Tara edged against him. "I like preparing my fiancé's favorite meals, with an occasional stir-fry or casserole thrown in."

"You, my dear, are a fantastic cook. Everything tastes great. Are the Hilliards awake?"

"The kids left for school. Carl's at the fellowship hall, and Annie took her mother shopping. Mrs. Kennedy beats dawn awake." Tara crooked her finger. "Follow me, lucky man. We're all alone."

Luke stopped at the place setting, which had a huge wrapped package on the floor beside the chair.

"Mine, secrets-lover?" Luke frowned as he lifted the box onto the table. "It's extremely heavy." Hesitating while unwrapping the box, he made eye contact with Tara. "Each day with you is an adventure. Mediocre living has passed me by. On to the gift."

Eight true-to-life replicas of Grandpa Burt's cars dazzled underneath a customized dome.

Luke sank onto a chair. "As Colton would say, whoa boy. Yesterday's word loss is meaningless today. I knew you were giving me miniature cars, but I didn't expect this."

Tara wrapped her arms around Luke from behind. Her face pressed against his neck. "Do you like it?"

"Like it? I'm mesmerized by it. I'll have to hide these cars from Colton. Is

234

this the last gift?" Luke maneuvered Tara onto his lap.

"Nope. There's one more tomorrow. Life is short. I want to show you how much I care every day."

Clearing his throat repeatedly, Luke coughed as if breath had caught inside his lungs.

"Even without the gifts, I've never felt so much love."

Tara hopped up to remove a platter from the oven, setting it on a trivet. Then she poured pineapple juice into their glasses.

"Talking to Carl while he ate breakfast brought back memories. I realized I no longer say grace before eating."

Luke immediately clasped her hand and closed his eyes. "Father, bless our meal and the life we share." He glanced at Tara. "Anything to add?"

"Father, teach us how to love you more. Remind us of lost lessons learned from our youth. Amen." She sighed loudly. "I blessed my food until I stopped eating meals with my parents. Many things have disrupted my relationship with God since January. I blindly allowed each one I could've prevented."

"That can happen when life becomes overloaded with problems. Understanding why makes the comeback easier."

Tara nodded, concentrating on eating. "This is spicy. Hope the rice isn't too hot."

Luke chuckled. "Perfect. I enjoy a singed tongue."

"So what's on this morning's agenda?"

The key ring Luke removed from his pocket had three color-coded keys attached. "Here are keys to my house and business. Blue opens house doors: front and back. Der-Jenca is green, and Cassidy Roofing black. Movers will arrive at your house by ten. We'll have the house cleared out and everything stored before noon."

"The man with the plan." Tara left the table and returned carrying an envelope filled with key rings. She laid a single key on the table in front of Luke. "Here's the key to my house. The rest are yours and Pete's copies for the shop and the other houses. They're marked. Duplicate keys are in the safe deposit box."

Tara kissed Luke on his way out the door. "Bye-bye. See you at one."

* * *

Later that evening, Abby and Tara lounged on Tara's stairs like teenagers. Sonya and Tad played hide-and-seek throughout the first floor. Yet Tara felt empty. Luke had spoken correctly about his drive to set his life in order. With boundless energy, he left no stones unturned. Her father would've loved him.

"Tomorrow's the rehearsal dinner," said Abby. "There's no going back then."

"Abby—"

"It's just a friendly reminder that other options still exist. You're exhausted. Cults recruit followers with sleep deprivation *and* sweets."

Busyness can make you disoriented and bring confusion. Had Annie made a similar comparison? "Abby—"

"Just saying. Do as you please. *But,* I can tell something's bothering you. Spill it, Tara."

Tara contemplated her next move while Abby watched her. Confiding in her best friend might unleash unresolved doubt.

I must know Abby's thoughts.

"The wedding. Give me your true opinion, best friend. *Please.*"

"Miracles happen. You love Luke, and Luke loves you. Nonetheless, bad timing could sink the ship. If you want to keep the wedding set for Saturday, then telling me what's bothering you is unwise. I would try to stall the wedding if I knew. At eighteen, no one could've persuaded me against marrying Craig."

"Through it all, you're still married."

"Throughout the highs and lows of life, we're teammates. Battling storms strengthened our marriage. But I'll teach my children that waiting's better. Craig and I made mistakes maturity would've prevented." Rising, Abby's palms slid over her thighs. "It's about dinnertime. Ready?"

"I'm ready to seal the relationship with Luke."

"Trust I understand the feeling."

Abby's infectious laugh was music to Tara's ears.

Chapter Twenty-Three

Luke watched as his brothers and sister rifled through his gifts. Andy read the gift cards, Benton rang the bells, and Steffi piddled with every item on the table. Colton went straightaway to the glass dome, scratching his head as Andy and Benton chuckled.

"Tara spent a boatload of money. Look at these unusually huge, perfect replicas. Someone performed an excellent job. It's a collector's dream." Colton crouched to get a better look. "And you say she has more pictures?"

"Several photo albums full. The car restorations spanned twenty years."

"After the honeymoon I'll select photos and build my own classic car collection. Tara is a treasure, man."

Tara's an excellent addition to what had been a futile life. Thank God I recognized my soulmate. She's the prize I don't deserve.

Steffi gestured toward the gift assortment. "These presents can't surpass the reasons they were given."

"Righto. Tomorrow is the last surprise?" Benton stared at Luke as he rang the stained-glass bell. "How can she outdo what's already here? Keep me posted."

Andy glanced at Luke. "Keep us all updated on the outcome."

"The outcome of what? Attend the wedding, Andy. That's Tara's finale." Steffi spread the gifts over the table. "Look at these personalized treasures. The giver's heart is in each one."

"Luke was the intended target, Missy. Not the gifts nor the gift giver."

Steffi blew into her hands until questioning eyes pinpointed Luke. "What is Andy referring to?"

Beats me. "How much I love my fiancée. What else?"

"Grandma saw a woman parked outside your house for hours the other day, then you sent her packing. Was it Leah?"

"She played her farewell scene. There you go."

"Uh-huh." Steffi pointed a finger at Luke. "That had better be the reason Leah came."

The reply baffled Luke. He hadn't lived a prudent lifestyle, but his character flaws didn't encompass vow breaking.

"You ... you believe I would cheat on Tara?" Luke paused. "Or that Leah came to break off the wedding?"

"Leah's capable of trying both. She'll use every trick to dispatch Tara and entice you into an affair."

"Luke won't succumb to her persuasion," said Andy. "I raised a different objection."

Benton replaced the handbell he rang back in line with the other bells. "Come on, guys. Let Luke and Andy speak privately."

Steffi's lips pursed into a pout. "I want to know what's going on. Tell me."

Walking across the floor, Colton stood beside his sister and pointed to the doorway. "You go first."

After the others left, Luke sat on the couch and pointed to an empty chair.

"It's been an exhausting day." Stretching his legs, Andy leaned onto the cushion. "So, what went on in the talk with Leah?"

Why did everyone's conversation include a woman from his past? *May as well get the examination over with.* "She went for broke: whined, begged, and flew into a rage. Her boss slash boyfriend is getting married on Saturday."

"Tell Tara the Leah story first thing. Secrets leak. Don't let anyone else inform her."

Luke shrugged. "We arranged to have the discussion after the wedding."

"That's rich. Why do women accept plans that favor you instead of them? How did you pull it off?"

"Tara knows we'll discuss a personal issue on our honeymoon. I assured her knowing beforehand wouldn't cause a wedding cancellation. I stand by that assessment."

"Your opinion doesn't count. You'd want to know if Tara had had a five-year fling that ended last year. It's her call. Trust Tara's love and inform her now."

Muscles twitched in Luke's face. Luke refused to traipse rainbows. Andy was asking too much.

About to speak, Andy hesitated. Sitting upright, he stared at Luke. "Man, you're the best older brother anyone could have."

"I needed that reassurance. I've tried." Luke leaned forward as his hand rose then dropped to his side.

His brother nodded. "And succeeded. You've always supported me. Steffi told me that you know she turned to me for advice concerning Scott. And how she'd questioned her oldest brother's judgment for a while."

"Stef provided a deserved shellacking. I continued dating Leah with one motive. Revenge. Leah became my punching bag."

"Gotcha. False guilt and regret can undermine sound judgment." His expression darkened. "I failed you at a crucial moment. I was too enmeshed within my own story to consider anyone else's. That wasn't the example you set for me. My brother was and is available whenever needed."

Luke glanced across the room while he spoke. "I fell lower than I ever thought I could land. Self-protection became my focus."

"Jesus is the only perfect man who walked on Earth. Flaws assail every person. I'll stand with you Saturday, whether you tell Tara or not."

Andy's vote of confidence demolished Luke's composure. "Thanks. I despise begging, but I would've."

"Get some sleep while I let myself out." Andy patted Luke's shoulder as he walked toward the door.

Alone, Luke relaxed on the couch, arms folded behind his head. Tara thoughts consumed his unsettled mind.

"God, I have a genuine family. Colton called, and they all descended. Various reasons brought each one, but everyone came. Tara doesn't have familial support. Who keeps her grounded?"

* * *

The cell phone rang as Tara scooted into bed. She'd waited on a call from Luke that hadn't come. Abby was on the other end. Her long night just became longer.

"Hi, Ab. Kids asleep?"

"Finally. Luke left?"

"Right after dinner. He was meeting up with his family tonight. He's late for his nightly call." Tara positioned herself on the headboard, thinking of how to direct the conversation. She wanted to unload on Abby but couldn't chance her friend blasting Luke.

"So what's with you and the fiancé?"

"Abby—"

"Please don't make me drive four blocks when most sane people are asleep."

Tara's shoulders drooped. Her mind went crazy. Abby was her forever confidante, but she needed to proceed with caution. Possible land mines were scattered ahead.

"Okay, I'll talk, but I don't want advice."

"Asking the impossible never works. Spill it."

Tara unburdened anxiety while Abby asked an occasional question until no words were left unsaid.

"You're quiet, Ab. Silence from you always makes me nervous. Thoughts?"

"I am … revisiting a similar conversation. Remember? The one where I sobbed on your bed, rolled into a ball."

"A vision I'm unlikely to forget. Craig told you he'd slept with some old girlfriend two weeks before the wedding."

"It still gets to me. Fourteen years ago, you and I worked out his deceit together. Sis, I appreciated good advice then *and* now. You said, 'Craig exposed the incident; take the ball. Either break off the engagement or marry as planned.' And then you listened as I hemmed and hawed for two hours, ranting against Craig and glorifying myself. Instead of dinging Craig, you labored to understand him. After I stated that I'd rather keep wedding plans intact, you said it won't be an easy climb, but mountain peaks belong to you. Those significant words carried me through numerous turbulent seasons."

Tara sighed into the phone. "Spot-on. I've never seen a happier couple."

"You also gave a projection about your life that day. Remember? You stated that you would marry a man who loved you back. And then you said, '*Abby!* We'll have four children and have a huge family. Our love will grow by leaps and bounds.' Tara, don't forget that self-proclamation. Nighty-night. Call anytime."

With her mind overflowing with thoughts of Luke, Tara laced fingers behind her head. Several people had asked her why she'd allowed Luke's pursuit. Her standard response had been that he never gave up the chase. Truth dawned. It was Luke's expression as their gazes met for the first time. He'd looked past her outer appearance and connected with her soul. The yearning in his eyes still invigorated Tara. Under Luke's influence, her existence transitioned from mundane to phenomenal. Destiny lay ahead.

Teardrops plopped onto her cheeks.

Trusting God was essential.

I'm learning, Lord. Don't let my faith falter.

* * *

The next morning Tara observed Luke park his car in the church's lot, but he remained inside the car. After sitting for ten minutes, Luke approached the duplex with slow, cautious steps, looking at the sidewalk the entire time.

Swinging open the door, Tara accepted his kiss, and slid a finger underneath his eyes.

"Shadows. Sleepless night? You should've called me back after your nightly call."

"My Tara thoughts are unending. Why ruin your rest along with mine?"

Even though Luke grinned the placating tone proved troubling.

"Happy thoughts? Care to share?"

Silence. Tara's conversation with Abby came to mind. What had ignited the Cassidy family date? *I'd figured siblings wanted time together before the wedding. Hmm ...*

Luke kissed Tara, pulling back slowly. "Ready to beat the brunch crowd at Kenny's?"

What's he thinking? Would Luke's present redirect his thoughts?

"I'll grab my purse." Tara went into the den and reappeared carrying a wrapped package with both hands. "This is the last gift before the ceremony."

When Luke peeled away the wrapping, various photos filled a wooden frame. Snapshots depicted the couple in unguarded moments.

Tara edged closer, viewing the collage through Luke's wonder-filled eyes.

He tore his gaze from the picture, staring at her. "These gifts. The preparations. Every effort proves my value. Thank you."

Oh Luke, I love you so much. Confide in me. Let me help.

Tara briefly closed her eyes and opened them with a wink. Her lips curved into a teasing grin. "My pleasure, sir."

Luke drew her into a bear hug, mastering control. "So we have rehearsal tonight. Nervous?"

Another subject change and moment of trust lost. I know the revelation can't be awful. What gives?

Tara smiled. "Jittery. All eyes will be on us."

* * *

Rehearsal ended without Tara tripping or any other mishaps. Luke distancing himself from the celebration was the only disappointment in the evening. His struggles to find the right words exposed a conflicted man. The morning's reticence was in full swing that evening. It wasn't Tara's imagination. Steffi's weary gaze followed her brother wherever he went.

At the rehearsal dinner, Kenny's waitstaff operated in organized synchrony. The private meeting room was decorated with hearts and flowers. Laughter sounded throughout the place.

Bruce raised his glass for a toast. "Tara and Luke: A match made in heaven. May love ignite the perseverance required for a lifetime commitment. God bless your marriage, children, and future endeavors. Obedience to Him safeguards relationships. Edna and I support this union."

Luke turned to Tara. "I love you. Tomorrow can't come fast enough."

"Ah. Today culminates the best two weeks of my year. I love you, Luke." Claps sounded around her.

Tara blinked. Had they spoken loud enough that others had heard?

* * *

Sometime later, Luke kissed Tara at the door, squeezing her fingers in his.

He sighed, staring at her. "Last chance to call off the wedding. Tomorrow at eleven we'll be husband and wife."

"Surely you joke. Right?" Her fingers shook upon her trembling lips.

"Half and half. I love you enough to want what's best for you. You matter more to me than I do. If you're sure, Kissimmee, Florida, is our honeymoon destination." The back of his hand stroked her cheek. "Tomorrow, love. Watch my progress from the window."

"Call me when you reach home. Bye-bye." Tara leaned her forehead on the glass as Luke made a U-turn and headed in the opposite direction. "What will tomorrow bring?"

"Tara and Luke's wedding," Kylie spoke from the doorway. "Me, Wes, and Stephen are eating strawberries in the kitchen. Want some?"

"Uh-huh. Then I need to hit the sack."

Tara's body followed behind Kylie, while her mind was on the road with Luke.

* * *

At the church, Suze stopped Luke from going inside the bride's dressing room an hour before the bridal march was set to begin.

"Tara's wearing her wedding gown. Grooms don't see their brides until the ceremony."

Eyes narrowed, Luke surveyed the room until lighting on Tara. "Ours isn't a traditional engagement. Excuse me."

Luke sidestepped Suze and faced the stunned woman fully dressed in her wedding gown. Pleading eyes implored Tara to grant his request. When the hand he held out shook, Luke shoved both hands into his pockets. "Please talk with me now. It's important, Tara. Otherwise, I wouldn't intrude."

Rachel sprang into action and led the children into the hallway.

"Last bathroom call." Megan joined behind the procession.

Her stomach sank. *Honeymoon discussion. Now? This is my fault. Every significant issue should've been voiced earlier.*

Closing her eyes, Tara inhaled a deep breath. Stillness surrounded her when they reopened. Steffi's woeful gaze focused on her brother. Suze glanced between the couple, and Annie stood at Tara's side.

Abby, wearing a bland expression, checked her watch. "Fifty-five minutes and counting, guys. Make it quick."

Inching out of the room using baby steps, Tara ignored Luke's extended hand, thankful she'd chosen a trainless gown, and wouldn't need assistance. Walking the opposite way of the sanctuary, she spoke over her shoulder. "The storage room is private."

As they veered down the hallway, Tara tried slowing her racing heartbeat. At the open door, she stepped inside, closing it behind Luke, arrested by the longing in his eyes.

Luke caressed her cheek. "My beautiful ladylove, I won't trap you into marriage."

The arms he placed on Tara's shoulders weighed her down until she stumbled.

Luke opted to hold hands. "Okay, here's the quick version. Five years ago, I met a woman who lives in California and visits her family that lives here during the summer. Her name is Leah. Our association was insignificant, just having off and on dates."

"Did you date her for five years? I'd say dating for five years makes it a relationship."

"Point taken. *But,* I was frank with you about my social life. There wasn't a special woman in it. Not ever. I don't buy every car test driven."

"Keep going."

"I need to tell you about the past to help explain the present. Leah dated a friend of mine who died two days before his twenty-sixth birthday. Paul passed away too young."

Something's off. Wait. Let Luke explain.

"Paul loved the woman, but she manipulated his heart. Pete, Paul, and I were inseparable in our youth. Peers called us the three musketeers behind our backs. Paul grew apart from us after high school and suffered from emotional problems in his twenties. Suicide threats became routine." Pain sharpened Luke's features. Massaging his forehead, he continued. "Pete and I grew weary from answering wolf calls. He would phone threatening suicide. We would run to his side. This played out numerous times until the day we couldn't make it. Our friend might be alive today if we had. Steffi was really sick with the flu, and Grandma wasn't home, so I had to stay to take care of Steffi. Pete was on a job he couldn't leave. We told Paul why we couldn't come. I guess he didn't believe us. Paul was dead when we arrived."

"Oh no." Tara clung to Luke's arm. She'd hadn't expected a death story. "Luke, tragedies happen. It's not your fault."

"I failed him. Paul was deserted while too vulnerable to protect himself." Luke grimaced.

"Uh-uh. You were at home taking care of Steffi. You couldn't just abandon her when she was so sick."

Glassy eyes focused above her head. "Pete's work had wound down around the same time The Grands came home. He was knocking on Paul's door when I pulled up. We entered the apartment through glass we broke in the bathroom window. We found pills. Paul's heart had ceased beating. Our friend expected Pete and me to rush in for the save, otherwise he would've used the gun on the nightstand. His first attempt at killing himself succeeded." Luke sagged against the wall.

"You did nothing wrong. Does Pete blame himself too?"

"He did until hearing my Leah plans. I hated the woman. She deserved the same fate as Paul: total isolation from everything good." Luke focused on Tara. "No, I didn't plan her death. She's a narcissist. There are other ways to cause pain."

Thank God for genuine friendships. "I take it Pete disagreed with whatever those were."

"Yes, even though Leah deserved destruction."

Unable to stand still, Tara's feet shuffled underneath her gown.

Luke's haunted eyes closed in an obvious attempt to regain self-control. "Paul battled multiple difficulties before dying. A lost job, failing the law school exam, his parents' divorce, and more stuff. Plus, Leah broke up with him; it pushed him over the edge. When we found him, while I called 911, Pete read Paul's messages. Leah's last text doomed him."

"What do you mean?"

A lone finger stroked her cheek. "We had told Paul that instead of crying over spilled milk, to pour from a different bottle. The toxic woman stole his hope. In her last text, she told Paul he was weak. Incapable. And wasn't worth the effort it took to love." Luke squeezed Tara's fingers, then shook his head. "Imagine reading those words while suicidal. He finally went through with suicide because of Leah."

"And you dated her because?"

"Paul always called her Sweet Lee. Pete and I had never met her. She wasn't interested in Paul's family nor his friends. It took a few dates to realize who she actually was. It wasn't until she mentioned Paul by name that I got it. Then I sought revenge. Leah became a perverse reality I'd accepted. That and every lie that defined the association."

"Luke, even with all this, you shared an intimate relationship with Leah five years. Why?"

"Guilt." His woebegone expression revealed a broken man. "Darkness had enmeshed me by the time we met. Initially I flirted with making her pay for Paul's death. Leah knew I despised her, yet her arrogance couldn't accept that I wasn't hooked. Her pursuit was gratifying on many levels; especially knowing the huntress had fallen into the trap. Later I regretted maintaining contact for that purpose."

Trying to comprehend, Tara rubbed achy temples. "You were sorry you aspired to hurt Leah?"

"My shame centered on Paul. Taking up with Leah for any purpose tarnished my friend's memory. For five years I slept with a woman who'd aided Paul's death." He took a deep breath. "Viewing inexcusable actions through your eyes is devastating."

His making this confession now was mind-boggling, even though Tara understood the man who gave it. The man Luke described was not the man she loved. He'd come a long way.

Luke clasped her hands within his palms, and he began to explain how the relationship had worked, including Leah's proposing to him in April and showing up at his home on Tuesday. His gaze was riveted to Tara's face as he answered each question she asked. Embarrassment highlighted his subdued features once she finished.

"Tara, let me prove those days are gone. I'm a better man."

Perhaps Tara was the only woman that would sympathize with Luke's shortcomings. Yet somehow, she understood his self-inflicted nightmare.

"I'm not upset with you. I asked. You answered."

"My masterplan was toying with her like she played Paul. However, that supplied limited gratification. Last September's repentance to God about my time with Leah inspired hope. When you opened the door, I knew He had forgiven me. Up until then, I wasn't sure."

Stiffening her arms, Tara disallowed Luke's attempt to pull her closer.

"Instead of leveling with Leah on Tuesday about Paul, you left her hanging. On purpose. Don't make light of bad behavior."

Sudden dismay dawned in Luke's eyes. "You think I should tell her about the Paul connection? I'd rather stay away from her."

"No. We'll pray for well-being for Leah and for us." Tara offered what she hoped was an encouraging smile. "Luke, I didn't lose the certain hope our love is real. God blessed us. Putting Him first keeps our relationship on track."

Luke kissed Tara until her knees wobbled.

Seeking composure, she fanned herself. Were her ears red or merely pink?

"Was that a prelude of what's to come later?" she whispered.

Luke's smile reached his eyes for the first time in two days. His teasing leer tickled Tara into laughter until he silenced her with a kiss. Returning to the lobby, the couple went their separate ways as Suze lined up the children outside the sanctuary.

Annie met Tara before she reached the dressing room. "Everything okay?"

"Yes. Thank God it is."

Satisfaction replaced Annie's gloomy countenance. "Deep breath. You guys sent me into a tizzy."

Tara locked her arms around Annie's neck. "You and Carl have always treated me special."

"Our ties run deeper than bloodlines. We love you," Annie whispered as Abby and Steffi left the dressing room.

"Are we on?" Steffi asked in a rush.

Pink imbued Tara's cheeks. "Luke is a godsend. I love him."

"Affirmation. Yay!" Steffi did everything but high kicks.

Annie linked Steffi's arm. "Let the ushers know it's walking time."

Tara winked at Abby after the other women moved away. "Ab—"

"Luke won me over today. Was what he told you not as bad as suspected?"

"Um, bad enough. But we can smooth it out. I hear the organ playing," Tara said before Abby replied. "It's official. Luke and I will tie the knot in just a few minutes. Yay, team Tara *and* Luke."

"Forever Tara. You won't change," Abby said, laughing.

The End

A Note From E. C. Jackson

"The Write Way: A Real Slice of Life" is the slogan on my website and Facebook author page. If every person reading my book feels connected to the characters, my job is done.

The Certain Hope is the third book in the hope-themed series. The unusual love affair between Tara and Luke reminded me of what trusting God is all about.

Book four of five standalone stories is coming soon. *The Certain Hope* will become my first audiobook and is due out soon.

If you liked reading this novel, please check out my other books and leave a review on the site of the retailer of your choice.

Thank you for your time!

Listed below are descriptions of my previous hope-themed books.

Book One: *A Gateway to Hope*
Nikhol "Neka" Lacey and James Copley
Twenty-one-year-old Neka is a bit of an introvert, she also happens to be stunningly beautiful. When she discovers her friend James is about to be dumped, she sees the perfect opportunity to escape from her quiet life. Can she summon the courage to leave it all behind?

James Copley comes from a ruthless family. It's rubbed off. Years ago, he disengaged from his brother's smear campaign, but now his father has offered him an ultimatum, "Get married or lose your seat at the table." Plotting to stamp his design on the family business, he proposes to a woman, even though he doesn't love her. But his carefully laid plans start to unravel when she leaves him on the day she's due to meet his family. Could years of planning his comeback vanish with her departure?

A possible solution comes in an unexpected form: Neka. She's not only a friend, but the daughter of his benefactor. And she's right there, offering to support him. But will her support stretch to marriage? He attempts to win her over to his plan but collides with her powerful father who wants to leverage the situation for his own gain.

In their fight for survival and love, they are forced to face some uncomfortable truths. Can they overcome thwarted dreams and missed chances to find true love, or does forcing destiny's hand only lead to misery?

Book Two: *A Living Hope*
Sadie Cummings and Kyle Franklin

It was a match made in heaven. Or so everyone thought. Sadie Mae Cummings is all set to marry her childhood sweetheart, Kyle, when she is assigned to tutor Lincoln, the new college football running back. This sophomore phenomenon has all the girls on campus knocking on his door. But Sadie isn't interested in his advances.

Lincoln's overblown ego doesn't take well to being shunned, and he resolves to make Sadie his own. He pursues her relentlessly, until finally Kyle finds himself shut out of Sadie's life, with their shared future crumbling around him.

After two years, Sadie's relationship with Lincoln ends, and she is left having to put the pieces of her life back together. She desires nothing more than to recapture her relationship with Kyle. He has stayed true to the dreams they had planned together, living the vision even without Sadie by his side.

When she moves back to her hometown, she labors to rekindle their love. But things have changed, and Kyle has moved on. Sadie quickly discovers how hard it is to rebuild burned bridges.

Follow Sadie's story as she fights for a chance to restore broken dreams. Will love endure?

Pajama Party: The Story
Companion book to *A Living Hope*

Pajama Party: The Story is adapted from a play I wrote many years ago.

Most sleepovers are simple. Food, fun, and pillow fights. But sixteen-year-old Karen Duncan has bigger plans for her slumber party. Family troubles have changed her over the past year, and she's no longer the petty, selfish girl she used to be. Now she's ready to shake things up with her friends. The guest list comes as a surprise to some and a slap in the face to others. This popular girl has invited some not-so-popular guests. Even more shocking, she's left out some of the girls she's hung out with since middle school.

Diane and Evette are outsiders, nervous about being stuck in a house with the same girls who tease them at school. Kathy, Lisa, and Joann come to the party with the confidence of the in-crowd, but they're masking inner turmoil that is bound to surface. Sandy and Angela are usually the voices of reason ... usually. And then there's Linda, the friend that got away. She may not ever forgive the girls who abandoned her years ago. Karen hopes to change her mind.

Her agenda is ambitious, and it could spell disaster. But Karen is convinced God will use this party to spark a new beginning for everyone involved. This companion book to *A Living Hope* gives us the inspired story Sadie Cummings wrote for the girls of Shiatown.

About the Author

E. C. Jackson began her writing career with the full-length play *Pajama Party*. For three and a half years she published the *Confidence in Life* newsletter for Alpha Production Ministries, in addition to writing tracts and devotionals. Teaching a women's Bible study at her church for eleven years led naturally to her current endeavor of writing inspirational romance novels and teen and young adult fiction. Her mission: spiritual maturity in the body of Christ through fiction.